THE
MIDNIGHT
PARTNER

ALSO BY BART DAVIS

Bart Davis

THE MIDNIGHT PARTNER

BANTAM BOOKS
NEW YORK TORONTO LONDON SYDNEY AUCKLAND

THE MIDNIGHT PARTNER
A Bantam Book / August 1995

LIBRARY OF CONGRESS CATALOGING-IN-PUBLICATION DATA

Davis, Bart, 1950–
    The midnight partner / Bart Davis.
        p.   cm.
    ISBN 0-553-09690-7
    I. Title.
PS3554.A9319M5   1995
813'.54—dc20   94-23599
                                                                CIP

Published simultaneously in the United States and Canada

PRINTED IN THE UNITED STATES OF AMERICA

BVG   0 9 8 7 6 5 4 3 2 1

For Robert Gottlieb

No better agent or friend,
anywhere.

When a man's partner is killed he's supposed to do something about it. It doesn't make a difference what you thought of him. He was your partner and you're supposed to do something about it.

Dashiell Hammett
The Maltese Falcon

THE
MIDNIGHT
PARTNER

ONE

1

I wish I'd been there that August night to stop my best friend and longtime partner, Jack Murphy, from taking his last dive off the roof of his house into his swimming pool. He often dove off his roof at the summer parties he held in his lavish home in the Bluff Point section of Port Adams, the wealthiest part of a wealthy town on the North Shore of Long Island. It was Jack's way of demonstrating his athletic prowess, his zest for life, his way of saying age won't slow *me* down.

It also attracted the three types of women who dominated Jack's life: the perfectly groomed housewives with their health club tans, tennis legs, and knowing bedroom tricks—barely a day went by when one of them didn't invite him to her castle of daylight isolation to watch private athletics in mirrored walls; the lady lawyers and accountants, skinny women in ankle-length skirts who tossed aside their silk blouses in Manhattan hotel rooms and got kinky because they liked the concept—Jack said their only drawback was that they talked too much, and if that was what he wanted, he said, he'd call *me*; and the Queens secretaries he claimed were best for a brief thing, tough girls who drove glossy black Firebirds with plastic beads hanging from the rearview mirror, their long loose hair piled high as waves in a storm, black thong bikinis cutting their butts like cheese wires. They were eager to use what they'd learned ten years out of high school before the knowledge atrophied along with the muscles in their waxed thighs.

They all vied for Jack's attention with shameless offers. The secretaries, the housewives, the divorcees. And my wife.

2

Who am I? Just an average man trying to succeed. A parent. A middle-class Jew locked in a comic, self-defeating struggle to be a Christian hero, a cowboy, a jet pilot, a detective. I've been told I have talent in several areas. I don't know. I was a bright kid, never a genius. I don't have any natural athletic ability, but I push myself.

My name is Phil Liebowitz. Friends call me Phillie.

Here is my story.

3

I got the call from Jack's wife, Jessica, at three in the morning on Monday. She was crying too hard to speak coherently. I heard male voices in the background. One of them finally took the phone and told me what happened. Jack was dead. Suicide. I found my voice and said I'd be right over. I woke Carolyn and told her. She looked scared and fragile in her oversize T-shirt.

"Not Jack," she said. "I can't believe it. How? And for God's sake, why?"

"I don't know yet. I'm going over."

"Should I go, too?"

"One of us has to stay here. Don't say anything to the kids till I get back, all right?"

She pushed her tangled brown hair back and nodded. There was a kind of stunned horror on her face.

I said, "I'll call you when I can."

Bluff Point was only a few miles from my part of town, farther by tax brackets than by distance. I needed to breathe, so I put the top down on my red Miata, which was parked in the driveway. It was late August. The last of summer. In a matter of weeks the air would turn cold, causing insolent leaves to fall, mortal challenges to the army of gardeners who air-hosed the lawns clean every day like a horde of angry elephants.

Nobody should die at three in the morning. It's like sneaking out. The shock of Jack's death gave me a shaken, hollow feeling as I drove past the big, dark, silent houses on my way to his. The madness in most of them was still at this hour; pressure-cooker lives simmering until morning. It's a devil's bargain out here. In exchange for the Holy Trinity of schools, space, and safety, we fight with our kids, who have too many things and too little respect, tolerate tradesmen and traffic and trains, and struggle to make ends meet because God, honey, nobody has money for *everything*; and Christ, what these houses cost! Sometimes we're too tired to live.

The suburban prayer? Just let me get a little ahead, Lord. The only truth: Nobody gets enough.

I put my dark thoughts aside when I pulled up in front of Jack's house. The outside lights were on and there were enough Port Adams and Nassau County police cars in the driveway to hold a convention. Uniformed officers flowed in and out like a line of ants at a picnic. An ambulance was there, and a Nassau County Crime Scene wagon. MEDICAL EXAMINER'S OFFICE was stenciled on the doors of a black Chevy.

I went around back. Strobes were flashing, washing out the

colors of the Norwegian pine and New Zealand impatiens. I tried not to look at what the crime scene techs were doing in the empty pool, drained just a few weeks ago for repairs, though sooner or later I'd have to. Instead, I gazed up to the landing where Jack had most likely come through the door of our second-story office onto the roof. At parties he held his arms straight out up there and waited till he was sure everyone was watching him. He loved the way the girls tracked the bulge in his spandex bathing suit. Jack was proud of his upper-body development and his surgically implanted new hair, done one clot at a time. He would have been sickened by the sight of himself mashed into an ocherous puddle at the bottom of the empty pool.

Later on, the poolman called to say he didn't clean up stuff like this. It turned out, neither did the police.

I went into the living room. A graying detective in his late forties with a square jaw, flat-top haircut, and wary, steel-gray eyes was giving orders to uniforms. His collar and forehead had deep creases, the former done by a bad Chinese laundry, the latter by experience. His eyes intimidated me. They made a mockery of my petty sins.

Jessica Murphy was sitting very still in a leather wing chair by the French doors that led out back. She had a white robe on over a filmy negligée and was too distraught to pull it all the way closed. She was very beautiful, model beautiful, even now, yanked out of bed as she must have been. The four years she'd been with Jack hadn't put an additional line on her face. The policemen made it a point to use the doors so they could look down her bodice.

Jessica saw me and flew out of the chair into my arms. She smelled of the potpourri she kept around the house. Jack smelled of it sometimes when he came to work. More often he smelled of other women. There was also a faint ammonia-like odor wafting in from the techs outside.

"Oh, God, Phillie. Jack . . . he . . ."

"I know, Jess. I'm here."

She looked at me wild-eyed. "How *could* he?"

"I don't know." I stroked her shiny blond hair. "Did he say anything?"

"Nothing. I just woke up, and—and—"

"Excuse me, sir. Who are you?"

It was the detective asking. He wore a plaid jacket, blue shirt, cotton tie, brown slacks, and loafers. The *sir* was automatic. Mac. Bud. Sir.

I was glad to have a question I could answer. "Phil Liebowitz. Jack's partner. Mrs. Murphy called me."

"I'm Detective Donnegan. Port Adams Police. I'd like to talk to you later."

"Sure."

His chin jerked upstairs. "Mr. Liebowitz, maybe you could—?"

Right. Sooner or later they were going to bring Jack out of the pool. She shouldn't see the sponge mop they'd be using.

"Did anyone call Mrs. Murphy's doctor?" Fred Marcus was one of Jack and Jessica's closest friends. He lived just a few miles away.

Donnegan smiled. Warm as winter. "He's on his way."

I steered Jessica up the long curving staircase to her bedroom, a vast white-carpeted chamber with pale walls, Queen Anne dressers, and a four-poster bed with a white linen canopy. An antique chair and writing desk sat in front of the balloon-shaded bay window. Brass lamps gleamed without any fingerprints. It amazed me how clean it all was, but of course the Murphys had no children.

I slid the robe off Jessica's shoulders and tucked her under the bedcovers the way I did my kids.

"Tell me *why*, Phillie."

"I wish I could, Jess. There wasn't any indication? No fight or anything?"

Tears brimmed in her eyes. "I woke up, and he wasn't here. I went to check the office—maybe he was working. The door was open. . . . Please, Phillie, the police already asked me all this. No more."

I went into their huge walk-in closet and hung up her robe.

One side was hers, the other Jack's. His jackets and pants and sports stuff and sneakers and shoes stared at me. That same smell was here. Would I ever get it out of my nose? I went back and sat beside Jess. Jack had lain here earlier tonight, maybe even slept at some point. What had driven him from his bed and this woman and sent him up to the roof to die?

"I can't figure it, Jess."

"Me neither." She wiped her eyes. "I loved him, Phillie. I know you did, too."

"He was my best friend, my partner."

I heard a noise behind me, and Fred Marcus strode in. Fred was a little shorter than me, with dark hair oiled straight back and a fleshy face that always smelled of skin lotion. He was a fitness and sports medicine specialist whose practice included the horse show crowd, the ice skating fraternity, and many of the local pro ballplayers. He also served as the doctor for lots of their events. I could never figure out why Jack and Jessica were so crazy about him. He was an obnoxious putz like most of the young doctors who had replaced the gracious old gentlemen who used to practice medicine on the North Shore. These new guys were the kids nobody had played with back in school, arrogant dwarfs suddenly come into power. At thirty-five they had a big house and a Porsche, and all the girls who once jilted them had come to realize the awful truth. *Sic transit pulchritudo mundi, sic manet per pecunia:* How fleeting are good looks, how permanent is money. Rock stars did less well than this complacent, dominating, let's-go-to-the-art-gallery snob.

Fred sat on the bed and took Jessica's hand. "I'm here now, dear. Don't worry." He lifted her chin. Her tears gave her a kind of Joan of Arc radiance. "This is terrible for you. Let me give you something."

"If you think so, Fred. You're a dear to come." She threw the last part in more sweetly than I would have liked.

Fred took out a little black zippered case with syringes and ampules inside. I didn't need to see this.

"I'll be back, Jess."

There was still a lot of commotion downstairs. I walked

along the carpeted second-floor hallway past the guest rooms and den to the bookcase at the end of the hall. I didn't have to push the spring-lock, which let the whole unit swing away revealing a short flight of stairs. It was partly ajar, indicating that the police had already been up there. I once asked Jack about the bookcase door. He said it gave him the feeling of being isolated within his own home. He said he felt like that a lot.

The office was hot and stuffy because whoever had searched the room had nudged a carton against the grill of the room's only air duct, effectively blocking the air conditioning. They'd also knocked out the plug for the limited old Mac Classic computer we only used for E-mail, short personal messages to each other, and our phone answering system. I replaced it. The blacked-out screen came back on, displaying a sign that said the power interruption had caused the loss of the last message and suggested that the SAVE command be used to prevent such a loss from happening again. With everything else going on, I barely registered it.

Jack's office was a duplicate of mine. We worked together most of the time, but having two offices allowed us to work at either house or alone. We'd built them at the same time, bought our furniture and computers together, shared software and games, and late at night typed stupid messages to each other across town on our new modems. FUCK YOU. FUCK YOU! FUCK. YOU?

The last time we'd worked here was Friday night. I felt the first stab of pain twist my guts. The *last* time. For a second it was hard to breathe but I had things to do. I squeezed off the pain the way you clamp a bleeder. I was willing to bet the police had been looking for a suicide note. I was also willing to bet they hadn't found one. Jack's personal computer was stone cold. It hadn't been turned on. If Jack had had anything important or substantial to say I was sure it would be in his computer, which was linked to mine. We roamed each other's files at will. In slack times he read the novel I'd been working on for more years than I care to mention, and I read the poetry he would never publish. We often left comments, usually profane. Back when we first started, Jack wanted to buy equipment for both of us but I refused, a matter of pride. We got them when we made money. Paper was mostly incoming stuff, screenplays with titles written on their bindings in black ink piled high on every shelf, letters, contracts, and research material.

I turned on the computer and slipped in a new floppy disk. The computer snicked and beeped like a sloppy eater. Nobody has no secrets, but up until tonight I thought we had fewer than most. I knew what he earned because it was the same as what I earned. The differences in our lifestyles came from Jack's inheriting a substantial trust fund and having no children to drain it dry. Carolyn and I had begun married life with an old VW Microbus, a box of books, and a hand-wired Dynaco stereo. We were considering training our kids to eat and wear money because of all the middle steps it would save.

There were three new files, one named DIRECTORY, another THOUGHTS, the third PHILLIE. What the hell did he have so much to say that he couldn't just tell me? The files had been loaded just the day before. He probably wrote them on his laptop. We each had one. I kept mine in the car for the not-so-rare brilliant flash while driving. I copied the three files onto the new disk and tossed the originals into the electronic trash. There was no trace they had ever been there.

I ejected the disk, pocketed it, and pulled up our current project. I was staring at the last scene we'd written when I felt a presence. Donnegan was watching me from the doorway.

"You've got light feet," I said.

"What are you doing?" he asked.

"This was where we worked," I said, as if that explained something. Maybe it did.

"You and Mr. Murphy wrote together."

Not a question. I just nodded.

He came around and looked at the screen. "What's this?"

"What we were working on."

He read over my shoulder and had the class not to comment on it. "Did you find a note or anything?" he asked casually.

"No. You?"

"No. Which is odd, because they usually leave one." An observation. Not unkind.

I pointed. "That's Jack's desk there."

Donnegan opened the drawers, touched the keyboard, peered into a mug of pencils, hefted Jack's favorite glass paperweight. I knew full well he wouldn't find anything. Whatever Jack had to say was now copied onto that disk and I didn't want to share it with Donnegan. The file didn't say SUICIDE NOTE FOR THE WORLD. It said PHILLIE. Donnegan rubbed his pepper-and-salt hair and looked around.

"That the door to the roof?"

"Yes."

"I've got the report, but I need to see it for myself."

I followed him outside into the summer night. The roof patio was bordered by a low decorative fence. The trees were so thick around the property you could barely see the neighboring houses. The cicadas in the branches were working overtime making noise. Donnegan looked down at the pool. Technicians were still taking pictures, filling it with light. I wondered how many times he'd stood at scenes like this, and what constant exposure to carnage did to you.

"Was he happily married?" he asked.

"As happy as anybody. More than most, I guess. They both married late. Jess is a quiet girl. Jack liked that."

"Any peculiarities in the marriage?"

"You're kidding," I said.

He looked at me a little deeper. "I mean more than usual."

"No." The cicadas were screaming.

"Why was the pool empty? Summer isn't over."

"Bottom cracked. It had to be fixed and repainted," I said idly, then with more force, "Look, this had to be an accident."

Donnegan went down on one knee. His fingers drifted over the roof tiles. "Clean as a whistle."

"Check it again."

"There's nothing here," he insisted. "I think he came out here and went down under his own power." He sounded sad when he said it, as if people diving into empty space, expecting

support and finding none, were all too common in the suburbs.

"No way," I said firmly. "Jack wasn't the type to commit
suicide."

"What type is?"

I got angry. "Don't ask me that like you think what I said
was bullshit. I knew him better than anybody. Maybe he was
pushed."

Donnegan looked interested. "Is that a possibility? Was
someone mad at him?"

"No, but it's a better bet than suicide."

"Why?"

"Jack was a Catholic. Suicide is unforgivable." The thought
of taking a shortcut to God only to have him turn you down
cold made me shudder.

Donnegan didn't believe in fairy tales. "The roof is slate.
There are no slip marks on it. The fence is clean, so are his
feet."

"Feet?"

"He was barefoot."

"Oh."

"The ground below is soft," Donnegan continued. "There
are no footprints. If it was a fall he would have landed short of
the pool, on his back. Headfirst, he was diving."

The flashes in the pool were fewer now. I wished I had more
arguments, or better ones, but I didn't.

"I'm going back in," I said.

It was quiet inside and still hot. Donnegan poked around,
leaning his head sideways to read the titles.

"*False Gods.* You guys wrote that?"

"We did a rewrite. That's mostly what we do—did. Studio
has a script it thinks is good but the story is weak, they call us.
We're sort of structuralists. We tell them what's right, what's
wrong, suggest plot changes. Not dialogue so much."

"For instance."

"We did one for Disney," I said, thinking back. "The writers
had Lancelot looking for Merlin in the present time, using a

piece of his magic wand. The studio thought it was too epi-
sodic. We put Merlin on top of the Empire State Building
drawing Lancelot to *him*. That way, anything that stopped
Lance added to the tension."

"I see."

"Sometimes we do it in reverse," I said. "Analyze why a
certain movie didn't work." Talking about this hurt. Jack and I
loved our work. I clamped harder on that bleeder.

"For instance."

"You see *Near and Beyond*?" I asked him.

"Yeah."

"What'd you think?"

"Tepid."

I was impressed with the word. I didn't say so. "Know why?"
He shook his head.

"You knew the hero won from the get-go. It should have
been told in real time. By the way, is Mrs. Murphy asleep?"

"Yes, but somebody should be here when she wakes up."

It was more sensitive than I expected from a cop. I'm not
sure why.

"Someone will be," I said.

He flicked some dust off the scripts. "You have no idea why
he did it?"

"He didn't do it," I said fiercely. "Does a guy who just spent
ten grand on a hair transplant sound like he's planning on
checking out?"

"Under ordinary circumstances, no."

"So?"

He said, "Suicide isn't rational, it's the refuge of the despondent."

"You need a German accent to say that."

"I'm not joking." He looked at me intently. "What do you
feel about it?"

I made my face still. "None of your business."

"Yeah," he said. "It is."

I waited. It was just the two of us in that hot room. "What
do *you* feel?" I asked.

He looked hard at me. "All this." He gestured around. It included the office, the house, the beautiful wife. He seemed discouraged. "Have everything, have nothing. Go figure."

"Are you going to investigate?" I asked.

"Not unless there's a real suggestion of foul play, and there doesn't seem to be. His motives don't really concern us. As long as no one helped him or tricked him into it, it's not a police matter. The medical examiner's office will—" He stopped. "Do you want to hear this?"

"Yes."

"They'll keep tissue samples from the internal organs for microscopic studies. The chief toxicologist will run a screen for diseases and drugs of abuse using the vitreous fluid."

"What's that?"

"The liquid in the eyeball."

"Why?" I was curious and disgusted at the same time.

"It's self-contained. Sort of a record of the body at the moment of death. The ME has to fix cause. See what's involved. Lot of jumpers are on PCP." He saw my scowl. "I didn't say your partner was. Maybe he had cancer or something. You know. A reason."

"How long does it take?"

"Less than a day. Then they'll release the body for burial. But like I say, it seems pretty clear-cut."

"Case closed," I said. Bitterness spilled out when I wasn't looking.

He handed me his card. "Look, you find something or you wanna talk, call me. Or if a note turns up," he added.

"Okay." I turned off the computer.

"Just don't take anything till we clear the house."

"How would you know?"

He smiled. "Polaroids. Only be a day or so. Just procedure."

"Fine."

I didn't want to go yet. Leaving felt like, well, leaving.

"Donnegan?"

"Yeah."

"What you asked me. I feel like I should have been here, maybe I could've done something to stop him." I didn't know why I said it, Donnegan was nothing to me. And I still wasn't accepting it was suicide.

His eyes thawed. "Most people feel like that. You couldn't have."

I felt a pain in the corner of my eye and knew it would be a tear if I let it. We stared at each other across the dry dusty silence. He turned to go.

I followed him out with the disk in my pocket.

TWO

1

I went to look at Jack before I left. Say my final good-bye. The technicians had finished their work and were taking him out. It wasn't pretty.

I watched him go, thinking about how easily we lose things.

Someone turned out the outside lights. Around front, cars and vans were beginning to pull out. A policeman told me I had to move my car.

There was nothing left to do but drive home.

THREE

1

A silent war is waged in my house over garbage. Carolyn and I let it sit in shiny brown plastic bags in the corner of the kitchen and try to ignore it long enough for the other to weaken and take it out to the trash cans. The bags can lie there for hours quietly leaking something more oily than water, and my thoughts grow darker and darker.

We live at the end of Forest Drive in an old house on a high bluff with a view of Adams Bay. You can see the city on the other side of the water, a jagged line of glistening towers that makes the western sky glow at night. Often I go out to the back yard and sit thinking long thoughts about how I got to this place, the middle of my life. The city lights reflect on the water, all different colors. Some nights it's like a rainbow out there. Rainbow City.

When Carolyn and I are in a cold silence over the garbage, or the kids, or life in general, I think about what it would be like to go to Rainbow City and be completely different from what I am. I imagine the craziness. Women in leather on bar-stools. Nights without time. But I'm afraid. There are germs there the size of small dogs waiting for me. Or maybe I'll get beat up and they'll take all my money and it will be in the papers so all my friends will know I went to Rainbow City to get crazy.

So what.

It was where Jack went, but I didn't know that till later.

2

The garbage was in two big bags in the kitchen when I got home and went to get a drink. I was too tired to be mad, so I took it out. I felt drained and angry and confused. I'd staunchly defended Jack to Donnegan, but privately I had to wonder: Had he really done it? If he did, how could he have left without talking to me? If it was something like cancer, I would have helped him. In spite of everything, he had enough credit for that. He didn't have to die alone.

I left Carolyn a note on our dresser to tell her I was in my office and to come wake me if I fell asleep. I wanted to be at Jessica's house when she woke up. I checked the kids before going up to my office. As usual, Ben, my eight-year-old, had thrown the covers off. He lay crosswise on the bed, his head butting the wall, his legs and arms dangling over the side. Ben slept the way he lived, frantically.

Beth was my three-year-old angel. She was also God's way of saying, "I know I sent you Ben—this will help you through." She was as beautiful in repose as she was awake. She had so much love in her she'd thank you for bringing her a rock, or for the sunshine, and in fact had done both. Beth of the Good Attitude.

I kissed them both and watched them for a while to let their vulnerability soften my heart.

My office, like the back yard, had a splendid view of the city, and the air pollution made for some spectacular sunsets. I turned on my Mac and pushed the floppy disk in to load. I viewed the daily *Far Side* cartoon while I waited. A spider was staring at the out-of-shape web he had constructed.

The caption read, "Whoa . . . that can't be right."

"It isn't," I said aloud. There were webs and there were webs.

The DIRECTORY file opened at once. I scrolled through a list of names and numbers and saw maybe ten I didn't know. Jack's parents were dead, he had no sisters or brothers or kids, only a fruitcake maiden aunt dying in a home in Florida. It was just him and Jessica, the girls of the afternoon, and me. I duped the file, deleted the names I knew, and generated a new list of unknowns which I named, cleverly, NEW DIRECTORY. I printed it out and put it in my wallet.

I opened the THOUGHTS file. The first entry was dated almost a year ago.

Thoughts come too fast, Phillie. Realizations. I'd sit opposite you and wonder if even you knew what madness was running through my mind. The truth? Sex dominates my life. As far as I can see, my one true talent is that I can spot surrender in a woman farther than most men can see hair color.

I never met a woman I didn't immediately measure for sexual conquest. Females of all ages, races, and cultures; tall, short, friends' mothers, cleaning ladies, women belonging to religious orders, waitresses, the blond girl on Sesame Street, nurses, neighbors, and all the others you can imagine. Every relationship I've ever had with man or woman had most, if not all, to do with sex.

Except ours, Phillie, my one true friend.

Sex is the most powerful force in my life. I think that's true for most of us, especially men. It doesn't really matter. It's true for me.

> And to think, I knew almost nothing about sex till a
> few days ago when I started a new life . . .

A new life? One that started a year ago? That took a while to
sink in. It felt like one of those talk shows where they bring out
the long lost twin brother the guy never knew about. What
new life was Jack talking about? And how had he kept it secret
from me? There was more, but I wanted to look at the PHILLIE
file. When I tried to open it I got the following admonition:

> The file named "Phillie" is locked. Please enter the
> correct password to open it.

I typed J-A-C-K. It said INCORRECT, and five flashing hyphens
appeared challengingly. I entered JACKM and PHILL and WRITE.
Nada. I went through letter combinations like MURPH and LIEBO
and BOWIT. I took a wild stab at MRXTL and KIJUF and NIKON.
None worked. Where was the password to open the file?

A horrible thought struck me. With a sinking feeling I
thought I knew what the last message in our old computer had
been, the one which the power failure had caused to vanish
forever down the electronic drain, and just who had left it
there on his way out.

Damn.

1

I went back to THOUGHTS. Jack's writing had a tone I'd never read from him before. Powerful, and desperate.

> In the suburbs, emotionally exhausted men and women tumble into bed at night lost in separate fantasy worlds, dreaming hot dreams with their backs turned to each other, needing release, waiting for it, not getting any, waking with sweaty loins, carrying erections like wheelbarrows. Another day of wish-I-coulds. Another day of I-can't-tell-her or -him. He sneaks into bathrooms and runs the water to hide the sounds. She waits to be alone to impale herself on the artillery shell in the top dresser drawer under the underwear, or in the suitcase in the closet so the kids don't find it. ''. . . Mom, what's this, a battery holder?''

Sometime in the past year, Jack and I must have diverged like Frost's two roads. How had it happened? What had changed him?

Fatigue hit me like a wave, but I was too ragged to sleep. I lay on the couch and lit a joint. Wispy tendrils curled around my head. The smoke made my thoughts come faster, my feelings more accessible. It let out the anger at Jack I had been so good at concealing from Donnegan. Had Jack known how much I hated him? Did he know I knew? I felt gypped that he died before we'd had things out. I didn't tell Donnegan, but the truth was Jack and I were in the midst of breaking up. We'd ceased to be effective partners, and the reason for it was the same reason why a cold silence had settled over Carolyn and me like dust on the furniture.

If only he had told me, I could have been there.

What would I have said? Hatred and sympathy are an odd combination.

They all feel that way, Donnegan had said. How little he knew about Jack and me.

I opened a window to clear the smoke. It was cool outside. The air off the bay wafted in fresh and clean. If Jack hadn't committed suicide, and it wasn't an accident, he was murdered. That had to be my starting point, even if all the physical evidence said it *was* suicide. Could suicide be murder? I didn't know. I also didn't know what I was going to do about it yet, but a nagging thought kept telling me I had to do something.

Love and hate warred within me. I told myself I was wrong. Jack did it and that was that. Forget him. The trouble was, I couldn't. In spite of everything, I loved him. He was my partner, and I loved him. I always had, for all that we'd meant to each other for over twenty years, despite the images that seared my mind, cost me sleep, and left me curled up on the couch clutching my stomach like an embryo in pain.

When a man's partner is killed, the script read, you're supposed to do something about it. It doesn't matter what you thought of him. You're supposed to do something about it.

I didn't like it, but there it was.

FIVE

1

"Phillie?"

"Hmm?"

"It's morning. You said to wake you."

"Hm."

"Mommy, can I kiss Daddy?"

"Sure, honey."

A little hand on my chin. Perfect lips on my cheek. I smiled.

"Daaad!!!"

Bony knees flew into my chest, and I managed to cover my groin a split second before size-two sneakers hit it.

"Mom says get up!"

"Right, Ben. Thanks."

I opened my eyes and regarded my family. No one was holding any weapons.

"Breakfast," Carolyn said, and went downstairs.

We had redone almost every inch of our old Victorian house, moving from room to room like architectural termites. Formerly a disaster of epic proportions, the kitchen was now a sun-filled, yellow room with white cabinets and blue Formica counters. The kids had set the big pine kitchen table, so a knife, fork, paper plate, deli napkin, and plastic Mickey Mouse cup with handles were piled in front of my chair. I snared a juice glass and sat down.

Beth immediately ratted on her brother. "Ben took him a knife."

"I did not!" Ben protested. "She's a liar."

I'd seen the same look of innocence on serial killers, but I let it go. He was unarmed now, and no one was dead. You fight every battle, they cart you off in a suit with very long sleeves.

"Don't play with knives, son," I said. "Hospital bills being what they are."

"I didn't."

Beth the Testimony Freak whispered out the corner of her mouth, "Ben took it."

"Sit down and eat," I suggested.

"Mom's niddy," Beth told me proudly.

"Excuse me?"

"Knitting," Ben translated. "I got stuck by the needles."

"Where?" I asked, concerned.

"On the couch."

"No, I mean—"

"Wanna see?"

"Of course. Must've hurt."

"No, Dad. What Mom's making."

I gave up. "Yes, please."

Knitting was Carolyn's most recent attempt to improve her domestic ability. Other projects included reading every design magazine published, antiquing used furniture, caning chairs, and canning fruit. We had ended up with, respectively, fuel for the fireplace, ugly used furniture that became fuel for the fireplace, scratched asses, and food poisoning.

Ben and Beth dragged in a pile of misshapen blue squares.

"Nice," I said. "What is it?"

"Two hundred and fifty more, it's a sweater," Carolyn said, as if she didn't believe it either. Her face was carefully controlled around the children, but I knew she was still deeply shaken. She'd had time to think about it. She wanted to know what I knew, wanted to address the void that had just opened in our lives. Deeper than that, I couldn't read. I could only wonder.

She set down a plate of crepes. Carolyn couldn't cook most things worth a damn, but she made crepes like a Parisian street vendor. She had an MBA from Columbia and had been a vice-president at Chase Manhattan. She'd given it all up to stay home and raise the kids. She was a fine mother, as directed in that endeavor as in everything else she'd ever done, but emotionally, even after all these years, she was still struggling to fit into domestic life.

Carolyn regarded the blue mess sadly. A lot of effort had gone into those tangled strands. I wondered if maybe she was recording the pain of our marriage like some modern Madame Defarge. She leaned over to put it away. She was the same size eight as when we were married, God love her, and still had a flat ass—as rare in the suburbs as hen's teeth.

"It'll probably take five years at the rate I'm going," she said. "I was a better banker."

"It'll turn out fine," I said.

"Fine, Mom," echoed Beth supportively.

"I think it's time to replace the wallpaper in here," Carolyn said, as if that were what we'd been discussing.

"If you think so," I said.

She hooked her feet under her chair and ate quietly.

She looked nice this morning, long legs bare, brown hair bound up with one of Beth's crumply elastics. Her T-shirt was so faded you could barely read the U CONN logo, a school neither of us had attended. The years had given Carolyn a richer, softer look. You wouldn't want to hop into the back seat with her right off, you'd want to take her to dinner first, find out what she thought, make that smile of hers come up a few times. She didn't smile often, so when she did, it meant something. *Then* the back seat. Her nose was too big, but her eyes made up for it, bright as beacons. They were the best feature of all, smart eyes, kind eyes, eyes that saw the truth in things.

I'd once loved her very much.

"Did you get any sleep, Phillie?"

Ben took a crepe and poured enough sugar on it to go into insulin shock. Beth daintily smeared jam on hers.

"Not much," I said, looking at my watch. "I gotta get back."

"Is he . . . ?"

I nodded. "Yes."

"Is he what?" Ben asked.

"Nothing."

"Is he what?" Ben insisted.

"Who he?" Beth wondered.

"I don't wish to discuss this." I ate some of my crepe.

"Who, Dad?"

"Forget it, Ben," I said.

"Dad, you always say you shouldn't talk at the table if you don't want us to hear. Don't you?"

"Doan you, Dad?" asked jam-lipped Beth happily.

I raised an eyebrow. Carolyn shrugged. I nodded. Carolyn thrust her chin at me. The unspoken conversation had actually gone:

Should we tell them?

Well, sooner or later they'll have to know. Death is part of life. We shouldn't hide it and make them afraid.

I agree.

Good. You tell them.

I put my knife and fork down and turned to the kids. "I don't quite know how to say this to you, but Uncle Jack died last night."

"Uncle Jack?" Ben's eyes got real narrow. They'd had quite a few fishing trips and bull sessions between them.

"He—he had a heart attack. It didn't hurt him at all. But Aunt Jess is very sad, and we all have to take good care of her now. Okay? I have to go over right after breakfast."

Ben poked at his food. He said, "Okay, Dad." A longer talk

would come later on the private spot on the staircase landing we reserved for very important personal issues.

Knowing only that something in our world had suddenly slipped out of place, Beth said, "I hate this."

I said I did, too.

2

The kids went to play outside. I went upstairs and took a shower and got dressed. Carolyn came into the bedroom.

"Tell me," she said.

"He jumped into the empty pool and mashed his head. The police can't find any foul play. That makes it suicide in their book. The body gets released after the medical examiner takes Jack's organs out to study them."

"Jack wouldn't have," she said firmly.

"I told them that. It was a tough argument to make with him lying there."

"Did he leave a note?"

Maybe, but I said, "No."

"Christ," she said. "Jack. It hurts." Her face got that tight, lost look, and the first tears came. Maybe not the first.

"You'll miss him a lot, huh?"

Her eyes got cold. "We've been all through that."

"Not enough."

She turned away and started to clean the dresser. When women don't want to talk about something, they clean.

"I'm taking Jess to make arrangements today," I said. "Unless you want to."

"I'll go over later. Bring the kids and some food."

"Be nice to her."

She looked annoyed. "I always am."

"There's nice and there's nice."

"I'm a lot warmer to her than she is to me. Probably because I'm not a man. It never stopped me from being friendly."

"Friendly—now there's a strong word."

She ran a brush through her hair. "I don't have time for this, Phillie, I gotta drive the kids to camp."

I didn't want to fight. I wanted her to hold me and tell me it was okay, that we'd all get through this. She didn't.

Why the hell don't you? I wondered.

I read the answer on her face: Because I've had it up to here with the kids' needs, and your needs, and my own needs don't get met, so what the hell are you complaining about?

"Where's my brush?" I asked.

"In Beth's room."

She didn't get it, so I did.

Six

1

Jessica was sitting up in bed when I got there. She was still in her nightgown. There was a half-drunk cup of coffee and some pills on her nightstand. I could see the phone stuffed under her mattress, along with the Caller ID box and the answering machine. She looked tired and drained from the drugs and the rest of it but relieved to see me.

"Hello, Phillie. Thanks for last night."

"People been calling?" I asked.

"I talked to Abe Finch, and Jimmy, and Belle, and Louise. That detective, Donnegan, called. He's coming over."

"Lee phoned," I said. Lee Miller was our agent, an intense hunter-killer in a gray business suit. Every deal was personal to him. Every negotiation a battle. He made the War College look relaxed. "He sends his love and condolences."

Her eyes brimmed. "Phillie, I don't know what to do about any of this."

I swept some of her golden hair off her forehead. "Take something?"

"Valium. Fred left it."

"Good man, that Fred."

She heard my tone. "I still don't understand why you dislike him."

My nostrils flared, a sure sign of acid building. "Jess, some things come with certain professions. That doesn't mean people deserve them. It has nothing to do with the kind of person they are. It's just the way the system is set up. Fred thinks he gets what he gets because he's special."

"He studied hard, and he works hard, too."

"His work is physically easier than any manual laborer's, and he didn't study much longer than any other grad student. It ain't him, hon. It's just the club he belongs to."

"He wants to help people."

I sighed. "You're right, of course."

She looked at me tenderly. "Poor Phillie. Always so angry. How did Jack put it?"

I knew what she meant. "He used to say I had no middle ground. Even back in college he kidded me about my absolutes. Black or white. Good or bad. Right or wrong."

"It's a hard way to be, Phillie."

"Maybe, but the way I see it, Fred's an impossible phony, and that's unmitigated by the good he does. What can I say? My lot in life. Cursed by the God of Either-Or."

It was her turn to rumple my longish brown hair. "Baby's so complicated. Always in knots." She leaned forward. Her nightgown fell away.

And there it was.

I had to fight to remember that Jack was barely room temperature in the medical examiner's jars. An internal voice that all men know is our dicks masquerading as our minds argued slyly that comforting her in the face of death would be an affirmation of life. We should drink to Jack's memory, and if the vessel happened to be Jessica, so what? Jack had no right to her fidelity before his death, much less after. And he owed you *big*, Phillie old son.

I said softly, "Jess, I can't. You know that."

"Phillie," she breathed. "I *need* somebody."

"Jess . . ."

"Take what you want for a change. Jack did."

"No, he didn't." Automatic after all these years.

She sighed. "Don't pretend with me. I've been alone in this house more times than I can count."

I went and got her robe from the closet. She was right, and there was nothing I could say. Lying seemed irrelevant now.

She saw her reflection in the mirror over the dresser and it curled her mouth briefly. She lay back on her pillows looking even tireder than before.

"Phillie?"

"Yes?"

"I'm sorry."

"Don't be. I look around, I'm the weird one."

She kissed my cheek, this time sisterly. "Don't ever think it." She roused herself, clutching the robe demurely. "I'll get dressed."

"I called Morgan's Funeral Home. I figured you'd want to use them. Okay?"

"Okay. But no wake. Let's do it and be done."

"If you say so. One thing, though."

"Yes?"

"The coffin. It'll have to be closed."

"Just as well," she said from the bathroom. "I don't want to have to look at him."

2

It was cold in Morgan's Funeral Home. Bill Morgan himself ushered us into a private office and offered us coffee. We said no. He was a balding man with a long face who spoke in soft, foregone tones.

"I'm so sorry for your loss. Did you know Jack and I knew each other as kids?"

I said we did, sort of.

I hadn't grown up in Port Adams. Jack had. We were room-mates in college, and he convinced me to move here when we graduated. We got jobs at a local TV station together, writing the copy that led to our first collaboration. He was a part of everything I'd done since. I was with him the night I met Carolyn, when the kids were born, when his parents and my father died. He was godfather to Ben and Beth.

People said two less likely friends you couldn't find. The wimpy Jew and the fiery Irishman. I was mild and restrained, Jack was wild as the wind. I read books, he hopped freight trains. On our college summer jaunts around Europe, he ran ahead to see what was over the next hill. I planned lunch. I used to needle him how he always did everything first. I guess we were sticking to our patterns. He even beat me to dying.

Morgan said, "Our families lived side by side when we were young. For a while. Then Jack's grandfather—well, he did *so* very well in that business of his, he bought them a much bigger house across town." He smiled conspiratorially. "Jack and I used to sneak into the mortuary and play hide-and-seek."

Among the coffins? Yuck.

Morgan said, "Once we got the tar whaled out of us for taking my father's saws and building a treehouse."

I couldn't help myself. "Wrong tree?"

"Oh, no. It was the saws. They were the *surgical* kind."

"Phillie?" It was Jessica, eyes pleading.

"Er, Mrs. Murphy would like a very simple aff—funeral. Can you do that?"

Morgan produced several plastic-covered cards like Pizza Hut menus and handed one to Jessica and me.

"State law requires me to explain all the costs. Then we can go down and select a casket."

The list of items included everything from limos to pallbear-ers' white gloves at five bucks a pair. Jessica took one look at it and gripped my hand for strength.

"Mr. Morgan, what did the church say?" It was her first complete sentence.

Morgan couldn't meet her eyes. "I spoke to the monsignor earlier. There's a—a question as to whether Jack can be buried in consecrated ground. I mean, as you know—"

Jessica got angry. "What question? He's got pieces of the place named after him. There's a goddamn Jack Murphy window. It was important to him. He even went to *confession* every damn week."

"I know, but they won't, I'm afraid. There are many other lovely places. Let me show you." He fished in his desk for some brochures.

I had a lot of trouble with this. A Jew can never really accept rules can't be bent.

"Isn't there some way—?" I began.

Morgan shook his head. "They're quite firm about this."

"And they don't grant rich people divorces either. No money in funeral plots?"

He ignored my sarcasm. "Maybe we should start downstairs. We have a lovely casket selection. So beautiful."

Jessica tossed the menu onto his desk. "It won't be necessary. Do you have any plain wooden boxes?"

Morgan turned to her quizzically. "Yes, but—"

"Put him in one," Jessica said flatly. "And burn it."

SEVEN

1

I took Jessica home and drove back to town. Learning what was in Jack's file was my next order of business. I was still surprised at his not being able to get into the church cemetery, despite his moral crime. His family had been members of St. Timothy's Church in Port Adams for generations. He had never been what I would call religious in the God-fearing sense of the word, but he paid close attention to the sacraments and it was a big part of his background. It was as though he'd been expelled from his favorite club, one he had fond affection for, if not necessarily the utmost respect.

I hoped the file would give me some answers, but opening it without the password was beyond my meager skills. I had loved very few people in my life. My heart had been broken by Jack's betrayal and now his loss, both so close. Despair, never far from my soul to begin with, reached for me. I batted it away and parked in front of Lester Kornbluth's electronics repair shop on Main Street, computers a specialty.

"Mr. Liebowitz, how ya doin'?" Lester called from his cluttered workbench back behind the counter. He wore coveralls with ELKAY REPAIRS embroidered on the pocket and a baseball cap turned backward. The guts of radios, TVs, and computers sat in front of him, a technological timeline.

"Fine, Lester. You?"

"They keep breakin'," he said happily.

"I got a problem. Maybe you could help me."

He put down his meters and came to the undecorated Formica counter. The store was no frills, all business. He sold a few electronic items but only halfheartedly. Repairs paid the rent.

"What's up?"

I gave him a floppy disk with the PHILLIE file I'd copied onto it from my hard drive. "Coded file. No password. Can you open it?"

"You did it on your Mac?"

"Mr. Murphy did."

"Cops were talking at the diner this morning. Sorry."

"Me, too."

He blinked a few times. "C'mon back. Let's see what's what."

He popped the disk into a computer and played with the hyphens, added other programs, got new screens set up, and tried all the copy breakers he owned. He shook his head sadly.

"Sorry, Mr. Liebowitz. No dice."

"How come?"

"They build these entry protection things different ways. This one has traps built in. You fool around with it the wrong way, you lose it all."

"Nobody can open it?"

"*Somebody* can," he admitted. "But I don't know who. Want me to ask around?"

"If it's not too much trouble."

He started to thumb through a little notebook. "It's got to be worth somebody's time, you understand?"

"Time as in hundreds or thousands?"

"Could well be thousands. Time is money."

"So you've billed me."

"One thing for sure, though," Lester said, handing me back the disk.

"Yes?"

"Mr. Murphy made sure nobody could get into this who wasn't supposed to. Kind of your industrial-strength protection."

"Thanks, Lester." I reached into my pocket.

"Hey, forget it."

I felt guilty accepting something for nothing. "I've got a remote that's not working . . ."

Lester smiled. "Bring it in anytime. See ya around, Mr. Liebowitz."

2

Lester had given me an idea. A few years ago, Lindsay Juarez had retired as head of computer security for some big government agency and now happily ran the computer room at the library. Jack and I both knew her. If he wanted "industrial-strength protection," as Lester put it, he might well have gone to her.

Walking past the library's typewriter room always reminded me of when Jack and I weren't making enough money to buy our own equipment and had to use theirs. Now we were patrons. It was like the time we went to Italy the summer of our junior year. Too poor to afford anything but student-type cafés, I stared enviously at the people eating in the chic restaurants behind the green hedges around the Piazza Navona. Three years ago, Carolyn and I went to Rome and ate in those same restaurants, watching the kids on the other side. It helped me to understand growing up. It's going from one side of the hedge to the other.

Lindsay had her head in a drawer of electronic spaghetti

when I walked in. Kids were waiting expectantly to go on line. Their computer screens were dark.

"Lindsay?"

"One sec. Almost got it. . . ."

I waited while she did something to make the screens come alive. The kids looked relieved. Mice started clicking like castanets.

"Happy campers," I said, watching them hack their way down dragon-filled mazes, sometimes eaten, sometimes not.

"Yes, they are," Lindsay said, turning. When she saw it was me, she changed from cheerful teacher to sober adult. Death is a lot easier to handle when it's in cyberspace.

"Oh, it's you, Phillie. I heard about Jack. I'm very sorry."

"Thank you. I'll tell Jess."

"Do that. When is the funeral?"

"Tomorrow."

"I'll be there. Can I do anything?"

"Maybe. Did Jack see you for some kind of program to protect his work? Something using a password."

She nodded. "A couple of months ago. Said it was to protect against plagiarism. He wanted the best. I got it for him."

"He left a couple of files I can't open. No password. Can you do something?"

She looked doubtful, launching into a complicated technical explanation of why the best was the best. I understood only two words, *I* and *can't*.

"The program came by way of a friend at the National Security Agency," she said. "Without the password, the data will stay encrypted virtually forever. There are two billion possible combinations for those five spaces."

"No small number."

"The NSA doesn't like hackers."

"How come I can copy it?" I asked.

"Copy all you like. You still can't open it. Is it very important?"

"To me it is."

The kids were starting to crowd around with questions. "I'll do what I can," she said. "Do you have a copy?"

I had the disk I'd showed Lester. I gave it to her.

"Promise me you won't count on it," she said honestly, and went to join her computer whizzes in a land that didn't exist when I was a kid.

3

When I got back home, Carolyn was studying her knitting manual as if there were a test later. She stopped cramming long enough to fix dinner. We ate, then cleaned up while the kids played hide-and-go-seek around the house. I pictured Jack playing it with Bill Morgan among the caskets and coffins. Ghastly. It hinted at a side of him I hadn't known about. A darker side.

Lester and Lindsay had given me no confidence that the file could be opened. I wasn't sure what to do if it was inaccessible. I went up to the office to think and was annoyed to find the door jammed. It sometimes happened if the window was left open and a breeze blew the door shut. I needed a screwdriver to open it, and I was just about to go downstairs to get one when I heard the window opening inside and felt heavy vibrations on the roof. Breeze, hell. I ran downstairs and scooted out the front door and made it around back just in time to see a heavyset man running across my neighbor's back yard. I couldn't see his face. He plunged into the woods on the other side of the adjoining property where the land curved around the bay.

I vaulted my neighbor's fence, shocking the hell out of my knees, stumbled, caught myself, and ran after the prowler. It was beginning to sink in that he had been in my house. I knew from the police blotter that break-ins were happening more often in town. It scared the hell out of me. I tore into the woods. The guy was fast, but I was in good shape. We ran through the dark woods to the sound of dead leaves mushing underfoot. He was about a hundred yards ahead. I lost him in the foliage, then caught sight of him again. I still couldn't see his face. I ducked under a tangle of branches and decreased the distance between us. I was mad. He'd been in *my* house. Anger lent me speed. I could hear him gasping for air, slowing. If I could just keep it up . . .

I never saw the tree branch. It was like I was poleaxed. I fell into empty space. The ground hit me. My lights must have gone out for a second or two. There was a funny roaring in my ears. I rolled over on my back, trying to get my wind back. My chest was on fire.

In the distance I heard a car start up and screech away.

There was nothing more I could do. I walked back to the house with sweat dripping off me.

"Why did you run out of here like that?" Carolyn asked when I walked back in.

"I heard the Mister Softee guy."

"Did you get us anything?" asked Ben.

"I couldn't catch him."

Beth said, "S'okay, Daddy," so I shouldn't feel bad.

I got a screwdriver and pried open the office door. He'd been up here all right. Drawers were open. Papers were scattered all over the floor. I got it all cleaned up. I didn't think anything had been taken, but with all the stuff we piled on top of things, I wasn't sure I'd know if it was.

I'd never had a burglary before. I felt violated. Was it connected to Jack? For the life of me I couldn't see how. No one knew I'd taken the files from his computer. I'd left Lester and Lindsay only an hour ago. It had to be a coincidence. I decided to go with that and not call the police. What would I tell them anyway? Besides, they would only scare Carolyn and the kids and spook the whole block. We'd looked at burglar alarms once, months back, and just never got around to buying one. Now I called the company and told them to put one in. Tomorrow, if they could.

Burglars and suicides, funeral parlors and angry churches. I was a sweaty mess, uptight and nervous.

Jack wouldn't, Carolyn had said, and I'd told Donnegan the same.

I searched my computer hard drive for anything else Jack might have left, just in case. Nothing. Then I checked for anything more tangible to point me in the right direction—a letter, an address, a canceled check, something to give me a clue about his "new life." Another blank. He'd kept whatever he was doing completely hidden from me. I made a mental note to check his office more carefully. I was going to have to retrace the steps he'd taken and try to fill in the pieces I'd missed this last year.

The only other person who knew Jack nearly as well as I did was Zack Cleland.

I called Zack and told him I was coming over.

EIGHT

1

The Seaview Tennis Club is a funky old place over by the railroad tracks on the south side of town, the aging queen of North Shore tennis training facilities. The carpets are stained, the offices old, and the mildewy lockers look as if someone imported them from a vocational school in the South Bronx, but the unmistakable aura of talented young athletes hard at work imbues it all with an earthy dignity. You came here to work. You want luxury, go to a country club.

Zack hugged me when I walked in. "I heard. I'm blown away, man."

Zack was the head pro and part owner, a gifted athlete whose life was as uncluttered as his tennis. He was unselfish and true, my second oldest friend besides Jack. He was also

Ben and Beth's other godfather. Their only godfather now, I reflected sadly.

"When's the funeral?" he asked.

"Tomorrow."

"Ellen can make some calls."

"That would be good."

I threw my bag in his office, a privilege stemming from our long relationship. Zack had taught me how to play, and I owed whatever ability I had, admittedly small, to his efforts.

"Jesus, who can figure these things?" he said. "I haven't been worth shit since I heard. Any idea why?"

"No."

"You okay?" he asked.

"No."

"Wanna hit some balls?"

"Yeah."

Therapy, Zack style.

We hit hard, both of us needing release. On the tennis court I substituted tenacity for talent, hurling my ungainly body around and refusing to give up. I got to every ball, it was just that when I got there, the messages my brain was supposed to transmit to my body arrived too late to do any good.

We hit for an hour and I was exhausted. My wet shirt weighed eight pounds when I stripped it off.

"My backhand sucks," I said.

"Your backhand's solid. Just stay under the ball. Bend your knees."

His litany of torment: Bend your knees. Get under the ball. Move your feet.

"Zack, if I could bend my knees, I would. I've heard it so often, I'm thinking about having my ass taped to my ankles so I can play in a crouch."

"Might work," Zack agreed.

I sighed. "Let's hit the Jacuzzi."

We settled into the hot water. Zack's body was lean, smooth, muscular, and black. I cleverly hid all those neat things beneath a carefully cultivated, off-white spare tire.

I wasn't ready to talk about Jack. "Tell me about the kids," I said.

"Got some talented juniors this term," he said, and ran off a list. I felt decent for the first time since the phone call from Jessica. Was it only last night? This morning, more accurately.

"We got a big endowment from Mel's will," Zack said. "We'll bring some more inner-city kids out with it."

"He told me he was going to do it. He loved this place."

"Played till he got too sick. You made it nice for him, too, Phillie."

"We enjoyed each other."

We were talking about a remarkable man named Mel Hazen who'd died a few months before. Mel had made a fortune in chemicals, a field as compelling to me as, say, paint drying. Yet we'd had a common bond as students of human nature. I still missed him. It occurred to me I was losing friends at an alarming rate.

I said to Zack, "Don't get hurt, will you?"

He understood. "How's Jessica?" he asked, opening it up.

"Shaky. She doesn't know how to deal with this. I don't either."

"He must have felt very alone to do it."

"Assuming he did."

Zack raised an eyebrow. "What I heard, there isn't any question."

"And you just accept that?"

He looked at me closely. "You don't?"

"I've been going through it over and over again in my mind since last night. Jack loved life. He gobbled it up like a bunch of grapes. On the other hand, the police aren't waffling. They say for sure he jumped. I can't make it add up."

"He never talked to you about it?"

"No."

"Maybe there's stuff we don't know."

"There's always stuff you don't know," I said as we got out and toweled off. "Guy's a pillar of the community one day, next he's busted for a thousand pounds of pot in his basement.

All of a sudden everyone can see why he had two houses and took lots of vacations to the islands. Broken deals. Affairs. Christ, look at *this* place."

"It's the pressure, Phillie. Tough to afford life on the North Shore. The men are always tired or away. The women come here frustrated from being alone all the time or from being married to old men. Jack knew about that. It isn't news to you he scored more than games here."

I knew, and it saddened me.

I like women. I talk to them, and I think I know something about them. Male lore holds that the terrible moment in a man's life is when he realizes he's not going to be a professional athlete. The moment is different for a woman. It comes when she realizes she isn't ever going to have romantic love. It's a killer moment, and the reason affairs are more dangerous for women than for men, and why women are wisely cautious about them. They'd sooner kill than return to a life without a full heart. Women know what's important. Unfortunately, most of them know it too late.

Too many suburban women marry for money despite every instinct telling them they need love. You see them driving up at tennis matches and club dances in their Jags and Mercedeses, hair and makeup perfect. They seem content, but the strongest desire of all rages inside, the desire to be loved with passion. Some pass through it to a comfortable old age, warmed by the fire, knowing the time for such is gone. They did it for the kids, and now the kids are grown. The house is paid for. Florida beckons with skeletal fingers. So what if they never had the real thing. So it goes. So it goes.

Some drive the desire way down deep, where it festers and rots. Middle age for these women is a dry thing. Bitterness shapes once full and pliant mouths. They live without sex and tell themselves it is not so important. They soon revile it, especially for what it has not done for them. In the end they pull books about rebellion from the library shelves and curse teenagers who ride fast in cool convertibles along moon-drenched back roads. They hate early and long.

Others indulge. Sex becomes a scorecard. So many golf pros,

so many tennis pros, so many. Chin tucks and liposuction and face-lifts and enough energy expended on the treadmill or the court or the track to power a small city. They work to forestall what they know is inevitable: Life with the bland moron they married. In a big house.

To be fair, many women are full and complete. Their children are blessed with mothers who are ripe like summer peaches. Their friends know them as the ones who are always there for them. They are the quiet strength of the community, neither bitter nor harried, who have taken advantage of life's essential goodness and come to terms with the rest. My heroes have never been ballplayers or movie stars. My heroes are these women, and men, who seem to exist without the conflicts of my life, the constant unanswered questions and the uneasiness of living discreetly even though I know I must. I've tried to be like them. Sometimes I've even succeeded.

I once believed Carolyn and I were among the most rare of couples, blessed with true love. Love that conquered. Love that cured. But in the end we weren't, and it didn't. Not when it mattered. I tried to let my anger at that float away with the bubbles. I was only partially successful.

"Something changed Jack," I said. "What do you think it was?"

"This is silly, Phillie. He was the same."

"Money problems?"

"You know he got left a bundle, and you guys did okay."

"Zack," I said patiently. "I know I know that. I'm thinking out loud. Try to help."

"Sorry."

"Any difference in the way he played?" I asked.

"Looked just as good on the court last week as ever."

"Women." It wasn't a question.

Zack put on his tennis gear and didn't answer, which was answer enough.

"Who?" I asked.

"Bethany Williams."

I shrugged. "I already know about her. Who else?"

"Rita Krownits."

"Her, too."

He thought for a second. "Judy Lane."

Her I didn't know about. "Red hair, leather skirts? Plays on Wednesdays. Mercedes convertible."

Zack grinned knowingly and changed his speech pattern. "Ya noticed, mon?"

"I notice them all," I said. "And don't go Island on me, I know you went to Princeton after a sterling youth on the courts of Stamford, Connecticut."

"I was just surprised, that's all."

"For Christ's sake, Zack, I'm married, not dead. I just don't do more than notice."

"Someday somebody gonna turn your head around."

"Nope. A deal's a deal," I said firmly.

"You an' me seem de only ones who tink so."

"Was his affair with Judy common knowledge?" I asked.

"Probably not. Me, I know the signs. Come in two cars, one's left in the parking lot till right before dinner. You know."

"Yeah. Judy's hot," I observed.

"Word is, more than hot."

"What's more than hot?" I asked.

"Kinky."

"Dogs and cats, whips and chains, more than one, female to female?"

"Yep."

I didn't think he'd heard me. "Which?"

"All de above, mon."

Jack had always been strictly conventional sexually, if not numerically. Had Judy changed him? I thought about what he wrote. *I knew almost nothing about sex till I started my new life. . . .*

It was a place to start.

Zack picked up his rackets. "I gotta get back on the court."

"I'll call you later."

"One thing, Phillie. If—and I think it's a big if—if someone hurt Jack and you get involved, you gotta stop to think you might get hurt, too. Be careful, huh?"

"Jews invented careful. Could be a pogrom any second."

Zack laughed and went out to the courts.

I ran into Mel's nephew, Robbie, upstairs in the lobby. We were about the same age, and he played here, too. Robbie was a lumbering hulk with a bad temper, addicted to the biggest drug on the North Shore. Money. Money warps values the same way drugs do, binds people together unwisely, and tears them apart unmercifully. It so often substitutes for intelligence and good taste that most people don't know the difference.

"How are you, Robbie?" I asked.

He grunted a curt hello and mumbled something about Jack, which I thanked him for.

"Funeral?"

"Tomorrow," I said.

He grimaced. "I hate funerals."

Robbie's parents were killed in a car crash when he was ten. Mel raised him, got him through school, and financed his business endeavors, all of which failed. In a way I felt bad for him. He was almost universally disliked. Except for his military service in Vietnam, which I'd heard had been no picnic, Robbie had always lived in Mel's house, spent Mel's money, and dispensed favors in Mel's name. It had given him a false sense of importance, and having earned none of these things on his own, he jealously guarded them as if fearing they could be taken away as easily as they'd been given.

"What time?" he asked.

"Noon."

"I might come."

I was surprised. "Jack's family will appreciate it."

"It's a small town, Phillie, you know?"

I wasn't sure what he meant. "In the sense of everybody knows everybody's business, or we all gotta stick together?"

"Tough when you lose somebody close," he said, as if that explained it, and walked away.

I said for the record, "He was my partner."

The reservation sheets were on a clipboard behind the

counter. I looked through them. Judy Lane was scheduled to play at ten on Wednesday. Clay court. I clicked the pencil against the counter.

The police said Jack killed himself.

I said he didn't.

I booked the court next to Judy's. Wednesday at ten.

NINE

1

The kids were in bed when I got home. Both clamored that they were still hungry. I was, too, after playing.

"Midnight snack," I announced, and they scampered downstairs happily.

Carolyn put a loaf of bread and a plate of cold cuts on the kitchen table, and the kids examined the slices like suspicious clerks checking for counterfeit bills.

"Did you wash your hands?" I asked.

"Yep," Ben said without a second thought. In the world of liars the kid was a natural.

"Yep," Beth said. Adding, "Outside."

"I see."

It was fun the way sudden meals can be. We talked about our day. Events at camp. Movies we wanted to see. I think

Jack's sudden death made us value our family's closeness all the more. It was an unexpected pleasure.

"May I be excused?" Ben asked. He bought the manners rap only as much as it worked. The notion of concern for others was as alien to him as cleaning his room. Like most parents, I settled for form without content gratefully.

"Brush your teeth. Help Beth."

"Be s'cused too, Daddy?" Beth asked.

"Sure, kid. Give Daddy a kiss."

" 'Kay."

I wiped the mayonnaise off my cheek. The kids went back upstairs and seemed to be doing fine by themselves, so Carolyn and I cleaned up. It was a rare quiet time. Carolyn plunged a dagger into it.

"Phillie, we have to talk."

"Why?"

That threw her. Talking was supposed to be an automatic good. Like giving. I no longer put great value on talking. It couldn't change the past.

"We can't keep doing this," she said.

"Yes, we can. Till both kids graduate from college. Then you want out, be my guest."

"I don't want out, Phillie," she said plaintively. "I want . . . back."

My face must have told her how little I wanted to go over this again. She turned away so I wouldn't see her crying. There was a time it would have made me want to hold her. Instead, I wiped the table.

"For God's sake, Phillie, one time—" she said tearfully.

"It doesn't matter one time!" I yelled. I caught myself. The kids were upstairs. "This isn't the time and place."

"When is?"

"I don't want them to hear us."

We couldn't shout, so we fought cleaning up. Dishes clinked hard into the sink, silverware crashed into the drawer, garbage got shoved harshly into the pail.

Carolyn slammed a cabinet with particular violence.

"Don't make me the bad guy in this," I warned her. "Because I'm not."

"Phillie, there aren't any bad guys. Just people. Helpless, fallible people." She looked at me sadly. "You're too damn tough on everybody. Even on you."

That threw me.

2

We are each at the center of a web of relationships that holds us in place. Without them we'd go spinning off into space alone and unconnected, homeless people baying at the moon. Although we may resent these ties, without them we are nothing but islands broken off the mainland, clods washed away by the sea, diminished or augmented by nothing because we are uninvolved.

I was bound to Carolyn by the children, to the children by love. By love to responsibility; by responsibility to maturity; by maturity to work. In my tight little sociometric diagram of a life, I was bound to my house and car by the bank, by the bank to my credit rating, and to my credit rating by the middle-class values to which I clung, sometimes by my fingernails. Each of these things represented choices, but they weren't why I stayed. I stayed because I knew if I let the vibrations of discontent throb down the strands, they would collide and spread until the whole web fell apart. To fix a single strand in the intricate weave of my life, I'd have to take the entire web apart, strand by strand, choice by choice.

I couldn't do that.

I didn't think I'd ever get it back together again.

3

It still felt strange to be in my office. I kept expecting Jack to walk in. I tried to open the PHILLIE file again using license plate numbers, addresses, birthdays. When that didn't work, I tried words that might have meaning for Jack, like PENIS and DILDO.

I settled down to work. Nights were usually good for me with the kids asleep and the phone quiet. Jack and I had been writing an original screenplay and it was only half finished. I didn't know if the studio would let me do it alone. In fact, I didn't know what kind of a career I had left without Jack. I hadn't felt so insecure in years. My hands froze on the keyboard. I was sure I couldn't face Hollywood alone. Somewhere scientists are working to take us to the real stars. *They* are important, and we'll be far better off when we realize it. Till then, come to plague-infested Los Angeles and make movies. You will plumb the depth of your depraved soul.

We had sold Fox on a comedy idea about two guys starting out making an independent film. It was based on us. In the early days we had gone to indecent lengths to break in. Looking back, it was funny. Then it was heartbreaking. We were young. We wanted to write. We thought we were ready.

We were wrong.

No experience we ever had as a team was as bad as making our first movie, and the screenplay we'd been writing about it —and the events that had led up to it—weren't completely fictional, although everyone thought it had to be. Orpheus and his pal Costello, we descended into hell and lost the damn girl, too.

The first project Jack and I had written together was a spec teleplay about a high-profile agent with a hard pitch and a soft heart. We took it to Alan King. He took it and disappeared. That wasn't so cruel or unusual, but it was devastating to us.

"I don't understand," I'd whined over matzoh ball soup in a Great Neck deli. "The meeting went great. King loved us. How come he hasn't called back?"

Jack shrugged. "His secretary said he was sick."

"Short of a heart attack, he should have called."

"Finish your soup, Phillie, we have to get back to work."

King and chicken soup sparked an idea for me. "Wasn't he the guy who coined the phrase Jewish penicillin?"

"So?"

"Let's send him some chicken soup!"

"And a note," Jack agreed enthusiastically. "Waitress, do you deliver?"

"Minimum twenty-dollar order."

"How much chicken soup is that?" I asked.

She tallied in the air. "Two gallons."

Jack didn't hesitate. "Send it!"

Looking back, I guess we sent the soup because we were at the point where doing anything made sense. Our mistake was sending *all* the soup. A quart would have left us some for dinner. King never called.

Later, we tried to co-produce a movie with a lunatic French-woman who had a matching film grant from the Canadian Film Board, and a retired FBI agent who knew an interested producer.

"I flew in as soon as Steve told me you had a million dollars," the producer said happily when we met him for breakfast in his hotel's dining room.

I gave the FBI man a sharp look. "Wait a second. Didn't you explain we get the million only after we put *in* a million?"

"Yeah, but we still get a million," he said.

"*After* we put in a million."

"Who's got the million?" Jack sang.

"Let me get this straight," said the producer, smelling the first rat. "You don't have a million?"

"I'm really sorry," I said, totally embarrassed. "I thought he explained all this."

"Sure, kid. Waiter?"

There were so many stories, I couldn't help smiling. We met a director who was going to produce our script. Phyllis—more about her later—took us to him because he was indebted to her rich husband. He was a pompous braggart with an unconscionable ego. His name was on every item in his office: on the director's chairs in front of his desk, on the one-sheets of his movies, on stuffed animals, on mugs, on the awards on his walls.

We said hello.

He said, "The company is in favor of your project. We believe in *Phyllis. She's* the reason you're here. We trust *her.* If *she* feels this script is producible, we'll back her. Now, remembering that I refuse to allow unintelligent characters from cocky writers who think they're better than their audience—"

"Now just a minute," Jack began.

The director peered at us over his glasses as if we were bugs. "My first film? I produced it for ten thousand dollars. Mortgaged everything. Couldn't go over budget. I had to break it all down day by day. Rain, snow, sleet, hail . . ."

On and on.

But of all the crazies we met, Phyllis was the ultimate, the *pièce de résistance.* Manic, manipulative, unhealthy, egocentric, self-indulgent, overemotional, and crass. We fought all the time. Carolyn and the kids are under strict orders to tell her, if she ever calls, that I died.

Picture Jack and me writing on our computer. Picture Phyllis, about fifty, flabby, dressed in a body stocking, popping vitamins into her mouth from a big Tupperware container while fastwalking on the noisiest treadmill in America, looking over our shoulders at the screen and "correcting" what we write.

Whir whir whir . . .

"No! She wouldn't wear a red sundress! She's the wife of a corporate executive. A Wasp. They don't wear red!"

"Why not?" I asked.

Whir whir whir . . . "I would never wear red."

"But this character isn't you," I protested.

"It's like hats."

"Hats?"

"She should be wearing one. A V-neck T-shirt and a hat and a low cut . . ." *Whir whir whir . . .*

"Who wears V-neck T-shirts?" Jack demanded.

It was too much for me.

"Just sneakers and a T-shirt," Phyllis pronounced.

"If it rains, we've got an R rating," observed Jack.

I moved on. "I like this next line," I said.

"So do I," agreed Jack.

"She wouldn't say that."

I jammed a pencil in my mouth. Jack paced. *Whir whir whir* . . .

Phyllis popped more pills. "You sure you don't want some of these?"

"No."

"This stuff is so good for you. No sugar. You know what sugar does to me? Rots my skin. Makes it fall off. Here. Look." She pulled up her shirt. "Just two candy bars, and—"

Jack said quickly, "We believe you."

"Phyllis," I said, "why not try eating some normal food for a change?"

She made a face. "I can't. I'm allergic to everything. Meat. Fish. If I ate an oyster, I'd die. Slimy little things. First I'd throw up, then I'd die. Ice cream? Like Kryptonite. My tits would shrink, then I'd throw up, then I'd die."

"About this scene, Phyl—"

"Look at this," she said. "I sweat like a pig. Did you know an alligator sweats through his mouth? Really. He lays there with his snout open, letting off heat. I wonder if it works?" She started to breathe heavily and noisily through her mouth.

I knew what had happened. It was the Twilight Zone.

Whir whir whir . . .

I couldn't believe Jack was gone. I shut off the computer. Enough for one night. Downstairs, everyone was asleep. After a few hits on a joint, my mind hit the clutch and disengaged. I lay on the office couch with my eyes closed, remembering more of the sad, painful, funny things Jack and I went through; casting sessions at old-age homes, plots to murder the director, Jack's unique retelling of a conference call we had where Phyllis phoned from her shrink's office and put him on the line. Without Jack, I would have gone insane. He was always there to pull me back from the edge and get me to go on, assuring me it would all be worth it in the end. He had a special gift for making me laugh, and it made the world not such a down and desperate place.

I drifted off to sleep thinking you lose a lot when a brother dies.

TEN

1

A black stretch limo took Jessica and me to the funeral Tuesday morning. It was a day for just about anything else. The August sun made the air buttery warm, and the breeze smelled of moist earth. Jess wore a black suit and gray silk blouse, black heels, and dark stockings. She kneaded a soft black, veiled hat nervously through her hands.

"I couldn't do this without you, Phillie."

I took her hand, stopping the hat. "We're family, Jess. Remember that. Anything you need, we'll be there."

"What did you tell the kids?"

"Uncle Jack had a heart attack, and we were all very sad."

"Is Carolyn bringing them?"

I nodded. "They won't understand what's going on, but in the long run they'll feel better to have been a part of it."

A sudden thought worried Jessica. "Phillie, what do we do afterward? I didn't even think . . . I mean, people—"

I patted her knee. "Carolyn and Ellen called a caterer. Afterward, anyone who wants to will go back to your house."

She pressed my hand gratefully, then turned inward again.

There were a lot of people at the funeral home. Carolyn and Ellen, Zack's wife, had been on the phone a good part of last night. Ellen was a gracious woman, expansive, warm, and loving, like the quilt you had when you were a kid. Zack was standing close to her on the front steps, their hands intertwined as usual. I spotted my agent, Lee Miller, smoking a cigarette. Nearby, Fred Marcus was checking his watch impatiently and wondering why God hadn't spoken to him in the last five minutes. It was a good crowd, maybe a hundred and fifty in all. Jessica seemed pleased.

I saw Judy Lane, alone, lift her dark glasses to dab at her eyes.

"Ready?" I asked Jessica.

"Don't leave me," she said, eyes pleading.

I installed Jessica in the front row. The coffin was a simple unfinished pine box. Flowers had been arranged to cover it, as if it weren't good enough.

Somebody tapped me. It was my son, Ben. He was wearing a blue blazer, white shirt, and tie. He looked spiffy as hell, but his eyes were wary.

"Hi, Dad."

"Hi, Ben. You okay?"

"Sort of. What's gonna happen here?"

"We're going to pay our respects to Uncle Jack. Somebody will offer a prayer, and then I'll say something."

" 'Cause he was your best friend?"

My eyes brimmed. "Yes."

"Where's Uncle Jack now?"

"In that—in heaven, son."

"Oh."

Beth was wearing a dress and looked scared. She kept her face pressed tightly against Carolyn's leg. Carolyn walked over to comfort Jessica, and they ended up hugging and sobbing.

Beth tugged on Carolyn's dress, and Carolyn picked her up so all three could hug. Ben watched the females curiously.

Bill Morgan waited till everyone was seated to address us from the podium.

"I knew Jack Murphy well, from a shared boyhood. It's especially sad when someone so young and vital passes on. . . ."

I only half listened. I was remembering when relatives died when I was a kid, and we would go out to the Jewish cemetery with my aunts, uncles, and cousins. It was the kids' job to get rocks to put on the headstones to let the dead know we had been there. My father's job was to locate one of the incredibly scruffy rabbis who inhabited the place to say some prayers. My father always made faces behind the rabbi's back when he chanted in Hebrew, and the kids fought not to laugh.

It took me years to realize how much my father hated being there.

When Bill finished, he summoned me to the podium. The crowd looked at me expectantly.

"On behalf of Mrs. Murphy," I began, "I'd like to thank you for coming today . . ."

I hesitated, and started again.

"Jack was my friend and partner—"

I stopped. My words hung dead in the air.

I heard Jack asking me, *Don't you ever just say what you feel?* Feet were shuffling. There was an uncomfortable silence. Carolyn moved her lips slowly and deliberately so I could read them. *Just say it, Phillie.* I put my notes in my suit pocket.

"Look," I said to them, "when you write together you share things. You expose what's important, what you believe in, what you're afraid of. Bill means well, but Jack wouldn't want you crying and wringing your hands and using words like *untimely* and *waste* and how only the good die young. We all die too young, don't you know? Ask a guy at eighty if he's ready to go, and he'll stare at you cold enough to freeze you where you stand. He's close, see? And he wants more. Nobody goes easy, and no matter how it looks, if I know Jack he didn't either."

I took a deep breath and pushed on, not really knowing where I was going.

"See, if life is a gift, it's just plain bad manners to gripe about the size of what you got, or the price of it, or how long you had it. You enjoy a gift. You push it and pull it and make it do what you want. You use it to the hilt. That's what Jack did. And by the time he was done, he'd used life better than most people ever do."

I'd told myself I wasn't going to cry. Not in front of all those people. Jack would have laughed at me, told me what a schmuck I was, the word sounding funny on his thin Irish lips, like me saying *blarney*. But when I looked at the well-dressed quiet people on the folding chairs, and Jessica and Carolyn and Ben and Beth, suddenly the whole place went glassy and my voice got all wobbly, like when I was in fourth grade and got sent to a speech class and was told to stand up and talk and I couldn't for all the trembling.

I said to people I could not see, "I wish I could tell you why a thing like this happens, but I can't. I don't know why. All I know is there are a lot of jerks around, and Jack wasn't one of them. He had character. That's a fine thing. I—I loved him very much."

I had to hold my eyes open wide to keep the tears back. Jessica was crying softly. I saw Carolyn biting her bottom lip the way she does when she's proud of me. I couldn't see why she should be.

When I got back to my seat, Ben surprised me by snuggling tightly against me.

It helped.

2

After the service I stood outside with Zack and Lee. Carolyn and the kids and Ellen had gone with Jessica in the limo back to her house.

Lee put an arm around my shoulder. "Very impressive eulogy. Did him justice. How are you?"

"Coping. Barely. What's new?"

"Studio says they'll judge the product when it comes in like always, with or without Jack. They send their sympathy. They're not being bastards for once."

"That's good to hear."

"Can you finish it? I said you could, no problem."

"Sure. No sweat." That's what you always say. If they ask you to do a rewrite in ten days, no sweat. Can you translate the Bible into Martian? No sweat.

"I'm trying to get you a rewrite from Fox. People feel good about you, Phillie. Don't worry too much."

"I worry the sun won't rise tomorrow, Lee."

"Try not to. It will."

"So you say."

He laughed. "The original optimist."

"Mr. Liebowitz?"

I turned, surprised to see Donnegan standing there. He was wearing a blue jacket and gray slacks. Black shoes. White shirt and tie. I didn't like him here. I realized why. We shouldn't have needed him.

"Hello, Detective."

"I came to pay my respects."

"Nice of you," I said, meaning it.

"Got a minute?"

"Sure."

Zack touched my shoulder. "Want company?"

He was so loyal. Should I ever get into a fistfight—God forbid—I want Zack at my back. If I get hit from behind, I'll know he's dead. I said no, thanks, and Donnegan and I went to the little garden alongside the building. He lit a smoke.

"Nice eulogy."

"Thanks."

"You cared about him."

I shrugged. "Wanna know something?"

"Yeah."

"Lately, I hated his guts."

"Why?"

I didn't answer.

"It didn't show," he said.

"It wasn't supposed to."

I moved some dirt with my shoe. "You know, I never really said in there what I liked best about Jack. I mean, what probably kept us together, being so dissimilar and all."

Donnegan looked interested. "Were you? Dissimilar, I mean."

"Pastrami and mayonnaise."

"Got it."

"He made me laugh," I said.

"That's all?" He sounded disappointed.

"Don't knock it," I said. "Most of the time I'm so angry, I make myself crazy thinking about all the things in the world I should be out there changing. I don't know why I give a shit, but I do. Then Jack would come charging in and power up his computer and tell me about some crazy woman who just sat on his face, or he'd be riled about some sports thing that made no sense to me. He made the world not so gloomy. Does that make sense?"

"Sure. You think cops look for a partner who shoots like Rambo? You want a guy who knows how fucked up you are in your own way and takes a little of it off your back." His eyes twinkled. "If he likes the same doughnuts, so much the better."

I laughed. I was beginning to like him. I had to watch it. Like and trust were inseparable for me.

"What did you want to talk to me about?" I asked.

"We got the initial toxicology report from the coroner's office. Did you know your partner used cocaine?"

"No way," I said flatly.

He was watching me closely. "One of the first things they do is swab the nose. His sinuses looked like fire pits."

I absorbed that slowly. It was deeply disturbing. I'd been to enough Hollywood parties to know that anyone who told you cocaine wasn't addicting was on it. I hadn't known Jack was doing it—part of his new life, I supposed. Was that what had changed him? Someone once predicted that all the bodies those Mafia types disposed of in the ocean would someday bob to the surface when the concrete holding them down dissolved, or the chains rusted through. I had that feeling here.

Another piece of Jack's secret life had bobbed to the surface, rotten and decayed. It didn't augur well for the other things I was going to find.

"Can I talk off the record?" I asked.

That amused him. "Do I look like a reporter?"

"I want to be able to say I never said it."

"You can always say *that*," he said.

"I guess. The only thing I ever knew about was we—he smoked a little pot."

"Nothing more?"

"No. What else did you find?"

"He was in perfect health," Donnegan said. "Organs okay. Good muscle tone. Screened negative for diseases."

"Of the body, anyway."

Donnegan looked interested. "What do you mean?"

"Whatever killed Jack was in his head. He loved life, he wouldn't just abandon it. Something drove him into a place he couldn't see any way out of."

"Do you know what it was?"

I shook my head. "No, but I'm going to."

Donnegan let out a long slow breath. "You're not gonna play detective, are you?"

I was about to be defensive, but something stopped me. I looked at him more closely and saw his uncertainty for the first time.

"You don't think so either," I said.

His face was impassive. "Think what?"

I was sure of it now. "That it was suicide. I know you think he did it and all, but something doesn't add up in the *way* he did it. Or the *whys*. Your policeman's mind is still figuring. I can see it. You're unhappy. That's why you came today. You're smelling the wind."

"Maybe."

"Look, I've rewritten more cop stories than I care to name. The thing I always take out is where somebody doesn't tell someone else what they know for some stupid reason that would have solved it all if they'd just been average smart enough to trust the other guy. So I'll make you a deal. Let's be real. You show me yours, I'll show you mine. Right from the beginning. No holdouts. Okay?"

He thought that over. Lit another cigarette from the first. I didn't think cop work relaxed him.

"Every week the chief medical examiner and the chief toxicologist and their pathologists and serologists and the rest of the staff sit down with the homicide detectives and the district attorneys and go over their cases. The ME's gotta rule one way or another on cause of death. Officially, your partner's listed as suicide, but a lot of people are arguing for ruling it undetermined or even homicide. There's the lack of a note. And cokeheads don't usually jump off roofs. Crazies using PCP and other hallucinogenics do. One other thing, too."

"What?"

"There were recent needle marks on his arm. Just days old, or we'd have missed them. We'd like to know why."

"Not more drugs?" I was still reeling from the cocaine.

"He screened negative for all other drugs of abuse."

"It makes no sense to me," I said.

"You find a suicide note yet?" Donnegan asked.

"Why are you so sure there was one?"

"Never met a writer in my life didn't run at the mouth when he had the chance."

I started to speak, didn't. Lost either way.

"If you find it," he said, walking away, "remember—I showed you mine."

I felt guilty as hell not telling him about the file.

I should have read my own script.

It would have saved a lot of lives.

ELEVEN

1

I was still digesting what Donnegan told me when I walked into Jessica's house. Lots of people had come over after the funeral, and the air was almost festive. Multicolored platters of smoked fish, meats, breads, and pastries were laid out on tables in the dining room. Less work went into the Sistine Chapel than goes on a yearly basis into food platters on the North Shore. Centuries from now when they are uncovered in archaeological digs, their number will foster the theory among archaeologists that we prayed to food. They'll be right.

A group of locals was talking in the living room, led by Sy Weidermeyer. I knew Sy from when we worked on a project for the school board together. Sy was a psychologist, which meant he was massively fucked up and had decided to help others. He was trim, youthful, and competitive as hell, very North

Shore. Tachini warm-up suits, a lover in the afternoon, a short nap on his own couch, then a quick drive home smug as a chipmunk with a hoard of nuts in his tree. I could hear him talking about the need to build more shelters for the homeless.

Where? somebody asked.

Sy thought there was a lot of land upstate.

Sy walked over to me as I was putting enough sturgeon on my plate to cover the Russian conversion to capitalism. He was wearing a tan ultrasuede jacket, white jeans, a shirt and tie, and New Balance running shoes. Fucking vanilla.

"Did you hear?" he asked, slithering some herring into his mouth. He reminded me of a moray eel.

"Nope," I mumbled, eating the delicate white fish that cost fifty dollars a pound. I was hard pressed to feel morally superior. I tried to slither less.

"Denise and Frank split up."

"No. Really? How come?"

He winked. Same old story. Behind the well-tended lawns . . .

"Him or her?" I asked.

"I hear her, but you never know," he said.

"Too bad. Kids and all. It hurts them."

"That's never been proven clinically, Phillie."

"C'mon, Sy. You know any kids saying, 'Gee, I'm happy as hell my mom and dad split'?"

"Health is a state of mind."

For this he got two hundred an hour? Health is a state of mind?

I said, "Kids need two parents. Working hard. Cooperating. Putting them first every day of their lives."

He speared some more fish. "Cultural trends differ. It's not the only way."

"I didn't say it was. I said it was the *best* way."

Sy stared myopically down his long vulture nose. "That's a value judgment, Phillie."

"You bet your ass it is, Sy."

He smiled. "I understand." More fish. "And how are *you* doing, Phillie?"

"Jim-dandy, Sy. Never better. Hot diggety dog. God damned great." I unclenched my teeth to smile.

He peered at me over his glasses. Fucking Big Bird.

"Phillie, have you ever asked yourself what you're so angry about?"

"I'm not angry except for my normal anger." It was probably my version of "Health is a state of mind."

"Come again?"

"Sy, I'm angry about so many things, I don't know where to start. I'm angry about how slow the fucking check-out line in the Grand Union is, and I'm angry about people who get more breaks than I do. I'm pissed as hell about the guy who tried to rob the school and fell through the roof and sued the district for negligence and *collected*, mind you, and I really have a case for liberal guys who hire women and then lord it over them that their husbands don't make enough money to support them. And maybe the thing I'm angry about most of all, Sy, is that maybe if I wasn't so goddamn angry, I wouldn't have any personality at all."

Sy looked at me closely. "We should talk."

"It won't change anything."

"It won't change the past, that's true."

"What else is there?" I scooped up some whitefish salad and walked off to cool down.

A man with a caterer's apron got in my way. "Excuse me, sir. Are you Mr. Liebowitz?"

"Yes."

He looked relieved. "I'm Henry, the caterer. Mrs. Murphy is indisposed. Someone said you might be able to make a decision."

"I don't know, Henry. I'm not feeling so good about my decisions these days."

"They're like food, Mr. Liebowitz. Some go down better than others."

Was everybody smarter than me or what? "What can I do for you, Henry?"

"We're out of wine, sir. It's my fault entirely."

"No problem. There's a wine cellar if you need more."

"I'm sorry to ask. Could you come and verify what I take?"

"Okay."

Downstairs wasn't a basement, it was another floor underground. There was a movie theater with a thirty-five-millimeter projector and a big screen. Also a pool room and a sauna. There was even a refrigerated closet for Jess's furs. I showed Henry where the wine was. He scanned the racks and started putting bottles in a box.

I waited for him in the big playroom. I'd always liked how Jack and Jessica had decorated it with old tools they'd bought during their antiquing days. The tools hung on hooks set into authentic barn siding, with little name tags underneath that Jess had hand-lettered. Eighteenth-century planes, hammers, ice tongs, a restored brace of tiny black-powder derringers with a leather powder-bag, even a blacksmith's tongs complete with the initials of the man who made it, CC, Charles Cornwall. An odd smell crinkled my nose when I walked in, and I wondered if the room was properly ventilated. The leather would rot if it wasn't. I opened the air-conditioning grate wider.

"Mr. Liebowitz? I'm ready."

Henry handed me a list and kept insisting that he would replace the bottles, that wine was included in his price and I shouldn't worry. I couldn't have cared less.

I followed him up, glad to see Sy was gone—that is, till I saw my mad friend Todd in the living room. He must have arrived when I was downstairs. His blue sport-jacket pockets were bulging with keys and stuff, which made the front droop and the back ride up his behind, splitting the vent wide. His tan chinos were as rumply as his face. His sad eyes were as sad as ever.

"Lousy thing," he said.

"Lousy," I agreed.

"Nice words today."

"Thanks. How's it going for you?"

"Going, going . . . gone," he replied. In his tax bracket, everybody's a comic. But I knew he wasn't talking about money.

Todd sold some kind of bonds in South Dakota and Texas.

Put away maybe a half million a year. Had parties with people who talked about boats and how nobody worked hard anymore. He'd been gazing out at the pool. Maybe he felt a kinship with Jack. He was trapped, too.

"I never figured him to go that way," he said.

"Me neither."

"I thought about doing it once," he confided softly. "When it got really bad."

"You made the right choice."

"I guess so. I appreciated your help, Phillie."

"Forget it."

What Todd was referring to was his having fallen in love with a long-legged horsewoman named Samantha from the Dakota plains, a love that had only one thing wrong with it— his wife, Marcia. Marcia was sweet and smart and hardworking, and she and Todd had loved each other through time and children, but Samantha awakened emotions in Todd he hadn't felt in years. He knew it was hopeless. He couldn't leave Marcia. She'd done nothing worse than grow older. But it was killing him. He sought my advice one day over beers, and I had to tell him the sad truth. Pain you get over, love you never do. If he left Marcia, it would kill her. If he didn't, he'd have to live with a cold, hard spot in his heart born of selling out passion to responsibility. On balance, I told him, stay. Honor his commitments. In the end, he did. Marcia's still good and kind and loving, and deep down Todd's pretty sure he made the right decision, but sometimes a tall willowy blonde in a crowd draws his attention and makes his stomach feel as if he swallowed a table, and he is quiet for days. My solace is real. In every man's heart there is a place for the one woman God sent us, the one timeless love we are entitled to. If we think it is the one we said no to, we are never quite so damn sure of anything in this life afterward.

"See ya, Phillie," he said.

"Take care, hear?"

"Hey, I'm okay," he insisted, his head bobbing like a cork on the water. "Really okay. Really."

That many *really*s, it wasn't me he was trying to convince.

2

I went upstairs. Jessica was sitting up on her bed in stockinged feet. Fred Marcus was with her.

"Phillie."

"Fred." Gnat. "How are you, Jess?" I asked.

She patted the bed beside her. I sat. "I don't know how to thank you for today, Phillie. What you said. It was straight from the heart. Everybody could tell. They all said so."

"Nice," Fred added effusively. His eyes were saying, Get out. I wondered about that. I said so.

"Isn't it a little soon, Jess?"

"That's none of your—" Fred started.

"Shush, Fred. Phillie is special. He and Jack were like brothers. That makes him family. He asks, I'll answer."

Fred sniffed. I loved that. Next he'd pull a hankie from his sleeve and put it to his nose. I wanted to pop him one. Jess saw it.

"Phillie, you should know that Fred and I were lovers before Jack died. I was never unfaithful till it got to the point where Jack was so around the bend I just couldn't depend on him anymore. When was he coming home? When was he going out? I never knew. We were split in too many ways to put it back together. We would've separated if he hadn't. . . . I hope you understand."

I hated the fact that I did. I'd been there too many times when Jack called to tell her we were working late and then cut out to meet someone.

"You were wrong, Jess. You should have—"

Her laugh was bitter. "Should have what? Gone to counseling? I asked him a million times. I even spoke to his priest. Can you imagine? *Me* going to a priest and asking for help?"

I couldn't. Jess hated the Church. Things in her past she'd hinted at but never really explained. Their rejecting Jack had only deepened her animosity.

Fred said, "I'll handle this, Jessica. Perhaps Phillie and I should step outside."

"Fred," I said. "That would be a mistake. The thought of

you in Jack's bed makes me so mad, I'd probably smack your little jowly face around."

He reddened. "I think that's quite enough, don't you?"

"Don't pull that take-charge hospital-doctor crap on me. I'm not some kid nurse makes twenty thou a year wants to bang you in the closet so maybe you'll take her out of bedpans and give her a house and a BMW."

He fumed but didn't say anything. Jessica put her hand on mine.

"I'm asking, Phillie. I love Fred. In time, we're going to get married." She squeezed. "Be my friend?"

It didn't sit well with me, but there wasn't a damn thing I could do about it.

"Sure, Jess."

I shook Fred's pasty little hand and didn't smack his face.

Shows you how wrong a person can be.

TWELVE

1

A brisk wind was shoving the clouds around Wednesday morning as I drove to the tennis center. I got there a few minutes before ten. Judy Lane was standing in the lobby talking to one of her doubles partners. Judy had shoulder-length red hair, narrow features, green eyes a cat would envy, and cheerleader legs. She wore a white tennis skirt and a pale green cotton shirt that surged over her breasts like a waterfall. She had always struck me as pretty easygoing. Today she looked nervous and haggard. Her makeup seemed like an afterthought. She glanced my way. She knew who I was—we had seen each other around, and she had been at the funeral—but she gave me a longer look than that.

Her partner went down to the courts. I ate the distance between us by going for the coffee machine.

"Excuse me," she said.

"Hmm?"

"Mr. Liebowitz, I was at the funeral yesterday. What you said, it was, well—right. I just wanted to tell you."

"Thanks. Friends call me Phillie."

"I know." She hesitated. "Jack and I were friends. He talked a lot about you."

"I wish I could say the same. Who are you playing with?"

"Just some of the girls. But I don't know. I don't really feel like it today." She plucked absently at her racket strings. "You're hitting with Zack?"

I smiled. "Part of his charity work."

She wanted to laugh, but emotional fatigue prevented it.

"Are you okay?" I asked.

"Don't I look it?"

"No," I said gently. "You look deathly tired and very near to crying."

Her hand fell away from the strings. "What Jack did. It, well, it hit me very hard."

"Me, too."

"You made me cry yesterday at the funeral," she said.

"I made me cry, too."

"I guess we have more in common than we knew."

I was about to agree when Zack came into the lobby. His expression said he was ready for me and what the hell was I doing? Judy turned to go meet her partner.

I said quickly, "Look, there are some things I'd like to talk about, but I don't know how to start."

"What things?"

"About Jack. But this isn't the place. Can we go some-where?"

She searched my face. "Maybe your being here is kind of an omen."

It was the first time I'd ever been one of those.

"Lunch?" I suggested.

She came to a decision. "I'll meet you after we play."

2

Judging from the noisy grunts and the clean hard smacks coming from our court, two U.S. Open champs were working out. Zack and I hit the ball a ton. Judy peeked through the curtains once or twice, and I did something dramatically athletic to show her how tough I was. Then I held my side till the pain went away.

I showered and told Zack I wasn't staying for lunch. Judy came into the parking lot as I was rolling down the Miata's side windows, unzipping the back plastic window, and hand-folding the top.

Judy got into her white Mercedes 500 and touched a button. Not only did the top slide away into a neat little compartment, a goddamn roll bar and windscreen popped out, god-forbid-her-rich-hair-should-get-messed-up. She pulled out of her space and waited for me to lead.

Looking back, I was already in trouble.

Pros will tell you. Timing is everything.

THIRTEEN

1

The restaurant was on the water with a great view and fair food, mostly a lot of herby fish for the diet crowd. Its saving grace was great drinks. If a place like this didn't have great drinks, it had no reason to exist.

The second round of strawberry daiquiris arrived in glasses with forties figures. I still wasn't sure how to proceed with Judy. According to Zack, she and Jack had been having an affair. Maybe Jack's last affair. I wanted to know all about it, just as I wanted to know about his involvement with drugs, but I didn't want to scare her away by asking.

"These are good," she said, meaning the drinks. She'd changed into a green warm-up jacket that showed lots of cleavage. It was a good show.

I smiled in a way I hoped was reassuring.

"What are you going to do now?" she asked me. "I mean, with Jack gone."

"Once a writer, always a writer," I said, wondering what the hell I was talking about. Her throat told me she was older than I'd originally figured. Throats tell you age the way rings on a tree do. A little Christmas surgery in sunny Florida. Bruises heal in a week.

"It's so exciting, the world of movies," she said. "Jack used to say it was so glamorous."

In fact, Jack used to say it was horseshit. She was probably reporting what his dick said. I went with it.

"You see your name up there on the screen, it's like no other feeling in the world. You know how to spot the writer at a premiere?"

"Tell me."

"He's watching the audience, not the screen."

She smiled knowingly. It sounded like a genuine insight. It wasn't. It wasn't even true. The way you tell a writer at a premiere is to find the guy begging decent seats from the director and producer.

"What are *you* going to do?" I asked gently.

The dam burst before I was ready for it.

"I don't know *what* to do. I can't believe he did it. I'm a wreck. I haven't slept in days. Not since—"

Her eyes slammed shut and tears squeezed out. Her real face was showing. She was deeply hurt. It surprised me. Usually, only love produces that.

"I have to get hold of myself." She stood up so abruptly her chair fell over and she walked-ran to the ladies' room holding a tissue under her nose.

I picked up her chair. I didn't know much about her, but she obviously cared for Jack, and she believed it was suicide. I was pondering this when the waitress brought our food. I held up my hand.

"Don't serve the food till the lady gets back, please."

"Why not?"

"First, because I asked you not to, if for no other reason. Second, because it's not right."

She looked at me like I was nuts.

"The same thing applies to clearing the table," I went on. "It shouldn't be done till everyone is finished."

"Is that so?" Obviously, she wished everyone were so helpful.

"Yes, it is."

She was working on the news when Judy came back, eliminating the problem.

"I'm sorry," Judy said. "I hate causing scenes."

"You didn't." I looked to the waitress. "Now."

The dishes hit the table hard enough to give them whiplash. If I had really heard the word *asshole*, I would have complained to the management, but I couldn't be sure.

I said to Judy, "Look, we're both on shaky ground here. Have something. I'll bet you haven't eaten since this morning."

She gave me a lopsided smile and poked her fish. "You're sweet. Jack always said you mothered him. What did he tell you about me?"

I took a shot. " 'Beauty too rich for use, for Earth too dear.' "

"Shakespeare?"

She wasn't dumb. Or had passed the ninth grade, anyway.

"*Romeo and Juliet*," I confirmed.

She was suddenly suspicious. "Jack never said that. 'An amazing slut,' maybe. Or the best lay he ever had. But not *that* fluff." She read something on my face. Confusion probably. I'm less than inscrutable lately. "You don't know much about us, do you?" she said.

"No. Other than the fact of it."

"Why the hell did you get me here, Phillie? You want to screw me?"

"I want to know why Jack killed himself, if he did."

"What do you mean, *if* he did?"

"Just that."

She regarded me closely. "Do you know something?"

"I don't know anything, yet."

She took a deep ragged breath. "Honestly, neither do I."

"Are you sure?"

"I was his lover, not his shrink."

"He didn't have a shrink. He had you."

Her laugh was bitter. "That didn't stop him."

"Maybe. We don't know. Help me," I said. "I'm running stupid. And blind. My best friend who loved life more than any man I ever met just went and threw it away one fine summer night. I don't buy it. Neither does a cop named Donnegan."

"The cops are the ones who called it a suicide."

"I know. But Donnegan doesn't think it adds up, and he's actually experienced in these matters."

"I see." She grew thoughtful.

"Hey." I reached over and fixed her collar. "Eat something."

She smiled. "It's nice you do things like that. Jack said you were tough as nails, but when you cared you were a pushover. He said caring would be your downfall."

He knew less about my downfall than about my wife, but I let it go.

"Tell me about you and Jack," I said.

Judy took a sip of her drink and made a face. "Enough of this syrup shit," she said. "Get me a double Jack Daniel's rocks."

In more ways than one, the hard stuff was coming.

2

"Jack and I met at a party at Fred Marcus's house," Judy began. "I've known Fred for a long time. He introduced us. Jack and I took to each other right away." Her eyes twinkled, remembering. "I could tell he liked my legs. I liked the way he laughed, and the fact that he wasn't shy about looking."

"You're married."

"My husband and I have sort of an open marriage. Do you know what that is?"

"Free to do as you please." I tried to say it value free, like an anthropologist discussing a native custom, but it came out "Nobody has to give a shit."

"You don't approve," she observed.

"Does it matter?"

"I don't know. If you're going to understand, maybe it does."

"I don't play pro sports, I still appreciate them." I didn't for the most part, but that was beside the point.

"That's different," she said. "Phillie, have you ever been totally free?"

It didn't take me long to answer. "Never. Not a single day in my life." For some reason I didn't like the sound of it, put that way. Maybe it was being proud of something you shouldn't be so proud of.

"Jack and I got free," she said simply, sincerely. "And it was wonderful."

"What do you mean free?" I asked.

She considered that for a while. "Jack had the words. He should tell you."

"Kind of tough now."

"Maybe not." She handed me a floppy disk.

"What's this?"

"I found it yesterday. Jack did a lot of writing at my place, on a little computer."

"His laptop?"

"Yes. It's still there. It's pretty obvious this is an early version of things he wanted to tell you. It's incomplete. You'll see."

"You've read it, then."

"He showed me how. We used to write poetry to each other. Erotic stuff."

She blushed for the first time. Go figure. She could drink and curse like a champion without blinking, but poetry made her blush.

"I've had it with me since I found it," she went on. "It's what I meant when I said maybe your being at tennis was an omen."

I went out and got my own laptop from the car, freeing at least fifty percent of the Miata's trunk space. I was excited. Maybe the file would tell me what I needed to know.

I got the screen up. The disk was labeled PHILLIE 1. We always marked early versions with numbers like that. Judy was right. She'd found a first draft of his last message to me.

What do you mean free? I'd asked.

Jack told me.

FOURTEEN

Phillie, I read.

I'm sitting here at Judy's house trying to get it right. I'm sorry I kept things from you. We never lied to each other before. Maybe if I'd told you the truth I wouldn't be here now.

Anyway . . .

My name is Jack Murphy. I'm forty-four. I know you know that, Phillie, but I want to make a complete record, like in court. What follows is true. I want to be honest. That's rare for me.

The truth is I was never sexually faithful to anyone. I tried, it wasn't possible. God gave man the tongue and erection. Both lie like champions to get to the same place. My sexual feelings were too strong to deny. And why should I deny them? I refuse to be some pasty-faced, balding yuppie taking orders and going to the grave a frustrated, neurotic mess. Or repress myself like some frightened schoolboy afraid to be chastised. Some people claim their sexual needs don't rise up and choke them as often as mine do. Maybe, but I think they're lying.

Phillie, you once told me the way you knew you were in love was that you wanted to hold the girl after you had sex with her. If you wanted to put your pants on afterward, you knew it was a passing thing. Women rarely if ever understand the truth behind this feeling. They believe we lie to them to get them into bed. False. We lie to ourselves to get them into bed. Our capacity to lie to ourselves is matched only by our belief that we actually believe the nonsense we are spewing. But it is our dicks speaking through our mouths. They can do that, you know. Possession is not by external body, it is by internal organ. Once our dick begins to speak ex cathedra we are putty in its hands. At three in the morning, my dick has actually changed the way a woman looked. But after we come we know the truth, instantly and without pretense. We were there for sex and we said anything.

There was more, lots more, bits and pieces, fragments Jack had let flow out of his mind without restraint and would have strung together cohesively in later versions. I read it exactly as he had left it.

They say the city's hot. Compared to the suburbs it's a cold day in January. There are crazy women out here, all the more eager because they are untrained. They're trapped in their houses dreaming strange hot dreams, alone and seething, trembling for someone to break down their doors.

You remember when I said I couldn't do the *Knights* rewrite because I had a meeting of the church council, Phillie? I didn't. Frank Morse got me to dinner by implying that he and Denise wanted to swing. You know Frank, a fat little lawyer with little eyes and a receding hairline. Around the house he wears stretch denim jeans and Nike T-shirts that say "Just do it." He actually took me on a tour of his house like it was a fucking museum or a national landmark. Nobody with a really big house would do that.

Frank had the hots for the other woman invited to dinner, Anita. After the kids went to sleep, we all smoked and talked about sexual freedom. Frank and Anita went upstairs.

exciting looking at Frank while I lay on top of his wife. It started me thinking about a kind of sex I had never had before. I'd had lots of women but suddenly I understood the difference between quantity and quality. A few months later, given what I was to learn, I would have asked Frank to join us. That was what he wanted, he just didn't know it. I heard later he and Denise got divorced. I hope she found someone who appreciated her.

And me, Phillie? I'd started down a new road, one less traveled to be sure. I wish I had known it led to a place that would kill me.

why Jessica and I had never had a great sex life. You know us Catholics. Wives and whores. Good girls and bad. Judy was different. Bold and adventurous. I didn't know a thing about real sex till her. Fred Marcus introduced us at a party at his house. Pushed us together on that big couch of his and gave me a big buildup. Judy was smart and funny, not to mention having great legs. Her skirt barely covered her ass. I wanted to get under that skirt from the start.

Relationships can be trivialized to death. Out here people kill over who left the soda uncovered, or ate the last cookie in the fridge, or drove which car. Judy didn't care about any of that. Her passion was sex. I did things with her I never did with Jess or any of the others. Fantasies, Phillie. That's what sex is made of.

It was an awakening. I could talk while my fingers were inside her. I could lift up her skirt and make her do things. Or hold one of her nipples while I

cocaine. Judy brought some over. Phillie, nothing can ever match the first high. It's captivating and mysterious. Euphoric. I'd never known I had so many boundaries, how conventional I'd been. Coke let me let go. I was totally without inhibitions. We snorted it off the glass coffee table in her living room. I opened her blouse. She pushed down my pants. I slid my fingers into her, breathing hard. We were like two tigers, powerful, unmindful of others, completely involved

rubbed and kissed and fondled. That night I found out I also love to be dominated. She made me hers. Did with me as she pleased. I liked being submissive, taken mind and body. It was completely new. Sex was power. Power became sex. Things got hotter. She told me to masturbate. I had never done it in front of anyone. She tied me up and whipped me, taught me about bondage and discipline and S&M.

I told Jessica you and I worked late.

It's going faster the more I write. Soon I'll put all the pieces together, Phillie. I'm sorry to burden you with this but there's not much time left.

The boundaries of everyday life began to fade. Judy and I opened each other up. Her husband, Ray, was in the city most of the time so we used her place. Soiled love in a clean house. It was Judy's idea for me to be her slave, dominating me for my pleasure. She wore garters, stockings and heels. No panties. She tied me to the bed with leather straps. She put her fingers in my mouth. She pulled her breasts free and made me lick them. I didn't know what was more erotic, her exposed, or me awaiting exposure at her pleasure.

I was completely helpless. She was already wet, and I hadn't even touched her. She raked her nails over my thighs. She rubbed her breasts, heaving them up and down, and spread her legs to show me. She put me into her mouth. I struggled against the ties. Later, I realized what I liked most was the feeling that I wasn't responsible for anything. I was in her hands.

She put a condom on me and mounted me, holding herself up to watch it slide in and out. She was stretched so tight. She told me to come. She demanded it. I had no choice. I came like crazy, shouting.

When it was over, she untied me and we held each other. We were free, free from all the have-to's you're always talking about, Phillie, free from feeling like everything always has to be in its place. "Dare I disturb the universe?" Wasn't that the Eliot quote we argued about and you said no one had the right to? Well, I've felt the power when you do. It's addicting. I couldn't breathe when Judy wasn't around. I thought of her all the time. Even when you and I worked, I was thinking about what I wanted her to do to me later. I wished I could've told you, but I couldn't. I knew you'd think it was too weird. Jessica kept asking me if anything was wrong. I couldn't tell her either. I didn't need a shrink the way she kept suggesting. I was beyond that. Judy and I were a new form of life. Nothing existed but sex. I didn't need to eat or sleep, only to be buried inside her.

visited by a guy we both know, so I don't want to say his name. Judy and he had been lovers. We had some drinks. Judy spread coke on a mirror, and we did it up. I added more of mine. Did you know I carried it all the time by then? In a little glass vial. Sometimes when you left the office I did a quick snort. I was a citizen of the world, just passing through. Judy opened her blouse. I kicked off my shoes. He took off his. Sex was in the air. It was hard to breathe. I knew what I wanted, knew what she wanted, too.

Judy slipped off her clothes. With him there it was like seeing her naked for the first time. Did you know the only true stimulant is a woman's own sexual discharge? Forget the joy jellies and the bullshit creams. Spread her own fluid over her, and she'll react like you've wired her to an electrical generator. I rubbed her, she stroked me, he masturbated. She got down on her knees and sucked me. Then she knelt in front of him and pressed him into her swollen breasts. The muscles in her legs were taut. He had this tattoo of a dagger on his arm, and she kept licking it. She told us to come into the bedroom. We lay down and played with her while she stroked herself. Pleasure raises blood pressure. It takes you into a world where suddenly you're a panting, grasping, groping thing that wants more and more and more. There is only one true sexual organ, the brain. Mine was on fire. Judy snorted through her nostrils like a racing horse. She pushed her fingers in deeper. I was insane. I knew it, and I didn't care. I was over the edge. She turned to give us a better view. She licked her wet fingers. She smeared her nipples with her own juices. I couldn't hold back any longer. I came in long gushes, shouting at the top of my lungs. I rubbed it over her face, her cheeks, her lips.

She drew him into her. Their sweat pooled on my belly. I knelt behind them until he came. Judy was still hot-eyed. She lay back and rubbed herself. A red flush crawled over her chest. She planted her feet on the bed and raised herself off the sheets. Her mouth was an open "O" when she came, crying out as the spasms hit, her whole body jerking.

We took her in our arms and kissed and stroked her. All three of us felt warm, almost grateful. Judy snuggled in our arms. Do you know how much tenderness there is on the other side of insanity? On the other side of pain? Try and understand.

I was over the edge, Phillie. They had brought me there, but I was staying. Let everybody else get up and go to work and come home and do what they're supposed to do. Not me. Or Judy. We were different. We shared a secret. No matter how conventional our lives might appear on the surface, underneath they weren't. Soon we found others like us.

My hands are trembling as I write this, remembering it all. Can you feel the heat? Do you blame me, Phillie? It wouldn't matter. I couldn't let go. I was hooked.

I'm not justifying.

Everything else had lost its meaning.

I felt no shame.

I felt no guilt.

I was a god, Phillie, beyond all that.

FIFTEEN

1

I shivered as much from contact as content. Jack back from the grave. I was hearing from a ghost.

"It's true?" I asked.

"What he wrote? Yes."

"Do you mind my knowing it?"

"No more than I did doing it."

She was bold. I had to give her that. I thought about the file I had at home. The rest would be in there, and I still needed the password to open it. I was lucky to get this much. I tried to hide my reaction—that much sex in one dose was too much for me—but my face must have shown it.

"Maybe I shouldn't have given it to you," she said. "I don't think you understand."

I looked at her sitting so demurely across from me. S&M,

bondage, group sex. She was like the suburbs, calm on the surface, turbulent beneath. You'd never suspect the craziness going on inside her, never see the inner heat that forced her hands between her thighs as she reached for leather straps.

"I'm trying to," I said. "Was it love?"

"In a way." She sipped her second bourbon. "Certainly more than he felt for Jessica or I felt for Ray. But it was beyond that. That's what I'm trying to make you see."

"What's beyond love?" I asked.

Her eyes got bright. "Obsession."

It was like trying to get my mouth around one of those Carnegie Deli sandwiches with eight pounds of meat on it. I just couldn't encompass it.

"What he wrote there isn't all of it. We went a lot further." She scored the condensation on her glass with a sharp pale fingernail. "But I know one thing. If dying was what he wanted, he should have asked me to die with him. I would have. They say death is the ultimate truth. Well, it's also supposed to be the ultimate orgasm. I hear that strangling is the way to do it."

I was shocked. I must have looked it.

"You have to understand it went that far," she went on. "It was total. It didn't start out that way, we didn't plan it, but things changed. We lived for each other. All the bullshit around us, the cars and houses and private schools, the people grubbing for money. We were above it. I used to blow him in his car on the Long Island Expressway. We'd pull to the side so we could snort some coke and he could fuck me. You want more? I put a plug inside me when we went out to dinner, and all the while we'd stare at each other across the table and know that for all the bullshit the people around us were throwing, only we were real. Die for him? Gladly. I may die *without* him. Him die without me? I can't tell you why he did. I just can't."

Seedy red sludge had settled to the bottom of my daiquiri glass. The afternoon sun was falling into the sea. Judy zipped up her jacket, staring out over the water. My legs were cramped from sitting so long.

"Was he doing other drugs besides coke?" I asked.

"What does he do?"

"He's an investment banker."

"And Jack wasn't as boring."

She reacted differently than I expected. "Ray isn't boring either, Phillie. It's not so black and white. For twenty years I raised Becky and looked good on his arm and sat on his silly boat, and in return he gave me a life of relative ease. I'm one of the few women around who actually respects my husband for making money, and if there wasn't much passion, and we both knew it and played around, well, who did we hurt? We were good to each other and raised a super kid. The synagogue didn't collapse when we walked in. You could do a lot less well in life."

I found myself liking her. Maybe I didn't agree with her choices, but she had enough character to stand by what she chose.

"Would money have been an issue?"

"No. Ray has a lot. It would have been amicable."

"You never know." I'd seen divorce turn lots of friends into enemies. Money and children suddenly became pawns. "One more thing." I pulled the list of phone numbers I'd printed from the NEW DIRECTORY file out of my wallet. "Any of these phone numbers ring a bell?"

"That's a joke?"

"Forgive me."

She read the list and something moved behind her eyes too fast for me to follow. "Try this one after midnight. That's all I'm going to say. Lunch is on me." She looked around as if seeing the restaurant for the first time and handed the waitress a platinum American Express card. I didn't like her paying, but I'm told it's now crass to object.

"Thanks for the talk, Phillie. Jack was right. Confession *is* good for the soul."

"Don't go yet. I need help."

"Up till an hour ago I thought Jack killed himself. I need to think." She hesitated, looking worried. "I could have problems myself."

"Alcohol. Makes for a nice head."

But not an explanation for needle marks. "Where did he buy the coke?"

"A biker bar down by the water." She pulled her gaze back from the sea and turned it on me. "I thought at first you wanted me. Do you?"

"No."

She touched my hand. Her eyes, no longer bright, were gentle.

"Jack was right. You're a nice man."

"I don't feel so nice. Did Jack have any enemies?"

"First tell me why you and one cop think he didn't commit suicide," she said.

I gave her the easy reasons—his love of life, the church, her, even his new hair. And the deeper one, my sense that he just wouldn't have done something so alien to his nature. As I spoke, I saw her doubts growing. She was replaying things in her mind. She and Jack had been together for almost a year. It occurred to me she might know more than she'd told me. Her next words confirmed it.

"You've got me thinking. I've told you the truth, Phillie, but I haven't told you all of it. I want to think things over before I say any more. If Jack didn't kill himself, if it's murder like you say, it changes things."

"How?" When she didn't say, I pressed. "You can trust me."

Her laugh was short and bitter. "I'm a little short on trust these days."

I couldn't really blame her. These were criminal matters we were talking about, besides the personal ones. She wasn't about to make me keeper of her secrets after spending only two hours together. For all I knew, she was an accomplice, something I hadn't considered till that moment.

"Did Ray know about you and Jack?"

"He knew. And it was okay. Our daughter, Becky, is away at college. It didn't affect her. If I wanted a divorce, he would have said fine. We have a condo in the city. He just would have moved in full-time. Ray's a nice man. I even like his girlfriend. Believe me, he wasn't lonely."

I'd briefly considered Judy as some kind of an accomplice. Till that moment I'd never thought of her as a potential victim in a wider conspiracy.

"Are you in danger?" I asked.

She took a deep breath. "I could be."

"Go to the police," I said. "Don't hesitate."

"I can't."

"Why?"

"Stop it, Phillie."

"Stopping isn't my best thing. Can you protect yourself?"

"Maybe. I have some . . . insurance."

"What kind of insurance?"

"Why won't you leave me alone?" she cried loud enough to turn heads.

I ignored the stares. "I can't. I need you. I'm at a dead end. In the file Jack said you found others. Who were they?"

"Don't expect me to betray them, Phillie. There are innocents involved."

"Somebody's not innocent. I need somewhere to go on this, Judy."

"Go home. Jack's dead. Nothing can change that."

"That's just words."

"Listen to me, Phillie. Let it go."

"Not until I know for sure what happened," I said angrily. "I don't owe him much, but I owe him that."

Her hand went to her neck, maybe to hide old scars of various kinds. "I'm sorry," she said.

I leaned closer. "I think I know the man Jack wrote about in the file."

"How can you?"

Because my mind finally delivered the information it had been dredging for since reading the PHILLIE 1 file.

"Men don't wear a lot in locker rooms, Judy. I've seen that dagger tattoo. Robbie told me he got it in the army. Some kind of special combat thing." Privately, you could have knocked me over with a feather. Robbie and Jack and Judy in bed together?

"I'm right, aren't I? Jack was talking about Robbie Hazen."

She seemed to be measuring my resolve, or maybe I'd just worn her down enough. "You won't say I said?"

"I swear."

She told me quickly, as if to reduce the sin. "All right. It was Robbie."

I said, "If Jack didn't kill himself, there's a murderer walking around. Maybe you even know who."

Her face remained guarded. I wasn't going to get any more, but at least I had another piece.

She signed the charge slip, absorbed in her own thoughts. "I'll call you after I've had some time to think."

"All right."

She put a card with her address on it on the table. "Now you know where I live."

The card was nicely engraved. Classy. Like her. The bus boy cast furtive glances at her behind as she walked away.

I may have underestimated someone, she had said.

I wondered who.

SIXTEEN

1

Judy's story had troubled my mind and body. That made it hard to concentrate as I tried to sort out the pieces driving home. The phone number she had told me to try after midnight had a 212 area code. Calling Rainbow City.

Sex and Jack and Judy and Robbie and Rainbow City. Where was it all heading?

The afternoon sun made the foliage shimmer. The road was twisted and hilly, and the driveways curved up to their houses on high. The fleet of slat-walled gardeners' pickup trucks was beginning to weigh anchor. I was tooling along in fourth gear, top down. My thoughts made me dreamy. Maybe that's why I missed seeing the big mustard-colored Chevy Suburban van suddenly swerve into my lane. It came around a parked truck the gardeners were filling and plowed toward me like an ocean liner.

There was nowhere to turn, no time to stop. The big Chevy van with its huge chrome bumpers and Christmas lights on the cab roof would have crushed my little roadster like a tin can. The gardeners and I both saw that if I tried to drive in between them and the Chevy, I would have hit one of them. They panicked and ran. I did the only thing I could, on reflex alone. I yanked the wheel hard to the right and hit one of the uphill driveways at almost forty miles an hour. The Suburban sliced by me, a blur at our combined speeds. It was no longer my biggest problem. I hit the driveway like a ski jump, swerved to avoid the house, and blasted through the hedges out into space.

The seat belt held me as my body and the car tried to go our separate ways. I jammed on the brake, but there was no road under me. Some part of my brain was yelling that when we hit ground again, it would be better to slide than to skid. I saw a pond off to my right and a downward-curving stretch of lawn to my left. In front of me was a statue of the Virgin in one of those Catholic sanctuaries, and you can bet your life I converted. I was a missile coming in for a landing, stages separating. The shuttle returning to Earth. I held on for dear life. We hit the ground with a shock that jarred me from my ass to my ears.

I have to say this for my little car. It skidded and rocked violently on a suspension that was never meant for ski jumping, but I felt the tires bite and the gears mesh, and suddenly I was in control again. I missed the Blessed Virgin with five feet to spare—Hail, Mary—and shot off the lawn back onto the pavement where I braked to a stop.

NASA Houston, this is Phillie. I have landed.

I was sweating as though I'd run twenty miles. My wrists and ankles hurt. My heart was pounding. I was probably in some kind of shock. The gardeners from the pickup ran over to me. Staccato Spanish poured out of their astonished faces. They made soaring motions with their hands, the way kids do with toy planes.

I couldn't take my hands off the wheel, they were shaking so hard. I looked at my lap. Surprisingly, my pants were dry.

I said, "Did you get the number of that truck?"

"No way, man. We watching *joo*," one said with a broad smile. He shook his fingers like he was trying to get something wet off the tips. "Man, the way you drive. What's your name?"

"Mario Andretti."

"Fucking someting, Mario," they agreed.

I waited till the sweat evaporated and my nerves settled. The houses and trees seemed very bright and clear, the way they say things do when you manage to avoid dying. I cursed the guy who ran me off the road. He never even stopped to see if I was all right. I thought about going to the police station to report it, but there were too many Suburbans like that around town, and I didn't have a plate number. I only had the impression of a man hunched over the wheel. Probably just as scared as I was.

I decided to shrug the whole thing off and not tell Carolyn. Accidents happen, right?

2

I made myself drive into town. Au pairs were pushing baby carriages back to the hangar. Commuters streamed off the early rush-hour trains. Men in suits with sweaty shirts, women in linen skirts and sneakers. They went into delis to join the lines of I-want-to-be-home-for-my-family wives in shorts and halters buying last-minute takeout for dinner.

I got fresh bread at the bakery. Then I walked over to the bookstore and bought a crossword puzzle dictionary. When I felt I had sufficiently mastered my subconscious fear of driving, I went home. The alarm company had just about finished installing the security system. They were making big bucks, these companies. A river of money flowed out of Manhattan to chic North Shore restaurants and Infiniti dealers. But we'd taken too much, sucked the city dry till it imploded. Only garbage was left to course down the empty streets after rush hour, and the violence we had left the city for had picked up its head and was trying to follow us home.

Maybe it was the aftermath of the near accident, some sort of adrenaline slump, but I felt lousy. A soul-wrenching weariness was creeping into everyday life. So many of the things we did month after month, year after year, were meaningless. Peace was hard to come by. Carolyn and I were on the rocks. Mel was dead. Jack was gone.

And I was beginning to depress myself.

I spent an hour inputting five-letter words from the crossword puzzle dictionary to open the PHILLIE file.

Still nothing, but my vocabulary was improving.

SEVENTEEN

1

Carolyn had made chicken lemon for dinner. It should have been lemon chicken, but she'd halved the chicken part on the recipe and forgotten to halve the lemons. Ben and Beth and I tried to see who could make the funniest puckered faces and argued who was dying first. Then we saw the look on Carolyn's face. We were treading on thin ice. Very thin.

Carolyn said, "Your sister called. She wants you to call her back."

"Why phone? It's a small town, she tells me."

Carolyn laughed. "The fact that Rhonda spends her entire day gossiping with the other housewives isn't a factor. It's a small *town*. But that's only one recurring theme."

"What's the other?"

"What she's buying."

Rhonda's husband had a perpetual stoop and looked twenty years older than he was. Fear of the debt he and Rhonda had accumulated kept him up at night staring at the ceiling wondering when he would be released.

It's not pleasant to have your brother-in-law looking forward to death.

"She bought Meredith's winter coat at Carby's."

"The little boutique up on Miracle Mile?"

Carolyn nodded. "I wouldn't shop there, and we aren't broke."

"Since when do you care about this stuff?" I asked.

"Few housewives talk spreadsheets."

"I can't talk spreadsheets."

"Skip it, Phillie."

As I said, thin ice.

We cleaned up dinner and got the kids to bed. It was an easy night, only twelve requests for drinks, bathroom calls, stories, fluffed pillows, lights on, lights off, five more minutes of TV, one last Nintendo game, kisses, hugs, sit with me, sing to me, read to me, stay with me; at last, good night.

Carolyn put on a big T-shirt, and we lay in bed watching television in silence. Communication was at a low ebb. A raised finger for stop, a lowered finger for flick on. I was still trying to figure out the three remotes we needed to operate the TV, VCR, and cable box, another way technology had simplified things.

I once talked at length to one of the men who invented part of the cable system as we know it. Over the course of dinner he worried about the homeless people and how he was going to furnish his three homes in the same breath, reduced Italian culture to a what-me-worry philosophy, and sounded off on how it didn't matter that low-income families who used to get TV for free now had to pay an increasingly large portion of their income just to watch a baseball game—they had more *choice*. This from a former leader of a radical political organization. Some saw this as a contradiction. I didn't. Either way, the man got off on doing it to the poor.

Carolyn broke the silence. "I can't go on like this."

"Marlene Dietrich, *The Blue Angel*, 1930."

"Cut it out, Phillie."

"I forgive you," I said. "Let's leave it at that."

"You aren't capable of forgiveness. It's just a word to you."

"You want sign language?"

"God, I hate it when you're glib like that. You're so full of shit."

"What the hell do you want?" I shouted. The sound echoed in the room, floating toward the children. It surprised me.

"Let me explain," she said softly. "Please."

I shook my head sadly. "It won't help. It sits in my guts and twists them every time I think about you and . . ."

"Why not say it?" she demanded. "Me and *Jack*. I can't stand being tortured about it anymore."

I walked out. Grabbed a joint from my office and smoked it on the chaise longue in the back yard. Rainbow City was glowing in the night, hellfire across the water. The smoke loosened the ties that bound my mind to my body. Images of Judy writhing naked on the bed played across the movie screen in my head. Carolyn's image took her place.

Carolyn was still inside. I wanted her to come out. If she asked me to talk again, I might. She didn't. I twisted my fist into my stomach to stop the pain. I wanted to scream. I did worse.

I remembered.

I remembered the moment when Beth emerged from Carolyn and I held her miraculous little hand. I also remembered the moment I knew something was wrong. With Carolyn. She had always been a clearheaded, crisp thinker. In the months that followed she became increasingly muddleheaded and absentminded. The simplest things were too much for her. She was unhappy most of the time. She loved Beth but resented her, which added guilt. She blamed me, which made us distant. No matter what I did, no matter how supportive and loving I was, she remained bitter and depressed.

I thought it would pass. It got worse. At the end of the first year I spoke to a psychiatrist friend of mine named Max Wagner, the smartest man I've ever known. We'd met during a film

Jack and I worked on. He explained to me just how serious postpartum depression could be and suggested therapy and medication. Carolyn refused. I did my best to help her, feeling more like her shrink than her husband for the next eighteen months. The only thing that seemed to lighten her up was Jack. He made her laugh, and Jesus, I was glad to hear it. Time dragged on, but being with him seemed to revive her. For the first time, things seemed better.

Then one day Carolyn said she had something important to talk about. After we got the kids to sleep, we went to the living room and poured some wine. We didn't even turn on the lights. She told me she hadn't felt like a complete woman since delivery, but it went deeper than that. She hadn't been happy since becoming a full-time mother. What happened hadn't been planned, it just happened. With Jack. She was truly sorry, but it had returned the good feeling she once had. She was ready to come back to me, to all of us, whole and alive and herself again.

If I would have her.

A hot blade savaged my guts. An affair? *My* wife?

Here I was trying to come to grips with being forty-three and yet to score a major hit, still trying to figure out how to be a decent parent and fit in sex and *The New York Times* and all the other cherished things that had vanished with the birth of the kids. I couldn't remember a decent night's sleep since Ben was born. Now Carolyn was telling me she'd just been to bed with my best friend. I saw her face. So much hurt had resided there. It was gone now, wiped out by one simple act. How could I hate them?

Easy.

The silence began. Since that night we hadn't been to bed together other than to sleep. We warred over garbage and mowing the lawn. We were covered by emotional antimacassars, unable to reach out or break free.

I went back upstairs. Carolyn was under the covers. I was choked with nervous tension. I had to dispel it. The room was pitch-dark. I couldn't see her face.

I said, "I want to hear about it."

"What?"

"I'm trying to get past it, and I can't. It's alien to me. If I hear about it, I'll be a part of it."

"Phillie, I won't, not now. I can't."

I slid in beside her, felt the tension of her body after all the frozen hurtful days. Our sharp silent rebuffs. The constant playacting in front of the kids.

I said, "If you could do it, you can damn well talk about it."

"Jack is dead. Why torture me? Why torture yourself?"

"It'll feel better when I stop."

"It's ghoulish, dredging it up now, like grave robbing. Let the dead rest. Let *me* rest."

"I can't. Not till I know."

"It's sick," she pleaded.

"We're living a lie, it's time we faced it."

"You'll hate me." She was sobbing now. I felt the first warm tears on my arm.

"I already hate you," I said. "I'm trying not to hate both of us."

The darkness was absolute, so was the distance. After a while she said, "It was late afternoon. We went for some ice cream after you guys worked. You were home with the kids. I felt lighthearted for the first time in a long time, Phillie. I felt like a woman, not just some baby-tending machine. Jess wasn't home. Jack lit a fire. We had a drink. Talked about nothing at all. I had feelings bubbling up inside me like they used to and I knew I just couldn't live my life the same way anymore. Jack was easy to be with. Full of life. He made me laugh. Not that you didn't. I love you, Phillie, I always have. I didn't love Jack, not that way. I just needed something different. Maybe every woman does once in her life. I needed to break free, to do something daring. Goddamn life, goddamn kids. My body almost killed me. I hated it. I wanted to die, do you understand? So I said, fuck it. For once in my whole rigid MBA life, I said fuck it, and if you want to kill me for one lousy moment of being free, then that's okay. Jack tried to stop me. We didn't even have condoms. It was dangerous. He said all the things to put me off that your best friend was supposed to say, but I needed him more and he knew it."

She shifted around. Her tears were coming harder.

"I think he went along because sending me back to you whole was the best thing he could do for both of us. You want more? Tell me, Phillie, because I'll tell you everything this once and then never again. You hear me? If you ever bring this up again, I'll kill you, or me, or both of us. I won't suffer for it any more. I won't suffer for the rest of my life. So tell me what you fucking want, or let me go."

I could barely breathe. I was sick and twisted inside. I knew if we backed down, we were finished. I could never bear to come this close again.

"Tell me."

"We went into the bedroom and lay down and kissed and felt each other through our clothes. He opened my blouse and rubbed my breasts. I pulled off his shirt, and we lay like that with our chests touching. He reached under my skirt and played with me through my panty hose. I rubbed him through his pants. He was so familiar, kind of docile, and I liked that because I felt in control. We took off our clothes. He got on top of me."

Her breathing got heavier. "I put my legs on his shoulders and let him rub against me. He said he wanted to take me . . . like that. I wanted to. It hurt, but all of a sudden I could feel him coming, spurting into me hard and hot. I told him to put some of it on me, and he did. I rubbed it into me and told him to lick me till I came."

I couldn't stand it any longer. Carolyn's nails ravaged my back as I rammed myself inside her. She was soaking wet. Our mouths were glued together. We fucked hard to relieve the tension, to exorcise our demons, for a host of reasons good and bad. My face was a mask of pain and lust. I was glad she couldn't see my eyes.

"Tell me it all," I gasped.

Carolyn gripped my arms, and her words came out in stops

and starts as I thrust harder and harder. We were punishing each other and we both knew it, but we couldn't stop.

She said, "I felt good for the first time in a long time, like I used to. The thing that was frozen in my chest finally released. I went to the bathroom, and when I came out Jack was hard again. I rested my elbows on the chair. He stood behind me and put himself in me. When he came, I came, too."

So did I, in hot spurts. Carolyn clutched at me and cried out and came again and again. I wanted to hold her. I wanted to comfort her, but I was in too much turmoil. I couldn't face the truth that the cure for her problems didn't include me. I was a part of it only because I demanded to be. I felt small and vituperative and mean-spirited. If I loved her unselfishly, I should forgive her. How come I couldn't? Ego. If I'd been honest, I would have told her so. But I didn't.

Carolyn was crying, her whole body wracked by deep sobs.

I got out of bed, packed a bag, and left.

EIGHTEEN

1

Zack opened his door and looked at me in surprise.

"I need a place to stay," I said. "I'm sorry I didn't call first."

He was shirtless and barefoot, wearing only gray sweat pants. "Forget it, man. Come in."

I flopped into a chair in the living room. I heard him upstairs, explaining to Ellen. He came back with a robe on and poured us both a drink.

"What's wrong?"

"Carolyn and I are separated," I said simply.

"You're an ass," he said.

"I appreciate your sympathy."

"Horseshit," he responded angrily. "You love each other. The kids are great. You feel about divorce the way most people feel about amputation. So what the fuck is going on?"

"She had an affair. I can't live with it."

"Carolyn?" He said it too weakly for me not to notice.

"You knew!" I said accusingly.

He nodded. "You mad?"

"How?"

"People have their own orbits. Sometimes you see two of them change direction and intersect. We all knew how screwed up she was after the baby. Suddenly she was okay again. She and Jack played one day and I heard them talking. You know how you feel so isolated, but there's only a curtain between courts." He looked away. "It was obviously over so I let it lie."

"How many others knew?"

"I don't know, Phillie. It didn't seem like a big thing."

"One time!"

"Okay, okay, one time." He settled down on the couch. "You want some advice?"

"No."

"Forget about it. That's the best advice you're going to get. Don't look at it too hard. Don't analyze it. Don't mess around with the why's and why nots. She's the best woman I know. You never made a mistake?"

"Not like that."

"Then you're a fucking saint. In which case she's the only one who can put up with you. Take her back, and don't be such a hardass for once in your life."

"Fuck you," I said.

"Fuck you, too."

Ellen said from the doorway, "You guys are *so* highbrow." She was holding sheets and a pillow.

"Hi," I said. "Sorry."

She dropped the linens on the couch, shuffled over, and kissed my cheek. "Better here than walking the streets."

"I'm employed," I said. "It would have been a hotel."

"You guys still gonna talk?" she asked.

"Nah." There was nothing to say. I pulled off my shirt. "Go get some sleep. Gotta be on the court early, I bet."

"You wanna hit some?"

"When?"

He went over his schedule mentally. "Eleven."

"If I can. I'll call you."

Zack held his hand out and Ellen pulled him off the couch. "C'mon, baby." He went happily. Kidless, their love for each other was undiminished by time or trial. It was nice to see.

I sat there feeling isolated and alone. I wanted my bed. I wanted my kids. Divorce. I cringed at the word. What would Beth and Ben say? What a mess I had made of my life. I had, let me count, eighty-two dollars and seven cents in my pocket, keys, credit cards, and a slip of paper: the New Directory I'd showed Judy.

It was one A.M. I picked up the phone and punched in one of the numbers. First there was background noise I couldn't make out.

"Hello?" said a voice. "Who's this?"

"Who's this?" I asked. "Even better, where's this?"

"If you don't know, fuck off."

The line went dead. Next I tried the number Judy had said to call after midnight. It was a tape. In the background there were the sounds of skin being slapped and people moaning, and a sexy female voice said, "Hello, you've reached Whips and Chains, New York's most unique club. If you're calling for Mistress service, please push number one on your phone now. Every Saturday we present our S&M show, the Black and Blue Revue. 'It gets better every week,' says the *Fetish Times*. The fiery W is your safe, clean, and friendly fetish playground. Our daily schedule is as follows. . . ."

I hung up.

Orbits, Zack had said. I was out of mine, spinning off into space. I had to find my way back, and this wasn't helping.

The nagging thought. Suicide or murder?

2

It was two A.M., and I still couldn't get to sleep. Soon enough, morning would put out the glowing windows in Rainbow City, and the buildings would blend into gray mist. My mind wandered back. I closed my eyes and went with the flow.

Jack had been a sexual athlete as long as I knew him, mowing down jocks and literary magazine types with equal ease. Sex came easy to him. For me it was a complex, gut-twisting set of contradictions. Parental voices warned me. Peers cajoled me. When I was a kid, my insides ached every sweet spring night I spent alone, burning for something I couldn't name. I felt the heat of adolescence so keenly, I had to masturbate five times a day to stay calm. Until I met Blythe, my true love. At least, I believed at the time she was my true love. Thirty years later I still dream about her, so she probably was.

I remember the first time Blythe and I made love with a clarity that astounds me. The summer moon painted the night sky streaky purple and cast film noir shadows through the fire escape into her living room, where the Castro convertible and our passion unfolded. I loved Blythe with greater purity and clarity than I had ever loved anyone. I loved her as only a seventeen-year-old can. We were seniors in high school. It was June. A Chinese dinner cost a dollar. A cab ride fifty cents. The smell of creosote and the sounds of the Four Seasons and the Beach Boys rode the wind. We had everything.

We went through the various stages of taking off our clothes, which really meant me taking hers off and trying to fight muscle cramps while I shucked mine one-handed, my lips never leaving hers so as not to be "obvious." Was being naked really my intention? Of course not. Love, not sex, was what this was about. Liar.

I had never seen her totally naked before, and her shadowy length is an indelible picture undimmed by decades. I had no real idea of what was required. Foreplay, tenderness, cajoling her into responsiveness, all were mysteries. As nervous as I was, I actually had an erection. I didn't really know what to do with it, but I had one. Then reality dawned. She asked me if I had protection.

Ha! I did! In fact, I had two kinds of protection in my wallet, which was hopelessly distorted from the bulk of them. There were two kinds of condoms back then, at least only two that I knew about. The kind in the little foil packages that left a ring on your wallet, and something quite extraordinary called a Four-Ex. Four-Exes came in little blue plastic cases. They were loose-fitting, wet, slimy sheaths that slipped on easily because they had no ring at the base. This stood in marked contrast to strangling your dick with the garrote on a Trojan. Assuring her I would be right back, I grabbed the Four-Ex and went into the bathroom to put it on. Why not right there? I don't know. Probably because the sight of such a necessary but possibly disquieting act as wrapping myself in sheep intestine would be unesthetic, and love was supposed to be beautiful. Rather than run the risk that this would put her off, I left her alone, brilliant tactician that I was, and went to figure things out.

I flicked on the light in the bathroom and had to confront myself as I really was, a panting, nervous, naked boy with a rapidly shrinking hard-on who could not find a way to open the blue plastic package that contained his passport to sexual maturity. Why weren't these fucking condoms like Life Savers or Band-Aids, with a little red string that opened the package? I tried yanking the container apart with my bare hands. I couldn't get a grip. I threw it against the wall. Nothing. I hit it. I rammed it against the sink. When it didn't break, I put it on the floor and stomped on it with my bare feet. I am one day going to write the Queen of England that she should store the crown jewels in one of those little blue plastic cases because if she does they will be unstealable. There are vaults in Swiss banks that could take less pounding than I gave that little blue plastic case that June night. I found scissors in the medicine cabinet and tried to stab it open. I ran it under hot water, thank you, Mother. I put it on the toilet rim and bashed it with the seat. Nothing could open that impenetrable blue case. Worse, by now my erection had shrunk to nothing.

Plan two. Get the other condom. It was in my pants pocket. I cursed the goddamn Four-Ex one last time and calmed down. All was not yet lost. I could still have my first sexual experience. I went back inside and slipped back under the covers. Where were you? she asked. I wanted to make sure of things for you, I said reassuringly, reaching for and—Thank You, God—finding the pack of Trojans with one hand. I didn't experience doing everything one-handed again till I had my first kid.

The moment rearrived. Regluing my lips to Blythe's, I tore open the foil packet of Trojans with such ease I felt like Samson. I slipped the ring on the head of my penis and pushed. Nothing. I pushed harder. All I was doing was driving my penis back into my body. The damn condom wouldn't unroll. I don't think by this time I was really functioning on all burners. Maybe if I had some patience it would have been okay, but nothing worked. I got the bright idea of reversing the condom. Success! It unrolled half an inch or so. I defied physics by actually unrolling the thing from underneath, one-handed, getting it on a few fractions of an inch at a time. In later years I realized that I had it on correctly in the first place, and in my frantic craziness changed it backward. Nevertheless, within a few seconds I got enough on to proceed.

I entered Blythe. I have never ever forgotten the exquisite feeling of her vagina slowly separating around my hard penis for the first time. The shortest and longest of journeys. When I had fully entered her I was as completely at peace as I had ever been, truly linked with another person, and happy. The sensation was glorious. Knowing as little as I did —as most of us did—I just pumped and heaved and kept my lips glued to hers until I came. Selfish, male-oriented, lust-driven, sure. Maybe that's the definition of being seventeen. It doesn't matter. To this day it was one of the sweetest, most powerful, and most loving moments of my life. I gave what I could. All I had.

Of course, Blythe didn't orgasm. That was totally out of our league. I wish I could have made her happier sexually. I don't even know if she really enjoyed it. Talking about it required a far deeper level of honesty than most seventeen-year-olds are capable of, certainly than we were. I've learned many lessons from sex, but the foremost one is this: Talk about the sex you're having with the person you're having sex with, and never stop talking, because if you withhold anything, there will be something you're not getting. This will eventually make you mad, and you will want to kill them, or at the least get whatever it is you're not getting from someone more willing to give it.

When the heaving and pumping were over, Blythe and I broke apart. There was blood on the sheets. I have never forgotten it, nor how it tore at me. Part of me understood how great was the gift I had been given. Blythe was crying. I did my best to comfort her. I loved her totally. I told her so. I said I would never leave her. I believed it. I reached down quietly to remove the condom.

It is likely that the day I see Jesus coming down the turnpike will not be as big a shock as the moment I looked down and saw that I wasn't wearing anything on my penis except a ring. I'd put my fingers through the damn condom while frantically unrolling it from underneath. The rest must have torn away during. But where was it? Dear God, it could only be one place. Deftly, one-handed, I reached down and fumbled around, pressing myself against her. Just taking it off, I assured her. At last I felt a recognizable shape and secured it with enormous relief.

The relief quickly changed to panic. What a fool I was! I had assured Blythe she was protected, but in my incredible ignorance and unforgivable clumsiness I had torn the condom to shreds. How could I tell her? How did one explain such a thing? I couldn't even find the tiny reservoir in the tip, much less see if it had spilled out. I felt guilty. I was frightened. The great joy of my first sexual experience with the girl I loved was suddenly transmuted into fear and anxiety.

I decided discretion was the better part of valor, or maybe brevity was the soul of wit, or some such nonsense. Anyway, I didn't tell her. There was nothing I could do about it at that moment, and what I wanted most was to comfort her, not provoke a nervous breakdown. We kissed and talked and later she even made me something to eat. I grabbed a bus home. I have never forgotten walking the few blocks back to my parents' apartment. I had completed the rites of passage only to discover an agonizing truth. Only in childhood are there any complete victories.

Blythe and I went steady for several more weeks, spending our time together, going to movies, double-dating, and walking past big houses picking out which one would be ours someday. This indicated both the blissful state of our romance and a profound lack of appreciation for down payments. She turned out not to be pregnant, and I became a firm believer in a God Who Loved Me.

Blythe and I separated for the summer, vowing to return to each other in September. She found someone else by late July. I pined. I brooded. I hurt. Every song on the radio spoke directly to my pain. But I learned a lesson. Girls are just as curious about sex as boys. I was a nice, clean-cut nebbish who didn't frighten her as much as most of the immature clods and hulking lifeguard monsters our age. Perhaps this, and not true love, was the real reason she had chosen me as her lover. I wasn't selfish. Quite the opposite. Despite an honest awareness of my own foibles, I was a sensitive person and I loved her. The reasons for that first time don't really matter now, I suppose. In one of the final moments before the fifties really ended and we entered the Age of Abuse, we were two children who did our best to love, innocently and with real concern. Having given each other that, we gave each other more than most.

I remain tied to Blythe even though I never saw her again. I would be happy if she knew how often I thought about her even now. No one ever forgets their first lover, so wherever Blythe is, I know I am stored somewhere in her memory. I hope she remembers me kindly, a boy who knew very little about loving but who loved her fully and to this day loves her still.

While the unambiguous Jack was rollicking through fields of girls like a healthy stallion, this experience set the tone for my sexual life.

Fulfilling, but introspective and complicated.

NINETEEN

1

I wasn't getting any rest tossing and turning on Zack's couch thinking about Jack and all the rest of it, so I got up and put my clothes back on. I had one small piece: Robbie Hazen. I decided to go try to find another. It was either that or coffee at the all-night diner.

It was a big decision. I couldn't remember the last time I'd been out by myself at three in the morning.

Where did he buy the coke? I had asked Judy.

A biker bar down by the water, she'd said.

I knew Jack sometimes hung out at a place called Augie's, which fit that description. It was in a commercial area by the harbor filled with boat supply stores, small marinas, and body shops. The only houses left there were converted summer bun-

galows with weeds creeping up the chain link fences and greasy
shades in the windows.

A pounding bass beat was pouring out of Augie's when I
drove up. Maybe fifteen full-dressed Harleys stood side by side
in the gravel lot. The air smelled of low tide and pot. I stood
outside working up the courage to go in. It made me mad that
I had to. Putting on Jack's swagger helped. And his attitude.

I was conscious of descending into a darker world as I
walked in. Following Jack's trail was leading me ever down-
ward. Drugs. Group sex. Biker bars. Jack and Carolyn. The last
thought twisted my guts. What right did he have to drag us all
down with him? If he'd wanted to go to hell, why couldn't he
have gone there on his own?

I took a stool at the bar. The bikers and bikerettes drinking
there wrinkled their noses as if a bad meal had been set down
before them.

"What can I getcha?" the bartender asked.

"Beer, thanks."

He pushed a bottle of Bud across the bar. The fishing nets
hanging from the ceiling were filled with bugs the citronella
candles on the tables had driven up there, a final catch. There
was enough cigarette smoke in the air for a smog alert. I was
wondering what to do next when one of the biker girls called
over, "Hey, I know you."

"Excuse me?" I looked around to make sure she was talking
to me. She looked vaguely familiar, but I couldn't place her.

She detached herself from the group and came over. "Don't
you remember? Over at Helen's? The bake sale?"

Helen ran the annual bake sale for the PTA. My mind made
the leap.

"Dr. Friedkin? June?"

"Surprised?"

Shocked. June Friedkin was a divorced dentist who lived a
few blocks from us. She had a nice split ranch with a flagstone
walkway and a Japanese cherry tree I liked in the middle of the
front lawn. A dentist's lawn. However, she was wearing a very
undentistlike studded leather vest with nothing but a lacy
black bra underneath. Her black hair was all frizzed out kind of

sexy, and her makeup was dark and heavy. She climbed onto the barstool next to me.

"Hi, Phillie. How's Carolyn and the kids?"

"Fine," I said, very taken aback. June had a kid in Ben's class, another in junior high. We'd made cupcakes that day.

"I didn't know you, er, rode," I said lamely.

"Years now," she said. Her jeans were skin-tight, and her boots had those little flaps on top like Wonder Woman's. She wore a studded leather belt, and chrome bike chains adorned her shoulders like bandoliers. There was a gold skull on a gold chain around her neck.

"My old man's in the club," she went on, climbing onto the stool next to mine. "It's kind of a hobby with me."

"Where are the kids?" I asked.

"Asleep," she said happily. "My au pair's on tonight, so I get to go out."

I started to say something, stopped. She knew my question and asked it for me.

"What's a nice dentist?"

"I wasn't going to ask," I lied.

"You would have, in time. It's simple. I work in spit and blood all day. Then I cook and do homework with the kids, run the bath and clean-up drill till they go to bed. When I can, the night's mine."

"Enough 'Rinse, please'?"

She made a perfect professional face. " 'Open' no more."

"The dental battle cry."

She laughed and stretched languidly, making the vest ride way up. A lot of skin was visible through the armholes. "I don't remember you ever being in here before."

"Never have."

"What do you usually do at night?" she asked.

"I usually just go to sleep."

"I hear some people can."

A few of the bikers were building beer can pyramids on the bar. They smashed empties into their foreheads and used them for decoration. I'm no art critic, but it was at least as good as most of what I've seen at the Whitney.

"Jack used to come here," I said.

June's face got solicitous. "Jack, yeah, I was sorry to hear. That man could party with the best. It was always a good time when he came in." She said it reverently, as if the talent were on a par with great scientific achievement.

"Hey, everybody," she called to her friends. "This is Phillie Liebowitz, Jack Murphy's partner. Ex-partner, I guess. He's okay. Phillie, this is Billy and Mike and Paulie and Dawn and Lucy and Janie."

"Nice to meet you," I said.

The bikers' attitude changed instantly. Some said hi, and the rest raised their beers to me and turned off their stomp-you stares. Jack was a good pedigree. The girl named Lucy, a short blonde with a square jaw and heavy hips, eyed me up and down and shot back her tequila in one long gulp, finishing with a mighty shudder. There was something primitive and inviting about the gesture, like the way an animal shows its strength for mating purposes.

"What brings you out, Phillie?" June asked.

I leaned closer. "I want to score some coke. Who do I talk to?"

"For real?"

I nodded. My idea was simple. *We found others like us.* Jack's autopsy had revealed cocaine, and his file confirmed it. If I could find whoever dealt drugs to him and Judy, maybe he could tell me who those others were.

"How much?"

I didn't have any idea how it was sold. "What Jack used to buy."

She looked me over. "Jack got it for you?"

I went with it. "Yeah. And now . . ."

She shrugged. "Okay. Go out back. That door over there. I'll send him."

"Thanks."

I needed to use the toilet. Meeting a dealer at four in the morning in the back room of Augie's wasn't what I'd had in mind when I got up today. Jack was taking me still deeper. I saw myself in the stained bathroom mirror. I looked scared. I used the last of the toilet paper, nervously twisting the cardboard tube out of shape.

June was gone when I came out. The door she'd pointed out led to a dimly lit storage room cum office. Cartons of beer and paper goods were stacked against the walls, and an old wooden desk and chair and a couple of old file cabinets stood in one corner. The biker, Billy, came in, big as a linebacker, with a massive chest, thin hair, a bushy beard, and small eyes. He wore a leather pouch and a Bowie knife on his belt.

"You want something?" he asked, closing the door. The chains on his leather jacket clinked like cowboy spurs as he walked.

"Jack sent me."

"So?"

"I'd like to buy what he did."

"What's that?"

"Coke."

Billy shrugged. It made his leather creak.

I took fifty dollars out of my pocket. "This much."

"You want to see it first?"

"Oh, sure."

Billy pulled out a rolled Baggie filled partway with white powder from the leather pouch. He pulled out the Bowie knife, too. I didn't know which one scared me more.

"Hey," I said. One of my more noteworthy remarks.

"Easy, fish." He dipped the long blade into the powder and brought it out with a tiny pile on the tip.

"This is the goods," he said, and held the heavy blade under my nose. I stood very still in the dark room.

"Smells nice," I said. "I'll take it."

"Smells . . . ?" Suspicion crossed his face. He pressed the blade against my upper lip. "Do it."

"Later. I just want—"

"You a cop?"

The pain of the blade backed me into the wall. I went up on my toes to keep from being cut.

"You wanna keep your nose, fish, you better do it."

I looked for a weapon of some kind. There was a dusty old marlin on the wall. Maybe I could pry it off. Charge of the Fish Brigade.

Billy's face was close enough to mine to smell his breath. He pressed harder. "I asked if you're a cop."

"Ow . . . writer!"

"What? With horses?"

"Writer." With the knife against my nose it came out *rider*. "With a T," I said.

His face got mean. "Good-bye, fish."

I reached into my pocket looking for a key to poke him in the eye with, or something equally lethal. All I came up with was the twisted toilet paper tube. I shoved it against his belly and said, "Back off, or I'll pull the trigger."

I was prepared for mostly anything but his laughing in my face. It got worse. His laughter rose to one of those can't-catch-your-breath shrieks, and he had to hold his sides, he was laughing so hard. He kept saying things like, "The toilet paper killer. Ow, it hurts." It was humiliating.

"I could have killed you with this," I said angrily, brandishing the cardboard roll. "You should be more careful."

"Back off, or I'll pull the trigger!" he screamed.

"Most men wouldn't have thought as quickly," I said with injured dignity. My pride was hurt.

He slid the knife back into its sheath, no easy task when you're laughing that hard. He wiped his eyes. "God, that's a classic."

June came out from behind a stack of cartons.

"Not one word," I warned her.

She put a friendly hand on my shoulder. "Phillie, you're lucky you're my neighbor and I like you, and you're too damn silly to be anything else but a writer. Otherwise you'd have left by the water exit, if you know what I mean."

"This was a test?"

"Yes, and you failed. Now, why not just tell us what you want. You obviously don't do coke, and you're not here for any action."

"Can we talk?" I asked.

"We always coulda done *that*," Billy said amiably.

2

We settled back at the bar, June and me and Billy. Billy still wore a bemused smile.

"I came here to find out who Jack did coke with," I told them over fresh beers.

There was a sudden vacant look on Billy's face that told me I might as well be asking the pope to admit to illegitimate kids. Well, it was a nice try.

June said, "I slept with Jack," so matter-of-factly I didn't have time to react. "It was a friendly thing. Kinda nice." She fingered the little gold skull on her neck chain. "He had this made for me. See?"

"Very nice. You met here?"

"I did some work on his mouth. Replaced a crown some-body else messed up. We talked. A few weeks later he walked in here." She smiled. "Just like you."

I heard invitation in her voice. First Judy, now June. I was having a banner day.

"Was he very kinky?" I asked.

"What a strange question."

"I have reasons for asking."

"They must be doozies. Actually, he was very conventional. Surprisingly so."

I drank some beer. "That changed radically."

"Did it?" She grinned. "I wish I'd been around."

"Did it last a long time?"

"We had an intense, absorbing relationship," she said, "and then he left me flat."

"Well, we share one thing," I said.

"What's that?"

"Jack screwed both of us."

She had a big laugh that came from deep in her belly. She

was genuine, smart, and interesting, not at all what I expected from a dentist. Bikers I didn't know as well.

We drank some more. I was beginning to like these people's sexy easy ways. Lucy came over, and we all talked for a while about the movies. She downed another shot with a shudder. Billy was drinking Jack Daniel's. His small eyes sparkled warmly when he thought something was funny, which was often.

"What do you do now that Jack's gone?" June asked.

"It changes things," I confided. "I lost my rudder. I still have motive power, but I'm having trouble steering."

June ordered another drink. "Phillie?"

"Sure. Beer."

Lucy drank again, shuddered, and hugged herself. It made her breasts swell.

"I've lost business partners," June said. "Husbands, too. Tough, but you survive."

"You do," agreed Lucy.

"Did Jack ride with you?" I asked.

"Sometimes," Billy said. "Jack was okay. Knew how to live. No bullshit."

"He was my partner."

"He was cute," said Lucy. "Like you."

I smiled sweetly. "Ah, but I'm taken."

She smiled back. "Too bad."

Call it beginner's luck.

The jukebox cut out, and the dancers dropped into booths to grope each other, alcohol close. June looked at me in the sudden quiet.

"What are you really doing here, Phillie?"

"I told you. Following Jack's trail. Trying to understand him."

"Understand him, or be him?"

The question caught me off guard. Was that what I wanted? To be like Jack? I enjoyed being here, and that did surprise me. I felt freed from the rules of the rest of the sleeping world. Was I discovering I was more like Jack than I'd cared to admit?

I said, "I need to know why Jack lived like he did."

Billy spread his huge arms. "Fuck *why*, man. You gotta *feel* it."

Have you ever been free? I heard Judy Lane ask, and Carolyn telling me that if she had to die for one lousy moment of being free, then so be it.

"Ever see the sunrise over the mountains, or wake up on a beach?" Billy asked me.

"In college I once—"

Billy looked at me narrowly. I shut up.

"You wanna know what Jack knew?" he said.

"Tell me."

"How to be what he was. You oughta think about that."

It was hard not to.

June looked at me thoughtfully. "Come inside. I'll show you something."

I plucked a little plastic sword from a container on the bar. "Careful, this time I'm armed."

"He's very funny," Billy said to Lucy.

June led me back to the storeroom and over to one of the file cabinets. She pointed to a drawer with a combination lock.

"What am I looking at?" I asked.

"That one was Jack's," she said.

"In here? Why?"

"Jack loaned the owner some money. In return, he got this private space where he could leave things. He showed me once."

"Drugs and things?"

"Boy, writers are sharp."

"Natural ability," I said humbly.

"By the way," she said. "Don't get the wrong idea. It's no secret what people do around here. And if that's your trip, it's fine with me. But I just wanted you to know I don't."

"Why tell me?"

"Because we're neighbors, and I still want our kids to play together. And I care about what people think, just like you do. I ride. I play. I keep the humdrums away. But that's all. Okay?"

"Okay, Doc. And by the way, I'm glad. Anything else?"

"One more thing. Be careful out there, Phillie. The night's

catchy. You gotta watch it. I've seen tougher guys than you get snagged. It's easy to forget who you are at three in the morning."

"I'll remember. Do you have the combination?"

"Sure." She went to the door. "Billy, come in here and bring a crowbar, will you?"

3

Billy pried the drawer open, and he and June left me alone. Inside there was a folded shirt with a Chinese laundry paper band still around it, socks and underwear, and a pair of sneakers. Things for a quick change on the way home to Jessica.

There was also some cash, a studded paddle, lady's bikini underwear, and a great paperback adventure novel, *Voyage of the Storm*, which I'd loaned him. I checked everything, even thumbed through the pages of the book, but there weren't any phone numbers written on the pages or any notes or letters inside. The only thing of interest in the drawer was a thin gold case about the size of a deck of cards, with some geometric lines engraved on it for chic. I pressed a tiny catch, and it swung open, revealing a glass vial. I unscrewed the black plastic cap. White powder clung to a tiny spoon fixed to it. It was either the breakfast cereal of midgets or Jack's stash. The drug had bothered me since I'd first heard about it from Donnegan and read about it in Jack's file. How much of the answer it provided I still had no way of knowing.

The vial fit into a little blue felt-lined pocket next to a raised mirror. Something rattled when I shook the case. I tried to pry up the mirror but only succeeded in cutting my finger. I'd have to get it out later. I slid the case into my jacket pocket and went back to the bar. It was time to go. June stopped me.

"Come out with us, Phillie. We're gonna ride. See what it's like."

"I don't think so."

Billy pounded me on the back. "You can ride with Lucy. Dawn'll drive your car. It'll be okay with Razor. He liked Jack."

"Who's Razor?"

"My old man," Lucy said happily.

I pondered the wisdom of going out on a motorcycle at five in the morning with the girlfriend of a biker named Razor. I had to be out of my mind, but I knew what Jack would have said.

I said it.

4

We poured out of Augie's in one surge and mounted the Harleys like cavalry. I tossed my keys to Dawn, an Asian beauty, who slipped into the Miata and looked damn good in it. June and some others rode off to get food and beer at an all-night deli in preparation for the ride out east. I got on the bike behind Lucy, and Billy tossed me a helmet.

"Cops snag you if you don't."

Lucy revved the huge engine, and I felt the vibrations from my crotch to my brain. I was wondering what to hold on to when she pulled my arms around her, making pommels of her firm breasts. The saddle pressed me against her behind. We roared through the night, a dark spear of energy. Strong. Lawless. Daring. The part of me that observed everything observed this: I was riding with a gang of bikers at five in the morning with my hands on the breasts of Razor's girlfriend and an erection from the vibration of the Harley that could have penetrated steel.

Things in my life were changing rapidly.

Billy said Jack knew how to be what he was.

I was beginning to wonder what I was.

Actually, we didn't go far. Less than a mile away, we stopped at the town dock to wait for June and the rest of the food brigade. Lucy and Billy and Dawn went swimming. I sat up by the road alone, looking at the boats in the harbor. I know the truth about boats, by the way. Boats are an excuse for lunch. Anyone who has ever asked me out on their boat invariably says, "We'll go out, we'll have a nice lunch, we'll come back." I mean, what's the point? That's not sailing. It's driving. To lunch. The entire aim of the boating community is to park the boat and eat shrimp salad.

The others played in the water, free as codfish. The sun had come up by now. It was a new day. Soon I'd be going back to my endless responsibilities. Or would I? The open road beckoned. I could go. The bikers' dark sexuality pulled at me. I fantasized about women in leather vests moaning in the night. Taking what I wanted. Not holding myself back anymore. It surprised me how easily such desires emerged. Maybe Jack was right. The hell with responsibility—freedom's the answer. Forget all the ties that kept me in place. I might have, too. I'll never know, because at that moment a white Mercedes 500 swerved past me in the road going way too fast, its tires screaming at their limit of adhesion. I knew the car. It was Judy's. I had a bad feeling. As I watched, the swerving got more pronounced. The driver was clearly in trouble. I pulled myself back from the abyss I contemplated, ran over to where Dawn had parked the Miata, and peeled out after her.

5

After about five blocks, I got close enough to the car to see Judy was indeed driving. I honked to get her attention, but she ran a red light without even slowing and I had to stop to avoid an early-morning delivery van that was taking no shit from my little car. When I pulled up again and got a longer glimpse, I was shocked because I realized she was naked, at least on top. The side of her face was red and puffy. She was in bad shape, staring fixedly ahead and driving as if her life depended on getting wherever she was going.

Obviously, the police were occupied elsewhere, because she was running lights and stop signs with impunity. I couldn't, and lost her again. We were very near her house, though, and I decided to take a chance that that was where she was headed. I cut through a shopping center and out a back road, found her street, and followed the numbers to her house.

The Mercedes was buried nosefirst in the shrubs bordering her driveway. The motor was still running. I jerked the Miata to a stop and ran over. Judy was in the front seat, her head thrown back, not partially but totally naked. Her chest was heaving like a bellows as if she couldn't get enough air into her lungs. I wanted to cry when I saw her. It was horrible. She was cut and bleeding, her breasts and thighs covered with weird crescent-shaped burns that prodded some dim memory in me that I had no time to think about.

I threw my jacket around her, yanked her keys out of the ignition, and carried her across the damp lawn to the front door. She was surprisingly light. Her eyes opened, filled with fear till she saw who it was.

"Phillie . . ."

"Gotta get you inside. Get help. Hold on."

I got the door open and carried her into the living room. She still didn't seem to be able to catch her breath. Her skin was paste white and clammy. I laid her on the sofa and found the light switch and the phone. The Port police answered right away. I steadied my voice despite the panic I was feeling. I gave them the address and told them to hurry.

"An ambulance, too," I said urgently. "She's been burned. I think she's in shock. She can't breathe. It's really bad."

There was no way to describe how bad it was. She was a beautiful woman, and the wounds were a disgrace to her flesh. I felt my stomach churn and got mad at myself because this wasn't about me, it was about her. I grabbed an afghan off an armchair and added it to the cover of my jacket. I remembered you were supposed to raise a shock victim's feet for some reason, so I propped them up on the arm of the sofa. She was still shivering. I put my arms around her for warmth, cradling her head in my lap.

"Easy now. I'm here."

"Phillie . . . ," she whimpered, ". . . can't breathe."

I reached under the covers to feel her heartbeat. My palm came away sticky with blood. Her pulse felt like a drum roll.

"Who did this to you?" I said.

"Can't breathe . . . hurt . . ."

"Help will be here soon. Please hold on."

Her eyes glazed with pain. She was in her own world.

"I didn't tell them . . . I didn't. . . . It was right under their noses."

"What was? Judy, who did this to you?"

". . . I waited . . . then I ran . . ."

She fought for breath. I didn't know if she could even hear me, but I told her everything was okay, she was safe now. I wanted to believe it. The sun was up. The living room was filled with light. C'mon, I thought, someone get the hell over here and save her. It's morning, the darkness is over. I felt a searing anger at my inability to do anything for her. I found myself praying. She had made it this far—God, let her make it all the way.

". . . monsters . . . all monsters . . . ," she babbled.

I rocked her like a child. Her head lolled weakly to the side.

"C'mon." I shook her. "Hold on."

She jerked back, still fighting. Words tumbled out.

"I thought . . . videotape would . . . protect us . . . but it didn't. . . ."

"I don't care about the tape. Damn it, who did this to you? Tell me."

She tried. I swear she did. Her eyes found mine, and for a moment there was cognition in them. Her lips began to move, but no sound came out. A terrible stillness seemed to descend on her. Fighting it, her hands came out from under the blanket and clawed at the air as if she could somehow scratch a message there.

Then her eyes opened wider than I'd ever seen anyone's open before, and she died in my arms.

TWENTY

1

Carolyn's worried voice penetrated my ragged sleep. "Phillie?"

"Hmmm."

"A policeman's here. Detective Donnegan. He wants to see you."

I dragged myself out from under the covers and cleared my throat. I sounded the way an old engine does, starting up. "All right. I'm awake."

"What do I do?"

"Tell him to wait. No, better. Make him some coffee."

"Are you all right?"

"My head feels like a swamp. What time is it?"

"Two in the afternoon."

"Where are the kids?"

"At camp. I want to know what's going on. Do you need help?"

More than you know, I wanted to say, but I shook my head no, and Carolyn went downstairs.

It was hard to get up. I felt drugged. In fact, I was. One of the EMTs at Judy's house had given me a couple of pills. He said I might need something to get to sleep. He was right. He just hadn't warned me about the dreams I might have.

That had been only a couple of hours ago.

I was still holding Judy when the cops and EMTs swarmed into her house. The ones who remembered me from Jack's looked at me strangely; I was getting to be a guest at all the best North Shore murders. The EMTs took Judy from me and rushed her to the hospital, but we all knew it was too late. My clothes had blood on them. Donnegan showed up a little while later looking tired and irritable. I told him what had happened. He looked at me the way a cop does when he's wondering what to make of someone, whether he's being played for a fool or not. Then he eased up. I guess he decided. He put me in a chair, and I sat there remembering what it felt like to have her die in my arms while the crime scene guys did a lot of the same things they'd done at Jack's a few nights ago, and someone tried to locate Judy's husband, Ray.

"Phillie," Carolyn asked as I headed for the bathroom, "what happened last night? Where did you go?"

"I'll explain later. Let me shower, get my head straight. I have to deal with Donnegan."

She was wearing white shorts and a blue top. Her dark hair was pulled back along the sides, and it accentuated her bangs the way I liked. Sometimes she struck me as so pretty. The lingering pain of Judy Lane's death had me wishing I could reach out to her. I couldn't. We were both too aware that I had walked out last night without anything being resolved. The problems in our relationship still hung between us.

"Are you back?" she asked me.

"I don't know."

"When will you?"

"I don't know that either."

It wasn't the time for this. She let it go. "You want some breakfast?"

I probed my stomach, still sour from Augie's beer. "Just a bagel and some juice."

I got into the shower and made it as hot as I could stand. I slumped my shoulders under the cascade and waited for life to return. It took a while.

When I got downstairs, Donnegan was waiting for me in the kitchen drinking the coffee Carolyn had served him.

"Good morning," I said.

"Afternoon. Did you sleep?" he asked.

"If you can call it that." I drank some juice, a blessing to my parched throat. "Want some? It's fresh squeezed."

"Sure."

"I didn't think you could drink on duty."

"The force has gone to hell."

"Bagel?"

He shrugged. "In for a penny."

I popped another one into the toaster and set the table.

"You have a nice house," he said. "Comfortable."

"Thanks. We redid most of it. The view in back's the thing."

"Port's a great town," he said. "I wish I could afford to live here."

"They don't pay you enough?"

He smiled. "Are any of your neighbors cops?"

I thought about it. A builder, a photographer, an up-and-coming lawyer. No cops. It seemed wrong, somehow.

"I think they should give the police homes in the community," I said. "You should be a part of it. For mutual self-interest, if nothing else."

"You," he said, "should run for office."

"I," I said, "would die."

"How come?"

"I'm allergic to bullshit."

He laughed and stretched in the warm light. We talked wives and kids for a while. Then houses. He'd done lots of construction around his place in East Meadow, he told me, especially since his only kid went off to college. When I'd first moved in, changing light bulbs had been too much for me. Despite some notable failures, I'd learned a lot over the years. We talked oak floors and cabinets and kitchen counters.

"I put that window in myself," I said proudly.

"You did a nice job. It's a good room. A family's room."

"Can you tell things about a person from his kitchen, being a cop and all?" I asked.

"You mean with my great insight into the human soul?"

"That's it."

He shook his head. "Not a fucking thing."

I spread some more cream cheese on my bagel. My hands felt rough. I'd washed them over and over to get the sticky blood off. They weren't so steady either. Donnegan must have seen that.

"It was very bad," he said after a while. "It'll take a while to feel normal."

"She was a nice lady. She didn't deserve what happened to her," I said.

He munched on his bagel. "This is your first exposure to it, I guess."

"To what?"

"Nice people getting hurt. People who don't deserve the pain life delivers, but they get it anyway."

"Yeah."

"Not like in the movies," he observed.

"No. One second she was alive, the next . . . Who does shit like that to another person, Donnegan? I mean, we all fantasize. We say 'I'll kill you' or 'You're dead' a hundred times a week, but who the hell really does it?"

"Good juice," he said, pouring more.

"That's an answer?"

"You won't like the real one," he said.

"Try me."

He picked up two bagels. Poppy-seeded. "They look alike, they were made the same way, but one's good and one's bad. No one knows why."

"*That's* fucking profound," I said.

"Maybe not, but it's as good as you're going to get from me."

"You won't be offended if I keep searching then?"

" 'Course not." He smiled. "By the way, that was a good bagel."

We cleaned up. He hadn't come for breakfast, and we both knew it. I was waiting for him to tell me what was on his mind when Carolyn came in to get her car keys.

"Carolyn, this is Detective Donnegan."

"We met," Carolyn said, uneasy at the presence of a cop in the house, wanting to know what it meant.

"Thanks for the coffee, Mrs. Liebowitz."

"You're welcome."

"Did you want me?" I asked her.

"I have some shopping to do, and then I have to get the kids at camp. Will you be here when I get back?"

I looked at Donnegan.

He shook his head. "We'd like you to come down to the station. You can follow me in your car."

"Why?" Carolyn began, concerned.

"Relax, I'm not under arrest yet, am I?" I said, meaning it as a joke. It fell flat.

"No," Donnegan said, but both Carolyn and I saw his eyes get a tiny glint harder.

2

The Port Adams Police Station was a single-story concrete building up on the main road into town. A female officer was working communications behind a glass-partitioned counter in the lobby. She looked like a deejay. Donnegan and I were snicked through the electric doors. Blue uniforms were hustling around with papers. There were notices on the walls about PBA benefits and reminders about insurance forms. Donnegan led me into the detectives' room. Four desks. Gray file cabinets. IBM typewriters. Windows that looked out on a greenbelt. We were the only ones there. He made a call from the phone on his desk, and a few moments later a woman wearing a gray business suit and a white blouse walked in. She looked about thirty-five. Severe black hair. Thin lips. Not much makeup. A youthful face that was dry from too much school. The business suit scared me.

"Mr. Liebowitz, this is Assistant District Attorney Paula Michelson."

"Hello, Mr. Liebowitz. Thank you for coming in."

"Charmed, I'm sure."

Donnegan gave me a narrow look, sat down, and pointed me to a chair. The ADA sat to his right.

"I should tell you it's a bit unusual for the district attorney's office to be present at this kind of conference," Donnegan said to me, "but Mrs. Lane's murder promises to be a high-profile case, and I guess the feeling in Mineola is that we local guys should get it right from the beginning."

"We'd like to ask you some questions," Michelson said, ignoring the barb with everything but her eyes. "We'd also like to videotape your answers."

I was so nervous I could feel my heart thumping without putting my hand over it. But I was angry, too. I grabbed on to that like a power connection and rode it to where I got stronger.

"No," I said firmly. "First you tell me why I'm here. Then you give me a good goddamn reason why I should answer your questions. Then I'll answer. Maybe."

Donnegan looked me over. "You write that?"

I nodded. "*Full Fathom Five*. Concorde, 1990."

"I saw it."

"What did you think?"

"Could Michael Moriarty have talked any faster?"

I grinned. "Not and gotten out of Peru. Shining Path guerrillas wanted script approval."

"Excuse me?" said Michelson, frowning.

Donnegan said, "Mr. Liebowitz writes movies."

"I see."

I waited.

"Mr. Liebowitz, how well did you know Judy Lane?" Michelson asked.

"No tape?"

She shrugged and turned off the VCR. "As you wish."

"And friendly?"

It took some doing for her to smile.

"I knew Judy from playing tennis," I said. "She was more a friend of my partner's than mine."

"But you were with her this morning," Michelson said.

"Tough for Jack to be."

"Can we dispense with the wisecracks, please?" Michelson didn't love my humor. Keep them in school long enough, they lose perspective.

I said, "I was out with friends."

Michelson was dubious. "At that hour?"

"I couldn't sleep."

"What friends?" she demanded.

"Some bikers I met."

"Can you produce them?"

I thought about the difficulty of finding Billy and the rest somewhere out on the road. June could account for a good part of the night, but there was the chunk of time after she left that I was alone and had no real alibi for, when I saw Judy's car. Was it long enough to torture a woman to death?

"I can find them if I have to," I said. "We were by the harbor about to ride out east when I saw Judy's car swerving all over the road. I was worried, so I followed it to her house. She was naked and cut when I got to her. I did the best I could. I took her inside and called the police. She died in my arms."

"Was Mrs. Lane cheating on her husband?" Donnegan asked.

"Cheating implies dishonesty. Judy was one of the most honest women I ever met. What did she die of exactly?"

Donnegan shot the ADA a questioning look. She nodded.

"Heart attack," he said, "brought on by an overdose of drugs and physical abuse."

"We want to find whoever gave her those drugs and beat her like that," Michelson said. "Did she tell you anything about who did it?"

"Monsters."

Michelson frowned. "I'd advise you to take this a little more seriously, Mr. Liebowitz."

"That's what she said."

I was remembering what Hans Helmut Kirst once wrote: The more violent the time, the more violent the crimes committed in it. I said sadly, "I had lunch with Judy yesterday."

"We know," Michelson said a little too smugly.

That surprised me. "We were followed?"

Donnegan actually laughed. "Her AmEx receipt. The waitress who served you was working again today. She ID'ed a picture of Mrs. Lane. She was able to describe her companion because of the helpful and much-appreciated serving instructions he gave."

I ignored that. "We had lunch. Talked about Jack. That's the extent of our relationship."

Michelson consulted a folder. "May tenth this year ring any bells?"

"None."

She read from a sheet. " 'Officers responded to a call from neighbors and removed two inebriated males, one the owner, from the rooftop of number 157 Hilltop Lane.' Now?"

"Oh, come on," I exploded. "Jack and I finished a project and had a few drinks and went out on his roof to—"

"—'howl at the moon,' " she finished, reading. "No charges filed. You went up there together often?"

"Sometimes, for air. The office door led out there. Why?"

"Were you up there together the night he jumped?"

"No, damn it." I was sweating, and mad that she made me so nervous. I told myself I was innocent, so I had nothing to fear. Then I thought that if I'd written that line for a character in a script, he'd be in jail by the next scene.

Donnegan took a clear plastic envelope out of his drawer. "I have to show you something."

"Go ahead."

There was a Polaroid of Carolyn inside. I looked at it once, and went for him.

"Hey, what?" he yelled as I grabbed for it. I got a kind of armlock on him, and we tussled around for a few seconds. It was no contest. Probably the only damage I could have done was give him a nuggie. He slammed me back into my chair and tugged his shirt back into place, glaring at me, not even breathing hard, more annoyed than angry.

"Give me that!" I shouted. "Give it to me now!"

"It's evidence." He shoved it back into his desk. "You knew?"

"Yes, I knew, damn you." My voice was wobbly. "I just didn't know he took *pictures.*"

Michelson had watched it all. I saw the word *violent* go off in her head. She could have added *stupid.*

"One, that's all we found," Donnegan said, "in a box with some other stuff." He went on more gently, "If it helps any, it looks like she didn't—I mean, it wasn't posed. She might not have known, see?"

Small comfort. I didn't say anything. My face was hot, and I was humiliated. How many others had seen the picture?

"You're an odd sort of prude," he observed.

"What's it to you?"

Michelson said, "How about this? Your partner and your wife were having an affair. You found out about it and couldn't handle it. So one night when you were on the roof together, you shoved him off. That's why there was no struggle. Mrs. Murphy was asleep—you could have been in the house and she wouldn't even have known."

"I was at home when Jessica called me to tell me about it, remember?"

"You live just a few miles apart. More than enough time to get back."

"In this fantasy am I supposed to be responsible for Judy, too?"

She fielded that more easily than I'd hoped. "There were pictures of Mrs. Lane also. With Jack Murphy. S&M stuff. Whips, chains, clamps. There are pictures of other people we can't identify because they're wearing hoods. Maybe you're wiping out everybody involved."

"You write for Clint Eastwood?" Donnegan asked.

"Detective," Michelson said sharply.

"Sorry."

I said, "I tried to *help* Judy. What was I supposed to do when I saw her driving like that? Go for a swim?"

"Assuming she ever drove her car," Michelson said.

"What's that supposed to mean?"

"There are hooks set into the ceiling of her basement playroom," Michelson said. "We found S&M instruments there, too. She could have been tied up and beaten in her own house. We have only your word that she wasn't. You could have done it right there in the basement, carried her upstairs, smeared some of her blood in her car and moved it, and then called us."

"Why did I kill her? Because I don't like S&Mers?"

"Maybe."

I made a face. "That wouldn't hold up past the first act. If we want to get everybody into this, why not have Judy jealous of Jack and Carolyn, then helping me kill Jack and getting wiped out by me because she knew?"

Michelson got real quiet. "Is that what you're telling us?"

"C'mon," I fumed. "This is bullshit. Get a polygraph in here right now. No lawyer. Nothing. I'll take it cold. Do it."

Donnegan's eyes narrowed to slits, like gunsights in a pillbox. "Did you kill Jack Murphy?"

"No."

"Did you kill Judy Lane?"

"No."

He searched my face for a time, then let out a deep breath and leaned back in his chair. "You are one dumb sonofabitch, you know that?"

"In what category?" I asked. "There are several to choose from."

"Glib as shit, too."

"You're not the first person to point that out."

Michelson said, "Mr. Liebowitz, I want to inform you we

will be continuing our investigation. You are a material witness. What else you are remains to be seen. I advise you to consult with a good criminal lawyer and not to leave the state. Thank you for coming in."

She walked out of the detectives' room.

"A real charmer," I said to Donnegan.

"You didn't help yourself, you know."

"Yeah. Probably not."

I was angry, but I was also badly shaken. I saw it through Michelson's eyes. It wasn't so crazy. She could actually believe I killed Jack and Judy.

"This is getting out of hand," I said.

"People are dying around you, and you're too stupid to keep your head down."

"The Paula Michelson school of social responsibility."

"You ever without a line?"

"Not when I'm this nervous."

He sighed the way my father did when he wanted to tell me I was trying his patience, and settled back in his chair. "You're right to this extent. It is serious. If Paula thinks you did it, she'll come after you with all the weight the Nassau County DA's office has. Believe me, it's considerable."

"It might help if you talked to Dr. June Friedkin. She's a dentist in Port. I was at a bar called Augie's with her from two A.M. on."

"I thought you said you were with bikers."

"She's a biker dentist."

"That's unusual, no?"

"Not lately. Is this going to make the media?"

Donnegan feigned innocence. " 'Course not. Who'd want to waste their time reporting an unsolved double suicide slash murder with S&M implications and pictures to prove it? If I were you, I'd start checking under my bed for Geraldo Rivera."

"It can't be that bad."

"It could be. You haven't been arrested or charged, so we have to keep your name out of it, and Mrs. Lane's husband is cooperating with us to keep a lid on the more sensational aspects while we investigate. But you never know. Leaks happen. Especially if an ambitious ADA wants to create an atmosphere of public outrage to try her case in."

"Would she do that?"

"I'm just telling you it's been done. So do what she said. Get a lawyer, and practice spelling Liebowitz for the reporters."

Reality began to hit me. "What's going to happen to me, Donnegan?"

He shrugged. "Like you said, our having gotten you at home the night your partner died makes us less than happy with you as a suspect, regardless of what Paula said. Officially, he's still listed as a suicide, but as I told you, the ME hasn't closed the books. You did call us about Judy Lane, which carries some weight, but she's clearly a homicide, and that means there's a perp walking around somewhere."

"You don't think it's me, do you?"

"No, but I don't make cases. The DA's office does. We'll be talking to family, collecting evidence, interviewing friends and business associates. Judy's murder is going to be very public fairly soon. I won't lie to you. If it lies around unsolved for too long, you may look real good to them. You want some coffee?"

"Black. Three sugars."

"That's not coffee, it's syrup. You don't drink it, do you?"

I shook my head. A dry smile came over his face. "Some tough guy. You hit me over a picture of your wife that isn't much worse than what you see on MTV, you don't even drink coffee."

"Can I have a Diet Coke?"

"Sure, John Wayne. Wait here."

Judy's folder was still on his desk. I flicked through it. In the pictures she looked fleshy and white. I read about cuts and bruises, splinters in her back and behind, burn marks that were crescent-shaped. That prodded some buried memory again. I was trying to bring it to the surface when I saw that Fred Marcus was one of the doctors who had signed the medical report. I slid it back onto Donnegan's desk.

"Here." He handed me the soda.

"Thanks." It settled my stomach with a gassy belch.

"The other day you said you hated Jack. Is this why?"

"It's complicated." I tried to explain about Carolyn's depression.

"We had a case where a woman killed her kid," he said. "She pleaded postpartum depression and was acquitted. They're strange creatures, females. I don't claim to understand them."

"Maybe that was my problem. I thought I did."

"Did you know your partner was so kinky?"

"No." Donnegan had seen Jack's photos. There was no point in denying it. "Judy said their relationship went beyond love, into obsession." It sounded like movie trailer copy. *What's past love?*

"Her husband evidently knew."

"She told me at lunch. She said it didn't matter to him. They had an open marriage."

"You know anything about S&M?" he asked.

"Only what I've read."

Donnegan ran a hand over his hair. He was seeing another place and time and didn't like what he saw. "I did a tour on Vice when I was a city cop. Most of it was murky as hell, but frankly, the S&M crowd didn't hurt anybody as a rule, despite all the show of it, so I had no real truck with them. It's quieter now, but there are still a lot of clubs in Manhattan you can go see a live show, or rent a submissive, or be dominated, whipped, humiliated. The works."

I remembered the phone number that activated the tape from Whips and Chains. *We found others.*

I said, "I figure Jack and Judy belonged to a group."

"Judging from the pictures." He rubbed his chin. "Question is, is one of them a killer?"

"Of Jack or Judy?"

"Either."

"You're the cop," I said. "You like it?"

"Only moderately."

"Why?"

"They have a saying. Murder is to S&M what rape is to sex. Their scene's about pleasure, not dying."

"Can I see the pictures?" I asked.

"I don't see what harm it would do." He handed me some Polaroids.

"No videotapes?"

Donnegan looked interested. "Why do you ask?"

Because Judy had mentioned one, but I didn't want to tell him yet. "Most of the houses on the North Shore have camcorders. Make a tape, you can play it on a big-screen TV anytime you want."

"No tapes."

I looked over the photos. In one, a woman in black stockings and a corset was whipping the buttocks of a naked man bound to the floor. In another, a naked woman was suspended from a hook in the ceiling and was being fondled by two men. One was of a naked woman lying facedown and being paddled. Hoods and masks and positioning made them all unidentifiable. No marks or tattoos, not even a birthmark. Just sagging flesh and hard-ons that looked like add-ons.

I looked for Carolyn's body, which I knew better than I knew my own. I was relieved not to see it.

"Recognize anybody?" Donnegan asked.

"No." I was tired. "Can I go now?"

"Like she said, no travel."

I was a fly passed from web to web. It startled me how true my response was.

"I'm not going anywhere."

Donnegan took the pictures back. "Here's my card if you want to call me. And by the way, if you ever hit me again, I will tear your head off and shit down your throat."

"Poetry lost a great one when you went into police work." I noticed my knees were weak. Maybe Donnegan noticed it, too.

"Mr. Liebowitz?"

"It's Phillie to people who almost arrest me."

"Phillie—I'm sorry about your wife."

I said I was, too.

TWENTY-ONE

1

Carolyn was waiting outside in the parking lot by our family car, a gray Volvo, when I walked out. I was glad to see her. I wanted to put my head on her shoulder and have her make it all go away. Instead, I asked her why she came.

"What do you mean, why? I'm your wife, Phillie. I thought you might need me."

"I'm sorry. It was a nice thought. Thanks. Who's with the kids?"

"Terry next door came over." She folded her arms across her chest. "I want to know what's going on."

"Last night Judy Lane had a heart attack in her car and died. I saw the crash and called the police." I left out the rest for the time being.

"Her poor family. That's terrible." She shivered the way

139

people do when death passes close. "For you, too. Is that why they wanted to talk to you?"

I nodded. "Did Jack ever talk to you about her?"

"A few times. Not so much detail or anything, and I never met her. Just how he felt. It was sexy and powerful, and in his way he loved her."

"She loved him, too," I said. "Funny, I didn't know anything about them. I didn't even know you knew."

"Jack and I were friends," she said. "And I didn't give him a hard time about it."

"I wish he would have told me," I said sadly.

"I'm sure he wanted to but . . . you know."

Yeah, I knew. Phillie's too hard.

Carolyn saw my hurt and softened a little. "Come in the car."

I felt safer inside the big enclosed car after the police interrogation. I didn't drive it that often, but the Volvo's heated leather seats were right up there on the list of things I loved, along with Peter Luger's steaks, sunsets, the Yankees, Judy Collins, lobsters at the Palm, Andel's sturgeon, Paris, New Orleans, the Villa d'Este on Lake Como, and just about everything edible in Zabar's. Until very recently, the woman next to me had topped the list.

It was strange sitting alone like this in the police station parking lot, oddly intimate. No kids. Just us. What a pair we were. The adulteress and the murder suspect. It made me laugh.

"What's funny?" she asked.

"Us."

"You think so?"

I looked at my wife. "Carolyn, you may not believe this, but I know you are the only woman in the world for me. Part of why I'm so screwed up is because if I can't love you anymore, I don't think I'll ever love anyone again."

"You can love me, Phillie." She said it with such sadness, it touched me.

"I'm trying. It's not something I can control."

"So what makes you think I could?" Her struggle turned

into anger. "You men, you think everything is you. All neat cause and effect. I did it, I get punished, like Beth or Ben. Our family means everything to me, Phillie. I gave up my career for it. There isn't a goddamn day that I don't eat and breathe you and those kids. Don't you see? You're punishing me for what I did so I could stay part of it. What goddamn sense does that make?"

"Adultery isn't on the list of AMA cures," I shot back out of pain, and instantly regretted it.

"Fuck the AMA." Her chin quivered with sorrow or anger, maybe both. "Someday you'll understand I had no choice."

We stopped, knowing we'd come to the same dead end.

"I haven't told you everything," I said.

"What else is there?"

"The police know that Judy had a relationship with Jack. They're wondering if their deaths are connected. They're also wondering if I might have killed one or both of them because you and Jack had an affair."

"That's ridiculous," she said automatically, but then the implications hit her. "Wait, how did they know?"

"Jack took a picture of you."

She was horrified. "Phillie, I swear I didn't know."

"That's what it looked like. It still wasn't my most happy moment. Yours either, I know that."

"Is it . . . very bad?"

"Worse than MTV. Better than *Playboy*."

Her cheeks were flaming red. "I'll die if anyone sees it."

"I'll do my best to prevent that."

Another reason to dig. Figure all this out, and no one would ever see the picture. First, though, there was something else I had to ask her. To be sure.

"Did you ever do S&M sex with Jack, or Jack and Judy?"

"Phillie!"

"Did you?"

"No! Jack never even mentioned it to me."

I was pretty sure of her. Carolyn didn't lie easily, or well, or often. "I'm sorry. I had to know."

"For God's sake, why?"

"It's a big part of this. And we're involved."

"Because of me," she said bitterly.

"Because of both of us. I've been asking questions. I went to lunch with Judy yesterday, and I was the one who found her last night. It's easy for the police to think we're a part of it."

"You looked pretty friendly with that policeman at the house."

"That's Donnegan. He was at Jack's the other night. And Judy's. He's on our side, I think."

"That's something, at least."

"Not enough. There's an assistant district attorney who could put together a pretty good circumstantial case that I was involved. I wasn't. And I don't want to be, not like this, but I don't see where I have any choice now."

She swallowed hard. "I'd rather everyone on Long Island see that picture than have you hurt."

It was a brave statement for her to make. She was a modest woman at heart.

"It's not just you," I said. "I want to protect all of us."

Her fine mind went down several pathways at once. "Yes, I see that."

"I've got to go," I said.

We got out of the car. As we passed each other, she grabbed me and put her face close to mine.

"Phillie, I'm going to fight for you. To keep us together."

Way deep down, part of me fluttered into awakening and hoped she could.

2

There's a game I've played since I was a kid. I check out all the women in a waiting room, or on the bus I'm riding, or on the check-out line ahead of me, and decide which one I'd pair up with if nuclear war broke out and everyone except this group were wiped out. If the girls are young, I try to imagine what they'll look like when they're older. It's in the cheekbones and the eyes.

I was playing the game in Fred Marcus's waiting room in Beachhaven Hospital. I was not in a good mood. I'd driven over from the police station and had to park my car in the hospital garage, which was a good half-mile away, and I'd been waiting for almost forty minutes to see Fred. I was tired of waiting.

"You don't have an appointment," the receptionist told me again. "And the doctor is running late."

"Tell him Phil Liebowitz is here. We're friends," I lied.

"But you don't have an appointment."

"It's a personal matter."

By now, the other patients were watching us. With all their special casts and fancy braces, it looked as if Fred was making robopeople. The nurse kept her stubborn face on, cheeks tight, eyes blank, lips firm. I hate stupid people. Even more, I hate stupid people who stand on ceremony.

I collapsed.

"Oh, my God," she cried, and hit some kind of emergency alarm.

I was rewarded by Fred's little form scurrying out from one of the examining rooms.

I stood up. "Thanks. I'm better now."

"But . . . Doctor?"

"It's all right, Edith. Hello, Phillie."

"Hi. Let's talk."

"Come into my office."

He led me into a gray room with bookshelves and a desk, a computer, and stacks of medical journals. Fred had graduated from one of the big Ivy League med schools in the seventies, the last decade I figured he read one.

"You're disrupting my practice, Phillie. Just like you're disrupting my life. I'd appreciate it if you stayed out of both."

I ignored him. "What happened to Judy Lane?"

"It's a police matter. I can't talk about it."

I opened the office door and shouted, "I had two *healthy* legs before you operated, you maniac. I'll sue you for every nickel you've got. Every nickel you'll ever have!"

His face turned white.

"And my poor wife can't walk because of you!"

He came out of his chair and slammed the door shut. "Stop it. What do you want to know?"

"Play journalism with me, Freddie. What, where, when, why, how." Or who. I wasn't sure.

"I was treating a broken wrist in the ER when they brought her in. One of the Mets had a biking accident. The team doctor called me—"

"Skip it."

"Judy was a friend of mine, Phillie. I wanted to help. I assisted the resident, but it had been too long. She'd had a massive infarction, and there was nothing we could do to get her started again."

"Heart attack's unlikely at her age, isn't it?"

"Not if you've done enough coke to pay off Colombia's national debt, if it has one. She was loaded."

"Why did she go home and not to a hospital?"

"Did she?"

"Yes."

"It's not so unusual. She might have gone into arrhythmia in the car but, like a lot of people, thought she'd be all right if she just got home. She should have come straight here. She was in bad shape."

"I know. I found her."

He seemed surprised. "You?"

"Tell me about the marks on her body."

"Why are you asking? How well did you know Judy?"

"Like a sister."

"I didn't know. I'm sorry."

"The marks, Fred."

"Abrasions and bruises around the wrists and ankles, lacerations on the buttocks, a lot of damage to breasts and nipples."

"Recent?"

He nodded. "Within hours."

"In short, she was bound, whipped, cut, and burned. Did she take the drug during the beating?"

"It's likely," he said. "She got too high, too crazy, and it killed her."

I shook my head. "I don't believe that."

"She wouldn't be the first, Phillie."

"I had lunch with her yesterday."

"Really? What did you talk about?"

"Let's just say it's a lot funkier world than I ever knew, Horatio. One last question, then I'll go."

"Name it." He wanted to be rid of me so bad it hurt.

"Be nice, Fred," I warned. "I might be giving the bride away at your wedding."

His soft white hands moved over the blotter, arranging things. "Phillie, I'm well aware of your friendship with Jessica. Believe it or not, I'm grateful for what you've done for her since Jack died. Now, what's the question?"

"Do you love her?"

He didn't hesitate. "Yes, I do."

I walked out.

TWENTY-TWO

1

I parked in Christopher Morley Park and let the sun warm my face. Kids were playing noisily in the big pool, and families were picnicking on the lawns. Traffic sped by on Searingtown Road. I sat in a side eddy letting it all go by. Things were happening too fast. I was genuinely worried. If I couldn't find out what had happened to Jack and Judy, Paula Michelson might well decide that *I* was what had happened.

No, Ben, I heard myself saying, Daddy's not a murderer. They just *think* he is.

Fact: Jack and Judy were lovers. They belonged to an S&M group. Ostensibly, Jack was a suicide. The overriding question: Was it murder?

I drifted. Carolyn in the parking lot, staunchly supportive. *I'd rather everyone on Long Island see that picture than have you*

146

hurt. Judy beaten and burned. Jack smashed into pudding. Were Judy's and Jack's deaths linked to the S&M group? Who was in the group besides Robbie Hazen? Were they in danger? From who? Whom? Why were there needle marks on Jack's arm?

A seagull landed on my hood as I was adding Fred and Jessica into the equation. I didn't like Fred. He was slimy, superior, and had too many women. I doubted Jess would stand for the last part again. That suggested an interesting angle.

"Fred and Judy were friends," I told the gull, who looked mildly interested. "He introduced her to Jack."

The bird wasn't much help. He flew away.

Fred knew Jack wouldn't have needed much coaching to go after Judy. Was Fred helping Jack to stray even further because he was pursuing Jessica? Did Fred know what Judy was into?

I thought the tape would protect us, but it didn't, Judy had said before she died. Assume "us" meant Jack and her. What was on the tape, who was it protecting them from, and why hadn't it worked?

Maybe the gold case had some answers.

Shit. I left it in my jacket at home.

I headed there.

TWENTY-THREE

1

There was no car in the driveway when I got home. I went upstairs and packed the things I'd been in too much of a hurry to get when I walked out last night. I felt like a stranger. I wanted to stay. I knew I couldn't.

The jacket I'd worn last night wasn't in the wash or the closet. Instead, a cleaning ticket sat on the dresser, and sure enough it was listed. Great. Normally, the cleaning could sit on a chair for a week. Now that we were separating, she did it the same day.

Maybe she was tidying up more than the bedroom.

I shoved the ticket into my pocket when I heard a sound in the house. I'm not one to panic, but I heard it clearly. Near the kids' rooms. I tried to pad noiselessly down the hall—no mean feat in a house where ancient floorboards groan everywhere. I ducked fast and low into Ben's room.

"Aaaagh!" Ben cried out in fear and burst into tears.

"Jeez, I'm sorry, honey," I said, hugging him. "I thought no one was in the house."

"I got a stuffed nose. Mom went out to get me medsin." He sniffled, calmer now that he wasn't going to be attacked by a crazy man.

I pressed my lips to his forehead. He wasn't hot, but I felt instantly guilty. Ben was alone because I wasn't here to go to the store or to stay and watch him.

"You okay?" I asked.

" 'Course. Dad, where were you dis mording?"

"I went to Zack's, honey."

"You home now?"

The question made my heart hurt. How could I tell him I was breaking us up?

"Stay and rest. Mommy'll be home soon." I turned his TV on. "I'll be in the office. If you need me, yell. I'll leave the door open."

" 'Kay."

My office was hot, but I wanted to be able to hear Ben so I didn't turn on the air conditioner. I tried to approach the Jack and Judy situation the way I had in the car, thinking of it like a plot, so I created a new file in the computer and made notes and listed possibilities. Tried to figure out where everybody was at the times people were dying. It wasn't easy to concentrate, but that ADA Michelson provided motivation. So did the thought of Carolyn's picture on *A Current Affair*. My life was already screwed up beyond belief. It could be ruined altogether.

I pulled up the PHILLIE file and input five-letter words. The hyphens still just flashed at me insolently. Then I called the phone number on Jack's list where the people kept asking me who I was. It answered after a few rings. Traffic noises almost obliterated the voice.

"Hello?"

I tried a new approach. "Phone company. Line check," I barked. "Location, please?"

"You got the Village, man," said a hard-edged voice. "A pay phone. Don't *you* know?"

A pay phone in Greenwich Village? "Who are you?" I asked.

"The fucking mayor." He hung up.

All right. Concentrate. I stared at the screen.

Everybody had a secret, that much I knew. Like the moon, we each had a dark side. Once you knew that, people became more interesting. I thought of all of us writing our deepest secret on a sign and walking with it so others could see. *Screwed my best friend's wife. Wear women's clothing. Like my husband to beat me. Heard shouts for help and did nothing. Defrauded my customers. Peeked in windows.* Hester Prynne Parade Day, all of us wearing our scarlet letters.

Jack had always said Jessica was a shy girl, not very sexual or adventurous. Yet she'd propositioned me before Jack was cold in the ground, and she was sleeping with Fred when Jack was still alive. Did Jack truly know his wife? Did anyone? I was happy when they met, it was late in life for both of them. I'd hoped Jess would end Jack's philandering. She was a local girl, just a year or so behind Jack in high school. She'd gone away to college and spent much of her adult life working for a big European company. Mostly in Amsterdam. One year she came home for the Christmas holidays, met Jack, and stayed.

I decided to get someone else's view of Jessica. I called Valerie Powell, the owner of Port Hardware, also a local girl and the same age as Jess. Val was one of those hardworking backbone-of-the-community people who, despite my cynicism, are in the majority around here. She'd be into deviant sex as deeply as Mother Teresa.

"Porrrt *Hard*ware." Val answered the phone with the same cadence as conductors say *Pennnnn Stat*ion!

"Val? Phil Liebowitz."

"You must have the wrong number," she said flatly.

"How come?"

"I won't be responsible for injuries if you turn do-it-your-selfer again."

"Actually, I need some information."

"In your hands even that could be dangerous."

"I've improved a lot."

"Stranger things have happened, I guess. S'okay, we're slow just now. Shoot."

"You went to school with Jessica Murphy. Jessica Salerno back then. Did you know her?"

"Sure I knew her. Transferred in from Catholic school in our junior year. Did some modeling, as I remember. Great looking. Still is. I saw her at the funeral. Lucky for her they invented the Pill back then. And I don't mean aspirin, Phillie."

"She was sexually active?"

"Does a bear crap in Wall Street?"

"Does that mean yes?"

"First tell me why you're asking."

"I can't."

Val was quiet for a second. "There's some interesting talk going around town. And my cop friends have gotten real close-mouthed all of a sudden, but they're doing lots of investigating *something*. Does this have anything to do with that?"

"I don't know."

"Maybe you don't, and maybe you do, eh?"

"I don't."

"Tell you what," she said slyly. "Nothing I like better than to scoop the girls at the Rotary. Promise me you'll tell me every-thing later, and I'll tell you what I know."

"Deal."

"Okay."

I felt her cast back in her memory.

"Jessica was a funny girl. Quiet and sort of shy. Kept to herself, mostly, but wild when she wanted to be. I remember we all went to the beach one time—lots of bodies under blan-kets, if you get what I mean. All of a sudden this girl was running all over the place dancing in the fires wearing next to nothing, lots of boys were following. Surprised the heck out of me it was Jessica. Typical Gemini. Two sides in everything."

"You're into astrology?"

"In a big way. You ever have your chart done?"

"I'm a wimp, fear rising."

"Silly, you're always putting yourself down."

"Experience is a great teacher."

"Stop. Those were weird years. You got me remembering. Some of the kids were into mystical stuff. Witches and covens and black magic. I never took to it myself. Most don't. Remember the cats?"

"I wasn't here then."

"Someone killed a bunch of cats belonged to Robbie Hazen and cut them up and put the parts on sticks at the beach. Really weird. Fetish stuff. Right around graduation. Nothing like it ever happened again, and I guess we all forgot about it. It was such a happy time with all the parties and proms."

"Did Robbie and Jessica know each other?"

"Probably. How well I can't say. But a lot of people knew Jessica, if you get my biblical meaning, eh? Nice speech at the funeral, by the way."

"Thanks." As an afterthought I asked, "You know Fred Marcus?"

"Sure. He's a townie like the rest of us. Parents had squat. He worked for my folks in this very store to get through college. He busted his butt to get into med school—no small feat back then for a working-class kid with no family connections. My dad used to say Fred still had the first buck he paid him. Word is he cuts a hangnail on himself, he sends in an insurance form."

"Paint him in one word for me."

She didn't hesitate. "Ambitious."

"Thanks, Val. I appreciate it."

"Don't hurt yourself painting, Phillie. 'Bye."

She hung up before I could protest that it was the fault of the electric sprayer she sold me that I had drenched those cars. I let it go.

I put the disk Judy gave me in the computer. I'd noticed at the restaurant that the scroll bar in the margin wasn't at the end. It meant there were more pages. Maybe I could coax something out of them. Turned out, I could. Judy hadn't scrolled far enough to see them. I read the scraps of text with the oddly familiar feeling of hearing from someone on the other side of the grave.

> the last part started with such a minor sin, Phillie. I swear I couldn't have known. Remember Todd and his lover Samantha? Well, she was in town, and Todd asked me if they could borrow my house. I gave him a key and told him Jessica and I would be out Saturday night, to make themselves at home.
>
> I shouldn't have done it, I know. I don't mean loaning them the house. That was okay. It was romantic. Sweet, even. I shouldn't have videotaped them. I hid the camera, put in a tape long enough to cover their entire visit, turned it on, and left. It was scurrilous, indecent, and improper. I'd like to say that stopped me.

I scrolled further, found more.

> wicked watching them without permission later on, but that didn't detract from my pleasure. Samantha had narrow hips and big blue eyes. He unhooked her bra. I smeared Vaseline on me and rubbed slowly, getting hard. Todd leaned over and licked her. She moaned and opened her jeans and pushed Todd's hand in.
>
> Phillie, I don't know how good in bed Todd's wife is, but she'd have to be a goddamn Superwoman to be better than Samantha. This was bravura sex. No wonder Todd was going nuts. When they were done, they started talking about their problems, their pain. I turned the sound off. Somehow, and I know it may sound crazy, I watched them have sex and I didn't feel like I'd betrayed them, but it didn't feel right listening to their private conversation. I don't ask you to understand, Phillie. I know you'll be appalled by the whole thing.
>
> I thought about keeping the tape, but one time was enough. I'd used them shamelessly in pursuit of my own pleasure—at least I gave them back part of their

privacy. I erased it before my dick made a better counterargument.

There was only one more time I taped them, Phillie, and Jesus fucking Christ I wish I hadn't because

WHY?! How could he cut it there? How did Todd and Samantha fit into this? It was unbelievable. Jack had actually taped his friends having sex in his bedroom. He was right about one thing. I didn't approve. It was a lousy thing to do.

Was it lousy enough to get him killed?

I was thinking about that when the world exploded.

TWENTY-FOUR

1

Plaster dust sifted down like fine rain. I was lying on the floor along with everything else that should have been on tables and shelves. It looked as though a hurricane had hit. I smelled smoke. It curled into my nostrils and galvanized me. My first thought was to get to Ben, but I couldn't get up because I was trapped by something big and cold and heavy. I pushed hard, got my legs into it, and managed to slide out. A four-drawer steel file cabinet had fallen over me and was resting partway on my desk. If it hadn't caught there, it would have crushed my back.

There was more smoke now, and alarms were screaming all over the house. I made it down the steps to the second floor. My left shoulder was numb, my legs weak. The corridor was on fire. With some surprise I saw that part of the side wall of the house was open to the air. I had no time to take it all in. The flames were already between me and Ben's room. I grabbed a towel in the hall bathroom and plunged it under water. Christ, you see fire on the TV, you never feel the heat. It made my skin blister. I wrapped the towel over my head and hit the fire running. I spun into Ben's room, gulping air. The towel was smoking. Ben was sitting in bed with the covers pulled up around him. My kid, obviously.

"Daddy, your shirt's on fire!"

I dropped to the floor and rolled around like a dog with fleas. Remembering instructions, Ben threw his blanket on me and stood back. When I didn't feel anything hot, I asked him, "Any more?"

"No more, Dad. But you got holes—"

"Forget them." I opened his window. "Out."

Do it like you drilled, my mind told me. I was one of those people who had bought the fire rap and had actually drilled the kids on how to get out in an emergency. Ben's window led out to the garage roof. I helped him out, crawled after him, and got my second shock.

Ben wailed out in fright, "Dad, where's Mom?"

"Mom?" I said stupidly.

"She was napping Beth."

Jesus, Carolyn's car was in the driveway. I hadn't heard her come home. She and Beth were still in the house, one or both taking a nap, according to Ben. I had to go back in. My neighbors were already in the street. I called to one and she ran over. I lowered Ben into her arms, and she hustled him out to the curb.

I climbed back into Ben's room. The corridor was a sheet of flames to my left, blocking the stairs. The rest of the bedrooms were to the right. I got down on my belly and crawled. The smoke was so thick, there was only six inches or so of clear space along the floor. I slid into Beth's room, next to Ben's. It was empty. That left our bedroom, across the hall.

The fire was loud now as well as hungry. I heard it eating. The bedroom door was closed. I wrenched it open. The outer wall was burning, and the room was filled with smoke. Carolyn

and Beth were lying on the floor with their eyes closed, over-
come in their attempt to get out. They looked dead. I couldn't
get near the window to let air in. I got a wet towel from our
bathroom and put it over Carolyn's face and shook her, then
did the same for Beth. Beth wasn't doing well. She moaned
and went slack. Carolyn came to, coughing.

"Phillie," Carolyn gasped, "tried—"

"I know," I said, coughing. "Gotta get out."

Her eyes went wide and frightened. "Where's Ben?"

"He's okay. We're not."

I drenched the remaining towels with water and draped one
over Carolyn's head and my own. We wrapped Beth in the rest,
and I slung her under my arm like a football. She needed air.
My lungs were on fire. Carolyn was coughing and choking. A
piece of ceiling fell. I stopped. There were flames outside our
room.

"Ben's room is the only way out," I said. "We've got to get
across the hallway."

"Put her in between us," Carolyn said.

I understood. The sacrifice play. Her voice was steady. We
weren't done yet. Not the Liebowitzes. We put Beth between
us. Whatever happened, that little face was going to be protected. Whatever happened.

I said, "Ready?"

"Get her out, you understand?" she yelled over the fire's
noise. I knew what she was saying.

I said, "Together. Now."

We put our heads down and burst through the fire in the
corridor. Flames licked at Carolyn's back, and I jerked us
around, and my hair singed with a wicked smell. We spun into
Ben's room. The fire hadn't consumed it yet. We smashed the
flames aside with the towels and made it to the window, then
to the clear air on the roof outside. Carolyn lowered herself
and dropped the last few feet, then reached up for Beth. I
passed her down and dropped after them, and we tore the
soaking towels off Beth to make sure she was okay. She wasn't.
Her little chest was still. Carolyn held her nose and blew into
her mouth, and I waited the longest seconds of my life until

Beth coughed a few times and spit up, and her eyes opened clear and wide.

"Mommy, how come you crying?"

Carolyn picked her up and hugged her and ran over to smother Ben against the two of them. That was it. Everybody was out. Volunteer firemen's vehicles with flashing blue lights and a big red hook and ladder were coming up the road. Smoke was still pouring out of the house. I headed back in. It was stupid, but this was my home. I wasn't going to sit in the street and let it burn without trying to save it. There was a fire extinguisher in the garage. I grabbed it and began spraying as the first firemen hustled in.

"Is everybody out?" one asked me.

"Yes."

"Good. We'll take it from here, sir."

They fanned out and worked through the house putting out the fire. I sprayed till my extinguisher was empty and went back outside. I was mad as hell. Not mad like I was in Donnegan's office about a false accusation I knew was false, but pure white-hot mad where I knew I was capable of violence.

A guy with CHIEF painted on his black helmet came over. "We pretty much have it under control, sir." He looked at my fire extinguisher, saw the silver KID'S ROOM stickers on the windows, and nodded approvingly.

"You were well prepared, Mr. Liebowitz."

"Me and the Boy Scouts. What the hell happened?"

"You have a gas grill?"

I nodded.

"Looks like the propane tank blew."

"That happen often?"

He thought it over for a moment. "No, it doesn't."

He didn't have to tell me.

TWENTY-FIVE

1

With Ben in my arms, and Beth in Carolyn's, we answered a lot of questions out on the lawn. I went into my neighbor's house and put in a call to our insurance agent, Joe Krass, whose office was just across town. Joe promised to get over before closing. It was lucky that it was the end of the summer and the gas tank was nearly empty, or the house would have been on the moon. As it was, the blast had taken out a good chunk of one side and shaken the kitchen and my office to pieces. The power and phones were out, and most of the second floor was a charred, smoky mess.

"Can we stay in the house?" I asked him.

"Hotel would be better," he said.

Carolyn knew what I was thinking. "But can we?" she asked.

He thought it over. "I suppose so, if you don't mind the

water and the smell. The fire's out. There's no structural damage to the main timbers. More like somebody took a nasty bite out of it. Mind if I ask why?"

"It's our home," Carolyn said flatly. "We have work to do."

"The kids should see that you stay and fight no matter what," I explained. "You don't run from things. It's an important lesson."

He stroked his chin a few times. "There's another theory that this is what hotels are for."

As good as room service and clean sheets sounded, I said I'd think it over, knowing I wouldn't.

He said, "Either way, Mr. Liebowitz, you need medical attention."

"Arms, Daddy," said Beth.

"Yuck," said Ben.

I looked.

For the first time, I hurt.

2

Zack came over, and so did one of our tennis buddies, an internist named Paul. Paul treated me and gave me pills for the pain. He showed Carolyn how to change the sterile dressings and told me I'd be fine. Zack culled events from the firemen and my neighbors. He'd probably played tennis with three-quarters of them or their kids at one time or another. He told me saving my family was a very brave thing. I said I didn't *save* them, I just *got* them.

He said I was a picky fuck.

Our neighbors came over with food and blankets and bedding, a cellular phone, and a battery-operated TV. It became a kind of neighborhood CARE project to get us back on our feet for the night. The older kids played with Ben and Beth, dressing them up in clothing too big for them. All the excitement seemed to have cured Ben, whose sniffles were miraculously gone, probably to be replaced by pneumonia later. Someone brought iced tea and cookies, and we all ended up having a picnic, if you can believe it, on our front lawn. It made me feel warm and nice. Part of something.

Before dark, Carolyn and I did our best to seal up the house with mulching plastic from the garage. The living room and den were on the other side of the house from the explosion and were largely undamaged. We lit candles and made a bed for the kids on the fold-out couch in the den. Carolyn held them until they fell asleep. I wanted to tell her how much it had meant to me today when we had Beth in that burning bedroom and she told me to make sure our child made it, no matter what happened to her. I wanted to tell her that in spite of everything I knew what a truly fine person she was, but when I looked in, she was sleeping, too.

I couldn't leave after all that had happened. I opened the big picture windows in the living room and made up the couch, becoming the next victim of Carolyn's knitting needles. I cursed and rubbed my behind and put the knitting on the fireplace mantel. Without power, the large-screen TV and VCR were out, and I didn't have enough light to read by. I cleaned up as best I could with my arms hurting like hell and changed into a soft old sweatshirt Zack had left.

If someone hurt Jack and you get involved, you gotta stop to think you might get hurt, too. Be careful, Phillie, huh?

Zack had said it, and I'd laughed it off.

I couldn't laugh it off anymore. This time my wife and kids were involved. I thought some more about near-accidents on back roads, and prowlers, and exploding propane tanks that weren't supposed to. About ADAs who didn't like me, and tapes, and naked pictures of my wife, and person or persons yet unknown who I suspected had already killed twice and seemed to have few qualms about killing again.

A Jew afraid is a dangerous thing. I couldn't walk away from this for fear of the guilt I'd feel if I didn't take precautions. I had to think ahead. In the long run, if things were getting serious, I needed a major weapon. Real help.

I put in a call to my cousin Morty.

TWENTY-SIX

1

I woke up the next morning feeling better for the night's sleep. The sun was out and a breeze was blowing through the house. Everything still reeked of smoke, though, and my arms were very sensitive, so I dressed gingerly in underwear and a warm-up suit that had fortunately been in the wash in the basement. Everything else I owned smelled like used ashtrays. Morty hadn't called me back yet, but I knew he would with a certainty I felt about few things.

Think about this. Besides Meyer Lansky and Bugsy Siegel, there aren't many criminal Jews. I'm not talking white-collar crime. That's accounting. I mean a two-fisted, gun-toting criminal who lives off the street, making his way by the force of his personality and his wits alone. That was my cousin Morty.

Morty's name alone got him past the first few indictments. What self-respecting judge wants to sentence a guy named Morty to jail? When Morty did go to Rikers, the inmates couldn't believe it either. For six months they were convinced he was a fed. Cons did his work for him. The warden had somebody to talk to. The real hardasses stayed away from him, assuming he must have been at least a serial killer or something even worse because short of that, no Jew went to jail.

When he got out, Morty returned to a life of crime but—as I thought about it while I shaved at the kitchen sink—he'd added a maturity and feral caution that continued to keep him out of jail. He lived in a small apartment in Manhattan and paid the rent every month, on time, in cash. In an era of TRW, Equifax, and the government invading our privacy at will, of computers crackling every time we cash a check or use a credit card, of photo IDs and insurance codes and the thousand natural numbers which citizens are heir to, Morty was a man who didn't exist, a twentieth-century anomaly. He had no phone, no phone number, no checking account or driver's license, no credit cards, no mortgage, no car, no car insurance or life insurance, or medical, homeowners, or any other kind of insurance for that matter. He got no paycheck, paid no taxes. I wasn't even sure if he had a social security number. Morty lived by his wits in a world of con artists, loan sharks, dealers, and thieves, specializing in highly discounted merchandise and some very questionable business ventures.

We had grown up together, Morty and I, opposite poles in the family, dark and light, the city and the suburbs. Ironically, he was the suburban kid, but he was happy only in the dark corridors and mean streets of the five boroughs. As soon as I could, I moved out of the Bronx to the suburbs, which he treated with total disdain. The middle classness of it all made him itch to hit something, to bring the conceits down to street level and *then* let's see who survives. He had killed people, I believed, though he had never confirmed it. Enigmatic, an individualist, a man out of time. He reminded me of a line in a Bob Dylan song: to live above the law you gotta be honest.

I valued his word over that of any man I knew.

Practical considerations meant nothing to Morty, so his word meant everything. He had no career to compromise for, no family to answer to or plan around—although I was one of the few who knew he did have a wife and daughter living down South to whom he sent a thousand dollars every month religiously. He had no union, no synagogue, no club. He rose with the darkness, sought bed with the sun. Ironically, it freed him to be a man of honor, his only stock in trade. He gave his word sparingly because it was his bond. Like Paladin, he had gun, traveled, and believed in a simple, fair, biblical justice. His word was law.

It didn't make sense to hang around waiting for his call. It would come when it came, and I had things to do this morning.

2

I walked around outside surveying the damage to the house in the morning light. Besides the gaping hole where the propane tank had been, a big black burn ran up the wall like, well, like it had been burned. Joe Krass had arranged for an emergency repair crew to come later. I made a mental note to call the landscaper to replant the tank area. It looked like a lunar crater.

During the night I'd realized I had to change the flow of things. Ever since I got the call that Jack died, I'd been reacting. To Jack and Judy, to the prowler and the Suburban. Even to Michelson and the police. I was not a fighter by nature— running always seemed the smarter course—but I figured I stood the best chance of turning things around if I started fighting back. Morty was the first step. Research was the second.

I'm a fanatic researcher. One time Jack and I needed a Cuban diplomat to talk to his American counterpart, and for plot reasons he couldn't use the usual channels. We wracked our brains till we uncovered the wonderful little fact that the United States had been sending Cuba a rent check for the

Guantánamo Bay Naval Base ever since 1902 but Castro had stopped cashing them in 1959. The diplomat simply cashed the check with a message on back, and it was picked up by the State Department.

I needed to know more about what I was dealing with. I drove over to the library and sat in the main lounge looking out over the harbor reading about bondage, sadomasochism, domination, and fetishism. The clerk who checked out my books gave me an interested look.

You never knew.

3

It was nearly lunchtime when I got back. LILCO had been to the house and turned the power back on, enabling Carolyn to do a wash. The rest of our clothes had been sent out to be cleaned. The battery-operated TV had been replaced by Ben's own, brought down from his room, and the kids were watching *Doug*, a funny, sensitive show just right to counter the nasty *Beavis and Butt-head*. At that moment Doug was being Quail Man—intelligent and still, or something. I wanted to be just like him.

I gave Ben and Beth the sandwiches I'd picked up on the way home. They seemed to be handling everything okay. They'd set up a tent using an old sheet, declaring the den *their* territory. They asked me if they could live there permanently after we fixed the house from the fire. I said we'd see. This allowed Ben to begin building traps to protect his domain, and Beth to select a place for her dolls. Kids can make just about anything right. I watched them play, thinking how close we'd come. That renewed my anger, so I retrieved my winter suit from the basement storage closet and went up to my room to change. It hurt to see the fire's scars. The staircase and landing looked the way Tara's did after the Union army stormed through.

Wearing a suit twice in three days was a record for me. I didn't relish the wool blend on my skin in the summer's heat, but the lightweight cotton shirt I'd bought in town would cut down on the friction. My bathroom was usable enough to shower in, and I had to, after all the smoke and sweat, despite the pain in my arms. Carolyn came in as I was trying to put new dressings on the burns. It required more contortions than I could manage, so she took over.

"Where are you going?" she asked, tearing the surgical tape with her teeth.

"To Judy's funeral."

"With everything else going on, I sort of forgot about her." She taped the last gauze pad into place. "There. Okay?"

"Yes. Thanks. Did you sleep okay?"

"Beth had her knee in my back most of the night and Ben kept crawling on my head, but then I thought about almost losing them." She shrugged with a sort of half smile. "I slept fine."

I looked at her standing there in the steam-filled bathroom all tired and unmade-up, and I wanted to love her at that moment so badly it tore me apart. This was the woman I'd had children with, bought my first new car with, who had seen me through career changes and midnight attacks of insecurity, and with whom I had grown into middle age.

I tried to find a way to say what I felt. "With Beth, in the fire . . . what you did. I was very proud of you. Of us."

"I know. Me, too."

"Joe said he'd have a crew over later this morning. They'll get the house cleaned up and pull the ruined carpet out, stuff like that. I put the renovation file in the hallway so we can reorder everything. Joe said just to go ahead and do it, anyone has a question call him."

"You're so organized," she said gratefully.

"Wasn't that the quality you used to refer to so lovingly as anal retentive?"

She grinned. "Sometimes it has its advantages." She pointed inside to the kids. "They seem okay."

"They take their cues from us."

"Phillie, what's going on? From the beginning, please. I want to understand it."

I leaned against the sink. "Rank in order all the men, cancel that, all the *people* you know, and tell me who's last on the list to commit suicide."

"You," she said instantly and without reservation.

It surprised me. "Why?" I asked.

"Suicide's giving up. You never do. Ever."

"Forget me. I'm not on the list."

"You said everybody."

"Everybody except me. And you," I added before she could say her.

"Then Jack."

"Right." I told her everything. Why I had started, why I stayed with it. She reacted with shock at Jack's secret life, and horror when I described Judy's body. And her fear and rage were terrible things to see when I told her about the prowler and the Suburban, and that I thought last night's explosion was deliberate. She asked a lot of questions. She wasn't satisfied till she had every detail. The police should be so good at interrogation.

"It's like one of those Russian dolls," she said, "where every one you open up, there's another one inside."

"It's beginning to feel like that," I agreed.

She saw the danger to me, to all of us. "But you'll keep opening them till you find the last one."

"I'm not clever. It's all I know how to do."

I drew a dumb smiley face in the mist on the mirror. It made her laugh. I hadn't heard her laugh for a long time. I realized how much I missed it.

"I never saw him use coke," she said, upset by it. "Just the two of you occasionally smoking some pot and getting stupid and laughing. And eating."

Late-night chocolate cake runs, the giggles over what struck us funny.

"Yeah, I remember."

It was the first time we had talked about Jack without its tearing us apart. It still stood between us, but it was out in the open and we were still talking. More to the point, I was still talking. Protecting the kids and doing the work we'd done together to make things okay after the fire made for a good glow. I let my hand touch her shoulder. She stood very still, suddenly very vulnerable. The steel bar inside me bent slightly, grew softer. I kissed her, smelled the familiar scent of her, never perfumed. It was a twenty-year smell; a smell of permanence, of firsts and lasts, of holding each other's heads while you puked and bled and made babies and wallowed in the muck of life together and came up clean and fresh smelling.

"The kids . . . ," she whispered under my lips, pulling me against her.

"We made them"—I slid her bikini briefs down—"they won't be surprised." My towel caught on my erection as it fell, twanging it like a diving board. She giggled. I lifted her up onto the vanity counter and she almost pushed the picture off the wall.

Small things betray us.

I thought of the picture in Donnegan's office.

My face got hot, and the bar hardened back into place. I fought to control it, to make it go away. Please, God, just this once let me be an easy person. But her flesh turned to clay under my hands, and my blood, once so hot, grew cold. I turned away.

"Phillie . . . ?" It was a cry. "Please . . . Don't."

I picked up my towel and wrapped it around me. "I'm sorry."

Her face fell as though the nerves had been severed.

"Dad?" Ben was yelling from downstairs. "Dad?"

I poked my head out. The air was very dry after the steam inside. "Yes?"

"Phone's working. It's for you."

"Who?"

"Cousin Morty."

I broke free of Carolyn and went to answer it.

TWENTY-SEVEN

1

Talking to Morty took longer than I expected, so I got to Judy Lane's funeral late and sat alone in back. The family was gathered tightly together in the front row, and Judy's husband, Ray, had the slightly baffled look death causes. His daughter, Becky, held his hand tightly. Her eyes were red and puffy, and she kept blotting them with a handkerchief she had pulled out of the breast pocket of his dark suit. She had her mother's hair and eyes. There were tan marks on her shoulders where the black dress she hadn't anticipated wearing didn't cover her skin. Up until a couple of mornings ago, she'd been a happy college kid, partying at the beach. I was sad to see her life unravel.

Family relationships were on my mind for another reason. Robbie Hazen was sitting across the aisle from me. I kept picturing him doing those things in bed with Jack and Judy. He was wearing a baggy jacket, chinos, and sneakers. I had never seen him so emotional. He looked positively explosive. His chin was pressed against his chest so tightly his jowls flared out. It looked as if his head were resting on a plate. He was fingering a gold chain the way Catholics do with their rosary beads. I don't think it was a conscious act because he suddenly seemed to realize he was doing it and stuffed it back in his pocket.

The rabbi kept it fairly short. He mostly talked about what a good wife and mother she was. How her family would miss her. None of this long-winded, open-coffin Catholic stuff. Judy would be in the ground in an hour. Then we'd do something for the living, like eat. The tone was different, too. For Christians, death means a beginning. Jews have seen enough death to know there's no glory in it.

I felt Donnegan's now-familiar presence slip in beside me.

"Hear anything about anything?" I asked quietly.

"I hear maybe you shouldn't be cooking with gas."

"I'm insured," I said.

"Phillie, don't ever think so. It's getting rough out there. This thing already has two deaths connected to it."

"I can handle myself."

He sighed. "Even you know how stupid that sounds."

One of Judy's friends started to deliver a eulogy. Donnegan and I slipped out back to the parking lot. He lit a cigarette as soon as we hit the open air.

"The rabbi was right. She was a nice person," I said.

He heard the uncertainty I was still grappling with. "That surprises you?"

"Let's say it challenges my worldview."

"Because of the sex."

"Because *despite* the sex, she still managed to hold on to important things. Family. Her daughter. Her place in the community. I didn't think you could."

"You can't," Donnegan said. "It killed her."

"There's that," I said soberly. "Did you talk to Ray?"

"Yes, but he's not a suspect, if that's what you mean. He

and Judy lived separate lives. She told you herself he wasn't part of her scene. Money wasn't involved. She didn't have more than the normal amount of life insurance, and he's got a bundle anyway. He's lived with his girlfriend in the city for months. He was with her all day Thursday. He's agreed to cooperate with the investigation and keep the circumstances of her death quiet for now. It'll keep the media maggots off us that much longer."

He lit another cigarette, plainly unhappy. He was a cop with an unsolved murder and a questionable suicide on his hands.

"Relax," I said lightly. "You still got me."

"So the ADA reminds me daily," he said wryly.

"Michelson will come to love me just as you do, wait and see."

"When pigs fly." Donnegan shook his head with a you-just-don't-seem-to-get-it look. "This is serious, Phillie. You can't fool with her."

I was indignant. "She makes me angry. I didn't do anything."

"You're a writer. You could have made up a better story."

"That's not writing, it's lying."

"God forbid you should do that, Saint Liebowitz."

"It's a canticle."

"What?"

"A *Canticle for Liebowitz*. Wherein he *becomes* a saint. Famous story."

I sensed I was trying Donnegan's patience. I changed the subject.

"Did you ever write?" I asked. It's usually a gimme. Almost everyone has at one time or another.

"In the army, a little," he admitted shyly. "Sort of a journal about the things going on." It was the first time I ever saw him embarrassed.

"It isn't like a sex crime," I told him. "Some real macho types write."

"Name one."

"Betsy Thorndike."

"Who's she?"

"Girl I knew in college. She could take any five guys I ever met."

"People usually say Hemingway."

"I never met him. Are you a decent pickpocket?"

He looked at me strangely. "Why?"

I told him.

2

When I went back inside, kaddish had already been recited, and the coffin was being taken away. The family rose to follow it to the cemetery. I drifted outside with the others. Robbie was heading for Mel's black Rolls. It was a rare car these days, archaic, along with Gold Coast mansions and white gloves. The chauffeur was waiting with the door open. Donnegan timed it just right, hitting Robbie from the side, helping to steady him. His hands were too quick to follow. A murmured *Excuse me,* and Donnegan was heading for the coffee shop across the street. I followed him in, blinded by the dimness till my eyes adjusted. He was in a booth with a coffee cup in front of him and a Diet Coke opposite.

"Too much ice," I said, "and you forgot the lemon."

"What?"

"In the Coke. I mean, if you're going to do it—"

He regarded me narrowly. "Do I look like your wife?"

"No, but—"

"Or your mother?"

"Now that you mention it . . ."

He sighed. "Here." He dropped something shiny and gold on the table. "You were right."

"It's a nipple chain," I said. "A bondage instrument. I saw one in a book this morning."

He nodded. "It's worn like jewelry, the nipples go through the loops. You tighten them like this. Some S&M folks practice piercing. This is"—he looked for the right word—"softer."

"Psychological effect without physical harm. Interesting."

He was amused. "You sound like you swallowed a textbook."

The fact that he was right embarrassed me. I was approaching S&M with my usual boldness, by reading about the Scene, as those in the know referred to the world of S&M. I'd braved biker dens and late-night hours, but when it came to the hard stuff, I went to the library. The time before lunch had taken me through two books and several articles. Used correctly, the chains and paddles did no damage, just as the whips left no scars. Bondage was over the minute the "safe" word was used, a word agreed on by the dominant and the submissive, more often called the Top and the Bottom. The goal was to create a "scene," a psychological play whose limits were set by the players, for the fulfillment of the submissive. I found that last part interesting. I'd pictured the dominant as a king with fawning courtiers all subservient to his nasty pleasures. Actually, submissives outnumbered dominants by a hundred to one. Most Dominatrices, usually called Dommes, were actually professionals, employed by and existing to "serve" the community of submissives.

"I should talk to Robbie," Donnegan said.

I shook my head. "You don't know him. He'll clam up like a, well"—I realized I was searching for a simile for no reason, a writer's curse—"a clam."

"What's it like to have such descriptive powers?" Donnegan asked.

"Invigorating. He's mistrustful of strangers, insulated by money, and I can't imagine he'll warm to you as quickly as I have."

"Why don't I simply beat it out of him?"

"I don't think that's a threat," I said, "if you think about it."

3

Robbie's house was on the other side of Bluff Point from Jack's, bordering the golf course. I'd have spent my life worrying about one-in-a-million head injuries to my kids, but as I say, I never choose to live dangerously when I have the choice. The house was a big white colonial with lots of oversize win-

dows Mel had put in so he could watch the golfers, or perhaps
so they could watch him. When Mel was alive, Robbie lived
alone in the gatehouse. I used to wonder if Mel had consigned
him there as an insult, but as even the gatehouse was much
bigger than my house, it was hard to see the dig. Robbie now
lived alone in the main house with a housekeeper who cleaned
and cooked his meals.

The housekeeper told me Robbie was in back and led me
through the house. I found him outside tending a big pigeon
coop. It was at least six feet high and eight wide, on stiltlike
legs, built with lots of glass so you could watch the birds doing
whatever it was birds did on their perches inside. There were
trays underneath to catch the droppings. The coop was a sign
of Robbie's newfound independence from his uncle. Mel had
been deathly allergic to so many things, he never permitted
animals in or around the house, fearing that hair or dander or
something equally lethal would float in. He mowed down lots
of flowers on this theory, too.

"Phillie," Robbie acknowledged me as I walked over.
"Haven't seen you around here in a while. Since Uncle Mel
died."

For Robbie, it was a long speech.

"We used to talk here the last few months," I said, "when
he couldn't get out."

"He liked those times. Nice of you."

It was a rare admission. Robbie had always thought I wanted
some of Mel's money. It took the fact that Mel and I were
friends till his dying day, that I had turned down every offer of
cash he ever made, and that he left me nothing in his will, to
prove we shared the one thing Robbie had never inspired—
unflagging personal loyalty.

I said, "He was a pretty remarkable man."

"He was a tyrant," Robbie said. "I hated him." He looked at
me with those crazy eyes of his. Only a fool's not afraid of a
man with crazy eyes.

I made my tone mild, inoffensive. "Most parents and kids
don't see each other clearly," I said. "I'm sure my kids will
think I'm a shithead around the age of fourteen."

His look indicated he already thought I was a shithead. "You didn't know him," he said.

I did, but I changed the subject. "When did you get into pigeons?"

He picked up a hose and filled the water trough. "Long time ago. Uncle Mel would never let me have pets, so I used to build cages and coops and stuff out in the woods. I moved this one back here a while ago. You know anything about pigeons?"

"Bronx knowledge. They're fat and eat anything and shit all over the car."

He opened the coop's doors and took one out, running a gentle hand over its iridescent crest. The rest whooped or warbled or whatever, producing a startling amount of flying feathers and pigeon shit.

"They're great. This is a Tumbler. Watch."

He threw the bird up, and it kept climbing into the sky. As I watched, it went into a stall and dropped like a stone, tumbling head over tail till it suddenly spread its wings and came out of the dive and flew back to the coop.

"See?"

"Very cool," I said. A perfect bird for him. Both crazy.

"These are homing pigeons," he said, showing me another.

"The ones that carry messages?"

"We have races. Take them out fifty, sixty miles and let them go. First one back wins." He rubbed the bird with more affection than any human ever got from him. "She's my best. My fastest."

I pointed to a bird perched on a milking stool next to a gas can and lawn mower. "Stool pigeon?" It was too far to reach. He looked at me blankly. "A joke," I said. "Just a joke."

"Oh."

"I was at Judy Lane's funeral," I said.

"I saw you there. I didn't know you knew her."

"She was a friend of Jack's. But you knew that, didn't you?"

"Why would I?"

"You used to have sex together," I said. "By the way, you dropped this." I showed him the gold chain. It was as if I'd thrown a switch. His hand flew to his pocket and found it empty. His defensiveness came on like an energy screen, frightening in its intensity. I'd wondered if he was capable of physical violence. I didn't wonder now.

"It isn't mine," he insisted, staring at the twin loops.

"Robbie, listen to me for a few minutes without getting crazy. Please?"

"I'm not crazy," he protested. "I'm very smart. I always see the other side and get to it first, and then the other guy has nowhere to stand."

"Er—right."

"I'm smarter than anyone thinks. Than *he* thought."

I knew who *he* was. "Robbie, if Mel made you crazy, why'd you stay?"

His eyes were sad and troubled. "Who else was going to? He needed me. So frail at the end. His mind was going. All those things I had to do for him. He didn't trust anybody else. Look, you think I didn't know what he said about me? He made me feel like shit. Well, so what. You gonna leave the guy who raised you over that?"

It was the first time I'd ever felt sympathy for him. Maybe it's easy to stay when your father or uncle is a great guy. Just like it's easy to be a parent when you have an easy kid. But when he's a difficult child like Robbie? Or when your father's a tough and exacting old bird like Mel? Maybe you're bound to him anyway. Maybe you're not supposed to leave even if it might be the best thing for you. Did Robbie have more character than I gave him credit for?

I was saved the problem of deciding. Robbie sent a hamhock-sized fist crashing out at me. I ducked, and his punch knocked the pigeon coop door off its hinges.

He picked up the stool, and I barely had enough time to backpedal out of the way before it came crashing down on the space I had just occupied. I had never been in a fistfight in my life, but generations of conflict have bred acute wariness into Jews. Backpedaling is second nature. Robbie's eyes were glazed, and his chest was heaving. He looked like an angry steam engine. I heard my heart in my eardrums, I was so afraid. I scampered under the coop. My hands slid in the muck underneath. Robbie was too big to follow me, so I came out on the other side alone. I had maybe two seconds. I looked for a weapon, any weapon. I couldn't hit him with a bird, I didn't think. This was outrageous. Undignified.

I yelled, "Stop it!" like that was going to matter. It didn't.

Robbie came around the coop with his hands held karate style. He chopped at me and splintered a board as I ducked again. He outweighed me by maybe eighty pounds, and those crazy eyes gave him an edge I couldn't match. In desperation I yanked out one of the bird trays and swung it at him. The tray missed, but he got showered with droppings. He made a gasping noise and fell to the ground, tearing at his eyes and coughing. He was covered with bird dung. It dripped off his face. Feathers were stuck to his hair. He threw up at the same time that he was trying to get air into his lungs. Mucus poured out of his nose. It was quite gratifying in a way. The Lone Ranger had his silver bullets, I had a tray of birdshit.

I turned the hose on him. He shuddered, rubbing his face clean. I wondered if he might come at me again, but his eyes looked dull and defeated. It surprised me he went down and stayed down. Actually, my cousin Morty had once told me that it was the very quality he looked for in a victim.

"Takes a smart man to know it's not worth it to get up again and maybe get himself killed or crippled," he said. "You, Phillie, are too stupid to stay down. You'd have some kind of crazy self-respect thing that makes you get up again. If I had to take you, I'd kill you first."

I supposed it was some kind of compliment.

"Go get cleaned up," I said to Robbie. When he didn't move, I kicked over the gasoline can next to the pigeon coop. Fumes boiled the air. I reached into my pants pocket for a match. "You come at me again, I'll burn them."

"No," he cried. "Okay. We'll talk."

He went into the house, and I put the cleaner's receipt back into my pocket. I didn't have a match. I hadn't smoked in fifteen years, since my mother died of cancer. I washed my hands off and picked up the gold chain. There was birdshit all over my suit. I could see why it might not be your weapon of choice.

It occurred to me I had just won the first fistfight of my life. My. My. My.

"Sit over there," I said when Robbie came back wearing a fresh polo shirt and jeans. We were just about the same age, but he seemed so much more worn and weary.

"Tell me about Judy. And Jack. And you," I said.

"Just don't hurt my birds."

Fuck your birds. "You're part of their group. Right?"

He nodded dully.

"Who else?"

A light flashed in his eyes, but it didn't stay on. "Can't tell you. I swore an oath. We all did. It's Family. But you'd be surprised, that's for sure."

"I'll bet I would. Where do you meet?"

"Sometimes here. Sometimes in the city, at a club or a hotel."

"Whips and Chains? That club?"

"How did you know?"

"Never mind. How did it start? The group, I mean."

He picked a feather out of his ear. "First Judy and me, then Jack, then the others."

I was asking questions without knowing what I was looking for, hoping that deeper meanings and patterns would emerge and lead to understanding. So far they hadn't.

"You keep saying family. You're related?"

He shook his head. "Not the way you're saying it. Like dinner with the brats. *Family*. The community. The Scene."

"Why did you try and hit me?" I asked.

"I don't like you."

Ace interrogator, that's me.

"You shouldn't be asking questions about us," he went on. "They won't like it."

I was in over my head. Information was piling up, but none of it meant anything. Robbie's sexuality wasn't something he put on for the weekend. It was part of him, coloring all his thoughts and perceptions.

"Are you a Top or a Bottom?" I asked.

He looked away. "Bottom."

This was just too crazy for me. Comic and dangerous wasn't a combination I liked or understood. And Robbie was growing more defiant.

"You don't know anything about us. The kiss of the whip or the cane. You're a pussy, Phillie. You don't have the balls for it. Control is the ultimate turn-on. I like to struggle when my Domme puts her cuffs and collar on me. I tell her what to do. You understand? Me. I tell *her*."

"You offer control of your orgasm to your dominant lover," I said, the Ludwig von Drake of sexology.

"Fuck that," he said hotly. "You got that out of some book. We're in the middle of it. At the gates of Hell. We worship surrender, Phillie. You don't know what that's like," he sneered at me. "You can't. You're not Family."

I felt a pervasive air of unreality talking about these things on a summer day on the lawn. How's the weather? How're the kids? Where'd you buy that neat whip?

"Jesus, Robbie," I said. "Aren't you worried about disease and stuff? I mean, sex is dangerous with all those people."

"We're careful. Blood tests. Condoms. Not supposed to share body fluids or blood, even though some people do."

It made me laugh. Break the rules, push the boundaries, knock on hell's very door, but make sure you do it in a condom and without germs so you don't lose the house and car. How timid. How painfully timid. How suburban.

"What do you know about Jack's death?"

"Nothing. I heard he killed himself, that's all."

I couldn't tell if he believed it or was hiding something. Maybe it was just that he hated me so much, he wouldn't even tell me the right time if I asked him. We went around in circles for a while and I didn't learn anything else. I was ready to go but I had one more thing to do and I didn't like having to do it. I screwed up my courage and grabbed the gas can and spilled it on him. It soaked his shirt and pants. He gagged and threw up his hands and rolled away.

"What are you doing—?" he gasped.

My hand came out of my pocket, and I thrust it under his face.

"Somebody tried to blow up my house. My kids were inside. If anything like that happens again I'm going to come after you and burn you to death. I won't think. I won't ask who. I won't wait to see. I'll just come after you and do it. You read in the paper one of my kids got hurt, you better start running because I'll be right behind you." The gas fumes roared through my sinuses. His face was twisted with fear. He tried to pull away. I realized he was whining.

"I didn't do anything," he cried.

I shoved my face into his. I hoped what was in my eyes would scare him. I was trying to scare him. *I* was scared.

"Doesn't matter. They get hurt, you burn. Bet on it. Be sure."

I slammed the can into the pigeon coop. It created a flurry of noisy stupid birds and flying feathers. Robbie scurried over to soothe them. I wasn't sure he even realized I was there anymore.

My suit was soiled by birdshit and gasoline. I walked straight at him, and he flinched as if expecting to be hit. I wondered what it would feel like to whip this brute into submission, to make him wallow in the dirt. I felt the start of a sexual urge. It disgusted me. It made me feel guilty for being part of his degradation.

I softened my voice. "You know, if you were half as good to people as you are to animals, you'd get a lot better reaction from them."

He had tears in his eyes. "Animals don't hurt you like people do."

I was hard pressed to give him an argument.

4

There were clouds gathering in the sky as I drove home trying to keep pigeon shit off the upholstery. So much for my winter suit. Carolyn was shopping and the kids were at camp, so only the construction crew was at the house when I pulled in. The workers were fast and good. Their first job was to seal the house against the elements, and they had already replaced the studs and the plywood siding. The foreman went with me to see if I had enough shingles in the garage to replace the burnt ones or if he needed to order more. I pressed fifty dollars into his hand and told him I'd thank him again when he was done. Then I gave him another twenty and told him to buy lunch for his crew. He thanked me, and we shook hands. It wasn't extravagant. I was just being a good guy to work for. We both knew I'd get the money back in extra effort and probably one or two items he wouldn't bill me for. Call it a mutual understanding of motivation. He left to unload a pile of wood and Sheetrock from the local lumberyard when their truck pulled up.

Carolyn had turned the answering machine back on. I had a message from Bob Marson, Jack's attorney. There'd be a reading of Jack's will Monday morning at ten in his office in Lake Success. I was mentioned in it, but he thought I might want to talk to him first. I returned his call, and we agreed that with the weekend at hand, now was the best time.

I changed into freshly laundered jeans and a clean shirt, left a note for Carolyn to have dinner with the kids without me, and headed for Bob's office.

On the way I had to pull over and put up the Miata's top. It had started to rain.

TWENTY-EIGHT

1

I drove into Lake Success, thinking as always that it was a pretentious name for a town. South, it turns into New Hyde Park where the houses look as though Bill Levitt, the man whose name was almost synonymous with suburbia, had built them in his declining years with a cookie cutter. Why not? Bill had built *his* office in Lake Success.

I'd known Bill Levitt fairly well, actually, having worked with him right about the time the loss of his fortune made him move from his sixty-eight-acre estate to a local condo. They'd have had to drag *me* out kicking and screaming, but I wasn't the gentleman Bill was. The loss never changed him or his beautiful and charming wife, Simone. They remained two of the most gracious people I'd ever known.

My favorite story about Bill took place in 1948 when Teddy

Kollek, the late mayor of Jerusalem, then a deputy of David Ben-Gurion's, asked Bill to loan the Provisional Government of Israel a million dollars without collateral or interest for a mission of such importance, he couldn't even be told what it was. Levitt wrote a check on the spot. A year later, Teddy told Bill what he'd paid for. Combat success with Czechoslovakian Me-109 jet fighters had convinced the embattled Israeli leaders they needed more planes, but the price had gone up. Bill's money secured the jets in time for Israel to use them to win the Battle of the Negev, a decisive event in the War of Liberation.

Neat to be part of history.

I parked in Bob Marson's lot and walked into the main lobby. A receptionist phoned my name in, and Bob's secretary came out and led me into the inner sanctum. Bob was writing, head down. His male pattern baldness looked as if someone had cut the hide of a baseball from his scalp. He had a spreading paunch and no style at all in his suits or shoes. His blond altar-boy face was still boyish at forty-five, but with lines and jowls. There were shelves of law books behind him, a glass-topped mahogany desk between us. The windows were wet with rain.

"What's the glass top for?" I asked.

"Protects the wood," he said.

"Why not get a glass desk?"

"Better this way."

"Why?"

He thought for a moment. "Drawers," he said after a while.

Bob had answers. Chaminade High School graduates who almost become priests but go to St. John's and become lawyers instead, know things. Like how to afford a house and five kids and not have your wife work. Or how to find real estate deals and take a little piece here, a little piece there, until you have some sizable pieces. Or who to call for St. John's basketball tickets. Bob had a first-rate brain and knew exactly what he wanted out of life. These days that took a lot of answers. I envied him somewhat.

"Much as I'd like to continue this witty exchange, Phillie," he said, "I thought we should talk."

"About Jack's will?"

"Yes."

"He was my partner."

"Yeah, that too." Bob leaned forward with his elbows on the desk. "Jack's will is pretty straightforward, bequests to people and charitable institutions. It's the codicil to the will that is unique in my experience, restrictions placed on the trust by his grandparents, who originated the estate that Jack ultimately inherited from his parents."

"What restrictions?"

"You know what the sacraments are?" he asked.

It was too sudden a turn. "Are we still talking will?"

"Ultimately."

He liked that word. Catholics would. I cast back in my memory. "Sacraments are the things you have to do to be a good Catholic. Like baptism and marriage. Do them all, and you wind up in a state of grace, the most perfect state a Catholic can be in besides Jersey."

"My, my."

"Medieval studies in college," I explained.

"Me, too. I wanted to be Lancelot," he said.

"I wanted to be Galahad."

"The pure, eh?"

"And noble." Talking about these things in a Catholic lawyer's office gave them all a sense of age and linkage and membership. As a Jew, it frightened the hell out of me.

"The sacraments," I prodded.

"Jack had to be in a technical state of grace to continue to receive the income from the trust and control its assets. The Eucharist, baptism, confirmation, penance—the forgiveness of sins—matrimony, orders, and extreme unction—anointing those in danger of death. Protestants believe those things are symbols of grace. We Catholics believe they actually *bestow* grace. You see the essential difference."

I always thought Jack's connection to the Church and his sexual excesses were incompatible. I understood better now.

"I know the others. What are orders?"

"The clergy is empowered to undertake its sacred duties by

receiving holy orders bestowed by the bishop, who inherits his power from being a member of the Collegiate of Bishops who, *in corpus,* are Christ's apostolic successors."

"Jack wasn't a priest."

"He was a deacon. Lay clergy."

"He gave money," I said. Bob started to say something, but I held up a hand to remind him I came from people who didn't think that was so bad. He sat back.

I said, "Jack had no children. Isn't family life one?"

"He probably counted you. But no, it isn't."

"And suicide?"

He looked pained. "It isn't one either. You see, Phillie, it isn't all up for grabs. Suicide. Divorce. They're unacceptable. We believe there are rules. So did Jack's grandparents, even if they were a little Old World about it. If Jack fell from a state of grace, he lost the income and control of the trust till he returned. Dying in a state of grace, he would have passed the estate on according to his bequests. But here's the kicker. Dying in transgression, he lost it forever. His will is void. Jack's grandparents left a provision for legitimately conceived and baptized children, which there aren't, and for a surviving wife, which there is, so it all passes to Jessica to do with as she pleases."

"Doesn't she have to be in a state of grace, too?"

"The codicil gives her time to put her house in order to comply with the terms of the trust. I'm sure she will."

"I guess it makes sense in a weird way. It was their money."

"Actually . . ." Bob looked uncomfortable for the first time. "Actually, Phillie, some of it was *your* money. Remember, none of Jack's bequests can be honored. It *all* goes to Jessica. Even what he left you."

My voice got very tight. "What did he leave me?"

"Twenty acres of Bluff Point."

A sense of unreality invaded me again. I picked up his phone and dialed one of the real estate guys I knew from working with Bill Levitt.

"Stu? Phil Liebowitz."

"Phillie? How are you?"

"Fine. I was sorry to hear about Bill."

"He had a great run," Stu said. "Better than most. What can I do for you?"

"What would twenty acres in Bluff Point go for?"

The delay was imperceptible, he was that fast. "Hundred an acre. Two million plus."

"Twenty times a hundred . . ."

"Hundred *thousand*," he said easily.

" 'Bye, Stu. Talk to you."

"Stop by, we'll drink to the old man."

"Promise." I hung up and turned back to Bob. My face must have registered my turmoil.

He shrugged. "I know. I'm sorry. There's no way to sugar-coat it. You lose important money." His sympathy widened. "The Church loses, too. He left part of the estate to the parish. If he had died in a state of grace, Jessica wouldn't be poor, but she wouldn't be nearly as rich."

Jessica's finances were the last thing on my mind. Two million dollars meant money in the bank, the kids' college paid for, a house with enough bathrooms and closets, peace of mind, an end to the eternal struggle. I felt sick.

"I'm curious what you think about Jack's suicide," Bob said offhandedly. "And about Jessica."

Bob would have been bothered by *anyone* committing suicide. It was a sin, an affront against the prerogatives of his God. Maybe I was being small-minded thinking anything else, but he sounded as if he wanted me to say I thought Jessica might have had something to do with it. As if he were pointing a finger.

"Are you pointing a finger?"

"No," he said. "There is no suspicion of foul play. . . ." He hesitated.

My hand made a come-hither motion. "Give."

"It's just . . . I suppose we in the Church thought his ties to us were stronger." He shrugged sadly. "That's all."

I said I felt that way, too.

We sat in silence for a moment, probably nursing the faint hope there was something we could do to change things. Bob turned the pages of the will on his desk. It was a thick document with all kinds of clauses and wherefores and seals. The last page caught my eye. Signatures are like pictures, and even upside down I knew I had seen this picture before—on a medical report in Donnegan's office.

"May I?"

He slid it over. I knew Jack's signature as well as I knew my own, I had signed it so many times, as he had mine, on letters and so on. There were two witnesses. I didn't know the first, but I sure knew the second, Fred Marcus, Jack's friend, doctor, party host, and cuckolder.

"What is it?" Bob asked.

"Do the witnesses usually know the contents of a will?"

"They don't have to. They're only attesting to the signature."

"What about Fred Marcus?"

"I'm certain he did," Bob said. "He and Jack had several business dealings. Dr. Marcus helped him put some of his money into art."

"For a fee, I'll bet."

"I wasn't privy to those details."

"Did Fred know about the codicil?"

Bob's face reddened slightly. "Yes. He joked about it. Said the kind of silly things about quick and easy forgiveness of sin that people do when they don't understand Catholic confession or contrition."

The way he said it, I wondered if *people* meant "Jews." It made me feel like an outsider. But Bob was a good guy, and that was probably too harsh.

We talked some more, and I thanked him and left.

It was still raining. I drove back to town peering through my streaky wet windshield, wondering how far an ambitious man would go to get all that money and trying not to think of how many ways two million dollars would have changed my life.

TWENTY-NINE

1

Northern Boulevard was jammed, so I cut south and took the Long Island Expressway home from Bob's office. It was a mistake. The new computerized road sign they put in to let you know about upcoming road conditions read TRAFFIC AHEAD NORMAL. I resigned myself. Everyone knew that meant bumper-to-bumper. Crawling along behind trucks and tankers, I started wondering about the extra fragments on the file Judy had given me, and whether the tape Jack said he'd made of Todd and Samantha when he loaned them his bedroom could have anything to do with the one Judy had mentioned before she died. That made talking to Todd the next step in things, so I changed my mind about going home right away and drove to his house. Todd's wife, Marcia, answered the door wearing a blue caftan and backless slippers that flopped when she walked. Her dyed brown hair had been piled high into a winged helmet by some Valkyrie at the beauty parlor. I'd noticed this odd tendency of women before, to make their hair bigger as they age. I had no explanation for it.

"Phillie, how nice to see you."

"You too, Marcia."

She ushered me into the front room. The house had been built in the fifties, a bunch of boxes stacked around each other. Split ranch, or splanch, I think it's called. Big, roomy, bland, and expensive. Kind of like Todd.

"Is he in?" I asked.

A shadow crossed her face, tightening her makeup. I remembered when Todd and Samantha were in their heyday and she had looked positively haunted, but this look was fleeting. I guess they were putting things back in order.

"He went over to Flynn's," she said, taking comfort in knowing she knew where he was.

Flynn's was an Irish bar on Main Street noted for heavy food, heavier drinks, and the professional athletes who came there to enjoy the monastic life for which they are known. It was a nice place to sit and drink on occasion.

"You working on a new piece?" I asked.

The shadow was replaced by pride. "Wanna see?"

"Sure."

She led me to her sculpture workshop in back. Her full hips made the caftan sway, and her slippers clicked on the polished wood floor in time. Todd's lover, Samantha, had been a knockout for sure, but there was a health and happiness about Marcia that went a long way. She was smart, and good company, and her sculptures hinted at depths a lot of the local shopping queens didn't have. I remembered what Jack had written, about Superwoman Sam and bravura sex. Superwomen came in lots of shapes and sizes.

Marcia went to a table covered with hammers, chisels, awls, torches, and other tools for sculpting mayhem. A stone piece about eighteen inches high was partly covered with a dropcloth.

"Ready?"

"You bet."

She whipped off the cloth, singing, "Ta-daaa!"

It was beautiful. A stunning curve of gray-white marble that reminded me of the Pietà in the Vatican. I said so.

"You see it? Really? Oh, I'm so pleased. You a writer and all."

"It's lovely, Marcia. Are you going to sell it?"

She looked horrified. "Oh, no. I *couldn't*. Not any of my pieces. They're a celebration of Todd and me. Kind of like . . . our love. I couldn't sell *that*."

"If you ever do," I hinted.

She beamed. "Oh, you."

I smiled.

She picked up a hammer and chisel. "It isn't actually finished yet. I was just about to do some work." She pushed up her sleeves and took a few whacks at it. Chips flew. Her fleshy arms were powerful. She studied what she had done and selected a different chisel from the array on the workbench. Some were straight, some were pointed, some had curved blades.

"See you soon, Marcia."

"Hmm? Oh, all right, Phillie." She pounded on the chisel, engrossed in her work. More chips flew. Sweat appeared on her brow. Her big breasts moved under the caftan in opposition to her thick right arm. More chips. Her face changed, got more intense. She hit the chisel with a sharp series of metallic peals. Hard stone, harder metal.

They're a celebration of Todd and me.

I said I'd let myself out, and she grunted approval, not really concentrating on me anymore.

All those chisels and tools.

I couldn't help thinking about the marks they'd make on a human body.

2

Todd was nursing a tumbler of whiskey and staring out the window when I slid into his booth at Flynn's. The wrinkles in his clothing had spread to his eyes.

"Phillie."

"Todd-o."

"How's Jessica?"

I thought about her and Fred. "Bad. What about you?"

"Away on business next week. Back in two." He lifted his glass and let the light play through it. "Life sucks, Phillie. You know?"

I did. I also told him I'd been to his house and loved Marcia's new piece.

"I wish I could convince her to sell some of them. Be good for her confidence. Get you something?"

"Thanks. Black and soda." A waitress had once told me that was the correct way to order Johnnie Walker Black Label Scotch and club soda. It felt overly hip to me, but it did the trick. I took a mouthful, swallowed it slowly.

"I've got to tell you something," I said.

"Okay."

I took a deep breath and said it straight out. "Jack secretly videotaped you and Samantha making love when you used his house."

The alcohol had deadened his nerves the way it was supposed to, but it would have taken a hammer to anesthetize him for that.

"Jesus Christ, Phillie," he said, eyes wide. "Jesus *Christ*."

"I just found out about it."

"What did he do with it?" Todd demanded. "Who has it?"

"I don't know."

His face lost its color. "It would kill Marcia if it got out. And ruin me." Todd took another swig. The glass shook. "Just when I thought I was back in control. Over Samantha. Now this."

"I'm sorry."

He was close to tears. "The bastard. I hope he burns in hell."

"He might, if the Church has anything to say about it."

"Why did he do it, Phillie? It's disgraceful. We were friends. I gave him bond advice. Marcia and I went to his parties."

"Jack changed. He lost his way." I looked Todd straight in the eyes and said with total conviction, "Like you and Judy."

He looked at me blankly. "Who?"

"Judy Lane."

The blank look continued. "I don't know her."

"She was Jack's lover. He told me you and Samantha were both in their S&M group. That you liked to share her."

He reacted like a bug had crawled out of his drink. "That's disgusting, Phillie. Even for a Hollywood writer."

"I wasn't the one committing adultery, pal. You want that tape shown to the world?" It was a crummy thing to threaten him, but as with Carolyn, I had to know.

Tears slid down his cheeks. "Phillie, are you nuts? Samantha was a virgin when I met her. I'm the only man she ever slept with. My being married killed her. She couldn't handle it."

"Don't lie to me, Todd."

His face twisted. "Share her? Not with anyone on God's green earth. We used Jack's house twice. That was it. If he taped us, he did it for reasons I can't imagine."

Maybe, but I had a funny scenario working in my head. Jack taped Todd and Samantha. Somehow Marcia found out about it. She wanted the tape for a divorce, or to torture him, or maybe even for blackmail. She tried to get the tape from Jack but he wouldn't give it to her, so she pushed him off the roof with those big beefy arms. She tried to get it from Judy next. Marcia was strong, and hell hath no fury. Those marks on Judy's body could easily have been made by her tools.

I let that roll around awhile, like the scotch on my tongue. It occurred to me that Todd also had a motive. He might well have known about the tape and gone after Jack and Judy to get it. Saying he didn't know about it didn't necessarily make it so. He could just be a good actor. It wasn't a real stretch to think a bond salesman in the Midwest would be.

"Help me, Phillie."

"I don't know if I can," I said honestly.

"You're one of the good guys, Phillie. Everybody thinks so. So do I."

"You know what e.e. cummings said about Everybody?"

"What?"

"If Everybody lived twice, they'd call it dying."

He tried to smile. His face couldn't make the transition from dread.

"I can't believe Jack taped us."

I said, "Me neither." But I was thinking about a picture of Carolyn when I said it.

Todd downed the last of his drink, deeply shaken. "Who can you trust anymore, Phillie?" he asked plaintively.

To that, I had no answer.

Todd left. I was frustrated and unhappy. Things were getting more complicated, not less. All of a sudden I had two new candidates for Jack's and Judy's murders: Todd and Marcia. The more I thought about it, the more I realized that all my poking and prodding had gotten me in over my head. I'm stubborn, I know, but I finally decided to follow my own advice, or at least what I thought I'd advise someone in my situation. It was time for the pros. You're sick, call a doctor. Busted pipes, get a plumber. If it's murder, go to the cops. I decided to talk to Donnegan and level with him. I trusted him, and I needed his help. Besides, I had to think of Carolyn and the kids. I wasn't the only one in danger. My playing cop was only going to get us all in trouble. How many more explosions or car accidents could we survive? The decision to talk to Donnegan made me feel better. I called the phone number on the card he had given me. He was at the station and about to go off duty. He agreed to meet me at Flynn's.

I needed to settle down. Exposing Todd to more pain had depressed me, losing two million bucks had screwed me up even more. Jack had willed me a life with no worry, then taken it away with a single swan dive. Images in my mind exploded like clay birds in a skeet shoot. Vacation condo. *Blam!* College tuition. *Blam!* Freedom to finish my novel. *Blam!* Trust funds. *Blam! Blam!* A black Porsche convertible for me. *Blam! Blam! Blam! Blam! Blam!*

I went to the crowded bar and put down a ten-dollar bill. The bartender tilted his head amiably. "What can I get ya?"

"Another Black and soda."

"Want to make a guess?"

"Excuse me?"

He pointed to a five-gallon jug filled with coins on the bar and a cardboard chart covered with numbers.

"We're just about to make the drawing. Buck lets you guess the amount in there. Closest wins the jar. Wanna try?"

"Two million dollars."

He laughed. "Be nice, wouldn't it?"

"You don't know the half of it."

I slid over a dollar from my change. "Six hundred forty-nine dollars, eighty-three cents."

He stuffed my dollar into a box by the register and wrote my guess on the chart. The drawing was evidently a big event, and the crowd was eager to hear him announce the winner, but every time he went to open the envelope with the exact amount, someone bought a round of drinks and the announcement got delayed. Then someone else bought another round. It was great fun. I was flying by the time Donnegan showed up —between rounds four and five, I think.

"Give me a dollar," I said.

"Is that why you called me?"

"See that jar? Guess how much is in there."

"Fourteen thousand dollars."

"Seriously."

"Eight hundred and twelve fifty."

"Write that down," I directed the bartender, sliding Donnegan's dollar across the bar.

"You got it."

"Phillie, my wife's waiting for me for dinner. Why did you call me?"

"I have to get some things off my chest."

"Talk louder. I can't hear you. What the hell is going on here anyway?"

People were pressed all around us. I said, almost shouting, "Port's version of the lottery. A dollar and a dream."

We couldn't talk in all the commotion. The bartender was waving the envelope, whipping the crowd to a frenzy.

I said into Donnegan's ear, "First let's see who wins. We'll talk over dinner. I'll buy."

He sighed. "I'll call my wife."

"Good. What are you drinking?"

"Vodka martini with a twist."

I bought him one, and then another when he finished the first, and by the third or fourth—who was counting?—he was one of us. We all got to talking about how neat it would be to win something like the lottery and be rich. The hot topic was whether you'd actually continue to work if you didn't have to. I was beginning to think I'd found a long-lost branch of my family. We were hugging, almost teary-eyed at the prospect of anyone having to lose the contest. Donnegan popped for hors d'oeuvres. A woman propositioned me, and I said thanks but no thanks, and she wasn't mad at all. Then the bartender opened the envelope and broke into my pleasant haze with an amazing announcement.

I won.

It floored me. You have to understand, I never win at these things. If there are only two lottery tickets sold, mine's the loser. I never win gambling. Not even a door prize. I was totally flabbergasted. I got kissed more times than Yassir Arafat. Donnegan pounded me on the back. More rounds. Speeches. It put Todd and the two million dollars I'd lost out of my mind. When it was time to go, Donnegan helped me out to the back parking lot with my heavy bottle of change. It took two of us. The bartender waved good-bye from the rear doorway.

Donnegan eyed the Miata suspiciously. "You sure the suspension can handle this?"

"Just pull the seat belt forward," I began, and then a funny thing happened.

The bottle exploded. I mean, not just shattered. Exploded. Glass and coins went flying, showering me and the Miata. My arms were suddenly empty, and a metallic flow was spilling all over the street and under the car. Coins were everywhere. Six hundred in change is a lot of nickels and dimes.

Donnegan cried out and spun around. I saw a hole blossom on his shoulder and finally understood what was happening. I jumped on him and pulled him to the ground, covering his body with my own.

"Get help," I yelled to the bartender. "He's been shot!"

The bartender didn't react for a second, then bolted back into the bar. I reached into Donnegan's coat looking for his gun. I knew how to use one. I'd taken a course. I felt his hand clamp down hard on my wrist.

"Just stay down, stupid," he said hoarsely. "We don't need any dead civilians. Especially the ones you might shoot."

"Are you okay?" I asked.

"If you'd get off me."

"I was trying to shield you."

"Don't think I don't appreciate being shot *and* crushed."

I was worried. Blood was seeping through his jacket.

"C'mon, Donnegan. Are you okay?" I asked again.

He seemed to be mentally taking stock. "Actually, no," he said, and his eyes closed.

It seemed like only seconds later I heard the police sirens.

3

The cops raced Donnegan off to the hospital. I stood there answering questions. Yes, I had called him. No, it wasn't about anything, only for a drink. It was easy to lie. I didn't trust anyone but Donnegan, and now he was on some operating table leaving me to fend for myself. I was lucky the bartender had seen the whole thing, or I was certain I would've been charged with Donnegan's shooting. I think the cops who recognized me from Jack's and Judy's would have liked to wrap up the investigation then and there and hang me on the spot. I wasn't responsible for Donnegan's being shot, but I felt guilty just the same. I had no doubt that the bullets had been meant for me. He'd just gotten in the way.

"Can I go now?" I asked the sergeant in charge.

"No, sir. District Attorney Michelson is on her way. She

asked you be held until she gets here. You can wait in your car
if you want."

More good news.

I sat in the Miata and watched the police gather up the
change and put it in plastic bags. They found the bullet that
had blown up the glass jar, a gray lump of lead all mush-
roomed out on one end. Bigger than I expected. Big enough to
blow me away if all that metal hadn't been in between us.

I was cold sober now and glad of the crowd that had come
out of the bar and was still milling around. I didn't think the
shooter would try again with so many cops and people around.
Had Todd come back to do it? Had Marcia put down her tools
and picked up a rifle? Was Robbie paying me back for before?
Was it someone I'd never even met? An icy chill seized my
guts.

The sky was showing red streaks over the harbor. That lump
of lead changed things for me for keeps. We all talk about
death, fool with it like kids playing with matches, ·attracted
and afraid at the same time. We think if we invoke it, we
establish some sort of control. I knew now that was an illusion.
Worse, it was vanity. Sitting in the car I imagined a future
where Carolyn was telling the kids what a great guy their father
had been, how he would have loved to be there when they
graduated from school, or got married, or had babies. If I
hadn't been holding that jar I'd be as dead as Jack or Judy, or
maybe Donnegan. I felt my mortality keenly. I had to put my
arms around myself to stop the shakes.

"Mr. Liebowitz?"

I'd seen Paula Michelson pull up in a green Toyota Camry.
She'd been talking to the sergeant. She didn't look happy.

"Hello, Ms. Michelson."

I stepped out of my car. She was wearing a beige suit over a
blouse with no collar. Matching heels. She had pretty good
legs.

"What happened here, Mr. Liebowitz?"

"I already told the police. I met Detective Donnegan for a
drink. We got involved in a lottery, sort of, which I won. A big
jar of coins. When we walked out, someone took at least two

shots at us. The first hit the jar I was carrying, the second hit Donnegan."

"How convenient for you."

"Convenient?"

"I think you get my meaning."

My anger flared before I could stop it. "Do I look like your husband?"

"Excuse me?"

"Why not save the shitty attitude for somebody who likes you?"

I shouldn't have said it, but I was tired and scared and worried about Donnegan, and all she could do was stand there and make lousy insinuations like I had shot him myself.

"Fuck you," she said clearly and distinctly—tough to do through clenched teeth.

"They teach you that in law school?"

She controlled herself tightly. "No, that I learned on the dock in Freeport hauling nets off my father's fishing boat. I also learned the difference between decent working-class people and liars and cheats. A lot of smart-ass guys like you used to come down and charter our boat. Guys who couldn't even bait a hook. Guys who'd spend the day complaining and drinking and throwing up on me. Guys who'd divorce their wife if she so much as looked at another man, but it was okay for them to try and screw every waitress on restaurant row."

"I'm not like that."

"Let me finish. What law school taught me was how to count, Mr. Liebowitz. At least to three. As in strike three. One, Jack Murphy. Two, Judy Lane. Three, Detective Donnegan. I think you set him up. I think you've killed two people because you couldn't keep your wife in your own bed. Then you got scared we were getting too close, so you got Donnegan out here and somebody from your sick little mess of a life shot him."

"Why?"

"To divert attention. 'Look, everybody, it couldn't have been me. I was shot at, too.' "

"And the jar, how did I set that up?"

"If it wasn't the jar, it could have been something else. A narrow miss, a hole in the car. As I said, you're a clever man."

This was getting us nowhere. "Look, I'm sorry. I have a bad attitude when someone comes at me as hard as you do. My best friend was murdered. My family was almost burned to death. Every time you accuse me, it makes me feel defensive even though I haven't done anything. So I react. I swear I haven't hurt anybody. I'm just trying to find out what's going on."

"I don't believe you," she said flatly.

So much for the honest approach. She saw me the way she saw me, and nothing I could do was going to change it. Maybe someone who looked like me had hurt her early on, or maybe she was just born like that. Either way, a distorting lens had been clamped over her eyes, and no matter what I did, she was going to see me through it. Sometimes it's like that.

"What have I got left if reason and logic won't work with you, Ms. Michelson?"

"I work with facts, Mr. Liebowitz. My personal opinion of you means very little."

That's never true, but it was no use arguing. "How's Detective Donnegan?"

"Why are you asking?"

"I like him. I'm concerned."

I don't think she believed that, but she said, "The wound is not life-threatening. He'll be going home later. He'll have to convalesce for some time."

"Can I go now?"

"Yes. Good day, Mr. Liebowitz."

I got in my car and drove off. I wanted to hide, but I knew I couldn't. It had become a shooting war, without subtlety. I didn't have Donnegan anymore. Michelson wanted me hung. Whoever didn't want me finding out about Jack and Judy was going to keep on trying to kill me to stop me. Sooner or later they would succeed, too. It was just a matter of time.

Unless I found them first.

THIRTY

1

Jessica was on her hands and knees when I pulled the Miata around back, dressed in shorts and a T-shirt planting stunning pots of mums in the beds around the brick patio. Gold. Purple. Red. It looked like a preview of autumn. I said so.

"Good," she responded, wiping her sleeve across her sweaty face and leaving a dirt smear. "It's been one piece of shit summer."

I dropped into one of the wrought-iron patio chairs. My memory of the shooting was still fresh. Fear made me angry.

"I want to talk about you and Jack."

"Still trying to find out why he did it?"

"Yes. If he did."

She didn't seem too surprised. "He said you were totally

tenacious, but I never really got to see it before. No wonder you're so good at everything."

"I'm not," I said, embarrassed.

"Good father, good husband, good writer, good friend, and you keep your dick in your pants. Around here that qualifies you for sainthood."

"Er—about Jack."

"Sorry. Go ahead."

"I have to know a few things, but I don't want to hurt you."

"You're sweet, Phillie, but I'm past that. Just ask."

"Did you know about Judy Lane?"

In spite of what she said, the question bothered her. She stuck a spade into the dirt to cover it.

"Sure. And about Ethel and Karen and Marissa and Holly and Sherrie and—do you want me to go on?"

"No. Did Jack know about you and Fred?"

"He never confronted me, and I suppose he would have if he did. You know. It was okay for him, not for his wife. The fact that he was screwing somebody else's wife was a contradiction he seemed to live with quite easily. Must be all that early training in accepting mysteries." She worked some fertilizer into the dirt. "I went to Catholic school as a kid, too. Did you know that?"

I remembered Val saying she had transferred in from one. "It doesn't seem your thing," I said.

"It wasn't. It was my father's. He was a pretty prominent guy, and the nuns were going to honor his wishes even if they had to beat me senseless. You know the old line, this hurts me more than it does you? That's what they used to say." She slapped the tool against her palm for emphasis. "Poor girl"— slap—"this hurts us"—slap—"more than it does you"—slap slap slap!

She looked at the red welt she had raised on her hand, and for a moment her eyes were filled with old angers. "Bullshit. I knew which one of us couldn't walk straight from that birch rod for days."

"Is that why you hate them?"

"It was the hypocrisy, mostly. Rejecting Jack is the final

straw," she said. She turned back to the flower bed and made a hole big enough for a root ball, shook a plant loose from its plastic container, and popped it in the ground. "I kept rebelling. Finally I got so outrageous, even my father couldn't keep me in. He gave up and sent me to the local high school. Believe me, I made up for lost time. Graduation and pregnancy were running neck and neck."

"Almost got thee back to a nunnery."

"Never again. I swore. Are you working?"

"I'm trying. It isn't the same," I admitted.

"What do the studios say?"

"Lee told me they'd let me work alone. See what the final product looked like. Sent condolences and all that."

"You thought they wouldn't take you without Jack?"

"Sure. Why not?"

She seemed surprised again. "Because everyone knew that you were the one with the talent, Phillie. Jack was just along for the ride."

"Untrue. We had different strengths, that's all."

"Phillie, knowing where the pencils are is not a strength on nearly the same level as being a creative writer. Jack was a rich man who liked the amount of pussy being a Hollywood screenwriter got him. That's all."

I changed the subject. "I talked to Bob Marson about the will."

She accepted that without much reaction. "He told me you were mentioned in it. It's complicated with the trust and all."

"It's big bucks, Jess. I never knew how big." I had to keep remembering the money wasn't mine and never would be.

"When Jack's grandparents moved here, this was the boonies." She gestured around with the garden tool. "They bought the land for a song."

"Five hundred acres. At a hundred thousand dollars an acre, a lot more for the water view parcels . . ."

"Roughly sixty million dollars. Bob told me. And that's not counting the income from another ten million or so in stocks and bonds, which is actually what Jack received. The land just sits."

"Will you sell it?"

"I don't know. Bob says I could, in time."

It took all the control I had not to ask her to please give me two million dollars.

She went on. "Since Jack . . . did what he did, Bob says it all comes to me."

"And Fred," I said.

She popped another plant out of its container. "Yes, I suppose."

"Fred knew all about the will, Jess."

She stopped planting and looked at me hard. "So?"

"So I'm just saying."

She squared her shoulders. "I don't like what your saying implies."

"You mean, motive."

"Yes."

"Well," I said, "it sort of does, doesn't it? You're going to be a very rich widow."

"Fred does very well on his own. He's got a big practice."

"There's a lot of difference between making two or three hundred thousand a year and owning seventy million dollars' worth of stocks and prime real estate. Sure he can eat where he wants to and drive a Jag and have a nice house. But he can't afford an estate on the water or have his own plane or collect the art he loves in any major way. He can't endow charities or sit on hospital boards or make the society columns. The trust is the difference between his *making* money and *having* money. Real money. Jet-set level, global bucks."

"I don't have to listen to this."

"I'm not trying to hurt you. I want to protect you."

"Money's not what motivates Fred," she insisted.

"I know. He wants to help people."

"Fine," she retorted. "You got motive. Great. Only tell me, where exactly is the crime?"

She had me there.

2

Later, on the patio, after the mums were planted, she made us drinks.

"Will you tell *me* something?" she asked.

"What?"

"Did you know about . . . ?"

I knew what she meant. "Yeah," I said.

"Can you handle it?"

"No."

3

Several drinks later, I kept noticing the way her breasts moved under her shirt, like another pair of hands. Her blond hair was pulled back loosely, and her blue eyes were the same color as the sky. We talked some more.

"Have you found out anything in your quest, Galahad?" she asked. We'd talked King Arthur before.

"Bob Marson told me he wanted to be Lancelot."

"Lancelot just wanted to get laid. Galahad had it tougher, with the Grail and everything." She laughed without humor. "I suppose I could qualify for Guinevere now. Adultery and all. The king is dead. Long live the king."

"Cut it out," I said. It was late, and I'd had too much to drink today. I was getting sleepy.

"You're still his best friend, in spite of everything," she said kindly.

"I'm a schmuck." I was getting maudlin, too.

"Now *you* cut it out," she admonished me. "I don't like to hear you talk about yourself that way."

"Maybe I deserve it. I'm not sure of anything, anymore. I don't even know what I expect to find."

"But you're doing it for Jack. And me. That means a lot."

"Yeah. Maybe." It was comforting sitting with her, talking

and drinking the way we had so often over the years, even with Jack gone.

"Can I help?" she asked.

I appreciated her asking. Lately, the only person taking care of me was me. "You already have," I assured her.

"Not so much."

My eyes traced the fine lines of her face and neck, down past her prominent collarbones to the freckled skin above her breasts. I wondered if she knew how lovely she was. How clean and carefully wrought.

"Would it help to talk about it?" she asked.

"No. Yes. I don't know." I shrugged. "Maybe."

Her eyes twinkled. "As long as you're sure."

I laughed for a change. Actually, I was glad to unburden myself. I told her some of what had been happening, about Judy and the tape, and Michelson threatening me, and about the fire and the shooting. I left out the Phillie file.

"God, that's horrible," she said. "I had no idea. Jack murdered?"

"It's a strong possibility."

"Do you know who?"

"Not yet. And I'm worried about Carolyn and the kids."

"Of course. You should be. Do you know what's on the tape?" she asked.

"No. I'm still looking for it."

"Or how it's connected to Jack?"

"I don't know that either," I said.

She shrugged and sat back. "Maybe it's not so important. Maybe Judy only thought it was."

"You could be right. It didn't save her."

"Could be the whole thing is just what Fred said. She got too high and played too hard. Like Jack."

"And they fell." It suited my morality to think so.

"Put it down, Phillie. That's my advice."

"Don't *you* want to know what happened?"

She said forcibly, "The honest truth? No, I can't say I really do. I mean, for what? Some state of grace crap I don't even care about? I was trapped in this marriage, and maybe the best thing Jack ever did for me was to jump off the roof that night. Maybe it makes me a bad person, but I'm content to let it go. You should be, too."

"I can't."

"You have to. Jack *always* left the rest of us to pick up the pieces," Jessica said. "And we all did. Well, I'm not going to keep doing it. I've got more important things to worry about now than what he did or didn't do, or who did it to him. I have my life. And Fred. You have your work, your family, you and Carolyn."

"I moved out," I said. "But I moved back in. The house and all."

"That's a piss-poor reason," she said.

"Maybe."

"Carolyn wasn't herself, Phillie. Don't you think she deserves another chance? You can't hold a person to something when they're not themselves. Sometimes, things make us—" She stopped because she saw I wasn't really listening.

Her long legs were stretched out in front of her. She was even more beautiful this way, slightly disheveled, gamine wisps of blond hair falling in her face.

I left before I got stupid.

THIRTY-ONE

1

I made it to the cleaners just before closing. They were open late Friday nights. The Korean couple who owned it greeted me with big smiles, behind which lurked the suspicion that I deliberately lost every ticket they gave me to make them crazy.

"I think I left something in the cleaning my wife brought in," I said.

The wife waggled a finger at me. "Yes, you did, Missa Liebowitz."

She reached behind the counter and pulled out the little gold case. "You lucky we found before it went into machine."

I said, "Are my shirts ready?"

She said, "You got ticket?"

I smiled.

2

I gave the owner lady my pigeon-soiled suit. She looked dubious and told me she would do her best with it. I was able to fit three shirts in the Miata's trunk and still close the lid. I put the rest of the cleaning on the seat next to me. Wrapped in plastic, it would slide to the floor as soon as I moved the car, which I did, to a spot where no one could shoot at me.

I took a screwdriver out of the glove compartment and managed to pry the mirror out of the gold case with slightly less effort than what it took to build the Panama Canal. I was right. There was something inside. It turned out to be a gold key, a blank, without teeth cut into it. On one side was the letter W, drawn kind of like it was on fire. On the other side was a number, 100.

Why are you doing this to me, Jack? I wondered plaintively. Locked computer files, secret tapes, maniac sculptresses, golden keys waiting to fit in. A suicide that my guts kept telling me had to be murder. Trust funds depending on heavenly virtue. Judy into pain. Robbie covered with birdshit. Jessica urging me to forgive Carolyn.

Someone trying to kill me.

A sea change occurred when I remembered the feeling of that big glass bottle suddenly going empty in my arms, as if my heart had fallen out. My stake in all this had grown too big. My life was on the line. My family's, too.

I turned the key over in my hands.

The fiery W is your safe clean and friendly fetish playground. Whips and Chains . . .

That was where the trail led next. In order to follow it, I had to leave my perfect peninsula, something I never did without dread or anxiety, and travel to the land of carnage, Rainbow City.

Rainbow City and Morty and Jack and Judy and Carolyn and Todd and Samantha and Marcia and Robbie and Fred and sex and bondage and dying.

And me.

Shit.

3

I got home wanting to check the house more carefully than I'd been able to that afternoon. Ben and Beth pulled me around showing me things. Very little escaped their notice.

"Hey, Dad, you should've seen them fix the hole in the wall," Ben proclaimed.

"My room, too," Beth said happily.

"They had this great gun that shot nails," Ben said. "Like in *Terminator*. Can I have one?"

"They're not toys, Ben."

"Have one, too, Daddy?"

Ben said, "He said no, stupid."

"Don't call your sister stupid. She isn't."

"Sorry. I asked Mom if they could build me a secret compartment in my room in the wall. You know, where I could keep stuff. She said to ask you."

"We'll see. Actually, I think it could be kind of cool."

"You do?"

"Ben, I was a kid once, too."

"You were? I mean I know that, it's just, usually—"

"Skip it. Let's take a tour. Lead on, Beth."

" 'Kay, Daddy."

The construction had gone well. The bedrooms were habitable. All the damaged carpet and Sheetrock had been pulled out, and a cleaning crew had gotten rid of a lot of the smoke damage. New bedding had arrived on one of those two-hour truck delivery vans. It was still a mess, but it was home.

The burglar alarm people had come back and fixed the system after the fire. It was actually the first time we'd had it on for any length of time, and we were supposed to program it. Carolyn had gotten the in-person demonstration, but being the thorough type, she was in the living room reading the manual. I asked her how it worked. She explained something I didn't understand about zones, then cut to the chase and just showed me how to punch in the on-off code, once we chose it.

"Any suggestions?" she asked.

"I always liked the one Jack picked for his, so he wouldn't forget."

"What is it?"

" 'On-off.' "

"In line with such creativity, what about *code?*"

"Inspired."

"By the way," she asked, "what's your best time in the hundred-yard dash?"

"Not great. Why?"

"Near as I can figure, if you open the front door, you'd better be pretty damn quick because you have mere seconds to get to the kitchen and press in the code, or you'll be taken for a burglar and lots of men will come and do very nasty things."

I decided to go into training. When I read the manual, I found that one of the nastiest things they did was the amount you got charged for a false alarm.

We had dinner and settled in. Ben resisted telling me about camp with a tenacity the CIA would envy. Beth hugged me and asked me to read her a bedtime story. I chose *Jack and the Beanstalk*. It seemed appropriate. She asked me if there ever was a goose that laid golden eggs.

I told her no, there wasn't.

After we got the kids resting in their own rooms for the first time since the fire, I went to the armoire in the living room where we kept the photo albums and selected a few recent pictures and folded them into my wallet. When I got back upstairs, Carolyn was sitting up in bed with the covers wrapped around her, gnashing her knitting needles together. She looked like a manic fly eating a small blue square.

"If you leave those needles in bed the way you do in the couch, I could have a second circumcision."

I meant it as a joke, but she threw the tangled mass down in frustration.

"It's hopeless. I'll never be a grown-up woman who loves her life like Donna Reed."

"Never say never."

"You'd think a mind capable of an MBA would be able to handle some damn yarn."

"Different set of skills. You'll get the domestic side some-day."

"We already own a Volvo." She sighed. "That must count for something."

She dropped her head to her pillow as if it were too heavy to hold up. I tried to see her clearly. As a woman, not just a mother or wife. She was spiritually tired. Isolated. She'd been deprived of her normal sources of nourishment. She'd looked for others and not found them. She'd asked my help, and I hadn't given it. How would I feel if that was my life? I wondered.

I sat beside her. "Carolyn, do you want to go back to work?"

"I thought that subject was taboo."

"I realize how unhappy you are."

"Phillie, I'm not."

But she was, and we both knew it. "Beth will be in school full-time in two years. Most of the women I see around town have a hard time deciding which highway to take. You're not like that. You need more."

She looked the way I figured Columbus must have looked when Isabella said sure, go. A new world opened.

"I'd make sure the family didn't suffer," she said seriously, hopefully.

"We would. But maybe we're supposed to spread the suffering around a little more. It shouldn't be so concentrated."

She stared at me curiously. "You're different somehow."

I didn't know what to say to that, so I changed into a blue oxford shirt and jeans and loafers and slipped on my gray windbreaker.

"Where are you going?"

"Out," I said. "To the city."

"About Jack?" she asked.

"Yes."

"Why there?"

I looked at the woman who once upon a time shared my belief that love conquered all. Well, once upon a time it had. "It's where he went. Do you know where that folding knife is?"

"You got it all messy trying to clean that tiny little fish you

and Ben caught, so you threw it away. You're taking a *knife?*"
She knew that for me, shaving was tricky.

"Forget it." Better to take Morty.

"I've never seen you like this," she said.

"It's gotten dangerous. I'm sorry I got us involved."

Carolyn lowered her eyes. "So am I."

I said, "I spoke to Bob Marson, Jack's lawyer. Jack left a fortune. It means there's money involved in this, as well as sex."

"They say that's what most people fight over."

"Die over, too." I slipped on my jacket. "I have to go."

She put her real feelings into one last question and threw it at me like a peg home.

"Phillie, why does it have to be you?"

I knew the answer. It didn't alleviate my guilt over the supreme arrogance with which I had walked into something that was serious enough to kill over. Or that I hadn't thought nearly enough about my safety or my family's. The reason was that with Donnegan down and out, if Michelson arrested me, there would be no one left to solve this thing, to take my side and prove I didn't do it and find out who did. I couldn't let that happen. The death toll was mounting, and I had to get to those responsible before they got to us. I'm fatalistic enough to believe major damage can happen in this life. I try and avoid crowds, watch the kids, and save serious action for when it's real. Well, now it was real. No matter how much I might want it all to go away, it wasn't going to. It was going only to get worse.

"I'm all that's left," I said.

I told her about Jack's will, and Robbie, and the shooting. About Todd and Samantha. And what Michelson had said.

"Goddamn it, Phillie," she said angrily. "You shouldn't have gotten involved."

"I'm sorry. I thought I was supposed to."

"See? Always you. You don't care about me or the kids, just your silly, stupid principles. Do you have any idea how selfish that is?"

"I've come to."

"Well, is it worth it? Is it worth ruining our life and maybe getting all of us killed?"

"No, it's not. But there's no way to go back and change things. I don't have that luxury. Neither of us does."

That made her stop. Her face grew thoughtful. "I've been yelling for that, haven't I? What's done is done."

"Yes."

"It's hard."

"Yes."

"But we have no other choice."

"I don't see any," I said.

Her hands knotted together. "I'm afraid, Phillie."

I held her for the first time in months and stroked her gently, trying to draw on the strength that used to come from our believing in each other.

"I'm afraid, too," I said. "But we're not done yet."

"No, I guess not. All right, then," she said, pulling away. "Let's go over this again."

I explained all my thinking, where I was going, and what I was looking for. She had a better mind than mine. Her questions were sharp and focused—who she could trust, who she couldn't. How best to protect the kids. At the end she took a deep breath.

"Okay, get it for me."

"You're sure?" She had fought me about this for a long time.

"Get it."

I went into the closet and reached up to where I had fitted the false board over the doors. The little .22 automatic came out in my hand the way I'd planned.

"You remember how to use it?" I asked.

Carolyn hit the clip into place with the palm of her hand just as I had taught her, worked the action to chamber a round, and flicked off the safety. She wrapped both hands around the stock and pointed it away from us.

I was desperately grateful. Despite her discomfort with firearms, there was no finicky get-that-thing-away-from-me. Just an answer to a question. Competence. Teamwork. Intelligence. Trust. Our marriage.

"Very good," I said. It occurred to me it was the nicest thing I had said to her in a long time. "Keep it near, okay? And make sure the burglar alarm's on."

She lowered the trigger with her thumb and flicked the safety back on. "You be careful, Phillie. You hear me?"

"I hear you. Any trouble"—I fished out the card with Donnegan's home number—"call him. He'll be back on his feet soon enough."

There was an uncomfortable silence. It was the moment I was supposed to kiss her good-bye.

I didn't. Ben came in rubbing his eyes to tell us the flashing lights outside were keeping him awake.

THIRTY-TWO

1

A police car was parked in my driveway, with Donnegan in the back seat. His sport jacket was draped over his bandaged shoulder like a cape.

"You're keeping my kid up," I said when he rolled his window down.

"Let's walk," he said.

"Should you?"

"Dennis," he said to his uniformed driver, "help me out of here. And kill the lights."

"Yes, sir."

We walked around to the patio. He sat on one of the webbed chairs. He was pale and weak and seemed close to collapse.

"You look like shit," I said.

"I feel worse. Fucking bullet was big enough to stop a moose."

"I was worried about you."

"Irish cops are indestructible. It's in the genes." He lit a cigarette. It made him cough hard enough to clutch his shoulder painfully.

"Indestructible," I said.

"Look, I'm supposed to be heading straight home, to bed and pain-killers and wife. I lost a lot of blood. But I owe you."

"Why?"

"I got to thinking. I almost needed one of your eulogies."

"I got one. 'Here lies Donnegan. Came back once, now he's gone again.'"

"Stop the wiseass stuff for a minute. If you think being shot's no big deal to a cop, you're wrong. It took me an hour to calm my wife down. My kid called from college. I told them it was okay, a flesh wound. I was with a lunatic who jumped on me, maybe prevented something worse."

"There were only two shots."

"You don't know what the fuck there was, and neither do I. With all that change crashing around, a fucking rocket could've passed by we wouldn't have heard it. You ever been shot at before?"

"Does Nintendo count?"

"There are generally two reactions. First one is you panic and run. Most do—it makes perfect sense. If you had, no one, including me, could have blamed you. But you didn't. You tried to protect me. I won't forget it."

"Cards at Christmas, Valentine's Day flowers, the works?"

"Stop making jokes."

"I'm sorry." I told him about my conversation with Michelson after he'd been taken to the hospital.

"Well, she's as good as her word," he said. "She's asked the chief to send men to watch your house."

"For what reason?"

"To keep a murder suspect under surveillance while she gets ready to arrest him."

I stood there for a second, breathing the cool night air to let the dizzy feeling pass.

"How does it work?" I asked.

"One of two ways. She can apply for an arrest warrant from a county judge by filing what we call an information, and giving probable cause, which really only means that she has reasonable suspicion to believe a crime has been committed and that a certain person did it, in this case, you."

"What about evidence?" I asked.

"It's not a trial. To make an arrest in a murder case, the accusatory information is often sufficient on its face."

"What the hell does that mean?"

" 'Your Honor, this person is dead, and this person did it.' "

I was beginning to wish it had been me who was shot.

"When the judge issues the warrant, you'll be arrested. Since it's murder, you'll probably be held without bail while Michelson presents her case to a grand jury for a criminal indictment.

"The other way she can do it is to skip the judge and go straight to the grand jury. It happens that way a lot in white-collar crime cases because a grand jury is partially an investigatory tool. It's rare in criminal proceedings."

"Why?"

"If you start calling witnesses and the guilty parties get wind of it, they tend to take off."

"What pushed her over the edge?"

"The shooting at Flynn's," he went on. "It blew the lid off everything. Reporters've got it and the Lane murder, and they're all over us. TV tonight. Papers by morning. Sooner or later, they'll link her to Jack."

"It wasn't what happened at Flynn's," I said with conviction. "Michelson leaked it."

"I don't know. It doesn't take long for that kind of incident to get around town, Phillie."

"She's after me."

"Well, it is kind of catchy." He spoke as if he were reading a headline: " 'S&M murders on Long Island. Police charge Port Adams man. Assistant District Attorney Paula Michelson saves the world. Film at eleven.' "

"Turn off the TV."

He shrugged. "One way or the other, somebody's got to go down."

"How does her final version read?"

"Short and simple. Motive, jealousy. You killed Jack because he was sleeping with your wife. There's evidence of the affair, you even admitted knowing about it. Judy loved Jack, found out, and threatened you. You met her at the restaurant, Michelson says to try and scare her off. You couldn't, so you killed her. You used the S&M stuff in her house to throw off suspicion."

"Not a bad plot," I said. "Speaking as a writer, of course."

"No, it isn't. Speaking as Maury Povich."

"So how come you believe me?"

"Forgetting Flynn's?"

"Yes."

"I hate circumstantial cases, and I have yet to see a shred of anything physical that links you to murder. Even more, I saw your face after you'd seen your partner in his swimming pool, and I heard you at the funeral. You had real feelings for Jack in spite of what he did. You can't fake that. Unless maybe you're a psycho with all kinds of screwy shit inside. But I never met one of those worth a damn when things got serious. Nobody who'd drag his wife and kids out of a burning house or put himself in danger to save a friend."

"Is that all?"

"No. In its own way, murder is giving up. I don't think you know how to."

"Maybe I'm just too dumb to know when to quit."

He shook his head. "Character."

"How long do I have?" I asked.

"It could happen over the weekend, Monday at the latest. As soon as she gets a warrant, they'll take you in. At that point you're subject to questioning, search of your body and the

immediate area, your house, the works. And your name is released to the media."

"Till then?"

He shrugged. "Can't do much without a warrant, can I?"

"Yeah," I said, "you could."

"We never had this conversation," he said.

I told him about Judy and Robbie, and Jack's will, and Todd
and Samantha and Marcia. He was tired. The mental effort
was almost too much for him.

"I'm beginning to be less enchanted with Todd and Marcia's
involvement, though," I said. "Todd was in love with Samantha. The thought of sharing her with anyone sickened him.
Besides, why would a tape of Todd and Samantha be insurance
for Judy and Jack?"

"You tell me."

"I can't. It couldn't be used to control Marcia—she knew
the affair was common knowledge. Marcia had no interest in
either Jack or Judy that I can see. And Todd and Samantha
hadn't been so discreet that either Marcia or Jack couldn't
have found other proof if they'd wanted to."

He lit another cigarette. "Back to square one."

"Not exactly." I explained the State of Grace provision, and
that Fred Marcus knew about it, and that Fred was sleeping
with Jessica before Jack died. "Suicide voids Jack's will. The
whole bundle goes to Jessica. And Fred, soon enough."

"Was Marcus the guy who treated Mrs. Murphy that night?"

I nodded. "What did you think of him?"

"He called me 'my good man.' I just love people who call
me 'my good man.' Does Dr. Marcus like money?"

"Nope. He became a doctor to help people."

Donnegan's laugh made smoke billow out. He dropped his
cigarette on the bricks. I ground it out.

"I wish I could help more," he said.

"I do, too. For a while I felt not so alone."

"You're smart enough to be scared. That's important. It
might make you careful enough not to get killed. You start
feeling brave, run for cover."

"Not much chance of that."

Donnegan went into a coughing spasm that doubled him over. I walked him to his car and helped him in. He had to lean on me.

"I hate being so helpless," he said through the open window.

"Go home. Heal. It's Carolyn and the kids I'm worried about. You can still help me there. Michelson is so set on indicting me, there's no way I can even ask for police protection. They'd just think I was setting something else up."

He cradled his bad arm. "I guess I'm gonna be off duty for a while. I'll do what I can on my own."

"I knew you would. I already told her to call you."

"One last thing. Do you know a good criminal lawyer?"

"No."

"Call Archie Dickenson in Mineola," he said.

"He's good?"

"He's connected, which is better. One of the DA's boys who went out on his own. Plays golf with the judges."

"All right."

He searched my face. "What are you gonna do?"

"I'm going inside to wait for the police to take me in, and fight this out in court."

"You're being smart for a change?"

"And not," I continued, "go to the city as I planned, to find out more about Jack's S&M club, and who he knew there, in hopes of figuring this thing out."

He sighed. "It won't help you to be dragged in hiding your face from the TV cameras under a raincoat."

I hated the image. "Michelson wants a killer. I have to deliver one. *Besides* me. No one else is even trying. Jack wasn't a suicide, he was murdered. I don't know how it happened yet, but I will."

"You could trust the system, you know. You've got alibis, good standing in the community."

I shook my head. "Once I'm indicted, I'll never be free of it. Neither will my family. You know that. I've got to find out who's responsible for all this. It's the only way I walk free and clear."

"As soon as you go, she'll have every cop from Brooklyn to Suffolk looking for you, so keep your head down and avoid the police. Tell Dickenson to call me. I'll give him what I can."

"Thanks, Donnegan."

"For nothing. Don't get killed, asshole."

"Sweet talker," I said as the police car took off.

I went inside and said good-bye to Carolyn, kissed the kids, and called a cab. A few minutes later, I was on my way to the train station.

THIRTY-THREE

1

I sat with my back to the wall in the car on the Long Island Rail Road heading for the city, watching faces. Whoever had tried to shoot me could try again. People were still going into the city for the start of the weekend. In Plandome and Manhasset, men came on the train in green pants and gold club jackets, with women in furs looking glazed from a last one at the bar. At Great Neck I couldn't breathe from the perfume and moussed-up hair of gum-crackling JAP teens who talked clothes and boys and what Daddy was going to do for them. Asians boarded in Queens, and Hispanics, and the tight-lipped, xenophobic people of Douglaston. The Irish got on in Woodside. I didn't go all the way to Penn Station. Strong is good; smart is better. On the spur of the moment, I jumped off as the doors slid shut and took a cab into Manhattan.

I'd called the lawyer, Dickenson, from the station pay phone, and his service beeped him and he called me back. I gave him a short quick fill-in. He gave me his private fax/ phone number and said he'd start poking holes in Michelson's case, maybe try to get to a judge and file something that sounded complicated and Latin. Motions and countermotions, the tides of my life.

Morty had said to meet him in a bar called Gallagher's on the West Side. With a name like that, it should have had character but it didn't. Just a keyhole store with a long bar, some tables in back, and an old quarter-a-rack pool table. Waitresses looked at my neat clothing. The hope in their eyes depressed me.

"Hi, cuz," Morty said, rising from one of the tables. We shook hands, and as always I felt the strength in him. We kissed each other on the cheek. Jews are kissers.

"How you doing?" I asked.

"Same, same," he said. "How's Carolyn and the kids?"

"Fine. Yours?"

"Going into fourth grade. Phillie, we're getting old."

"You got that right. That's new, though," I pointed to the slim cellular phone on the table next to his cigarettes.

"It's not in my name," he said. After all, he had an image to maintain. "I gave one of the waitresses I know pretty well money for a credit card, and she put the thing in hers. I pay her, she pays the bills. Nobody knows but her. Nice and easy. No strings. I'll give you the number."

I shook my head ruefully. "I don't know. First a phone. Next thing you'll want a house and a mortgage."

"The neighbors would love me."

"It'd be interesting," I admitted.

Morty was wearing clean blue jeans, Reebok sneakers, a white polo shirt, and a suede jacket that looked well made and buttery soft. He had small features, and his hair was a rusty color that pops up every now and then in our family and usually turns dark, except Morty's hadn't. He was surprisingly little for one so physically powerful, pound for pound the strongest man I ever met. Bantam, you'd call him. Game. Not overmuscled, but solid. His power came from his density. Big guys tended to underestimate him and liked to dare him to go punch for punch with them for money or drinks. Once.

I gave him the vial.

He said, "Hmmm," tapped a bit onto his finger, and snorted it right there out in the open. I cringed while he did it, but no one said anything.

"Couple of grams here," he said, surprised. "Good product."

"Present," I said.

"Where'd you get it? You don't do blow."

It annoyed me he was so confident. "Aren't I just as much a man of mystery as anyone?"

"No," he said. "You are many things, my dear cuz, but a man of mystery you are not. Then again, you are honest and not a schmuck, and that is saying a lot." He called the waitress over. "Drink?" he asked me.

"Diet Coke with lemon—no. Lime."

He sighed.

"I like to talk tough when I first get in a bar," I said.

"That the lime?"

"Uh-huh."

"Have a drink drink, Phillie," he said.

"All right. Scotch and soda."

"Two beers," he said to the waitress, who was amused by all this. "What scotch you drink?"

"Johnnie Walker Black."

"Make it Dewar's," he decided—I don't know why—and the waitress left.

Morty was the older brother I never had, and even at this stage of our lives we fell into the rhythms of that relationship naturally. The first bite of pizza I ever had was when Morty took me to a place on Kingsbridge Road. Slices were a dime, sodas and ices a nickel. For a buck we ate like kings. I was a crier as a kid. Morty was tough, even then. Whenever I fell down and scraped my knees, which was often, natural athlete that I am, Morty would distract me by pointing to a crack in the sidewalk and telling me I had broken it. By the time I looked, I wasn't crying. We had a simple relationship. Despite all our differences, we loved each other.

He hefted the vial. "Wanna talk about it?"

"Soon. But I haven't seen you in a while."

"How's Jack?"

I told him.

"I always thought Jack was a prick," he said when I was done.

"Hey."

"Hey, my ass. He dabbled. I hate dabblers. Life is commitment, Phillie. You have it. I have it. He was a rich smug trust-funded goy sonofabitch, and I never liked him. In the end, I knew he wouldn't come through for you. You have all the drive and talent. I never saw what you did in Jack."

"He was my partner."

"I think that meant more to you than it did to him."

"Maybe. I don't know. It's gone past that now. Someone shot at me. And blew up my house. Could've hurt my wife and kids. That means a lot."

I saw Morty think about that. He said, "Maybe you'd better tell me the rest."

I recited the whole thing. From Jack's suicide and how I didn't buy it, to Judy's death, and the S&M group, and Robbie and Fred, and the locked computer file, and the tape of Todd and Samantha, and Donnegan who I thought was on my side, and the attempts on my life by people I was sure were not. The only thing I left out was Carolyn.

When I finished talking, he looked me over with those street-smart eyes of his that saw deeper than an MRI and said, "It's no game anymore, and you're frightened. You think maybe you started something you can't finish."

"Yes."

"That's why you called me."

"Yes."

"And why you're not as fucking glib as usual."

I stood for it all, knowing that was part of it. "Yes."

He looked me over again and nodded. "Okay."

That was all. He'd decided. He was on my side, totally, and I knew it. He'd never make a bullshit speech about something as important as this. The one word sealed our compact, and the chance of his breaking it was smaller than a personal injury lawyer's code of ethics.

"You look well," I observed, business completed.

"Philosophy," he responded airily as the waitress brought our drinks.

"Meaning?"

He settled back with a beer in his hand. I settled back for the ride. The ability to do a great rap has always impressed me. Morty had the talent. He started to roll.

"Lookit, I figure there are five things a human being needs to do, see? A yardstick for health. If you can do them you are okay. If not, you're screwed up. They are"—he ticked them off on his fingers—"eat, breathe, shit, fuck, and sleep. Let me give it to you again. A healthy person can eat, breathe, shit, fuck, and sleep. These are basic animal functions. The physical foundation of our lives. I can't answer the great questions of our age, and neither can anybody else, but I *do* know that if you can do these five things, you are well on the road to being a happy person. Forget the imponderables. Think of how many people you know who can't eat, or eat too much, or spend their lives worrying about food. There are the anorexics, and the bulimics, and the obese people, and the fad dieters, and the wild-eyed yuppie moms who swoop down on sugar like it's rat poison.

"Breathing? Check the drugstores for the number of medicines for people who can't breathe. Allergists are making a fortune, and they can't cure a fucking thing. How many people can take a good solid deep breath without choking? We have a whole state called Arizona filled with people who went there because they couldn't breathe anywhere else."

The waitress came by, and Morty put his arm around her waist and looked up to her like a lover. "We make our chests narrow so we can pass through the dangerous corridors of life. Don't be afraid. Fill your lungs! Deep breathing is the first and best form of relaxation known to man."

"Besides oral sex?" she said.

"I'm getting to that."

She grinned and swished away, nodding at his signal to do it again.

He downed the second beer. She brought his third and fourth that I knew about, and my second scotch. I was beginning to feel that lightness of head and spirit that says those wonderful little alcohol nodules are beginning to gobble up those big bad inhibitions. Heads turned. People were listening to Morty's rap. He felt the audience take shape, and it pushed him to a higher level. I was gauging the need to run, but they looked pleasant, so I relaxed.

He stood up and addressed the bar like a preacher. "Sleep? Watch the commercials. We're selling everything from Sominex to Valium, Halcion to hot soup. There are nighttime cold medications to let you sleep after you've taken the pills that keep you up. There are sleep disorder centers, for god's sake. Think about that. Something you have no choice but to do sooner or later, as simple and completely natural a biological function as there is, and we've managed to screw it up. There are people too filled with worries to sleep, people who need to get their eyes too tired to stay open, or who can't turn out the light, people who dream, people who can't dream, people who have nightmares, people who wake up too early, or cranky, or worry that they won't wake up at all. It goes on. Shitting? Can I talk about this . . . ?" He looked around, playing his audience like a talk-show host.

Someone called out, "It's in the interest of science!" and the rest yelled, "Sure!" Morty went on boldly. I gave him ten seconds to be up on the table, and he beat me by five.

"When I sit down to shit, it is a pleasurable experience," he crowed to the farthest reaches of the place. "I relax, nature takes its course. Firmly. Then I'm done. Empty. Go check out the shelves for the incredible amount of medication for this end of things. Too hard, too soft, too often, not often enough, the wrong color, the wrong texture, it goes on and on and on.

"Fucking? This is certainly the most mishandled. We screw up sex so bad, it's no wonder we abuse our wives, our kids, and our friends. We've taken a happy, healthy exercise and turned

it into a horror show. Sex should be freely given and enjoyed."
That was met by cheers. "Every proctologist in the country,"
he informed the bar, "will tell you the secret of a healthy
prostate is one orgasm a day, every day, no matter how old you
are or how you reach it. Let's come of age, folks! Teach your
children that sex is a joy and that Mommy and Daddy love to
do it, and you'll save them thousands of hours on the psychiatrist's couch. If you doubt it, just think about how happy *you*
are and what *you* were taught."

He let the laughter flow around him, and I thought about
what a great politician or salesman or entertainer he could be.
I supposed in his life he was a little of all three. He let the
laughter settle. Every face in the bar was smiling, wrapped up
in him.

He shrugged eloquently and said, "Eat, breathe, shit, fuck,
and sleep. That's the ticket."

This night he could have run on it. He bowed graciously.
"Ladies and gentlemen, I rest my case."

The applause was thunderous.

We didn't pay for a drink the rest of the night.

That's my cousin Morty.

2

I phoned Carolyn around midnight. No one had called, the
alarm had not been tripped. She still had the gun. The kids
were fine, both sleeping in our bed. At least somebody was. I
told her I was with Morty and I didn't know when I'd be back,
not to worry or wait up.

"Phillie?"

"Yes."

"I love you."

I didn't know what to say, so I said good-bye.

3

I went back to the table and shook my head when Morty tried to get me another scotch.

"I don't wanna get that fucked up."

"Too late," he said.

I was relaxed for the first time since the shooting. I felt safe with my cousin, and the friendly atmosphere the Morty Show had produced in the bar made me feel like I'd been coming here for years. People had made a pile of singles on our table. There had to be at least fifty.

I was thinking of bringing my kids here when Morty said, "The marks on his arms weren't from drugs."

"How do you know?"

"First-time users don't mainline. Even users for a while. And if he did inject it, he'd choose a site like between the toes or in the rump. Less visible. Besides, easier these days to smoke it, freebase. He was carrying it like this, he snorted it."

"So?"

"If I had to guess, I'd say blood test."

I liked it. What had Robbie said? *We were careful. Frequent blood tests.*

"Maybe they found something, that's why he croaked."

"The medical examiner said he had no diseases, Morty. He was clean."

Morty shrugged. "I don't know then. Show me the key."

I passed it to him.

He looked at it, turned it over.

"Fiery W," I said.

"I know the place. What do you expect to find there?"

"I haven't a clue, Morty."

He laughed. "Sam Fucking Spade."

"I didn't mean it that way."

"Forget it. It's part of why I like you. This Jack thing. You'd do the same for me."

"Of course. So would you."

He looked at me. "Maybe. I'd have to see a percentage in it, though. You don't. That's a difference."

"He was my—"

"Stop saying that. It doesn't mean shit. Out on the streets you live or die 'cause you do the right thing or not. This partner stuff is just another stupid prejudice, like 'I can't be beaten,' or 'I won't let someone spit on me.' Phillie, conditions are right, you let someone piss all over you and tell him you'll be back for more, thank you, 'cause anything is better than being dead."

"Maybe—"

"Maybe bullshit. You know what I learned back in the joint? That I'm fucking mortal. I could die out here. And it's my job not to. So I'm a little lower level than I used to be. More careful. I started out making the other guy afraid, now I'm smarter. I have to make him afraid of making *me* afraid. Make him know I'll go berserk, never end it. Never. On a rip-off or a scam, you gotta know what'll the guy do, when he'll give up and know it's over. Then you make him so scared, he never comes after you. It's over, it's *over*. Back to Daddy's safe business. Back to the suburbs. Whatever."

"Okay."

He sighed. "You say okay, but I don't know. There's a trigger inside you gotta be able to pull. Can you?"

I remembered a long silver stream of coins that could have been my guts. And Judy asking me if I had ever been free and answering her no.

"I want to go to Whips and Chains, Morty."

"And you don't want to go alone," he surmised correctly.

"Will you make sure I get out? Protect me?"

"You're scared?"

"Yes."

"You don't have any trouble saying it?"

"Why should I? It's true. It won't stop me, but it's true."

He looked at me curiously. "Do you ever lie?"

"Sure."

He shook his head. "That's a lie, isn't it?"

"Well, yeah, sort of."

He separated a big part of the pile of singles on the table for a tip and laughed. "It don't qualify." He downed the rest of his beer. "Phillie, you are a pistol. I will get you back to wimpville in one piece. You ready?"

I nodded.

On the way out the waitress pressed a piece of paper with her phone number on it into my hand.

I gave it to the taxi driver.

THIRTY-FOUR

1

Whips and Chains was in the old warehouse district on the West Side. The buildings all had loading docks, and any windows still intact were opaqued with dirt. Cobblestones had broken through the moist pavement like sores. The occasional driver coming east from what was left of the highway snicked his electric door locks down if they weren't already, and raced for the bright lights of Midtown. I checked my watch. It was two in the morning. I felt like I was on the moon.

The entrance was just a doorway marked W in the side of an old brick building.

"C'mon," Morty said. "We'll take a walk first."

I looked around. It was the edge of the earth. Homeless people loomed in doorways. "Are you crazy?"

"You're with me."

"Yes, but—"

"Isn't this why I'm here?"

"Yes, but—"

"Look." A wicked four-inch needle attached to a wooden knob was in his hand. I hadn't known it was there. In wood shop we called it an awl, for punching holes in metal. I pictured the holes it would make in somebody's chest.

"The rest of it's attitude," he said, swaggering down the block like it was noon in the mall instead of midnight on the moon. "It's a jungle. There are predators here. They select you. You got to show them you don't care. They smell that. It makes them think twice. Better they move on. Attitude, see?"

I was watching two mean tough-looking guys approach. My heart was in my throat. Morty was ready, I could feel it. I wondered if I'd have to do something if he did something. It occurred to me I didn't have the slightest idea what that might be.

"C'mon," he said, heading for them like an icebreaker, refusing to change course.

"Morty—"

"C'mon!" It was a yell, an insult to the night, a challenge. He roared it to the other animals, and they heard and fell back, afraid. The toughs passed, and we continued down the dark street lined with broken glass and garbage.

"Morty?"

"Hmm?" He lit a joint and smoked for a while, enjoying the head. High in the jungle. I wished we had a Sherman tank.

"I gotta pee," I said.

"So pee."

"Where?"

He stopped and pointed to a Dumpster. "There."

"I can't."

"Stop it, will you?"

"Morty, I *can't.*"

He pointed back toward the club. "Better here than there."

I peed. The Dumpster was pushed up against the wall of a building, and I wedged myself into the corner. I could see headlights over the stained black metal lid. None of them came down the block. I peed in timid little squirts with my head watching everywhere at once like a chicken's. Despite myself, a funny thought occurred to me, and an unexpected chuckle came out.

"What?"

"I was just thinking," I said. "It's like we're still the same kids in the Bronx thirty years ago. I'm whining, you're pushing me to go on get brave. Funny, that's all. Kinda nice, in a way."

Morty looked at the combat zone around us. "Only you," he said.

"I'm finished."

"Good," Morty said, seeing me eye the wetness on the black Dumpster. "Don't get the guilts. The only thing you did bad was you probably peed on somebody's house."

"Let's go in now?"

"Okay."

A meaty man in a leather vest and tattoos took our money. His belly flowed over his belt like sauce. We walked down a short flight of iron steps, past dirty plastic strips hanging in the doorway like the ones in a carwash or that keep in the cold air in a refrigerator case in the market.

Music flowed out hot and hard and swallowed us inside. My senses were immediately assaulted by the noise and a hot wet heat that smelled of body fluids. I had no way of encompassing all the information that I was receiving. It swelled over me like the tide. The narrow, green-painted, cracked-plaster corridors were crowded with bodies that made no move not to touch as they passed. A stream of young men in jeans with their flies open and their organs exposed went into dark rooms with women in corsets carrying whips. A steady din of noise, slaps, moans, and music blended into a constant pulse. We passed into the main room where perhaps a hundred or so people were milling about, shuffling from one scene to another. The bar served soft drinks and had a good view of the stage, where a skinny old gray-haired man was being whipped across his withered buttocks by a tall woman in a gold corset that barely contained her breasts. She taunted the man with a steady stream of verbal abuse, then used her whip with a figure-eight motion that gave it a mean whistle before it landed.

A sign over the bar read HAVE YOU FLOGGED YOUR CREW TODAY?

"You're nervous again," Morty observed correctly. He took out Jack's vial and tapped a line of coke onto the bar and did it up with a drink straw he pulled from a glass filled with them. No one said anything.

I tried to step back from the heat and noise. How was I supposed to proceed here?

"Drink something," Morty advised. When I hesitated, he added, "You can't get AIDS from a straw."

I said, "My mother told me not to touch anything."

"There's worse advice."

We had just gotten drinks when I felt a hand on my foot. I looked down. A near-naked man had his face pressed against my shoe, an absolutely beatific expression on his face.

"May I lick it?" he said brightly. "Please?"

"What?"

"May I lick your shoe? It's what I get off on."

"No!"

"I'm sorry," he cried, seeming to enjoy the rejection as much as anything. He crawled down the bar and tried to suck a black pump belonging to a well-dressed black woman. She kicked him in the chest harder than I would have liked to be kicked. I thought she was saying no also, but I didn't have the signals right. He sat up and begged like a dog, and this time the woman nodded and let him put her shoe in his mouth.

"What's here to scare you?" Morty asked me. "It's just people. Some folks like ball games, some like this. It's consenting. They don't hurt anyone, really."

Just people. I took a sip and tried to explain it. "I'm scared because I judge instantly that this is not good," I said. "But at the same time the tits of that woman onstage are giving me an erection, and all this is pretty heady, and suddenly I'm getting some twitches I'm not used to. So my judgment is at war with my body, and that worries me. It's the wimp's dilemma. If I let myself go, who knows what might happen?"

"You worried you'll make the wrong decision?"

"My dick can make some pretty convincing arguments."

He smiled dryly. "Well, fuck, yours ain't the only one."

I laughed and eased up a little.

Morty spilled out another line of coke. The pair onstage was replaced by a woman who climbed into a sling that rendered her wide open. A man in a leather jumpsuit put clips on her nipples.

"So you see some of this in you," Morty said mildly. "It's not surprising, Phillie. We're all the same schmuck. Try and relax."

"I am relaxed," I shouted.

"Of course. Forgive me."

The coke was still on the bar. "Aren't you going to finish that?" I asked nervously. I saw more headlines: MURDER SUSPECT BUSTED IN RAINBOW CITY. A night in jail. Large men wanting to be my friends.

"It's yours if you want it."

I shook my head emphatically. "I don't do that."

"How the fuck you know what you do if you don't try it? You've been smoking reefer for twenty years—don't tell me no. You never once wanted to see what all the fuss is about? Where's your curiosity?"

I admit I was curious. There would probably never be a better time. Carolyn wasn't here, and Morty would take care of me if I had a heart attack or went schizophrenic or something. I looked around. The gyrations in the room had built the heat up to where I was sweating. I draped my jacket over the back of the barstool. I was safe for now, but I was nervous. I wished they served alcohol. The pleasant buzz from the drinks at Gallagher's was fading fast. I needed a pick-me-up. Why the hell not?

"No thanks," I said. "I gotta pee."

"Phillie, wait—"

But I was anxious to get away from that line on the bar. It was calling to me too loudly. I remembered what Judy said. *The coke freed us, Phillie. Were you ever free?*

Never.

I ignored Morty's call and went into the corridor. "Men's room?" I asked a guy with his dick hanging out.

"Down there. Can I come?"

I said no and was again rewarded with that look of pleasure at rejection. I began to understand. It was the first step in an intricate ballet. Reject. Humiliate. Make the other come back for more. Take control by degrees till the mental and emotional pressure is unbearable. Only then does the physical part come into play.

I went down a short flight of steps to the john, a moldy-smelling wet room with bare light bulbs hanging from wires. You didn't have to be a genius to figure out the fire codes weren't being met here. There were three stalls, all locked. Splashing sounds were coming out of them. I looked around, and what I saw really didn't come into focus for a few seconds, like when you meet someone you haven't seen in a long time and it takes a second to run them through your mental computer. There were two bathtubs over by the scarred and stained wall, and people were lining up to pee in them. Men and women, it didn't matter, they just took turns standing or squatting. I watched a woman lift up her skirt. She wore nothing underneath. She got a leg over each side of the tub and rubbed herself for a while. Then a long stream began. I had never seen anyone do this before. I was transfixed, horrified, disgusted. I felt my ties sever as though cut by a razor blade. My first thought was they were doing this because the stalls were being used. Then I saw a hand reach over the rim of the tub, from the inside. . . .

I walked out quickly. This wasn't the moon. It was farther. My mind was busy harshly rejecting what I had seen. I wished I was drunk again. I needed some insulation. I couldn't handle all this sober. I made my way through the bodies. It was cooler back in the main room, though not by much. At least the smell was better. The crowd was almost shoulder to shoulder. People talked to me. I talked back. Services were offered and declined. Easily. I met Mistress Rianda. Lord Snow. Baroness Lea. I was here for a reason. I kept mentioning Jack's name, hoping for someone to point me in a direction. Any direction. I

heard a lot of names in return. They meant nothing to me.
The few who knew Jack—it was only a vague thing. A time or
two here or at a hotel. A few drinks somewhere. All the while a
woman onstage was penetrating a man with a large object. I
was finding it hard to breathe. I leaned against a wall and took
out a tissue and mopped my face.

"Are you all right?"

I opened my eyes. A girl about twenty-five in a white silk
blouse with French-style blossomy sleeves was looking at me
with concern. Her features were fresh and clean, and she
wasn't wearing much makeup or jewelry, only a simple gold
chain around her neck. She had blue eyes, and her long blond
hair was brushed back under a white headband that I immediately liked because it reminded me of cheerleaders in high
school, sock hops and innocence, days long gone. She wore
dark stockings under her short black skirt, and black heels. She
looked like a lady lawyer, or an advertising executive, or a
model, or a kid, with qualities of each.

"Are you all right?" she asked again.

"Yes, thanks. It's a little much," I said.

She smiled. "Some people feel that way their first time. It is,
isn't it? I mean, your first time."

We had to lean close to hear each other. "Does it show?"

She had a nice laugh. "Green and sweating? A dead give-
away. But it's kind of sweet."

A man naked but for old army boots walked by and dragged
his hand across the rear of her skirt. She didn't seem to mind.

"My name's Cee," she said.

"See?"

"The letter. Cee. Like in chains." She searched my face for
understanding.

Having none, I said, "Oh."

I was taken aback. This girl wasn't just pretty, she was a
knockout. Fine upturned nose, full mouth. Sparkling eyes.
There wasn't a blemish on her pale skin. She was maybe five
foot five with a great figure and a behind that swayed entic-
ingly when she moved. While I was taking her all in, a man
crawled over and curled up at my feet. I kicked him away. It

bothered me that I wasn't as offended by doing that anymore. I yelled, "Sorry."

"You don't have to apologize," she said. "It's what he's here for."

"I'm still getting used to it."

"That means you're still trying to figure out what you want."

I wondered if that was what it meant. I should have been out of here a long time ago. Hard drugs, harder sex. Was Jack worth this? I had a mission, but I'd lost sight of it. The place was getting to me. I struggled to stay on top of it.

"Is Cee your real name?" I asked.

"As real as any."

"Where are you from?"

"Does it matter?" she asked.

I hate cryptic conversations. They make me feel insecure. If she had said Brooklyn, I'd have had a follow-up. As it was, I felt like I was working, not talking.

"Do you want a drink?" I asked.

She looked at me deliberately. "You're asking?"

"Yes—I guess."

She deflated slightly. "Then, no . . . thank you."

I don't know why I said it. Maybe there was something wicked in the hot, stained bricks of this place, and I was picking it up by osmosis.

"What if I *told* you to?"

Suddenly the same light I had seen in other eyes here was in hers. She was waiting for me to tell her what to do. Wanted me to. She was a submissive. I looked over her shoulder. Morty was watching from the bar. He eyed me a question. I shook my head. I can handle this, thanks.

"If you told me to . . . ," she began. "If you really *could* . . ."

"Lift up your skirt," I said. I was on shaky ground here. Maybe I was experimenting. I don't know. I was crazy and scared and excited. Mostly scared. I tried to hide my timidity and ride both feelings to somewhere new.

She said, "No."

"No?"

"You don't really mean it," she said, and walked away.

Did I feel like a schmuck or what? The whole power scene was lost on me. I felt like apologizing, but that was submissive, so maybe I should have just popped her one to be dominant, but I had never hit a woman in my life. So what was I supposed to do? I didn't know the rules. The more I thought about it, I figured maybe it was like what they said about cost. If you had to ask, forget about it.

My head was spinning. I went back to Morty. He'd kept my chair empty and free of shoe-lickers. "Well?" he asked.

"Beats me."

"You could, you know."

"What?"

"Beat her."

"Yeah, I worked that out. But she dumped me."

"You're kidding. Guys without heads could score here."

"Make me feel better," I sulked. "Christ, why don't they sell booze here?"

"City would close them down."

"You mean *that's* legal?"—I nodded to a man squatting on the stage with a ball gag in his mouth while a corseted woman mounted him—"and alcohol isn't?"

"Logic abounds in this city. What do you mean, she dumped you?"

"I wasn't master material." I pointed to the line of coke on the bar. "Is that still mine?"

He was my guardian but not my savior. He made no move to stop me. "If you want."

I wanted a quart of scotch, but it wasn't available. This was. I looked at the coke. I was here to follow Jack. How much was this a part of it? Endless debate, my curse. I was sick of it. I held one end of the straw to the powder and inhaled. I looked down, and it was gone. My nose burned slightly. That was all.

"That's it?" I asked. Somehow major transgressions should be accompanied by greater fanfare. Or pain.

He laid out another line. "For the other side."

I snorted it.

"Nothing," I said.

"Wait."

Another letdown, I thought. All the people I'd heard raving about this drug, and all it did was make me feel guilty. I seemed to be getting more used to the place, however. The suburbs were far away. Far away. A near-naked man crawled through a sea of boots and heels and pointy toes. Onstage, a master had bent his slave over an ottoman and invited all comers. Yet it didn't throw me now that I had been here for a while. Amazing what you can get used to. Three feet away, a man was masturbating onto a woman's thigh-high black boots. Posters proclaimed the new Mr. International Leather contest. A slave was being strapped onto a catherine wheel. But it was different from when I first came in. Now it existed as one big show, a supermarket of perversion to do with as I pleased. Morty was eyeing me steadily. I felt deeply composed. Centered. I was an ambassador from another land, the suburbs. I had diplomatic immunity. I thought about Carolyn for no reason, and a hot stab of anger ran through me.

"Carolyn and I are separated," I said abruptly to Morty.

"Fuck. Why?"

"Reasons."

He looked at me like I was stupid. "She's one of the few decent women around. I hate women. You know that. Carolyn's different."

"She was. She changed." Interesting. My gums and teeth were numb. It was a pleasant feeling.

"How?"

"I don't know," I said. "Can I do another?"

"Up to you." He laid out parallel lines like tire skids.

I snorted them up.

It was amazing. My sinuses were the size of caverns. I was taking in huge amounts of air without even opening my mouth. I felt like an engine charged full of steam chugging through life. All my problems were forgotten. I was powerful. Endless. The master of my fate and others'. The Master. I was more clearheaded than I had ever been. I was one of the few who really *knew* what life was all about. Watching the churning mass around me, I understood for the first time what it was to be down there, how much it made the rest of it clean and pure.

I watched a lot of people in the room, but it was Cee who interested me.

"Carolyn betrayed me," I said to Morty, not knowing why I said it except that suddenly I was running at the mouth.

He looked at me sourly. "What is this, the Middle Ages? Betrayed you? What the fuck does that mean?"

"She slept with another man."

Morty was unsympathetic. "That's all? So fucking what? After all the shit you two've been through that's humiliating, like most of everyday life with two kids, what the fuck does a little sex matter, really?"

Cee was standing with a muscular, bare-chested, balding man in a leather vest. His hand was under her skirt. Her ass swayed gently to the beat of the loud music and him. My dick and my mind held a conference and agreed to stop fighting. We were all in this together, a unified force for the first time in my life.

"I don't know," I said to Morty. "I used to know, but I don't anymore." I got off the stool.

"Where are you going?" Morty asked quickly.

"I see a friend. A friend of a friend. A friend of a friend of a—"

"Easy, Phillie. You're high as a kite. You don't realize it."

"One more."

"Wait."

"One more!"

He sighed. "Okay." Twin lines again. Deep, thick, rich. Textures changed. I was invulnerable. Free. It hit me like a ton of bricks. For the first time in my life, I was free! I was finally feeling what Jack had felt. I was a god, too. I walked over to Cee, knowing she would feel the force of my presence behind her. She did, and turned. She was mine. I could do anything. I broadcast that message.

"Come with me," I said.

She searched my face again, this time finding whatever had been missing before. But she didn't move. I understood.

"Now," I said.

The balding man took his hand off her. He was thick-muscled with slabby arms. He uncoiled the whip hanging from the wide leather belt on his leather pants.

"You have bad manners, slave," he said to me.

"I'm invulnerable," I said, feeling electricity course through me.

He flicked the whip out Indiana Jones–style and swung it toward me, but I stood my ground, knowing it was true.

Morty moved. He caught the whip and turned it aside and jerked Leatherman's hand up behind him in an armlock, turning him around. His fist shot out no more than six inches into the small of Leatherman's back. The guy stiffened like he'd been shot. Morty whispered a few words in his ear. He went pale and nodded. Morty released him, and he walked away.

I said, "I could have done that."

Morty drifted in behind me as I steered Cee back to the bar.

"Your friend's fast," she said.

"Runs in the family," I said. "Do a line."

"If it pleases you."

Morty laid it out. I did more, too. My heart was pounding, but I felt wonderful. Better than I had in my whole life. The back of my throat was numb, same as my teeth. It felt great. I gave Cee a drink. She accepted it demurely, waiting for me.

"Open your blouse," I said, drunk with power. Emboldened.

She put down her drink. There was no hesitation, no girlish shyness. She popped the buttons, revealing perfect white skin. The swell of her breasts was beautiful in her lacy black bra. The noise around us forced us closer.

"I have my chains on. Do you want to see them?" she asked.

"Yes."

She pulled one breast free of her bra. A chain exactly like the one I had taken from Robbie was looped around her nipples, joining them. I reached out and touched one. Her nipple grew harder, and she sighed happily. I twisted it sharply. She winced in pain and gratitude.

"The other?" she asked.

Standing there with her chained breasts free for me and Morty and everyone else in the room to look at, she was even more intoxicating. I jerked the chain. Her breasts danced on the line like prey. Somewhere in my mind was a voice that wondered what the hell I was doing, but I silenced it with a twist of that chain. Her breasts were firm, supple. I was wild. I felt it. I knew it. Phillie the conqueror.

Cee was excited, lips moist. Her eyes were shaded with pain and longing. The precious vulnerability in her face made me even harder. I had a spike in my pants, and it wanted to be as free as the rest of me. I stroked it. She was mine. Totally. Bound to me, tied to me. The responsibility made me love her. I wanted to cherish her, to protect her.

"Here is all right," Cee said. "Or I have a room . . ."

Morty leaned over and whispered something to her, and she nodded. She looked back at him. "Sure. You too, if you want."

He shook his head.

I let her lead me from the room with its nerve-destroying music and constant din of moans and slaps, into the relative quiet of the corridor. A man walked by. She said, "May I?"

I nodded. He stood there gratefully, holding on to her hair. Others stopped to watch.

I said, "Enough," and she let him go.

I took her by the chain and batted the rest away. I had her lift up her skirt to show her garter belt and stockings. I liked other people looking at what I owned. I liked their envy. I was over the line, over the line, over the line. I was flying. I knew it, and I didn't care.

I understood Jack for the first time.

Cee's room was quiet and austere. Bare brick walls. A bed and a sink. An ottoman. A night table and lamp. A collection of bondage instruments hung on the walls. Whips and chains, plugs and dildos, gags and leather straps, canes and paddles. Hooks were set into the wall and floor. Cee sat on the bed in front of me. There was moisture between her thighs. My total freedom made me go slow. I suddenly knew the answer to why a woman is sexy. It's because sex excites her long before a man ever does.

She was already wet, excited, ready. Her lips opened for me. Her breathing increased. I put two fingers inside her, spread her juices inside and out. Her nostrils flared like a racehorse's. I was on fire. My brain was filled with her.

I leaned over. She was sweet-tasting, fresh and clean. She moaned and pushed her hips into my face. I licked the sides of her lips and heard her gasp in surprise and delight. I felt her first orgasm and smiled as wave after wave hit her until she finally collapsed against me. I waited, giving her time to come down. This was just a prelude.

I was still fully dressed, and to some degree, so was she. I told her to stand in the middle of the room.

"Masturbate for me," I ordered.

I stood there unmoving as she took off her shirt and bra. Her breasts were wonderful, upturned and firm, with lovely pink nipples and small crinkled areolas. She caressed herself, using the chain to pull the nipples and twist them and make her breasts bounce like a dancer's. She pushed her breasts together and rubbed them. She put her fingers into her mouth and sucked on them and tweaked her nipples with her wet fingers.

She pulled off her skirt and lay back. I unbuckled my belt and opened my pants. I stroked myself, watching her. She had one hand on her breasts, the other inside her. I posed her with her legs spread wide open. I had her kneel on all fours and watched her from behind. I had her stand and bend over. She told me I could tell her to do anything, that she was my slave. She kneeled before me. I was a god to be worshiped. I stroked her hair and rubbed myself along her cheeks and lips.

"Master, may I . . . ?"

"Yes."

She had barely slipped the condom on and taken me into her mouth before I came in a way that I never had with anyone before. I exploded, standing there in the middle of that room with my hands wrapped in her hair, ramming myself into her mouth while sirens went off in my head.

"Here." She went to her nightstand and took out a vial of coke. My best friend. My love. She poured some on her belly, and I snorted it off her, then forced her to the floor in front of me. I felt my emotions stir. Tenderness. Sweetness. I held her face and kissed it. Love was a part of it, but so was bondage. We were inside each other. Owned in owning. *We were obsessed,* Judy had said. I understood now. Cee and I lay there, and I held her chains, and we talked. Words spilled out of me. Everything I said was new and wise. We were in a room in my temple. She was quick-witted and intoxicatingly beautiful. While we talked, I played with her breasts and she fondled me.

When I was hard again, she pointed to the racks. "The whip," she said. "Now use the whip."

"Show me," I said softly. "Teach me."

"Yes, Master." She went to the wall and removed a leather collar and leash and studded leather wrist cuffs. She put them on and handed me the leash. "I'll do anything you ask, Master. Only . . ."

"Only what?"

"If I say no, you can ignore it. If I say stop, you can ignore it, too, because part of my pleasure is struggling against the bonds. But if I say *mercy*, you must stop. That is our safe word. Will you, Master?"

I held her face up to me, glorying in her. "Yes."

Holding the leash, I felt power coursing up my arm.

"Bend over."

She bent over the ottoman. Her long blond hair fell along the sides of her face. She was so vulnerable. I wanted to ravish her every orifice, give her to a hundred men, beat her senseless. There was a roaring in my mind and a pounding in my temples as I cracked the whip, almost took my eye out, changed my mind on weapon of choice, and took a thin reedy cane. Her ass was the perfect target. I struck her across those fleshy globes. Another boundary fell.

"Harder," she asked. "Please, Master."

It wasn't easy to hit a woman, but I was that far over the edge. I brought the cane down harder and she winced and clenched against the pain. "Yes," she cried. "Oh, yes." I hit her again and again. Every red welt was a badge of courage. I took the whip and managed to hit myself in the face, then got the feel of it and brought it across her ass in a satisfying *thwack*. I whipped her and spanked her and paddled her and made her suck me and lick my feet.

"Please, Master. Behind," she cried.

I was beside myself with sexual intensity. She reached back and rubbed herself. I rammed a condom on and pushed against the incredible tightness. Suddenly there was a tiny pop, and I was inside her, passing a narrow channel into a vast cavern beyond. The feeling of lust and power was indescribable.

Cee went wild, rubbing herself and moaning, crying out for me not to stop, not to stop. I held her by the hips and pushed deeper, going in all the way. I thought I would split her in two, but she yelled for me to keep it up. I plunged in and out, each thrust into an unknown world. She folded against me in the middle, and if I had gotten up and walked around, she would have remained a part of me, so deeply was I embedded within her. I felt her grip tighter, and I knew she was going to come. I drove deeper and shouted and moaned, and when I came, each spurt brought a long, drawn-out scream of pleasure that seemed to last forever.

I learned how much a part of sex is fury that night. God, how I learned. I hit Cee, but sometimes I was hitting Carolyn, and sometimes I was hitting anyone who had ever hurt me, and sometimes I was hitting myself. I did things I never dreamed I could do, things she showed me willingly, with clips and blunt instruments, and finally, when she begged me at the end to release myself on her, I did, with all the pent-up control and rage and fury and love I ever had.

We lay there huddled together at the end, vowing never to let each other go. We were soiled and clean, spent and energized, ruined and re-created.

I slept.

THIRTY-FIVE

1

I woke up alone.

My head was pounding. My face was hot. My hands trembled. I was sweaty and encrusted with body fluids. Memories of the night before came rushing back. Self-disgust and guilt rose up to choke me. I can't think of a moment I felt worse in my entire life than when I looked at myself in the mirror and remembered what I'd done.

I held my head in my hands and tried to piece it together. My watch said six-twenty. I assumed it was Saturday morning, but there weren't any windows in hell to let in the light. My clothes were draped over the ottoman. I washed in the sink and dried myself on the bedding and put on my pants. My wallet and cash were all there. I was glad. At least I hadn't been rolled.

I stuck my head out the door. "Morty?"

"Here, boss."

I looked down. He was sitting with his back against the wall, alone. The corridor was deserted. Someone had mopped it. You could still smell the ammonia.

"I don't feel so good, Morty."

He walked in and looked around. "No, you wouldn't."

He tossed me my shirt and sat on the bed. I put on my windbreaker. There was a piece of paper in the pocket with a phone number written on it in a neat, precise hand. Cee's, I was sure. I put it back. Morty was watching me. I didn't know what to say. I said so.

"What's to say?" He shrugged philosophically. "You still have my good will, if that matters."

"Right now, it does. A lot."

"This is between us, Phillie," he said. "It goes no further. You stepped out, that's all. You're human. With all the weaknesses. The place. The blow—"

"I don't want to talk about this here. Can we go?"

"Sure."

"I've still got my wallet and cash."

He smiled. "I know. I paid her. You owe me four hundred dollars."

I thought about that while I put on my shoes.

"Let's get some breakfast, okay?"

2

Morty took me to a place that looked exactly like a suburban diner transplanted into the city, deco chrome and everything.

"So you got *some* good things," he said.

We ordered. I was still quiet. Morty got the morning paper, and we both read about the suburban torture murder and the man the police were looking for. At least my name was still being kept out of it. So far. I was only identified as a "white male in his middle forties." Carolyn must have been frantic.

"You wanna talk?" he asked.

"No. I hate myself. I can't believe what I did. I betrayed everything I believe in, including Carolyn. I saw a side of me I never ever want to see again. I'm a barbarian. A degenerate. Morty, the things I did to her—"

"Can the histrionics. By my standards, you're still a virgin. Did anybody die? No. Are you still in one piece? Yes. You treated her fair. And it wasn't anything she doesn't do on a regular basis. She's a pro. You didn't know that, did you?"

"No."

"I figured. I told her to take care of you and I'd settle the bill. She did right by you. Honest. You got no complaints."

"You waited there all night, outside in the hallway?"

"Yes."

"Anyone try and get in?"

"A few. I spoke to them."

"Thanks." I meant it deeply, and he knew it, even though he shrugged it off.

I ate some pancakes because the thought of eggs made me sick. The juice was fresh squeezed. I ordered more. Morty had a cheeseburger and fries.

"You look bad, son," he said. "No relief?"

"My guts are in a knot. I think I should go get tested for AIDS. I did despicable things to another human being. Worst of all, definitely worst of all, is that I've put Carolyn through hell because of what she did, and now I've gone and done the same thing."

He munched his burger thoughtfully. "So what's the problem? Doing it, or not being able to blame her for doing it?"

"Maybe now I have to blame both of us."

"I hate psychobabble." He pointed a french fry at me. "You know what the streets are, Phillie?"

"No, not really."

"They're the place where things are real. Where people reveal what they want. Humans want a lot of ugly things, cuz."

"So I've learned."

He went on philosophically, "Suburbia tries to deny this is true. But lawns and fences and BMW station wagons don't change anything. Rich people in pretty houses still bubble and burn. You got the same ugly things, Phillie, you just got 'em gift-wrapped."

"Maybe I always knew that to some extent, Morty. But to see it so raw . . ." I shuddered. "I'm not sure it's good knowledge. I was so *different*. I'm over forty years old and I have to look at somebody new in the mirror all of a sudden. It's a lot to think about."

Morty nodded. We shared something now that we hadn't before. I'd left the clean suburbs and walked in his land.

"Welcome to the streets, cuz."

I managed to eat. It was good to see the sunshine outside. Some families were out early. They looked healthy and tanned and purposeful. One man's white polo shirt was a beacon of all that was healthy and normal. I wanted to buy it from him and put it on right there. My need to get back to the suburbs was a physical ache. I felt so dirty. We ate for a while in silence.

"Morty?"

"Yes."

"I lied. What I said before about Carolyn, that isn't the worst."

He looked up from his cheeseburger.

"Worst is, I want to do it again."

3

Morty said, "I told her how to reach me."

"For me?"

He nodded. "I wasn't sure I should've."

"Wouldn't have mattered." I showed him the piece of paper. "She left me her number."

"Maybe you should lose it."

"Maybe I should."

"What are you going to do?" he asked.

"See her." I knew it, and he knew it, too.

I used the pay phone for privacy. She should have sounded

bleary and sleepless, but she didn't. We talked for a while. I got her address. When I got back, Morty had paid the check. I didn't sit down.

"You going?" he asked.

I nodded. "You coming?"

He drained his coffee. "Yep."

4

I sat in Cee's living room unable to reconcile her physical beauty with the degradation I had put her through. She was even more beautiful in the morning light. Her hair was tied with a pink yarn in a simple ponytail. She had on jeans and a yellow crew neck sweater. She looked even prettier and more fragile than last night. Her apartment was an expensive two-bedroom in a glass high-rise in the West Sixties, with a marble lobby and a uniformed doorman. She had decorated it tastefully. A pale beige sectional sofa. Chintz chairs. Nice lamps. Paintings on silk-papered walls. Hardwood floors and Oriental rugs.

"I wanted to talk to you," I said. "You left before I could."

"The place was closing. I had to."

I was too tired to fence. My words came out in a rush. "Look, I don't understand any of this. I feel a connection to you. Like we're tied together. Something stretching from your guts to mine. I can't break it."

She nodded. "It's like that sometimes."

"What do we do?"

She went and poured us some orange juice and sat back on the couch with her legs curled under her. She looked like a teenager waiting for a phone call from her boyfriend.

"What do you *want* to do?" she asked me.

"I don't know. No, I do know. I want to do it again—but I can't."

Something flickered in her eyes. I wondered how many other men with ties elsewhere had said, *but I can't.*

"You're still seeing me through the sex," she said. "I'm a

person. That's only part of me. I eat, and read books, and go to movies, and have friends, and won't use chopsticks, and bank at Chase. I have a mother in Charleston and a sister back in the Midwest. I was married once, to a man named Lew who was a social studies teacher. I do some free-lance artwork. I have a life. An identity. Let me show it to you. Then see."

"Show me yours and I'll show you mine?"

She laughed. It was like the sea, strong and clean. "I've already seen yours."

"It's not my best part."

"I don't know about that."

I suddenly realized what was wrong and tried to explain it.

"Look, I feel all intimate again, and I want you to put your head on my shoulder and let me hold you and kiss you. It's like I've been imprinted, you know? One of those baby birds who comes out of the egg and the scientist shows them a wire model and they think forever it's their mother. You got past my defenses, past my mind and my critical faculties. One night together, and I feel things for you that are totally out of proportion to knowing you. Or you, me. It's weird. Unnatural. Is that what bondage does to you?"

"Think about the word," she said, uncurling those wonderful legs. "What we went through. Once bound, we're part of each other. Joined. It can never be undone. It's what we gave last night, what we shared. Not lives, souls. That's what you feel."

"God, help me."

"He can't." The embers smoldering in her eyes flared. "I can."

You can get over pain, but you never get over love, isn't that what I'd told Todd? Poor Todd. Poor Jack. Poor Carolyn. Poor Judy. Poor Phillie. Poor little sheep who have lost their way. I sipped the juice, not knowing where to go. Was I doomed to spend the rest of my life with Cee in my guts, reminding me of what had been, of all that was possible, of a territory that would always call me, as cocaine would? Odysseus might have escaped the sirens, but he never forgot them.

"We've started where we should have ended," I said.

"Why did you come back?" she asked.

"Not for all the reasons you think." I handed her the key from the gold case. "It came to me last night. It took a while, but I have been more clearheaded. This is for you." It wasn't a question.

She turned it over in her hands. "He told me he was having it made. He thought it was clever. C is the Roman numeral for one hundred."

"What does it tell you?" I asked.

"That we both knew Jack Murphy."

I had a sense of coming home.

5

Cee said, "Jack liked to buy little trinkets for members of the group. Rings, clips. Mine were always engraved with that number. I guess he never got around to giving me the key."

I remembered the skull he'd given June. "No, he died."

"I read it in the obits. I was sorry. He was a client, but a friend, too," she said. "Sometimes he hired me to be part of his group. He and Judy liked me to—"

"That's okay. Where'd you meet?"

"At the club usually. Sometimes a suite at the Plaza."

"Who else was there?"

"Jack. Judy. Do you know Robbie Hazen?" she asked.

"Intimately."

"He was there. A few others. It was a good scene."

"Will you look at some pictures?"

"If you want."

I took out of my wallet the pictures I had pulled from our photo album. Jessica had taken them at one of Jack's parties, posing everybody around a picnic table.

"Do you know any of these people?"

"Besides you and Jack, them."

Todd and Marcia were there, but she hadn't pointed to either. She'd picked two ex-neighbors of mine, Dave and Myra

Zindler, an insurance broker and his wife who'd moved to Florida last winter. More secrets.

Cee was still looking at the pictures.

"Not him?" I asked, pointing to Fred Marcus. It was the connection I hoped to make.

"Yes and no," she said.

"What does that mean?"

"He was never at the parties. Jack introduced me to him at the clinic."

"What clinic?"

"The one we use on the East Side."

"A hospital clinic?"

"It's more of a lab. Private. Lots of our people go there for tests because they understand, make it easy. All you have to do is ask for a 'full spectrum.' They do the lab work right there, and they mail the results to you and not a doctor." She gave me the address.

"What was Fred doing there?"

"I was under the impression that he owned part of it."

"Did Jack mention Fred was a doctor?"

She nodded. "He said they were great friends. And that Fred always handled his tests personally."

I had a weird thought. It was about as devious as anything I'd ever contemplated. I remembered something Donnegan said to me that very first night. Ever since this whole thing began, I'd been asking myself one question over and over: How could suicide be murder? I suddenly thought I might know how.

"When was the last time you saw Jack?"

"Couple of weeks ago, at the hotel."

"But things weren't the same." Statement, not question.

She seemed surprised I could know that. "No, they weren't. He was upset. Worried. Didn't take part like he used to. Later on, I heard him and Judy arguing. Something about a tape and who should keep it."

The tape again. "Did they mention any names?"

"No."

If the tape was insurance, it hadn't worked. Maybe it just wasn't insurance enough.

A theory was forming in my mind. I didn't like what I'd have to do to prove it, but that's why God invented Morty.

6

"Will I see you again?" Cee asked. She wanted to keep her hands folded in her lap, but they fluttered like captured birds. It was very quiet. The street was a long way from here.

I made a guess as to how far. "Kansas?"

She smiled. "I was born in Nebraska. That's where I studied art." She stayed very still. "Phillie, what I do, it's more than part of me. You know that now."

"I don't think I can live with it."

"I care for you," she said simply, hopefully.

"How can you?" I asked.

"Let's not kid ourselves. What we shared—"

"Was for money."

Her face moved as if I'd slapped her, but she turned back gamely. "You know better."

"Maybe. I'd want to do it again."

"I'd want you to."

Her hand went to the hem of her sweater. I tried not to notice it. "Are you happily married?" she asked me.

"No. But I'm married. Two kids."

"Nice. What was Jack to you? You never said."

"Jack was my partner, among other things."

"Oh."

"I want to know why he killed himself. If he did."

"You have doubts?"

"Yes, and I can't put it down till I know for sure."

She looked out the window, looked far away. "You're very tough on yourself. Life can be hard if you don't bend."

"Tell me about it."

The morning sun gave her a pool of butterscotch to sit in. "Do you want to be with me?" she asked.

I didn't know what to say. Sitting with Cee that morning, Cee of the bright smile and unbridled passion, Cee of the wild nights, I craved her the way an addict craves his drug. I wanted more, regardless of the cost. Only one thing held me back, and it wasn't the difficulty of divorce, nor even the children and all they would have suffered. It was simply that at that moment, in Cee's quiet sun-filled apartment high up in the air of Rainbow City, I realized I loved Carolyn.

"May I use your phone?"

"In the kitchen."

I went and called Donnegan at home.

"It's me," I said.

"Where are you?"

"Up in the sky."

"You're okay?"

"Sort of. You?"

"My shoulder hurts like hell. My wife keeps trying to feed me oatmeal in bed, and Saturday morning TV sucks."

"Try *Doug*. Did Michelson get the arrest warrant yet?"

"No, but things are very hot. My friends in Mineola tell me she's eating people for breakfast. Your lawyer is giving her a really hard time. She wants to know what cop he has in his pocket he knows so much. She told her whole staff no one is going home for the weekend."

I grunted my thanks.

"Have you read the papers?" he asked.

"Too tied up."

"Stop being a jerk. My advice is to give yourself up."

"I can't. I have a hunch I want to go with."

"What is it?"

"Let me see if it works out first. I'll call you later. Are you well enough to go over and check on my wife and kids?"

"Couple hours, sure."

I hung up, thought a bit, and called Jessica. I said she should stay away from Fred—he wasn't what he seemed to be, and I was sure of it now. I'd explain when I got back. She thanked me and told me she was glad I was her friend.

I hung up and thought of Cee waiting for me on the other side of the door.

What had happened to me? I wondered as I stood there in the kitchen looking out at the city. Tall buildings made huge pits. Last night would take a long time to understand, much less accept. I'd discovered a taste for depravity I never knew about. Maybe I'd sensed it as far back as the biker bar, or when I got around Jessica, but I'd played it safe, like most everyone else never admitting what I wanted, hiding my fantasies, certainly never acting on them and having to face myself in the morning. Now I had to. I had met the midnight partner. We all had: Jack and I and Judy, and Robbie and Cee and Morty, and maybe even Carolyn, too. Those hidden fantasies, the secrets we love and hate and covet and despise in the dark stretching hours before dawn—this is the partner who waits deep within all of us, and once we have gone on his beckoning midnight ride, we are never the same again.

I saw my reflection in the black glass of the oven door as though I was inside, looking out. Had Cee taken off her clothes? Would she be lying naked in that honey sun all wet and ready for me to use? So many doors yet to open. I knew what would happen if I walked through this one. Being with Cee had helped me to understand a lot of things. Jack was more complicated than I'd ever known, but in the end maybe he wasn't any more complicated than anyone else. He and Morty had said it wasn't bad to feel such things. And they were right, we were human, sure. But in the rest they were wrong. Act on those dark needs, and you take the first step into hell. June had said it best: Watch the night, it gets harder and harder to get back to the day. I knew now how true that was.

I pulled myself back from the pit.

There was a pad by the phone. I wrote Cee a note.

Dear Cee,

Forgive me, but I have promises to keep. I will always remember you,

With love,
Phillie Liebowitz

Still, I held back. She was so wild and restless. A thousand adventures and nights without end called to me. A different road, one without school trips and homework. But did I love her?

No.

I would just miss her for a long, long time.

One step at a time. One step at a time.

I still had an ending to make.

I left the note on the counter and let myself out the back door.

7

Morty was waiting when I got off the elevator. I told him what I needed to do next.

He thought about it. "Have to get some things, but can do."

I said, "I want to buy some clothes. Then shower and change."

So many doors yet to open . . .

He said, "My place," and took my arm, and when I stopped, he made me go forward.

THIRTY-SIX

1

I showered and shaved at Morty's and put on fresh socks and underwear and a new blue oxford broadcloth button-down shirt I'd bought at a local men's store, one with lots of blue blazers and polo crap in the window. My jeans and windbreaker were fresh from a one-hour cleaners. Jeans can make it through anything.

Morty's furniture was old but clean. Rummage sale stuff. A brown couch. A Naugahyde recliner. A lamp table with an inlaid mosaic bird that looked made from a kit. Thin carpet and black-out shades. A small TV-radio perched on a bookshelf. A pile of racing papers in the corner. Nothing you'd run for in case of fire.

I called Carolyn.

"Where are you?" she asked.

"Morty's."

"How is it going?"

"I'm a step closer," I said. "At least I think so."

"It's in the papers. On television, too. They make it sound horrible. I keep thinking I'm going to hear our names."

"You won't." Not yet, anyway. "Are you okay?"

"I don't know, Phillie. I feel like my life is coming apart around me. Nothing's the way it was. Police cars keep driving past the house. Every so often, someone calls for you, and when I tell them you're not here, they just hang up."

"I know it's hard on you. How are the kids?"

"They're kids. They're mad I won't let them play in the yard. I bribe them with ice cream and cookies, so they stay quiet. Ben is building something lethal in his room. Beth is coloring. They miss you."

"I spoke to Donnegan," I said. "He'll come over later if he can."

"All right."

"It helps me, you holding down the fort."

"Does it?"

"A lot."

I felt such a struggle within myself. I wanted to talk to her, tell her what I'd done, to confess and ask forgiveness, to forgive her. But I couldn't. I'd always prided myself on knowing what I felt. A simple quality, but an important one. Unlike most people, I knew what I loved, what I hated, what scared me, what made me mad, what made me happy. That knowledge had evaporated. I was off balance and frightened. The natural rhythms of my life seemed completely out of sync.

"Phillie, are you there?"

I wished I could bridge the gap between Carolyn and me with something positive. Support. Hope. Maybe even love. I didn't know how. We were locked into the kind of messages we sent as kids. How are you? I am fine. No way to share the important feelings, the ones that might change things.

"I have to go now," I said.

I heard the deadness on the line as her throat constricted.

"Please don't worry," I said. "I'm going to get us through this."

"What do we do if you're arrested?"

"It won't happen. I promise."

"How can you?"

"Trust me."

"The great Phillie Liebowitz," she said bitterly. "So goddamn sure. What if you screw up?"

I didn't blame her for saying it, not under this much pressure. She instantly regretted it.

"I'm sorry, Phillie. I know you're trying."

"Forget it. You're allowed. I'll call later."

"Be careful."

"You, too."

The line went dead. I called for an appointment at Fred's clinic, then read some of Morty's racing papers. The horses had great names. I'd have loved to know the story behind the one called *Shut Up, Shirley*. Morty came in half an hour later carrying a box from an art store and a brown paper bag filled with sodas, cold cuts, bread, and newspapers. He told me to make lunch, then took the stuff from the box into his bedroom and fiddled with it till I called him to eat.

We read the papers and ate ham and cheese sandwiches. Details were leaking steadily, but still not names. He looked over the top edge of the *News*.

"I like when they call you a 'successful Hollywood writer.' It adds spice."

"This one says 'entertainment industry insider.' "

I could see his mind turning. "You know, if you actually confessed, you could make a fortune."

"Tough to spend residuals in jail," I said.

"Amortize it. Crimes of passion are worth millions these days. We're so bored and confused with life, we're making serial killers stars. Figure five million."

"Too high."

"Even with book rights? All right, four. And maybe you spend five years in jail. That's eight hundred thou a year. Not bad."

"So *you* confess." I went back to reading. I could tell he was thinking about it.

"What did Carolyn say?"

I put down the paper. "How do you know I called her?"

"Tell me I'm wrong."

"You're wrong." I tried reading for a while and gave up. "She knows I'm doing my best, but she's scared. She'll be okay until they name names."

"They will as soon as your ADA gets an arrest warrant."

"I know. We're down to the wire, Morty. I'd better be right about this."

"Think who'd play you," he said, and went to take a nap.

I was too keyed up to sleep. I stood a good chance of going to jail. Carolyn's taunt hurt. In that small walk-up apartment, I didn't feel great at all, I felt small and vulnerable. My stomach knotted when I thought about seeing my family destroyed. Losing the house to legal fees. Forced to move so the kids could start over with different names. The pain in Beth's incredibly perfect face. The way Ben would hurt, like me, way down deep where nobody saw.

My stomach heaved, and I barely made it into the bathroom to throw up. On my knees with my arms clutching the toilet, I prayed like a little kid.

2

At three o'clock, Morty came out of the bedroom. "You set?"

"Define that."

"Let's go."

We took a cab over to the East Side. "How are we going to do this in broad daylight?" I asked him.

"Audaciously," he said happily.

Was it any wonder I loved him?

The clinic was on the ground floor of a cream-colored stone building between Park and Lexington. Morty and I parted at the delivery entrance. The clinic was crowded. I guess Saturday was a good day to take care of things like this. All the chairs in the reception area were filled, and lots more people were standing. A butch receptionist with a short haircut and forearms like Popeye asked me in a surprisingly gentle way what I was there for.

"Full spectrum, please."

"Your name?"

"Irwin Kleinman. I'm a new patient. I have an appointment."

"Please have a seat, Mr. Kleinman, and fill out this chart. We'll be with you shortly."

"They told me you do all the lab work here. Doesn't seem big enough."

She smiled tolerantly. "The labs are behind our technicians' stations." She pointed through the archway behind her to a row of cubicles. Beyond them, I could see the doorways to the labs where they ran suspicious blood and urine through their paces.

"Right. Thanks."

"No problem."

Filling out the chart was an exercise in creative writing. Afterward, I read *The New Yorker* for twenty minutes. I didn't understand a word of it. Not even the cartoons. I wondered if it was me. Then a nurse called me in and handed me over to a medical technician in a white lab coat, who ushered me into a cubicle and told me to roll up my right sleeve. I rested my arm on a support like the ones the desk-chairs had in high school. The medtech, a fat boy with a shaved head and a moustache, consulted my chart and eyed me with familiarity.

"Full spectrum, eh? Must make sure of things, mustn't we?" He produced a needle the size of an Apollo rocket.

Where the hell was Morty?

"How much blood do you need?" I asked.

He heard stalls every day. "Be brave now." He tied a rubber tube around my arm.

"Watch the fuck out!!!"

The crash in the corridor that followed Morty's imprecation

was so loud and glassy, it sounded as though someone had shot out all the windows in the place at once.

His voice rose to a shriek. "Jesus Christ, those samples are contaminated! Don't touch them. We got an emergency! Emergency!"

"What the hell—?" The tech leaned out of the cubicle and his face literally went white.

"What is it?" I demanded.

"There's specimens all over the floor! Some fool pushed over a cart. We deal with HIV and hepatitis B here, man! And TB's spread airborne! I'm sorry. I didn't stick to one man all these years to die in *this* place. I'm outta here."

He wasn't the only one. People streamed out of the labs and cubicles, making a bottleneck where the fluids pooled across the floor. Men and women in casual chic, street kids, secretaries, sad-eyed stick-thin patients, all were trying not to touch anything, least of all each other. Doctors and nurses were yelling for the janitors, who yelled right back that they weren't doing any damn thing at all without protective gear. It was a madhouse. The crowd surged back, looking for a way out. They held their noses and mouths. Morty was in a white lab coat shouting, "Do something! Why doesn't somebody do something? I don't wanna die!"

I let the crowd carry me along in its search for an exit. The delivery entrance in back was mysteriously blocked. I found a door marked RECORDS that opened on a stairwell leading to the basement. At the bottom, I felt for the light switch, went down a musty corridor, and came to the records room. The only problem was that it was locked.

I undid the tape holding the pry-bar to my calf and slid it out. I remembered Morty's instructions for a door of this type: "Lock, schmock. Rip out the jamb."

The wooden frame around the door separated from the wall as if it were cardboard, exposing the bolt. I worked the bar in. The door popped open. I closed it behind me and hit the light switch. File cabinets lined every wall. The clinic records were well organized and clearly labeled, which helped. I found the right cabinet, and three drawers down, MR to MU. There was a lot of yelling still going on upstairs. Sooner or later, the panicked crowd streaming into the street was going to bring the police.

MUGANS, MULLER, MULLET—I flicked past file after file till I came to MURPHY, JACK. I pulled it. All the office copies for the various lab tests were filed there. I didn't understand things like CBCs and all the numbers, but there was one form letter I didn't need any scientific training to figure out.

Dear Mr. Murphy, In accordance with our testing procedures, we regret to inform you . . .

I suppose it was the moment I had been waiting for since the night Jack died. You wander around poking and prodding, never sure. When I saw the preliminary and confirmation reports telling Jack he was HIV positive, the first signed by Dr. Fred Marcus, and the second, for a confirming test called a "Western blot," signed by a doctor I didn't know, but *both* listing Fred as the supervising physician on the clinic's private internal record, it gave me the gift of certainty. There was an additional diagnosis of something called P. carinii pneumonia, and the notation that it meant that the HIV infection had produced AIDS. I felt deathly cold. Jack had been in perfect health. The medical examiner had confirmed it. Fred had tricked Jack into committing suicide by making him believe he had AIDS. He'd murdered Jack as surely as if he had pushed him off the roof. The murder weapon was despair.

I shoved the file into my pants and went back up the stairs. There were still some people trying to make their way out and avoid the spill Morty had made from the stuff he'd bought at the art store. I gave him the high sign. I heard him yelling as I pushed my way out front.

"Jesus, I got it all wrong. That stuff was from the lab supply room. It isn't blood *or* piss! Hey, is that funny, or what?"

THIRTY-SEVEN

1

I sat writing a letter in Morty's living room while he brewed tea for us in the kitchen. I had to write it longhand. I missed my computer.

He called to me through the pass-through, "You got what you came for?"

"I think so. Fred was very smart. If Jessica divorced Jack, she'd void the trust. By tricking Jack into suicide, Fred could have her *and* seventy million dollars."

"World-class money," Morty said, setting mugs on the mosaic top. "People do a lot more for a lot less."

"I suppose."

"Want some advice?"

"Sure."

"You've come this far okay. Call it quits. Give the file to the police. Let them handle it."

"I'm going to," I said. "But it has to be set up right. The police and Michelson don't trust me worth shit."

"How come you always got an answer for everything?"

"I don't know," I said. "What worries me is, lately it's the wrong answer."

"What do you want me to do?"

I handed him the letter. "I'm taking no chances. Go find one of those places with a fax machine and fax this letter and Jack's file to my lawyer. The number's on it. I've asked him to use the file as leverage to block the warrant and set up a meeting with Michelson and a judge first thing Monday morning. I'll surrender and give them the originals."

He scanned it quickly, nodding. "That's it?"

"For now." I felt dreamy and unreal. I wanted to stretch out on the couch and get to sleep. But I couldn't.

"Is it easy to kill, Morty?"

"Depends," he said, "on what's in it for you."

My tea was cold in my cup. I pushed myself off the couch and grabbed my jacket.

"You going back home?" he asked.

"Not yet," I said.

"Why?"

"Gotta see a man about a head, first."

"Yours?"

I nodded.

"I got some business to do outside. Take your key."

"I put it back in the jar."

He went and got it. "You sure you're all right?"

I shrugged.

"Is this about Cee and last night?"

"Partly."

He exploded. "Don't talk so much, Phillie, it gets on my nerves."

I understood his frustration. He was worried about me, and he couldn't get through to me or help me. All our lives I was the one who was supposed to have a lock on life. I had a talent to let me ride through it. The ability to play it straight and still prosper. He never said so, but I knew he envied me.

"Morty," I said, "I'm enormously fucked up, and I have to go deal with it before I can do anything else."

"So go, who's stopping you?"

I walked over and hugged him. "Thank you for everything you've done for me so far. I know you did it because you love me. I love you, too."

He tasted his tea and made a face. "Too damn sweet for me, you know?"

"Sure."

He tossed me the key. "Let yourself back in, Phillie."

It sounded like good advice all the way around.

2

I took a cab to the Parker Meridien on West Fifty-seventh. I hadn't spoken to Max—actually, Dr. Maximilian Fordham Wagner—in a long time, not since I had gone to him about Carolyn's depression, but he told me to come right over. I was lucky to find him in New York. As I say, Max was probably the smartest man I ever met. He was a psychiatrist, a lawyer, and a mathematician; the world's leading expert on degenerative brain disease. He spent so much time consulting, expert witnessing, and lecturing at universities around the world that he had given up any permanent residence years ago. He just maintained suites at hotels he liked.

The Parker Meridien's atrium lobby was lined with trees. Mirrored walls and two floors of balustrades and columns curved up to a vast skylight. The polished marble floor looked like water flowing over black diamonds. In the lobby a pretty girl was handing out French chocolates, and I sampled one. I heard no slaps or moans anywhere, just the soft tinkle of glasses and silverware coming from the rich dark bar and the click of my heels on the marble, clean and precise.

Max's suite had a name, Tuscany. He met me at the door.

"Phillie, come in. How long has it been?"

"Too long, Max."

"Sit. Relax. Some champagne?"

"Yes, thank you."

I took my jacket off. The suite was decorated in beige and black. Beige carpet and furnishings, black furniture. The living room had a sweeping view of Central Park and most of uptown Manhattan. Streetlamps were going on as night fell across the city. I'd been very near the bottom of Manhattan last night. A day later and a quick elevator ride, I was near the top. What a difference a day makes.

Max pulled a bottle from an ice bucket on a black table and filled two flutes.

"How are you, Phillie? Make any more movies?"

"A few."

"What ever happened to the one we worked on together?"

Max had been the medical adviser on a psychological thriller about a serial killer Jack and I had been signed to rewrite.

"The studio went into bankruptcy. It was never released."

"After all that work? Seems a pity."

"You didn't see the final cut. How about you? Still globe-trotting?"

He sipped his champagne. "More than ever. I just got back from Paris. The APA symposium."

"I'm glad I caught you."

"Lucky you did. I'm not here much anymore. New York's changed. One senses the decay almost everywhere."

There were books all over. Piled on the furniture, lying on shelves, sitting on the dining-room table beside the remains of his dinner.

"I'm heading to Denver next week," Max said. "Interesting case there." He started to tell me about it, saw my lack of interest, and let it go.

He was a portly man with a big chest and a white tonsure of hair who sported suspenders and checked coats. He had the face of a religious supplicant. Soft-featured, smooth and tan, like fine suede. Always freshly shaved and powdered. Then you saw his eyes. He had a hawk's eyes, and his brow furrowed the way a hawk's did when it narrowed on prey. Max was smarter than almost everybody and knew it, but he didn't hold it against us. His great brain was devoted to larger mysteries.

"You look well, Max," I said.

He sat opposite me. "I feel well. I just wish I had more time. So many things to think about. But you don't want to chat, I can see that."

"No."

"What can I do for you, Phillie?"

"I need a shrink." He started to say something, but I held up my hand. "I don't want a recommendation. I want you. For one night. I won't spend years on the couch. Either I figure it out tonight, or I don't."

"Tough terms," he said.

"That's them. Or they."

He thought it over. "In my professional opinion your terms are self-defeating. Which is very likely their purpose."

I'd forgotten how beautiful his voice was. His native Afro-American rhythms blended with the Oxford accent of his university days.

"I don't think so. Do I have a deal or not?"

His lips pursed. "If it's what you want. But let's up the ante, shall we? Fifteen minutes. That's all I'll give you. If you want to do it, then do it, my troubled friend. Get to the heart of it, pin it down. In and out. Anything more would just be persiflage anyway. Willing?"

"Yes."

He settled back and put his fingers on his temples. "Clock's ticking."

I told him everything, concisely. He listened carefully, without speaking. A few nods of his head were all that punctuated my retelling.

"I'm very sorry about Jack," he said when I was finished. "Dying that way, he left a big hole in your life."

I thought about the last week. "Among other things."

"Four minutes gone. Eleven left. Is Jack your problem? Or deviant sex?"

"No. They're symptoms, I think. It's Carolyn. And me."

"Tell me."

"She's deeply unhappy. I don't know why I didn't see it sooner. I mean, I did, so I guess I just ignored it. She's doing what she thinks *I* want, not what she wants."

"How do you know?"

"She's knitting, for God's sake."

"Many women knit."

"Not Carolyn. She's doing it because she thinks she's supposed to. Like loving carpools and cooking and beauty parlors. A fifties TV show."

"Is that your model?"

"I guess, sort of. We always say it as a joke."

"I've studied the brain all my life," Max said. "It doesn't joke. Describe the model."

I thought about it. "Traditional family. Everything works. Problems get solved. Nothing's bigger than the people involved."

"Her depression was bigger."

"Yes, I realize that now."

"Go further," Max said.

I was beginning to sweat. This was hard work.

"The model couldn't handle her kind of problem," I said.

"Right. The model is all acceptance and no complexity. It leaves no way to adapt to new circumstances." He mimicked a helpless woman: "What is one to do?"

I frowned. "You're saying when things got too complex, too hard, there was no way to solve them because of the constraints I put on her, or that she put on herself for me?"

"Very good, Phillie. Eight minutes left. Carolyn had no way to solve her problem within the parameters you established."

"All right. But why did she have to solve it with sex? Why not car racing or skydiving? Why pick the one I can't handle?"

"Go with that," he said.

I let words spill freely. "I can't handle it, so that's the thing she does. Why? To hurt me? To kill me?"

"Did it kill you?"

"In a way. I'm not the same. Neither of us is."

"Ah," he said.

I began to see the vague outlines of it. Realizations seemed poised at the edge of my conscious mind, waiting for me.

"She killed me to free herself," I said.

"Bravo, Phillie." Max tipped his glass to me. "Six minutes left. What about you?"

"What about me?"

"What is *your* nature?"

Have you ever been free, Phillie . . .

"Closed," I said. I didn't know the word was coming out till it did.

"Ah," he said again.

"Ah?"

"Stop it," he said sharply. "What does the closed man want?"

"Not to be so closed, I guess. You think I wanted to break out, too? That I went to the club not so much because I wanted to find out about Jack but because I wanted to get nuts and have bizarre sex? To break out the way she did? And he did? That maybe this is all about me and not about Jack at all? That's crazy," I said flatly.

"Is it?"

"Isn't it?"

His mind slid over solutions as smoothly as a skater on a frozen pond.

"Phillie, Jack's death presented a very complex set of demands. Your psyche used this complexity to fulfill a pressing but unacceptable agenda by linking it to an acceptable one. These are the deepest needs, my friend, make no mistake. The mind may take a circuitous journey to get where it wants, but it will get there in the end."

"Given what I saw in that club, is that a joke?"

"Hmm? Oh, I see. No. Sorry."

I thought it over. I remembered how I felt. So free and wise. So *new*. Now I had guilt with a dash of torment thrown in for good measure. But he was right. I was different.

"Did I want to hurt Carolyn?" I asked.

"Only in very small part, I think. You are not vindictive by nature. If you wanted to hurt her at all, it was probably because you were angry she'd left you behind."

"Because I needed to break out just as much as she did."

"Yes."

"I trapped us both," I said sadly, seeing it.

"And you were very good at it," Max said. "You're strong. And tenacious. Everybody else but you just accepted Jack's death as suicide. Race cars and skydiving, as you suggested, wouldn't have broken you."

"You know, sometimes I get tired of so much understanding. What about something as simple as right and wrong? Justice. Doing what you're supposed to, and being punished if you don't."

"Justice," Max mused, "is a stern concept. You remember what the judge said to the Merchant of Venice when *he* demanded it?"

"No."

" 'Therefore, Jew, if justice be thy plea, consider this, that in the course of justice none of us should see Salvation.' "

"I won't take the Jew part personally, Max."

"It's universal. Justice is a cold thing without mercy."

I sighed. "She asked me why I was so tough on everybody."

He nodded.

"She tried to tell me," I said.

"Probably many times."

"It's about change, isn't it?" I said. "That's why I went to the club. To kill myself into something new." It was quite a thought.

He looked pleased. "Your agility isn't surprising. Emotional accessibility is often the root of talent."

"Gosh," I said.

"Don't be facetious. Just a few steps more. Work at it now. Three minutes left."

The park was glowing in the night. Beautiful and dangerous. Not the park of my youth. A different park. Things changed. Had *I* wanted to all along?

I said, "I can change my life if I want to, and not die."

Max clapped his hands delightedly. "Well done, Phillie." He

got up and poured us more wine. He was in good spirits. "You've given me quite an enjoyable night. Remarkable, really. We may have invented a whole new approach to therapy."

"Evelyn Wood Speedshrinking."

Max laughed, but then grew serious. "Listen to me. Here is a gift. I will put it together for you because you are one of the few people with the capacity to hear it all and use it. Take a stiff drink."

I did.

Max leaned forward in his chair. "You and Carolyn needed to reinvent yourselves. To be reborn. To change your lives. But couldn't. You killed yourselves, or killed each other, it's the same thing really, to be free. That must be your central understanding."

I nodded.

"What's next is up to you both. You can wallow in collective guilt, blaming each other and yourselves till you break apart. Or you can understand what your psyches drove you to do and grab the opportunity for a new life with both hands. It takes strong minds to do it. And love. And something equally important."

"Forgiving."

His eyes were bright. "Phillie, you're a joy. Time's up. I salute you."

I was exhausted and drained. It all had a ring of truth. I couldn't deny it. I didn't want to. I felt the first tentative healing of the cracks in my life. It would take a while for it all to sink in, for me to be able to work with Carolyn on it. It was one thing to understand intellectually. Emotions didn't always follow so easily. But it was a beginning.

Max went into the bedroom, came back out smiling.

"In my capacity as your doctor, I prescribe one last thing."

"Whatever you say, Max."

He tossed me a bathing suit. "Let's go swim in the sky."

3

I dove into the hotel's glass-enclosed rooftop swimming pool and let the water buoy me like good news. I felt clean and clear. Max and I were alone but for a young couple whose hands never left each other. Max did an ungainly cannonball into the water. The couple laughed. He made an impression, Max did.

A waiter set up the champagne and caviar Max had ordered. We wrapped ourselves in big fluffy towels and ate in the over-stuffed chairs by the side of the pool.

Truth bothers and changes you. That's how you can tell it's truth.

"Thank you," I said gratefully.

"De nada."

The youngsters watched us enviously from across the pool. Champagne and caviar were beyond their finances. Max saw their look and invited them over. They were delighted. They turned out to be nice kids from Michigan on their honeymoon. They made me feel old but good.

Every hour or so, the hotel turned out all the pool lights for a few minutes, and I had been waiting for it. The kids oohed and aahed, seeing it for the first time. Plunged into absolute darkness, the glass rooftop and windows disappeared, letting Manhattan sparkle all around us. We had a full three-hundred-sixty-degree panoramic view. It was glorious there in the darkness. I was a consciousness alone, without form, free to keep learning, evolving, becoming.

If I survived, I reminded myself. One more day. I was cutting it close, but it couldn't be helped.

We were down to the wire.

THIRTY-EIGHT

1

I stopped into Wolf's deli on Fifty-seventh Street and got some soup and sandwiches to take back to Morty's, and called Carolyn to check on things. If not for telephone credit cards, I'd have had to carry ten pounds of change with all this phoning home. The kids picked up first. I was thrilled to hear their voices.

"Hi, Dad, where are you?" asked Ben.

"Where, Daddy?" Beth echoed on an extension.

"Away on business. I'll be back soon. You guys taking care of Mom?"

"I am, Daddy," Beth assured me.

"I built a trap in my room, Dad," Ben said. His agenda was his own, as usual. "You should see. It's really cool. You walk in, and a big block falls off the door and hits you in the head, and a rope drags you into the closet, where a monster eats you."

"Call Harvard," I said.

"Who's that?"

"Never mind. Could the block hit Beth?"

"Nope," Ben said firmly. "I put up a warning sign."

"Honey, Beth can't read."

"Oh. Yeah."

"Beth, you there?"

"Yep."

"Don't go in Ben's room for a while, okay?"

" 'Kay, Daddy. I made you a flower."

"Keep it for me till I get back?"

"Okay."

"Put Mom on."

"When you coming home, Daddy?"

"Soon, baby. Very soon."

"I miss you."

"I miss you, too."

There was a pause, then Carolyn got on and the extension clicked off.

"Phillie?"

"Hi. The kids sound okay," I said.

"They are. How are you?"

"I'm okay. I think I have most of the answers."

"That's good. I want it to be over."

I heard the fatigue in her voice. She'd been under stress too long. "I should be back tomorrow," I said.

"Is Morty with you?"

"I'm going to his place now."

"It all seems so unreal, Phillie. Us here. You there. I don't know. I'm so tired."

"Put the kids to bed. Lie down, too. Okay?"

"Every sound outside, I jump to the window."

"Can you hold on a little while longer?"

"If I have to. Donnegan was here. It helped to talk to him. He thinks pretty highly of you."

My obligation to Donnegan was growing daily.

"Phillie, he said to tell you if you call, Monday is D-Day. What does that mean?"

"That's when Michelson will ask for an arrest warrant," I said. "But it won't happen. Trust me."

"I do, Phillie."

"I'm glad."

"What are you doing now?" she asked.

"I just got some food. Before that, I went to see Max."

"Your psychiatrist friend?"

"Yes. He helped me. I understand some stuff now I didn't."

"I'm glad, Phillie."

"I'm sorry for a lot of things," I said.

I heard her stifling tears. In the background, muffled, Beth asked her what was the matter, and Carolyn told her nothing was wrong. How dearly I wanted to be there with them.

"We'll talk when I get back," I said.

"I'd like that."

Neither one of us wanted to hang up. We talked for a while about nothing in particular, the kids, the house, summer nights in Rainbow City. Outside, couples were going to dinner and shows. A sea of yellow taxis and red brakelights.

"Carolyn," I said.

"I know. You have to go. Be careful."

"You, too."

I hung up the phone and caught a cab back to Morty's.

2

Morty was reading a racing paper when I got back to the apartment.

"Hi, cuz," I said.

"Phillie." He didn't look up. Two could play at the terse game.

I said, "I brought some sandwiches."

"Good."

"From Wolf's."

"Can't get decent pastrami in the suburbs," he said.

"Ben's is okay."

He made a face and said it couldn't compare to Katz's. For Jews, rating pastrami is second only to the continuing and more global debate on natural grass versus Astroturf.

He studied me. "You look looser."

"I have a better handle on things. I'll be okay."

"Good." I could see he was pleased. I'd restored the balance.

"I owe you," I said. "A lot."

"Fuck that."

"You reading Emily Post again?"

"Miss Manners."

"It's done you a lot of good." I still had my jacket on. "I think I'm gonna go home, Morty."

"It's late. Why don't you stay?"

"I don't think so." On my way over I'd decided it was time to go. Spend Sunday with Carolyn and the kids, circle the wagons, get ready for Monday morning.

I tried to find the right words to tell Morty what I felt, all my gratitude. I'd almost found them when his phone beeped. He answered it, and his face darkened. He hesitated as if he wanted to disconnect the caller, then handed me the phone.

"For you," he said, obviously unhappy. "It's Cee."

3

"Phillie?"

The sound of her voice made my chest tight. I had to take a deep breath.

"Hello, Cee. How are you?" Christ, I sounded fourteen.

"Fine, I guess. It was a nice note."

I felt a stab of guilt at not having had the decency to say good-bye in person. "I'm sorry. I couldn't risk staying. I might not have left."

"Would that have been so bad?"

"Yes."

"Why?"

"I have to go home."

Her laugh was short and bitter. When she spoke again, she sounded tired and sad.

"Forget about us. It wasn't why I called anyway."

"Why did you?"

"I remembered something. About Jack and Fred."

"What?"

"It's complicated, and I can't talk now."

"Cee, it takes the same amount of time to tell me what you want to say as to tell me you don't have the time to say it."

"It's not that." She paused and I heard a rustle of clothing. "I have someone here. We're, er—going out."

"Go into the bedroom."

"Phillie, I'm *in* the bedroom."

I pictured her tied up on the bed. What man was there? Had he used her already? Would he again? Did she want him to? I cut off those questions and the pictures they brought to my mind.

"I have to go," she said.

"Don't," I began, but she kept talking.

"I won't be back till tomorrow night." She told me where to meet her. "Say you'll come."

"I—"

"Good. See you there."

"Cee, damn it, I haven't said—"

"Phillie?"

I sighed. "What?"

"Remember me."

That was all. My heart was pounding. I turned off the phone. I realized my hands were trembling, too.

4

"Well?" Morty said flatly.

I was unsettled. "She wants me to meet her at the Garden tomorrow night. Tonight, actually." It was after midnight.

"I heard that part. Why?"

"She said she has more to tell me about Fred. Something she remembered. She said it was important."

"I don't like it."

"I'm not crazy about it either."

"What's going on there?"

"Some kind of charity all-star exhibition game. She'll leave a ticket for me."

"Why couldn't she tell you now?"

"Because."

"Because why?"

"Forget it," I said.

"Your face is all red. Why?"

I tossed him the phone harder than I meant to. "She had a date with her, that's all. She's leaving, and she won't be back till tomorrow night."

"He wouldn't have waited?"

"Get off it, will you?"

He was surprised. "Jesus, you're *jealous*."

I tried to recapture the calm I'd felt after talking to Max. *Damn* that call.

"You *are*," he insisted.

"Fuck you," I said.

He taunted me using my own tone. "You read that in Emily Post?"

"Fuck you *and* Emily."

"Nice mouth."

Cee had upset my equilibrium. The siren's song was back, calling to me. Watch the night. It was catchy. Was I ever going to be free?

"What are you gonna do?" Morty asked.

"I don't know."

I thought it over, staring at a calendar on the back of Morty's bathroom door. It was from the local liquor store, with the recipes of exotic drinks for every season. Ten minutes ago, I'd wanted to go home—now I felt I had to stay. Was I staying for a real reason, or only to see her again? I had an erection from just the sound of her voice. I tried to sort it out logically. Cee had provided the connection between Fred and the clinic.

This could be just as important. Besides, I'd be safe with all the people around. I knew the Garden extremely well because Jack and I had once been hired by the public relations director to write about it. And I didn't have to be back in Port till Monday morning.

And I had Morty.

"Will you back me up?" I asked him. "One last time?"

"What do you need *me* for?"

I let out a long breath. The moody fuck was going to break my balls until I asked nicely.

"Please."

"It's not my area. You did a whole damn book on the place."

"C'mon, Morty."

He simmered. "Sure, tell me to fuck myself, then ask for help. Lotta fucking manners *you* got. I mean it, Phillie. You hear me?"

I pinched his cheek the way our grandmother used to. "You're so cute when you're angry. Thanks, cuz."

The veins in his neck swelled ominously. "Sometimes I want to hit you *so* bad."

I grinned.

He made a strangled sound, and his fist lashed out. If I ever hit a wall as hard as he did, I'd break my hand.

THIRTY-NINE

1

Morty and I spent most of Sunday in his apartment watching current events shows and eating the soup and sandwiches from Wolf's. It had been almost a week since Jack died. I felt I'd spent a year living it. Around two I called Archie Dickenson in Mineola. He'd gotten my fax. He said he could probably get what I wanted by tomorrow morning if he assured the judge I was going to turn myself in. I told him to offer the judge me, Jack the Ripper, and a criminal to be named later in a package deal if he needed to, but block the damn warrant and get me the meeting.

Donnegan sounded major league worn-out when I telephoned him. I hated to do it, but I asked him to please go over to see Carolyn again today. He said his wife and doctor were both screaming at him to stay in bed. Of the two, he was a lot more scared of his wife, but he'd try. He asked me what I was doing.

I said I was going to a basketball game.

2

It was still warm and light out when Morty and I left his place around seven that night. He'd slipped past the doorman and "checked"—a polite term for breaking into—Cee's apartment twice since she'd called, under the theory that it was safer to catch her there by surprise than in the Garden if anything about the meeting wasn't on the up and up. She'd never come back.

I milled around the Garden alone for a while. If I'd have been smart, I would have walked down to Penn Station and taken the train back to Port and turned myself in. I'd have trusted my smart lawyer to get me off. Instead, I took the escalator up to Madison Square Garden and got the ticket that was waiting for me at the will-call window. Maybe being lucky so far had made me careless. Probably. I never saw it coming.

When I was a kid in the Bronx, the subway got us to the old Garden in twenty minutes. I never forgot the day my father picked me up at school when I was in the second grade and took me to the rodeo there. He never took me to ball games or on trips, but for some reason he decided to take me to the rodeo. I held his hand when we walked and felt very important and loved.

One day can last a lifetime.

A guard I knew passed me through the turnstile early so I could watch the arena fill. The Garden was more complex than a small city, with a devoted staff and a history and secrets all its own. Jack and I had met a lot of the great old characters who were part of the Garden's history when we researched our piece here, former coaches and PR men and the crews who could change the Garden from a national convention to the circus in a few hours and make it look easy. In fact, an exhibition hockey game was scheduled for the next day, so they'd be setting up the ice rink right after the game.

They'd told us some great stories, those old Garden hands. Like the one about the Garden employee and his fiancée who left the game early to retrieve their coats from his office and walked into a dead guy who had been stored there after he expired during the game. Or the night a hockey player needed stitches while the house doctor was playing a winning gin hand. Folks said he was the only man in the world who could stitch, play cards, and smoke a cigar at the same time.

I caught a glimpse of Ewing, Mullen, Jordan, and Magic Johnson, the last one retired but still doing events like these, hanging up their street clothes and changing into uniforms inside the locker room as I went through the players' exit out onto the court. Watching the Garden go from a silent arena to a packed house fascinated me. The technicians came first, paving the way for the reporters and sportscasters. Wires were patched, plugs connected, cable strung, cameras set, lights fixed. T-shirts said NEWS-12 and ESPN. The house lights came up, and I could see the upper tiers for the first time, where the TV studio was. The first few fans trickled in.

TV newscasters stood in front of their videocam operators wearing nice jackets and crummy pants because they were never shot below the waist. Security men and ushers took up positions. The team personnel in business suits came in and stood by the scorer's table. Up in the press room the reporters finished their free buffet dinner and drinks and picked up their laptops. The trickle of fans into the seats became a stream, and there was real noise in the air for the first time.

The players' wives and kids came next, dressed to the max, royalty in leather and gold. Coaches came over to joke with the kids. Photographers squatted on their spots at both ends of the court, rummaging through their equipment bags filled with film and lenses. The official Garden photographer was a gifted man who by long tenure owned the best spot in the house, right under the boards. He was wired directly into the Garden's lights so they'd flash when he shot, too quick for all but the most knowledgeable to notice.

By now, the noise was heading for din level. Fans of twenty or more years made their way to courtside seats and talked this team and that, new notes and past glories. They were so well versed in the sport that reporters asked their opinion during the game. Celebrities got folding chairs on the side line. Spike Lee, Peter Falk, Woody Allen, Robert Klein. Bodyguards stood quietly behind them to intercept anyone yelling, "Yo, Spike!"

The raucous buzzers, well—buzzed. Air horns bleated. In the lobby downstairs the crowd burst the turnstile dam and fast broke into a river that filled the arena. The air was thick with sound and motion and cheers. The players came out to warm up, and suddenly long men were sailing across the boards bouncing balls. Final positions. Cameras. Lights. The scoreboard welcomed us. The organ blasted a song everybody's heard and no one knows the name of. Vendors hawked. Strobes popped. Feet stomped. Music. Horns. Screams. Intros. The Garden reached critical mass, the buzzer sounded, and the game began.

"*Give it up. Seal 'em off! Backdoor. Set the pick! High post. Atta boy! Atta boy! Great shot. Two hands. Two hands! You getting paid by the call, ref? You getting paid on a piecework basis? Is that your real face, ref? Oh . . . Yeah!*"

I was getting edgy. Every seat was filled except the one next to mine. I wondered where Cee was. The crowd kept rising to its feet to cheer. Jordan was putting on a show. Even though he was triple teamed, he'd suddenly accelerate out of the pack and execute a 360 slam. Some people do what they do so much better than anyone else, they raise the level of skill to art. I said as much to the man next to me.

"Yeah," he said, looking at me oddly. "Great fucking shot, too."

Fred Marcus sat down next to me. He was wearing a suit and tie, with a stethoscope folded in his breast pocket.

"Hello, Phillie," he said.

A lot of thoughts went through my mind. The foremost one was the realization that I'd been set up.

"Fred, what are you doing here?"

"Working. I'm the doctor for this event. Sorry to be late, but a guy just slipped on some mustard and broke his arm."

"But I was supposed to meet—"

"Cee. I know that. I'm here instead. We have to talk."

It wasn't time to panic yet. There were twenty thousand people around us, and Morty was somewhere near, although I didn't see him. On the other hand, Fred's calm confidence scared me. I tried to crack it by playing my big gun first. I didn't have any others.

"Whatever you're planning, don't," I warned him. "I have Jack's medical file from the clinic."

"I know that, too."

Maybe I hadn't heard him right. The crowd was screaming because Magic Johnson hit a three pointer. I leaned closer to make myself heard over the noise.

"I said it's over, Fred. I have Jack's medical file. I know you rigged the tests to trick him into killing himself."

He wasn't thrown at all. "Phillie, I was at Jessica's when you phoned her from Cee's. The number registered on that Caller ID box she has, and I tried it later. I knew Cee. I'd met her at the clinic with Jack. Credit me with a little intelligence. When I learned about the problem at the clinic, and the custodian reported the broken jamb on the file room door, it wasn't hard to figure out who was behind it and why. I checked and found Jack's file was missing with the duplicate reports. That was smart, Phillie. It never occurred to me to throw them out."

"You're too late," I said, as tough as I could manage. "I already faxed them to my lawyer. He's giving them to the police."

Fred took that in stride. "They'll ask me about it, for sure. But without the originals they have no case. Even *with* them I bet I can beat it. A new file's already in place, and who knows what lengths you'd go to to clear your name? Even forgery, I suspect. After all, lots of forms are missing. It'll be my file against yours."

Given Michelson's opinion of me, he might well come out on top. I was liking the odds less and less.

"What did you do to Cee to make her call me?" Maybe it

was just my pride, but I didn't think she'd be a willing conspir-
ator.

Fred's smile was brutal. "A friend of mine just gave her a
little bit more of what she already liked. And a little bit harder.
You know all about that, don't you, Phillie? Did you like doing
those things to her? Will you tell your wife?"

"You're a maggot, Fred."

• "And you're a hypocrite."

For all I knew, we were both right. The crowd went to its
feet again, and a sudden ugly thought hit me hard. Morty said
Cee hadn't been home since her phone call to me.

"Where is Cee?"

Fred talked easily, the sound of the crowd insulating us.
"The police find people like her dead all the time, Phillie. You
should see the interesting museum the ME put together. A
whole display case of bondage gear from people who got too
rough. Just like Judy."

I was very cold.

"There's a lot of money at stake, Phillie. You can make
things easier for me if you give me the file. Are you going to be
reasonable?"

I laughed. "Sure."

He said into my ear, "I'll give you five million dollars after
Jessica inherits and we're married. That's better than you
would have done in the original will. You'll be a rich man. No
more worries ever."

Funny, I always thought that kind of money would tempt
me. I mean, whenever I wrote a scene like this where the
money was that big, I figured the guy would at least be con-
flicted. But I wasn't. Not for a second. Five million or fifty
million wouldn't let Fred get away with killing my best friend.
I guess I was a wimp even in the corruption market.

"Well?" he said.

"Get up, Fred. We're going to the police."

Out on the floor Jordan dribbled through the defense as if it
were standing still and drove for the basket. The crowd surged
to its feet again, but this time we didn't. Goes to show you, I
should have had more spirit.

I heard Fred say, "Sorry, Phillie," and I felt a sharp pain in my behind. I managed to get a look around and saw Robbie in the seat behind me wearing a baseball cap and dark glasses pull a hypo back under his jacket like a snake's tongue. I knew I had seconds, maybe less. I surged to my feet—and twenty thousand frenzied people in the stands got up with me as Ewing blocked Jordan's shot, drowning out my cry for help.

Then everything went dark and far away, and all that noise became just a pleasant *whoosh*, like the surf on a moonlit night. Hands steadied me, walked me out.

"The excitement must be too much for him," I heard Robbie say.

I was wondering where the hell Morty was when darkness dropped over my head like a hood.

3

I came to in a swimming pool.

It was nice. I couldn't feel my arms or legs, but why should that matter? It was nighttime. A full moon glowed overhead, and the stars blazed red and inviting. I felt warm and cozy. My head rested comfortably on the bottom. Get me a strawberry daiquiri, waiter, and keep 'em coming. I tried to sidestroke, but my legs couldn't quite get it straight. Fuck it. I floated.

"Raise his head a little," Fred's voice said, followed by a sharp prick on my scalp. What was Fred doing in my pool? I wondered.

"What is that?" I heard Robbie ask the words, but none of it made any real sense. It was a radio talk show. It had nothing to do with me.

"A mixture of alcohol and a cobra venom derivative. It will make him lose heat fast, and he won't be able to do anything about it." I heard the rustle of a sleeve as he checked his watch. "The changeover crew comes back in two hours. He'll be done by then."

"I hate funerals," Robbie said.

I knew that.

"You made sure the guard saw him sleeping it off in my office?" Fred asked.

"He said Phillie smelled like a distillery."

I giggled.

"Why's he laughing?" Robbie demanded.

"He's flying," Fred said.

I felt Fred lean close. "So long, Phillie."

My last impression was that they were walking on water as they splashed away. I wondered how they did that. Didn't matter. There was a song in my head. Merrily, merrily, merrily, merrily. Life is but a dream. I snuggled into the water. I felt fine. Merrily, merrily, merrily, merrily. Everything and nothing. What was important? Nothing. Not Fred or Robbie or Judy or Jack. Freddie-Robbie-Judy-Jack, step-on-a-line-and-break-your-back. I liked the rhythm. Carolyn and Ben and Beth didn't work as well. Carolyn. Ben. Beth. Something there. Had to think. Cee saw, Marjorie Daw. That wasn't it. Poor Cee. Poor lost Cee. And Carolyn. Always Carolyn. Forget it. Keep swimming. But the thought of her persisted, and suddenly it all came together, and the fog lifted, and I knew where I was and what was happening.

I was lying on my back in the ice rink at Madison Square Garden freezing to death.

Reality reoriented itself. It wasn't the moon, just a distant spotlight. Not night, just the darkness of the deserted arena. Not stars. Exit signs. And I wasn't in a pool, I was lying in three inches of water that was slowly being turned into ice by the giant Freezing Room one story below. My head was resting against the bottom of the rink. I had to get out of here before I froze to death. The drugs Fred gave me were hastening the process and keeping me immobile. I tried forcing my limbs to work, without success. I had to keep the water from freezing around me. I started to rock. It was the wrong move. The motion carried me off into dreamland.

Merrily, merrily, merrily, merrily. Life is but a dream. Merrily, merrily, merrily, merrily . . .

I came out of the fog again, felt myself slipping, and tried to hold on but couldn't. Merrily, merrily, merrily, merrily . . .

Carolyn. That was the thought to hold on to. Concentrate, for her. I cursed myself. I had forgotten my cardinal rule: Be afraid of everything, and leave nothing to chance.

I had to get out of here. I forced energy into my limbs. One advantage the drugs seemed to give me was that I didn't feel the cold. I managed to move my fingers. I could move my head a little. I saw Robbie and Fred sitting about ten rows back in the semidarkness, behind the Plexiglas shield they put up to protect the audience from flying pucks. The water was starting to crystallize. I could feel the vibration from the freezing units downstairs through the water in my ears. I wanted to shout, but I had no voice. I wanted to run, but I had no legs. I rocked again, and the water slapped my face with a freezing hand.

Even without the ice, how long could I last in water this cold? Not long, my mind supplied. Poor Phillie, with all the pressure he was under, he got drunk, wandered in here, and fell. They even had witnesses as to my condition. I remembered Donnegan telling me that the medical examiner would screen for drugs of abuse using the vitreous fluid. I pictured needles being stuck into my eyeballs. I wanted to scream. Cobra venom wasn't a drug of abuse. All they'd find was the alcohol, the injection sites cleverly hidden in my hair, as natural a cause as my own damn arrogance in coming here. I had to get going. Metabolize the drugs. I tried working one muscle against another, anything to build heat. I kept slipping in and out of a fog. I knew I had to get out of here soon or not at all. I tried to shiver to build up heat. It must have triggered some nerve reaction, because for the first time I felt cold seeping in, and suddenly I was shaking all over. It galvanized me into greater motion, not too great, I reminded myself, or they would come from the shadows to stop me. The cold was insidious, creeping in like a false friend telling me to relax, not to fight it, the long sleep was a good one. Just take it easy and rest. . . .

Carolyn and Beth and Ben, I concentrated on them. It gave me strength. Time passed. Feeling was returning to my limbs. I could move them an inch or two now. Merrily. Merrily. The drugs and the cold made me want to give up, but I couldn't. I had to get out of here. It was a race against time. I was being frozen into place. Frozen to death.

Then I saw something that gave me heart for the first time. Morty was slipping down from the upper rows, a shadowy wraith.

4

When Morty hadn't shown up, I figured he might not have seen them take me, or he figured I was going with them under my own power, or he hadn't found me in the medical office where Fred and Robbie had probably stored me till the changeover crew put up the rink. I'd put him out of my mind, not wanting even to pray lest it dispose God to my destruction. Till now.

If I cried with relief, the tears would freeze on my face, so I just kept up the struggle while he descended. He was going after Fred and Robbie. It was brave and all, but I wanted to yell, just get Security! No heroes! Didn't you tell me that? Maybe he knew best. I was in no position to argue. I went back to working my muscles. It still felt as though my limbs were detached from my mind, but I thought maybe in a few more minutes I could crawl an inch or two. It felt like progress.

Morty drifted lower. In the semidarkness it looked to me as if Fred was dozing, and Robbie was fiddling with a broken hockey stick. The players throw them down as soon as they crack, and this one must have been left behind. I felt such hatred for them that it was followed by a surge of adrenaline that galvanized me. They were watching me freeze to death, probably impatient it couldn't happen sooner. Cold comes in different varieties, ice being the warmest.

I was shivering so thoroughly now that every part of me was vibrating like one of those magic fingers beds. I succeeded in rolling over. Thank God. Good dog. I did it again, making quietly for the edge. Another roll, and I'd be there. I was quiet as snow, and I kept checking to make sure I hadn't alerted Fred and Robbie. I couldn't feel my feet anymore. The drugs might be wearing off, but the cold was killing me fast.

Morty was close now. Maybe ten rows. I heard no sound from his feet—maybe he'd taken off his shoes. Go on, I urged Morty. Get the bastards. Stick the awl's wicked needle in them. I wanted to see them dead for doing this to me, for making me more afraid. For trying to hurt my wife and kids. I didn't know if Robbie had a Suburban, but he'd certainly had enough military experience to fire a rifle or rig a propane tank to blow. I rolled once more and hit the edge of the rink. The six-inch lip might well have been a mountain. Morty was seven rows away. Five rows. Three.

Nobody paid off on heroics. Morty forgot his own lesson from the streets. Before he could make it all the way, Fred saw him.

"Robbie, behind you!"

Morty had committed himself to the leap, and Fred's yell screwed up his timing. Robbie was fast and strong, I'd seen that at his house. The needle of the awl gleamed in Morty's hand like a bee's stinger, but Robbie swung the broken hockey stick in his hand and caught Morty right across the face. I heard the crack clear across the arena. Morty went down with blood streaming from him. Then Robbie was on him. I heard Morty cry out as the jagged end of the broken hockey stick rose and fell. Then there was silence except for Robbie's heavy breathing and the sound of Fred rushing over. I put everything I had into one last effort and rolled over the lip onto the rubber matted walkway next to the rink.

I had one shot left. I crawled toward the exit with my face on the floor like a plow. I pushed forward five or six times and made twenty of the forty or so feet I needed, but I couldn't get anything more than that into my legs. They were coming back, but too damn slowly. I could hear Fred and Robbie's questions. Who is this guy? They searched him for a wallet. Fat chance. I was glad of it, though. They didn't notice I'd left the ice.

The entire rink area is actually on the fifth floor of the building, surrounded by a vast rotunda that holds all the animals and a lunch wagon and even a small hospital when the circus is in town, or endless security when the pope or some dignitary comes in. You can reach it by car directly from the street through a special entrance that leads to a ramp. You can stack a basketball floor inside the rotunda or run a bicycle race because it's nearly a mile around. But during hockey games they store other things there, and it was for one of them that I was headed. I crept my snaillike way toward the corner exit, a curtained portal fifteen feet high and wide, a mere ten feet away and down a few metal stairs. Unfortunately, like my fellow snail I was leaving a slimy wet trail anyone could follow. As soon as Fred and Robbie were done with Morty, they were going to be all over me.

I got to the stairs and couldn't quite navigate them, so I rolled down and hit the concrete floor hard. I waited for the world to stop spinning and took aim for the exit, five feet away, sliding across the painted concrete. I waddled like a seal on my hands and knees the last few feet and slid past the curtain into the rotunda.

Mecca. What I sought stood before me like a shiny mountain. Huge. Formidable. My hands slid over the polished surface. I got one hand up on the rim and pulled. I lost my grip and fell back to the floor, but I got up and felt for the rim again. I pulled myself up and made it into the seat. My head was spinning. I was terrified. By now, Fred and Robbie must have noticed I was gone. They'd be coming soon. I had to time things just right because this mountain had no speed. I had to get them both with it, and there was only one time I figured I could—when they came through the exit following the trail I'd left. My hand hovered over the ignition switch of the Garden's giant Zamboni ice machine, and I waited, shuddering from the cold and exhaustion, fueled by hate, ready to kill.

A lot of thoughts came fast and hard. How the PR people had let me drive this gleaming monster one brief time over the ice that it smoothed out at every hockey game or IceCapades or whatever else chewed up an ice rink. It needed no key, it was unlikely anyone would ever try and joyride it or use it for a murder weapon. You just hit a switch, and its Volkswagen en-

gine turned over. It was a gleaming ten-ton stainless-steel be-
hemoth, and I thought of the big hand it always got when it
came out to spray a film of hot water on the ice, which refroze
in a perfect sheet immediately behind it. I thought of my wife
and kids, too, and how I should have said I was sorry to Carolyn sooner and loved her more and better. Blood was running
down the front of my sopping wet shirt, and I realized my
chattering teeth were probably chewing my lips to shreds. I
heard voices. I waited. Not too soon, or they'd hear me. My
finger hovered over the start button, shaking like a leaf.

I heard them coming, their steps slow but not cautious.
What could a drunken frozen hophead do to them, anyway?

"Phillie?" It was Fred's voice. "Come on back. We can talk."

I still couldn't speak. Didn't matter. For once in my life I
had nothing to say. I focused on the patch of light at the base
of the curtain. The air chilled me so deeply, I almost blacked
out. I worried that if they didn't come soon, I might not have
enough strength to push the button and steer the thing. I
locked my hand around the steering wheel and bent the fingers
down with my chin. I used my chest for leverage.

"C'mon out, Phillie," Robbie's voice said sweetly, "or I go
back and shove this stake through the other guy's eye."

Sudden weakness hit me, and I almost fell off the Zamboni.

"Phillie, don't you doubt I'll do it."

Shadows crossed the lighted patch on the floor by the exit,
and I stabbed at the ON button. I missed. My hands were
shaking so much, I couldn't aim. I tried again and missed, so I
slammed my wrist against it and felt something crack, but this
time the engine started with a throbbing roar. I slammed it
into gear, and it lunged forward just as Robbie and Fred came
through the curtain.

I hit the big front lights and held on for dear life as the
Zamboni rumbled forward quicker than I expected or remembered. For a second they were framed in the exit. Robbie was
holding the wicked shaft of wood. Fred was behind him.
Blinded by the lights, Robbie raised the stick in defense, and
the big machine drove it right back into his chest and shoved
him aside with its chrome bumper. The Zamboni and I

plunged through the doorway. Fred turned and ran, and maybe it was ironic that the very ice he had meant to kill me with was his undoing, but I didn't have time to think irony. I steered right for him, using my chest to guide my lifeless hands, and when he slipped and went down I drove the Zamboni right up the metal stairs and over him. He screamed, "Nooo!!!" and I heard a wet popping sound that would stay with me always.

I tried to stop the Zamboni, but it was on a rampage. It had its first taste of killing, and like any hungry animal it wasn't about to turn back. I didn't have the strength to yank the gear lever. We rode over the metal stands, scattering folding chairs, and crashed through the rink wall. The Plexiglas shattered, spraying all over me. We skidded sideways on the ice and crashed into the far wall, splintering it, too. With nothing else to kill, the machine gave out with a howl and stopped in a throbbing idle, muttering how it could have gotten more.

Garden Security had heard the racket. Lights came on. Guards appeared at the floor entrances and ran toward us. I pried my hands off the steering wheel and dropped down clumsily. Steaming water was leaking from the Zamboni. I slid on the ice, climbed up the stairs, and found Morty, who had saved my life by risking his. He was lying under the seats, bleeding. I let them help me get him out and knelt over him. A six-inch splinter of wood stuck out of his side, and his blood was dripping down to the next row like a spilled Coke. I put my hand on his chest but I couldn't feel anything, and I wanted to cry till I realized my hands wouldn't have felt sandpaper, the shape they were in. I put my head against his chest. I heard it then, a heartbeat, fluttery, but still there.

"Hospital," I managed to croak. "Quick."

"Sure. Okay," said a florid-faced Irish guard. "We'll get an ambulance quick. But who the hell are you?"

It was a while before I could tell them.

FORTY

1

They said I had frostbite in my fingers and toes, and a fractured wrist, which was why I got the cast. My feet and hands were bandaged, my chest strapped when the X-rays showed several ribs were cracked. A nurse confirmed I'd be breathing without pain in less than a century. The rest was ugly but superficial. Morty wasn't as good. The hockey stick had punctured his spleen. They'd operated, and he'd be okay in time, but he had a way to go. When I visited him, his face looked like it had been used as a backboard. He'd need reconstructive surgery. He told me he wanted to be handsome.

I told him he was beautiful.

He didn't speak for a while behind his bandages, and I thought he was asleep. Then he said very quietly:

"I let you down. I'm sorry."

"You didn't," I objected.

"If not for you, Phillie—"

"They're dead, we're not. Nothing else counts, right?"

He looked at me admiringly. "Right."

"Want some water?"

"Okay."

I got the cup and held the straw to his lips.

"What about Cee?" he asked.

I shook my head.

"I'm sorry."

I still didn't know what to feel about that, so I left it alone for now.

"The doctors say you're going to be fine, Morty."

"I can't stay here that long. I gotta get out. Do business. Although," he said, glancing thoughtfully in the direction of the nurses' station, "I wonder if they take calls."

I grinned. "In a week everybody here will be working for you."

"Wanna hear what happened?"

"If you want to tell me."

He looked positively shamefaced. "I got to the Garden on time and went right to the scalper I use—I mean, I knew the game would be a sellout, and can you believe it? I got arrested. After all I do in my life, I get arrested for buying scalped tickets." I could tell it really embarrassed him.

"It took so damn long that by the time they issued me an appearance ticket, the game was letting out. I tried to pick you up outside, but that's impossible with all those exits. Then I got the bright idea that if it was a setup, it was probably Fred behind it, so I called his service, and the number they gave me confirmed he *was* at the Garden, and in fact he was still inside."

"Why would they give *you* his number?"

"They didn't." It was his turn to sound clever. "I had the waitress who leases my phone for me call. She said she was the doc's girlfriend and she'd been waiting for him for an hour, he was supposed to meet her. She had to call *him* because she was at one of those pay phones that don't receive calls, only make them."

He told me it had taken him the rest of the time to sneak back in. Security kept pressing him to tell them how he did.

I said, "You jimmied the lock on the street entrance to the rotunda and came up the ramp."

The part of his face that could, smiled. "Have a good trip back, Phillie. I owe you."

"I'd say we're even."

The Manhattan police had questioned me for several hours, more than a little disturbed I had mashed two people with the Garden's Zamboni machine and not the least bit happy with my story even though Morty corroborated it. Finally a flurry of calls from here to Nassau, including my getting Donnegan to reach out to his city brethren; a conference call with my lawyer, the judge, a Manhattan ADA, Michelson, and me; and my lawyer's faxing Jack's medical file to everybody concerned, resulted in the arrest warrant not being issued, which cleared the way for me to return to Port under my own power.

I called Carolyn from Morty's room and told her it was over. I said I'd been hurt a little but not to worry. I was coming home on the 6:15 train like a normal person. For a change.

A social worker came in with a bunch of forms for Morty to sign. I left when she started having apoplexy over a grown man who didn't have a social security number for record pulling, or any other numbers for that matter. He winked his good eye at me.

I said, "Take care, cuz."

2

I should have taken a cab back to the suburbs because I was a mess, but for some reason it felt important to finish it the way I started. People stared at me when I got on the train tattered and bandaged. The cast was heavy. My wrist hurt. I had a whole seat to myself, even in rush hour.

A lot of things passed through my mind as the train ran from the city. I realized Carolyn had been right from the start

—my heart had grown hard. It wasn't just me, though. There was an epidemic of heart-hardening. The symptoms were easy to spot. Faces immune to suffering. Angry letters in small-town papers. Handgun permits soaring. We accepted anything happening to anybody as long as it didn't happen to us. We expected terror. Most of our conversations were variations on one theme: how disappointed we were in people.

Sitting on that evening rush hour train I felt real pain for us —and deep compassion—because I remembered a time when our hearts were not hard, when we loved if not wisely at least much, and when suggesting we care about one another wasn't greeted by the cynical curl of lip and the thought that the other person was out of touch with reality. See, I remembered when even reality was up for grabs.

Carolyn was waiting for me at the station. Our tears mingled as we threw our arms around each other and embraced.

"Oh, Phillie. Thank God."

"It's all right. I'm back. It's okay."

For a long time we just held each other. My defenses fell away. My chest unclenched. I had come back to life.

"I love you," I said.

"Me, too." She wiped her eyes. "You're hurt worse than you said."

"I'll heal."

"Let me take you home."

"First let's find someplace quiet and talk. We won't be able to with the kids and all. Who's with them?"

"Donnegan."

"Is he ready for Ben?"

She smiled. "He says Ben is just like you."

"Poor Ben. How's Donnegan doing?"

"A lot better. He came over to tell me you were okay. Is it really true?"

"Yes. It's all over."

We drove to a quiet little pub. Over a glass of wine I told her what had happened in the city. How Fred had tricked Jack into suicide, which made it murder. About Morty and the clinic and the Garden. And about Cee.

She listened to it all. Shadows crossed her face, but they were fleeting, the way clouds cross the sun.

"You needed her," she said. "I guess deep down I understand. It was the same way with me."

"I know that now."

"It still hurts, though," she said.

"*You* know that now."

She nodded. "I'm sorry for that."

"How come," I said, "we only seem to learn from things that hurt?"

"If getting burned was fun, everybody'd want to do it."

"Can we get past this?" I asked her.

"You know, it's funny," Carolyn said. "I thought if we ever got back together, we'd be starting brand new. Sell the house, move to Iowa, start farming or something. And I suppose we can if we want to. But it's more like letting these past months drop away. Being what we used to be. Loving. Trusting. Devoted to each other's welfare. We were sick, but we got better. We don't have to keep the waste material."

"You don't hate me?" I asked.

One of those shadows crossed her face. "I do, a little. It's something I'm going to have to live with. Find a place for. I guess I can. What about you?"

"I've had more time with it than you," I said. "I'll still be a little weird for a while, but at least I know that what happened with you and Jack had nothing to do with me."

"The farther away we get, it's almost like a dream. Fading. Was it really me?"

"Yes," I said. "And no. Either way, it's over."

"Thank you for that, Phillie."

I said, "Let's go home."

3

I was grateful to see my house when we pulled up. Jessica's car was in our driveway. Maybe she'd come over to give me two million dollars. Probably not. I wondered when I'd get over *that* loss.

Carolyn and I walked in, and the lights went out. Not the electric ones, the ones in my head from whatever hit it. I came to lying on the living-room floor. Donnegan was slumped over in a chair with his hands cuffed. Carolyn was sitting next to Jessica on the couch, anxiously holding Beth and Ben. Jessica was holding a nine-millimeter automatic.

"Hello, Phillie," Jessica said. "The last act. Sit, won't you?"

What the hell was going on? Carolyn had a nasty red welt on her cheek, and the kids looked scared. My head hurt like hell. Jess looked beautiful as always. She was wearing a tight black dress with stockings and heels. Her face was perfectly made up. The sunlight from the big picture window made her hair shine. A million things went through my mind. None of this made any sense.

I made my voice neutral. "Hi, kids. Daddy's home."

In chorus: "Hi, Dad."

I saw my .22 on the couch, on the other side of Jessica. Carolyn followed my gaze. "She knew we had it. I had to get it, or . . ." She held the kids tighter.

"It's okay." Sure Jessica knew. As with most everything, Jack and I had gotten our target licenses and guns at the same time. "What happened to your face?"

"She hit me."

"Silly bitch wouldn't listen," Jessica said sharply. "You should train her better. The brats, too."

"Daddy?" said Ben weakly. He tried to come to me, but Jessica shoved the gun roughly into Carolyn's side.

"Hold on to him, damn it."

"Jess, he's your godchild!"

"Jack's, really. I hate the little bastards personally."

"Easy now, Mrs. Murphy. We can work this out." Donnegan had come to. Blood glistened on his scalp.

"Shut up," Jessica snapped. She turned back to me. "Your police friend here was kind enough to call to tell me that Jack wasn't listed as suicide anymore. He thought I'd be glad to hear it—good old Jack back in a state of grace. Jesus. He told me about Fred and Robbie, too."

"Nice work," I said to Donnegan.

He shrugged.

Jessica said, "You have to pay for it, Phillie."

"Does it matter they were trying to kill me, Jess?"

"What did you expect? Asking all those questions. Poking around. Poking around." She made a jabbing motion like the Wicked Witch. "I wanted you to be one of us. You turned me down cold. Too damn straight for your own good. Even Jack knew it."

"What are you going to do?"

"What would you do if I killed *your* family?" Her face got less pretty. "I don't forgive either, Phillie."

Her family? Christ, I'd missed it completely. Events suddenly realigned themselves in my mind. I'd made a basic mistake, the mistake of my life. I'd disliked Fred so much, I'd been predisposed to believe he was the one who planned it all from the start. I had his motive—money—and I'd even found his murder weapon. But Fred hadn't been in charge. I should have realized he wasn't the leader type. He was brutal but not corrupt enough. Not for a scheme like this. It had to be someone evil enough to torture Judy and—it hit me hard—Cee to death, or depraved enough to try to seduce me the morning after her husband died, or maybe even cut the heads off a bunch of cats in some weird occult ritual back all those years ago. Someone ruthless enough to use Fred and Robbie and Judy and anyone else to get what she wanted.

"You fooled me completely, Jess. All these years. Jack, too, I'll bet."

Her laugh was scornful. "Jack! He thought he was getting a perfect little Catholic wife who'd stay home and tend to the house while he ran around and did whatever the hell he wanted."

"When did he find out otherwise?"

This time her laugh was cruel. "When he accidentally taped me. He had a fit. All those lovely things. The ultimate truth.

He tried to make me stop. He should have *worshiped* me like the others."

The tape. There it was again. I'd forgotten about the tape. The last piece. Insurance, Judy had said. Right under their noses. C'mon, Phillie, think. I knew Jack had taped Todd and Samantha, but Jessica was saying he taped *her*. The ultimate truth. Where had I heard that phrase before?

"You're a Top?" I asked. "The head Domme?"

She looked at me condescendingly. "Those are children's games, Phillie. I'm much more."

"Do you have one of those silly names like Baroness Banana? Why can't you people just call yourselves Jill or Flo or Bruce or something?"

It stung her, but she knew what I was up to. She was too smart to let me distract her and give Donnegan room to move. She never forgot he was the one to worry about, even cuffed. Her eyes tracked him no matter what I said.

"You don't understand ritual, Phillie. Most men don't, even though they invented it."

I glanced at the fireplace. The irons were too far away to do me any good.

Donnegan spoke up. "Mrs. Murphy, what do you think you're going to do with all of us? You kill a cop, it won't be forgotten."

Jessica smiled that beautiful seductive smile of hers. Now it was easy to see the corruption behind it. It must have always been there. How profound Jack's shock must have been when he discovered it.

"Actually, Detective, your being here makes what I have in mind work. We all know Carolyn slept with Jack. Nobody will think it couldn't happen twice. Phillie came home and found his slut wife in bed with you, so he burned the house down with everybody in it. There's already one fire on record."

"What about me?" I asked.

"Mentally unbalanced. You shot yourself."

Well, she had the first part right.

"Daddy?" Beth sounded very small.

"Shh, precious. Everything will be okay," I said.

" 'Kay, Daddy."

Ben blurted out, "Aunty Jess, are you mad at us?"

Carolyn held him tighter. "Don't bother Aunt Jess now, honey. She's just mad."

I coughed.

Donnegan said, "No one will believe it happened that way."

"We'll have to see about that, won't we?"

I was scared. Her confidence wasn't so misplaced. She'd already gotten away with murder. If she pulled it off, my friend Michelson might be happy to believe she'd been right all along, that I really *was* guilty. I was desperate to figure a way out of this. Carolyn caught my eye as if she wanted to tell me something but I didn't know what.

Jess put a hand on Beth's shoulder. I said quickly, "Even the money doesn't make it all fit. There has to be more. Was it to pay him back for all his running around?"

"You're the smart half of the team, Phillie, but you don't know anything at all. Jack wouldn't do the things I wanted. Wouldn't let me do them either. The hypocrite! Deep down he was no different from the nuns I hated. He left me no choice." She smiled that evil smile again. "It became a kind of contest. Jack trying to make me pure. Me wanting to corrupt him. Such beautiful symmetry. It was easy to figure out what to do. I knew Robbie's tastes as far back as high school. Fred knew Judy. I made them into a Family and set them onto Jack. You know what he was like. All they had to do was show him the way."

"But there was still the tape."

"A damn stupid accident. I told Judy to get it back."

"I know what she must have said," I told her. "She wouldn't, right? She and Jack were in love by then, and she knew enough not to trust you anymore. So you had to back off. They probably thought it was all over and they could be together. They underestimated your cleverness. You didn't retreat, you attacked instead."

She nodded, caught up in spite of herself. I was a good storyteller, and I was telling her story.

"It makes sense when you look at it from your perspective," I said. "You killed Jack because he threatened to expose you. You killed him the *way* you did for the money. Then you went after Judy for the tape, no holds barred this time. *You* tortured her, Jess. But it got out of hand. Her heart failed. It's what they call bad work."

"The bitch kept lying to me. I got angry and, well . . ." She realized she was talking too much and stopped.

"You tortured Cee, too, so she'd get me to the Garden for Fred." By the look on her face, I saw I was right. "But there's still the tape," I went on. "Jack made it, I don't know how. It showed him the truth. The ultimate truth. That's what's on it, right? It's not S&M. It's death."

Her face contorted into raw despising fury. I had never seen such hatred before, and I hope this side of hell I never will again. Just as suddenly, it subsided, covered by her beauty. She touched a sharp red nail to her lip. It reminded me of a cat.

"To each his own, eh, Phillie?"

There wasn't a trace of guilt or remorse. I was willing to bet she'd sent Robbie to rifle my office that day to see if Jack had hidden the tape there.

Jessica looked genuinely pleased. "Phillie, I always said you had all the talent."

I took a deep breath. "I know where the tape is."

"You're lying."

"Judy told me before she died. I lied to you when I said she didn't. I never had a chance to get it. I wish I had. Then I'd have known all about you."

She was watching me closely. I desperately needed her to believe me. "Where is it?" she demanded.

"In a place where it will be found eventually. Then they'll come for you, Jess. You're this close to seventy million dollars. Fred and Robbie took the fall for Jack and Judy. All that's left is the tape. Do you want to live the rest of your life wondering when the ax is going to fall? Can you handle that?"

Her eyes narrowed. "What do you want?"

"My family. The police can't do a damn thing once the

tape's destroyed. It's our word against Donnegan's. This afternoon never happened."

The rage in her eyes was terrifying. I didn't know whether or not I had her. It was a dangerous time. Carolyn wouldn't let her kids go without a struggle. Donnegan was looking for an opening. We were fast reaching critical mass.

Jessica grabbed Beth hard enough to make her cry out. "I'll kill her unless you tell me."

Carolyn clutched Beth and cried out, "No!"

Jessica cocked the gun. "Phillie?"

They held my daughter between them. I was surprised how steady my voice sounded in the great and roaring silence between us.

"I'm all or nothing, Jess. You said so yourself. You pull that trigger, you better keep pulling it."

She tried to read my face. "Most people would fold, but you . . . I don't know. You never stop, do you?"

"Time to find out. Do we have a deal?"

"Get the tape, Phillie," Jessica said, "or they die. You've got one hour."

4

I jumped into the Miata and roared out of the driveway. It was hard to handle the wheel with the cast on, and shifting hurt my bandaged hand, but I barely noticed. It was eight-fifteen.

I couldn't call the police. Jessica was insane. If it ended up in a hostage situation, I had no doubt she'd shoot the kids. This had to be played a lot closer. I'd staked our lives on a bet that I actually knew where the tape was.

I didn't.

What I knew was where I had seen the crescent-shaped marks before. Marcia's sculpture chisels put me on the right track. The mark wasn't a moon or even a design. It was a signature. Charles Cornwall's, the man who, two hundred years ago, had made the tools hanging in Jack's playroom, including a pair of blacksmith's tongs complete with his initials.

He signed his work with two C's so close together, they looked like a crescent. Jessica had burned Judy with those tongs, leaving the marks. The splinters in Judy's back and behind were from the barn siding.

It was eight-thirty when I got to Jack's. It was getting dark. The door was locked, so I threw a potted plant through a window and crawled in, racing to the alarm and punching in the on-off code before it summoned the police. The room downstairs had the same musty smell. I searched the closet. Nothing. I pulled tools off the wall and checked for hidden compartments. I pulled back the rug and yanked the furniture aside. I was just about to start ripping the boards off the wall when it hit me.

The musty smell.

I got on a chair and peered into the air duct. A black videotape case was lodged about a foot or so in, blocking the shaft. It was why the room was musty despite my opening the louvers. The grate came out of the siding easily. I pulled out the tape case. Somebody had painted the letter J on it with red nail polish. It looked like blood. I ran into the projection room.

It was eight-fifty.

I ran the tape at high speed. First I saw Todd and Samantha, which still confused me, till I saw the rest of it. It explained everything. In high-speed search mode, Jessica and a leatherbound boy came into the bedroom a compressed hour or so after Todd and Samantha left. Jack had set his camera to capture one couple and had accidentally gotten two. Things were blurry at high speed, just as well, but I knew murder when I saw it.

It was nine o'clock.

One last thing, and I was back in the car. I sent gravel spraying. Fifteen minutes left. I screeched around the corners of Bluff Point and raced across town, barely slowing at stop signs. There was a traffic jam in front of the shopping center, and I sped into the parking lot to avoid it, narrowly missing a woman. I skidded out the other end, caught the light at the intersection, and sped through it in second gear with the engine screaming.

Nine-ten. Five minutes left. The tape and its case were on the seat next to me. Jessica was crazy enough to hurt them if I was late. A gasoline truck was heading for the last light before my turn. I passed it on the shoulder. It was a stupid thing to do, but my kids were on the line and I wasn't stopping for anything. The driver blasted his big air horn. I downshifted into third and roared past him.

Nine-fifteen.

I roared up the street and fishtailed into my driveway and leaped out with the tape and the case. The front door was unlocked. I went in low and fast, hoping to catch her by surprise, but she was way ahead of me.

"Stop there, Phillie."

Jessica was standing by the fireplace holding Ben against her. Her gun was pressed to his head. Carolyn and Beth were on the couch. Donnegan was still in the chair.

"Strip," she ordered me.

"What?"

"You heard me."

"Jess, I got it. Look." I held up the tape and the case with the red J.

"You could have brought other things. Do it."

I took off my clothes. Socks and shoes, too. Naked, most of me was black and blue. Carolyn winced when she saw the bandages around my ribs.

"Fred and Robbie did that?" Jessica asked.

"Yes."

"Good," she said. "Now put your arm on the table."

"What for, Jess?"

She pulled Ben closer. I did it.

"Not that one. The one with the cast."

I started to sweat. "Please, Jess."

She picked up a poker and brought it down on my arm hard enough to break the plaster and the bones underneath, except that the blow was deflected by the iron spike I had shoved in there to kill her with. As it was, I almost passed out.

She looked triumphant. "You can't fool me. No man can."

Ben yelled, "Stop hurting him!"

"Shut up," Jessica said sharply.

Beth cried out, "Daddy!" Carolyn held her back.

"I gotta sit, Jess." I was going to faint.

"Give me the tape."

A black pit yawned before me. There were limits. Carolyn's eyes were pleading. I wanted to tell her I'd tried, I just didn't have anything else to give.

"Daddy," Beth said. "Mommy niddy."

For a few seconds it was just words. Then I suddenly realized what Carolyn had been trying to tell me. I fought the blackness, the cold sweat, the shakes. I held on. My vision cleared. Jessica and Ben were still in front of me. Carolyn and Beth were behind them, still on the couch.

"Give me the tape, Phillie."

Instead, I slid it into the VCR, hit the power button, and pushed the volume to max. The wide-screen TV was wired to my stereo speakers. Screams blasted through the room, and the screen was suddenly filled with a naked, bloody Jessica riding her victim. It was too shocking, too powerful. Like seeing God. For a split second Jessica was transfixed. The gun moved away from Ben.

Jessica's rage had frightened me, but it was nothing compared to Carolyn's snarling fury as she sprang off the couch clutching her knitting needles like daggers and drove them into Jessica's back with such force that one broke in half. Jessica stood bolt upright, and her face contorted with shock and pain. I knocked Ben away just as Jessica's gun went off. The roar was deafening.

Hellish sounds and images from the tape filled the living room. Carolyn ran the kids out the front door. Jessica clawed at her back to dislodge the needles. I lowered my shoulder and drove into her. The gun flew out of her hand, and we hit the couch so hard, it flipped over and I landed on top of her. My good hand found her throat. The tape was still screaming bloody murder. Fear washed out of my bowels and tightened my fingers. I wanted her to die. I wanted to kill her. Everything

I'd been through, all the killing, it was all because of her. She had enough strength to get her hand around my wrist, then that too faded.

She lay still.

Fighting the black rage that darkened my vision, I let go.

I crawled out from behind the couch. Donnegan was on one knee with Jessica's gun in his cuffed hands. When he saw me, he lowered it. I put it on the mantel and helped him up.

He turned off the TV. Blessed silence.

"Key's on the table," he said.

I unlocked the cuffs. I was wavering again.

"Hold on, Phillie. I'll have an ambulance here in five minutes. I didn't think—"

His eyes widened, and he shoved me down and leaped aside at the same moment a gun went off behind me. Carolyn's gun. It must have fallen behind the couch when we did. The shot missed Donnegan, but he crashed into the wall hard enough to stun him.

"Phillie . . ." A growl from Jessica's torn throat as she crawled out from behind the couch. "Die now . . ."

The tape case was on the floor between us, and I dove for it. Jack's antique derringer fell into my hand. I didn't know if I'd loaded it right back at his house—Jack had only showed me once—but I shoved it at her and pulled the trigger at the same time she did. The explosion was the loudest thing I'd ever heard. There was a blinding flash and billowing black smoke. Jessica screamed. Something hot scored my thigh, and I pitched forward, unable to see a thing. It didn't matter. I had nothing left. I waited for her to sever my ties to the world, as naked as the day I'd come into it. My hand hurt a lot. The bandages were burning from the derringer. I smothered the flames on the carpet and turned on my side.

Jessica was lying there without a face.

5

It was late by the time all the crime scene vans left. I was propped up by pain-killers and relief. The EMTs wanted to take me to the hospital, but I said no, I was staying home. Carolyn and I had held the kids for a long time, comforting and talking to them, loving them. Donnegan had read Beth stories and gotten Ben one of those little badges cops give to family members. The kids were remarkably resilient, and a lot of what happened had gone over their heads, anyway. Both of them were asleep in their rooms now. We'd have a long talk in our private spot on the staircase landing tomorrow. Maybe we'd go to a counselor if there were any lasting effects, but I thought it would be okay. Villains had come at our house and family, but we were all still standing.

Donnegan was the last to go. A police car was waiting to take him home. We walked him out.

He shook his head ruefully. "I dunno. Zamboni machines, antique derringers, knitting needles. You guys make it interesting."

"I'm going to send you the sweater when it's finished," Carolyn said. "For everything you did."

"It'll be one of a kind," I assured him.

He smiled. "I'll treasure it."

I said, "Thanks, Donnegan."

"I didn't do much, really."

"You believed."

He looked at us with real admiration. "The city cops said they don't know how you did what you did, Phillie, being in that shape and all. And I never saw anything like you with those knitting needles, Carolyn."

Carolyn shrugged. "She had my kids."

"Lucky she isn't still canning," I said. "Would've been peaches all over."

That should have been all, but I saw it wasn't. Donnegan hesitated.

"Phillie, I was thinking. I got some ideas from being on the force and all for a long time. Maybe we could talk?"

"Sure. Call me tomorrow. As partners go, I guess I have an opening."

"Okay. Thanks." He said it brightly, like we had found something. Maybe we had.

Carolyn and I went inside. We checked on the kids again. They were fine. She moved around the kitchen, straightening. I made us some food. She took out the garbage.

Small things, that maybe weren't so small at all.

FORTY-ONE

I went up to my office. The computer asked me for the password when I tried to open the PHILLIE file. I figured I knew it now. Jack's last advice to me and, I expect, a plea to the God he was about to be judged by.

M E R C Y.

The safe word opened the file, and I read it all, the end a few times. It helped me understand.

> . . . Judy was mad I erased the first tape without showing her, so when Todd asked me for the house again, I made another. It went just like the first time. Later, I watched Todd and Samantha come into my bedroom and bend each other into love knots. When there was no more to watch, I went to take a shower. When I came back, I saw I'd stupidly left the tape play-

ing. The image of my bed was still on the TV screen, neat and remade. I was about to shut it off when somebody came in. On the screen, I mean. I had set my camcorder for one tryst and gotten two. Jess was supposed to have been in the city that night, but here she was walking in with a teenage boy. He was naked except for a leather hood over his head with a zipper across the mouth that looked like another set of teeth. Jessica—my God, she had on a black corset that left her breasts bare, black stockings, stiletto heels, and studded leather wristbands. She was bare from belly to thigh. I couldn't believe it was my wife. And before you call me a hypocrite, you think I'm the only man ever had a double standard—good for me, bad for her? Spare me your Jewish logic, Phillie. I don't need to tear everything apart and examine it from every angle. The rule is clear. Wives are from Mary. Holy. Inviolable.

Jessica put a collar on the boy and cuffed his hands behind his back. You ever hear of a snuff film, Phillie? It's when somebody is killed so others can watch it. Believe me, murder is no part of S&M. It's horrible. Disgusting. I never knew Jessica was into this, I swear it. I won't describe what she did to that boy. It was truly evil.

I couldn't call the police. They would have arrested her for murder. But I had to stop her. I confronted her with the tape. She said she found the boy and others like him by calling a pay phone in the Village. If the conversation went right, she sent a limo. Impressed, the boy became a willing victim. I said I'd give the tape to the cops if she didn't stop. Phillie, it was like I'd never known her, she was so crazy. So wild and ugly. But I was firm. She swore she'd never do it again.

It made me sick. Sick of what I had become, sick of what I was a part of, even by association. I wanted to talk to you about it, but I couldn't. Sex was dragging me down. I was doing too much coke. I was obsessed with Judy. I had lost Jess; I realized she was insane. You were doing most of the work for us, carrying me, and I knew it. Worst of all, I had the weight of that boy's murder on my conscience. I was lost.

That's when Carolyn came to me.

You must listen, Phillie, and try to forgive. You'd think confession would be easy for me. Doing it every week, I should be in practice. But since this involves Carolyn and you, it's different.

Sex can hurt and sex can free. That afternoon, I learned it can heal. Carolyn was so unhappy. I'd hoped maybe our friendship would cure her, but it hadn't. The depression had gone on too long, she said. She needed to find herself again, or life just wasn't worth living anymore. I wasn't so surprised. She was always scared of having kids, of being "fat and ugly," of giving up her career. You were the one who wanted it, Phillie, remember? She went along because she loved you. Now she was reaching out for one last surge of life, for her alone, and you couldn't be part of it. She wasn't going into the deep darkness of insanity without a fight.

But she was your wife.

I used to kid Carolyn that she went to extremes just like you did, only quietly. I was honored she chose me. I could have been anyone, but I think she knew in a funny way that afterward it would never have happened. No stranger would call her with hope in his voice. That was important. I knew if I put up a big fuss, she'd have gone away, yet that seemed so unfair. She'd elected to try for a cure that even all your love and patience had been unable to produce. If I respected her as an individual at all, I had to accept her on those terms.

Did my dick trick me, Phillie? Was it male ego? Did I want her because she was yours? I searched my heart in a way I rarely did. You're the talented one. We both know it. I got in on a pass. You could have done any project of ours alone, and it would have been just as good, maybe better. You never took any money from me even though I offered. So proud. So rule bound. So inflexible. Me? I took the money and ran.

So if I couldn't give you talent or money, at least I could give you this, a slightly used but healthy wife returned to the land of the living. I risked your eternal enmity, but even if you never spoke to me again, your career wouldn't be any worse off.

When it was over, I saw the light was back on her eyes. I needed to see that after what I'd been through with Jess. I took a picture of her without her knowing so I'd remember maybe I had done some good for once. Don't blame her, Phillie. She had to. Bend or you'll break. I know, because when I found out what I'd really done, I had no choice. It's the last part, and the worst.

I tested positive for HIV. It wasn't a mistake. I got a confirming test. Same diagnosis. I'll spare you the gory details, but Fred diagnosed other infections that meant it had already begun to turn into AIDS. Full-blown, highly contagious. It was a death sentence. He said I could start an experimental treatment, but the long and short of it was that I was facing a slow painful death. I'm no guinea pig. I swore him and the other doctor to secrecy, doctor-patient privilege and so on. But even that isn't what's going to make me do it to-night, Phillie. It's Carolyn and you. I had the infection when I was with her. We didn't have safe sex, no-where near, so if I have it, she has it, and that means you may well have it, too. I've killed you both. Con-demned my godkids to grow up orphans. That's what I can't live with. Sex can hurt, and free, and heal, but now we've grown so far from ourselves that it can kill. So I'm going to walk out onto the roof we used to howl from and take a last dive. I'll make it look like an acci-dent to keep my will intact—I'll smear enough grease on my sneakers and the roof to convince the police and the Church I slipped—but I want you to know the truth. I owe you that. No lies at the end. That's why I'm leav-ing the file. I hope the money helps a little in what is to come.

I'm sorry, but I can't be here to face you when it starts for any of us.

Good-bye, Phillie. I loved you more than anyone.
>   Your partner,
>   Jack

The final irony. All of Jessica's planning and even Fred's false positives wouldn't have doomed Jack but for his act of altruism toward my wife. Despondent, unbalanced by drugs and the actions of others, he couldn't see any other way out. Some odd final pieces made sense now. The cleaning fluid smell that night wasn't from the techs. Jessica had come out and wiped off the roof, then cleaned his sneakers and put them away. That's why he was barefoot, and why the closet smelled. In a few days when I had the strength, I'd call Bob Marson and find out how to take up Jack's case with the Church. It wasn't suicide, not legally anyway. It was murder, by despair.

I turned off the computer.

It was quiet and lonely, so I went outside and lay down on the last of summer's lush grass. Rainbow City glistened on the horizon far away. For a long time I watched it sparkle, remembering.

"Phillie?"

"Out here."

Carolyn was holding our big quilt. "Want some company?"

I smiled and put my good arm out. "Sure."

She covered us, and we curled up against each other, and that's the way the kids found us, fast asleep, when they woke up.

AUTHOR'S NOTE

I was able to write this book for three reasons. First and foremost because my wife, Sharon, insisted that deeper meaning was important and worthwhile and shouldn't be ignored, no matter where the economics led. She has always been my first critic and best friend, and if they ever hand out an award for loyalty, integrity, and sense of humor in the face of disaster, she's got it won hands down.

Second, because Robert Gottlieb, my friend and agent for more than fifteen years, always had faith in the book. By placing it with one of the finest editors in publishing, Ann Harris, and with Bantam Books, he gave Phillie the kind of launching my former protagonists can only envy.

Third, because friends and family gave their unflagging support. Anything you need, they said, and proved they meant it. Ann Harris inspired me by providing brilliant editorial notes and never backing down from the hard questions; my brother, Brandon Davis, and my friends Paul McCarthy and Stu Kobak gave invaluable reactions to early drafts; Bob Binns lent me his insight and sports knowledge; Deb Goldstein of William Morris held my hand through the hard times, and did so much more; Nara Nahm buoyed me over the phone; Jordan and Ally, my super kids, gave me lots of hugs and were great about all the nights I spent working; V. K. McCarty and Brad Hodges pointed the way; Dr. Irving Glick and Dr. Maurice Teitel explained medical matters; Michael Zausner let me use some of our treasured memories; George Kalinsky, while I worked on his book, showed me Madison Square Garden the way only he knows it; Dr. Leslie Lukash, Chief Medical Examiner of Nassau County, and Dr. Tom Manning, Chief Toxicologist of Nassau County, gave generously of their time and knowledge; Ruth Adams translated; the Dolphin Book Store and the Port Washington Public Library got books for me magic-quick; my old friend, Paula Frome, Esq., and Chief Frank Donoghue (ret.) and Captain James Ellerby of the Port Washington Police Department gave me the benefit of their experience; and people in the bondage scene shared with me openly and showed me they are us.

A special thanks is owed to Robert Moscowitz, who gave me his inimitable self, going the distance for me again just as he always has. He knows how very much he meant to the writing of this novel and how joyous it was to be with him, like old times, on those hot summer nights in Rainbow City.

One last note. Even though this is a work of fiction, you may be tempted to say, "I recognize that place or person" or "Isn't that . . . ?" or "I was there." You don't. It isn't. You weren't.

Only Phillie was.

And me.

Bart Davis

ABOUT THE AUTHOR

BART DAVIS has written ten novels, including the five books of the Captain Peter MacKenzie series, and two feature films, and collaborated on a nonfiction book about Madison Square Garden. He lives in New York with his wife, Sharon, and their two children.